"Obsessed . . . Spectacular and authentic [with] surprising (and hilarious) moments of finding community and connection."

—***Hey Alma***

"Fresh and revelatory. A joy to read . . . Hazel helps us see that the bad things that happen to us, no matter how terrible, don't need to define us."

—***Lilith***

"Such a delight . . . I loved the Blum family so much . . . Basically, I was smiling ear to ear the whole way through this book."

—***Read Receipts***

"[A] funny, fast-paced debut novel that feels familiar to right now."

—***Heeb***

Also by Jessica Berger Gross

Estranged: Leaving Family and Finding Home

Praise and Acclaim for *Hazel Says No*

A Today *Best Upcoming Book*
A July 2025 Indie Next Pick
A Spotify Best Book of the Year So Far
An R.J. Julia Best Book of 2025 So Far
A Jewish Book Council Book Club Pick
An Unlikely Story Bookstore Best Fiction of 2025
An Athena Books Favorite of 2025

"Add it to your list immediately . . . Funny, sharply observed, and very timely."

—Jennifer Weiner, #1 *New York Times* bestselling author

"Jessica Berger Gross has written an exuberant and big-hearted novel that encompasses an entire transplanted Brooklyn-to-Maine family. This book manages the neat trick of being both timely and timeless, and is a powerful and witty exploration of what it's like to find and claim your spot in a confusing world."

—Cynthia D'Aprix Sweeney, *New York Times* bestselling author of *The Nest* and *Lake Effect*

"I wolfed down *Hazel Says No* in two giddy sittings. Jessica Berger Gross has created one of contemporary fiction's great new families—a cast of characters whose struggles are resonant, hilarious, and poignant as they struggle to assimilate to their new lives. It's a big hearted and expertly crafted debut, one that celebrates the beauty of home, no matter where you happen to find it, and the power that comes with finding your voice."

—Grant Ginder, bestselling author of *So Old, So Young*

"Filled with spiky humor (I was grinning every time I turned a page) and characters so real, you expect them to show up for lunch, Gross' book is the irresistible story of a big city Brooklyn family relocating to a small rural town in Maine . . . An absolutely wonderful novel about figuring out who and what we want to be, and who we truly are."

—Caroline Leavitt, *New York Times* bestselling author of *Pictures of You* and *Days of Wonder*

"Hazel is in bloom. *Hazel Says No* is the book you're looking for right now—smart, funny, hopeful. Hazel herself is a protagonist for writers and dreamers of all ages who see themselves in her—and wish for her bravery while cheering her on!"

—Erin O. White, author of *Like Family*

"*Hazel Says No* is a smart, fun and thoroughly engaging novel about a family's move to a small town in Maine, where they are pulled apart then brought back together. The setting is vivid and colorful, the themes are timely and thought-provoking and the characters are all brimming with life."

—Tova Mirvis, national bestselling author of *The Ladies Auxiliary* and *We Would Never*

"This smart, well-written novel made me literally laugh and literally cry . . . A beautiful novel!"

—Amy Shearn, author of *Animal Instinct*

"I loved it. It reminded me of a cross between *Prep* by Curtis Sittenfeld and *Modern Lovers* by Emma Straub."

—Grace Farris, author of *See One, Do One, Teach One: The Art of Becoming a Doctor*

"*Hazel Says No* pulled me in from the first witty page . . . Great, skillful, and funny. Fans of Catherine Newman will love it!"

—Alice Elliott Dark, national bestselling author of *Fellowship Point*

"With humor and heart, Berger Gross introduces readers to Hazel Greenberg Blum and her family . . . and readers will root for all of them."

—*Booklist*, starred review

"Embraces the joy and light that can be found in moments both big and small."

—*Kirkus Reviews*

"Funny and compulsively readable."

—*Shelf Awareness*

"The brilliance of this novel is how it so deftly deals with very real and heavy issues and yet is ultimately so witty, empathetic and heartfelt."

—*San Diego Union-Tribune*

HAZEL SAYS NO

a novel

JESSICA BERGER GROSS

HANOVER
SQUARE
PRESS

For Lucien

ISBN-13: 978-1-335-00303-4

Hazel Says No

First published in 2025. This edition published in 2026.

Hanover Square Press
22 Adelaide St. West, 41st Floor
Toronto, Ontario M5H 4E3, Canada
HanoverSqPress.com

HarperCollins Publishers
Macken House, 39/40 Mayor Street Upper,
Dublin 1, D01 C9W8, Ireland
www.HarperCollins.com

Printed in U.S.A.

26 27 28 29 30 LBC 5 4 3 2 1

A spider's web is stronger than it looks.

—E.B. White, *Charlotte's Web*

PART ONE

hazel says no

1

the principal's office

Hazel Blum, please report to the principal's office. Hazel Blum.

People say—high school English teachers, grandmothers on the crosstown bus, Joan Didion, Hazel's mother—that everything can change in an instant. In Hazel's (admittedly limited) experience, this wasn't true. Change, whether political or personal, took an eternity, and generally didn't amount to much. We plod along like caterpillars until we're squashed under the boot of patriarchy and homework. It wasn't until one morning in Maine on the first day of her senior year at Riverburg High School that Hazel realized her naiveté. Of course, change could happen in an instant. It just hadn't happened to her. Not yet.

Hazel Blum, please report to the principal's office. Hazel Blum.

Hazel sank into her seat, wondering if she could get away with pretending not to hear her name over the loudspeaker. Moving senior year was awkward enough. To be called out in front of the entire student body on the first day of school was more humiliation than a human could take.

Hazel Blum.

There was nothing to do but half-heartedly raise her hand.

"That's me," she told her statistics teacher. "I'm Hazel."

"Then off you go."

Hazel grabbed her Books are Magic tote bag—containing one composition notebook, a #2 pencil, a black pen, her house key, a tampon, and a copy of Sally Rooney's latest novel. She headed out the homeroom door, past the media center (which looked like your basic prison library), past the auditorium with its black cinder-block walls and crumbling, more-likely-than-not asbestos-riddled ceiling, past classrooms in various states of disrepair, circling around to the main office where the guidance counselors sat. Coming from the New York City public schools, Hazel was used to peeling paint and institutional lack. Riverburg High, though, was next-level. A sign painted directly on the wall said Administrative Offices with an oversized arrow pointing down the hall. She turned the corner.

The principal was sitting at his desk. They knew one another. Not well. He'd given Hazel and her parents a tour of the school at the start of the summer, something her mother had insisted on. Not that there was the option of some other high school in town to attend. But Hazel supposed this made her parents feel like they had the illusion of choice. Like they were taking care of her. After that, the principal had made a point of talking to her at the town pool.

Since she hadn't bothered to find a summer job, Hazel had been forced to take her brother, Wolf, swimming during the weeks he wasn't in theater camp, in charge of making sure he didn't drown, literally or socially. That July and August, Hazel became something of a fixture at the pool, sitting with her legs dangling in the deep end like a pair of straws in a glass of iced lemonade; or else sprawled out on one of the plastic Adirondack chairs dotting the unshaded lawn, or lying facedown on her ratty owl beach towel, reading her way through the public library's uneven fiction section. It was cheaper, and probably as effective, she figured, as having her parents shell out for one of those pre-college summer programs for would-be English majors. The principal was a regular there, too—she'd noticed he was one of the few fathers.

When they encountered each other in the blazing afternoons, he'd stop by her towel or chair or poolside perch and ask what she was reading, and then about other books she'd read, and the future ones she wanted to read later that summer.

One day, the principal surprised Hazel by showing up with a Zadie Smith novel she'd casually recommended. Like they were having some chlorinated book club.

Now she lingered in the forty-five-degree angle of the open office door, framed by the doorway. He beckoned her.

"Hazel! Come," he said. He looked different than he had at the pool. Hazel couldn't put her finger on whether he looked older or younger in his school clothes. But definitely different.

The aforementioned pencil her mother handed her that morning was still sharp. Her stomach, still empty. She was a good student, with an A minus average at her old school (because, math), and a near-perfect verbal SAT score (believe it), and there was nothing left to do besides apply to college. Not that Hazel was a complete stranger to the principal's office in New York. (For talking back to a particularly sadistic geometry teacher.) But it was just third period. Hazel scanned the morning for any possible infraction. Spanish, then AP Government. Then a ten-minute break where she sat outside and kept to herself, pretending to read while checking out the other kids. It was 10:47 a.m. She'd hardly spoken to anyone yet.

The principal was her father's age, with a determined full head of brown hair. Tall. White. A strong jaw. At the pool he'd worn baggy shorts and concert T-shirts. Here he had on a blue button-down with a khaki blazer and dad jeans. A director might have cast him as a crush-worthy high school drama teacher. He was attractive maybe, for like, her mom, but Hazel didn't harbor a kink for middle-aged men.

"Have a seat," the principal said, pointing to one of the two chairs opposite the desk.

Hazel sat on the chair's edge. The late-morning sun streamed through the window. She had on a vintage black-and-white gingham cotton sundress her mother had unearthed at the Brooklyn Flea and red rubber Birkenstock sandals. She was growing out a pixie cut with bits and pieces held off her face by drugstore bobby pins, while she worked her way to a shaggy mullet or a mullet-y shag, à la her favorite '90s actor, Winona Ryder. In high school—in *life*—how you presented yourself seemed to matter. But she felt kind of naked. Maybe she should have worn something more basic, like sweat shorts.

"How's your first day going?" the principal asked. "Settling in all right?"

"Fine, I guess. It just started."

"I wanted to check on you. It must be quite a change."

It was and it wasn't, thought Hazel. School was school.

Hazel blamed her mother for the move. Maine *felt* like her mother's idea. That wasn't the whole story, though. The truth was that her family had come, in large part, for Hazel. Her dad, a professor, had been offered a job at the College, which came with a ridiculously amazing, practically unbelievable, faculty tuition benefit. Money that could make the difference between Hazel ending up at a big state school where she feared being hopelessly lost in a sea of large lecture halls, and her fantasized matriculation at another academically nurturing SLAC (selective liberal arts college).

"Not what you're used to, I'd imagine," the principal continued.

"I've gone to public school my entire life," she said. "I prefer it. I'm a socialist," Hazel added for good measure.

"Oh?" he said.

She vowed not to say anything else incriminating.

★ ★ ★

Toward the middle of August, Hazel had asked the principal if there was a school literary magazine. When he said there wasn't, he'd suggested that they start one together. Which would a) give her a way to meet some like-minded kids (if there were any in Riverburg?), and b) look good for college. Before the pool closed for the season, they'd talked a couple more times about the idea, the principal catching Hazel in various states of coming in or out of the water, or in or out of her book. She wasn't sure if anything would materialize from it. Some adults could be all talk.

That summer, he'd acted like it was somehow remarkable or noteworthy for a teenager to care about anything other than their phone. Like she was a genius for reading a novel. But now, in the harsh institutional light of his office, Hazel was realizing that the principal had paid more attention to her at the pool than was perhaps normal. Hazel was pretty sure kids read books in Maine, too.

The principal came out from behind his desk and slid himself on top of it.

"You can call me Richard, by the way."

At the pool she'd never called him anything.

That was possibly strange. Or maybe not? Outside of school, she called adults by their first names. Her parents' friends, of course. Why should Principal White be any different? Perhaps Riverburg High was less regressive than she'd figured.

He clapped his hands together and walked over to the door, gently shutting it. Hazel registered the metal click.

"Well, we're very happy to have you. We count ourselves the lucky ones. I've seen your transcript. Not that I needed to. I could tell by looking at you. By talking to you over the summer."

Hazel crossed her legs and then her arms.

"—And when I saw the books you were reading, and heard the way you discuss them? You sound like a college student. Plus, you're a New York City girl. They don't make them better, in my humble opinion. I should know. I grew up on Long Island."

"Thanks?" Hazel mumbled, immediately regretting the up-talk. "My mom is from there."

"Is that right? You hadn't mentioned that. What a coincidence. Let me guess: North Shore?"

"South Shore," said Hazel.

"Me too," said the principal. "There aren't that many of us around here. New Yorkers, I mean. On the coast, yeah, but not here. Now tell me, Hazel. I've been meaning to ask you. Where are you thinking of applying?"

Okay then, thought Hazel. Down to business. This made sense. He wanted to talk college applications. She remembered how her second-grade teacher had taught her to memorize the difference in spelling between *principal* and *principle. The principal is your pal.*

"Um. Some liberal arts schools, I think. Vassar. Wesleyan and Oberlin. Maybe Bard. Bennington. Maybe the University of Iowa, too."

"Vassar, huh? Good. You know, most of our kids don't make it to schools like that. Lots of students here go to the U of Maine, or community college. Some straight to work." He looked at her seriously. "I don't want that to worry you. I get you. I want you to know that. You're a star."

Hazel shook her head. She was *not* a star. Girls like her, with good grades and test scores, were a dime a dozen in Brownstone Brooklyn. She had gone to preschool with kids who were now on *TV shows.*

So no, Hazel wasn't special.

"You might be surprised to hear this, but every year we have a couple of students who get into the Ivy League."

Hazel wasn't surprised. Not even a little bit. She'd done her research.

That was the other reason why she'd been okay with the

move. Maine was considered a "sparse state" by admissions offices. According to Hazel's bedside stack of college guides and obsessive late-night online deep dives, her chances of acceptance to said SLAC, when applying from Maine versus Brooklyn, were raised by approximately 1000 percent. Colleges wanted "geographical diversity." Which meant an A minus Riverburg student could maybe hold her own against an A plus student from her old school. It wasn't a sure thing, far from it—but it felt like Hazel's best bet. She'd scrolled through two decades' worth of lists in the local newspaper chronicling where Riverburg High's top ten students went to college. It was legitimately impressive. And sort of warped that going to a worse public school meant you got to go to a better college. Or maybe, come to think of it, that was fairer? In any case, Hazel couldn't afford to be sentimental about the geography of her senior year. She'd miss her friends and her life in the city. *Of course* she would. But it wasn't that deep, she told herself. She could do this. All around the world people were suffering. She could suck it up for one year. What mattered was her future.

Because Hazel wanted to be a writer. To write novels, or be part of a writer's room, or work on staff at a magazine, or in the arts section of a newspaper. She was a word nerd, a bookworm. Books—stories—were everything to her. Half the time she cared more about the characters in her favorite novels (and shows) than she did about people in the real world.

Her ambition was far-fetched, clichéd, and therefore embarrassing to admit, like wanting to be an actor, or an organic farmer. But some people *do* get to become writers. Why not Hazel? That's what her parents said. Hazel herself had serious doubts. She wasn't sure she had anything of interest to say. But she knew one thing: The literary world was cutthroat. That shit took connections. Publishing industry connections. Connections formed at practically impossible-to-get-into colleges like her dream school, Vassar.

The college admissions system wasn't fair. Neither was publishing! (Or capitalism!!) But it was the way things worked. It's not like Hazel could do anything about it. Her plan was to glide through senior year as painlessly as possible, get accepted into college, collect her high school diploma, and survive her one and only Arctic hinterland winter in Maine.

"When it comes to your applications, what I'm saying is: Don't sell yourself short. I can make some calls. I went to Brown myself. And look at me now." The principal waved his arms in a self-deprecating and all-encompassing sweep, gesturing to the dingy office, run-down school, and the seen-better-days town beyond.

This was when she was supposed to laugh. She was tempted to tell him her dad went to Brown for graduate school. That her parents met in Providence. Another coincidence, what a small world, etc. But Hazel was silent. She wondered how much longer this could possibly take and what she was missing in class. Legacy or no, Hazel could never get into Brown. And if she needed strings pulled elsewhere, she had her father, who was friendly with what seemed like half the professoriate in the country. Vassar was already a reach, sparse state or not.

"We need to talk about the literary magazine, too, don't we? I have some ideas for us." He took a swig from his plastic coffee mug. "We should brainstorm. Think about the themes we want to explore. Genres, too. Let's figure out what you're into, but also what your fellow students would respond to, right? Get some readers, some contributors."

Hazel nodded, uncertain.

"And I was thinking, we should start meeting after school. Regularly, you know? So that we can make this happen. Get our first issue off the ground by Thanksgiving. We could use my office. Or, maybe better, find a place where we can really dig in. Where we won't be constantly interrupted because some kid is vaping in the bathroom. Are you free on Saturday?"

"Oh yeah, that's a good idea. I'll have to see. But I should probably be getting back to math."

Hazel's stomach was starting to hurt. She didn't know what to make of him. Was he one of those dedicated live-for-teaching teachers who change your life and inspire you to find your best self? The kind of teacher you never forget? Or was he supremely sketchy?

"It's my first day. And my worst subject. I don't want to miss anything."

"You don't need to worry about that," he said.

Hazel eyed the door, slung her bag over her shoulder and contemplated standing up.

"I could write you a letter."

"A letter?"

"A letter of recommendation. I'd like to, as a matter of fact. For Vassar. I know someone in admissions. That sort of thing can be make-or-break."

Oh.

He moved off the desk and into the chair next to hers.

"A letter of recommendation would be good," she said, although his invasion of her personal space was making her uncomfortable. "A letter would be great." It would be. At least it couldn't hurt.

"We both know you're special, Hazel."

Okay? But again, *no*. She was not special.

She was *fine*. Decently smart, decently talented. Smart enough to be fully aware that she was not particularly extraordinary. Hazel had never felt extraordinary.

What she had felt, for some time—years? Since the ninth grade, at least—was anxious. The steady hum of dread. A sense of doom, even. Like something bad was about to happen. Raised on screens and toxins and a constant barrage of horrific news stories, she felt like the world, her world, could implode at any time.

Sweat glued Hazel's thighs to her chair.

"I have one last question for you. Before I let you go. Can you keep a secret?" he asked, his voice dropping to a conspiratorial whisper.

"Sure," said Hazel. She could. She was, in fact, a great secret keeper.

"Here's the thing—"

"Yes?"

The principal inched closer to her.

"Here's the thing."

He reached out his hand, brushing her thigh. And then his fingers began to crawl back and forth. Purposefully. Pathologically.

He was *touching* her—and he was disgusting—and he was an adult and her *principal*—and she wanted to scream. Instead, Hazel froze, gripped by some sort of catatonic terror.

White lifted her chin with his fingers and stared into her eyes.

"Every year I choose one student to have sex with. This year, I pick you."

2

wolf starts junior high

The handmade poster in his homeroom read, and he was NOT MAKING THIS UP:

> Say *This is hard.* Not *This is gay.*
>
> Say *Do you want to practice throwing?* Not *You throw like a girl.*
>
> Instead of laughing at or teasing a Black student, ask *What's it like to be Black in a mostly White school?*
>
> Say *I like your outfit/haircut* even if it's a girl in sports clothes or a boy with long hair.

Wolf had a hard time believing this remedial level of instruction could possibly be necessary. Like the sign that said All Are Welcome in front of the school. Well, yeah. Wasn't that the whole point of public school? Did they really need to (literally) spell it out? His mother kept saying Riverburg Junior High would be different from his old school. Easier, for one thing. By a lot. Which he doubted since he was going from elementary to the big leagues: middle school. His mother had heard the teachers would assign dumb worksheets and lots of state exam prep and not enough challenging material. He welcomed worksheets! The simpler, the better.

His homeroom teacher, Mrs. Gilbert, handed out their class schedules, a page of names and room numbers with his locker number and combination at the top. He'd never changed classes before or had a locker. Wolf scanned the paper. Everyone—at the theater camp he'd attended the summer before, and at the town pool—said there was one sixth-grade teacher you had to have, Mr. Woods. He taught language arts and was the drama teacher and loved Rick Riordan books and decorated his classroom walls with Marvel posters. CRAP, Wolf thought the second he saw he was stuck with Mrs. Gilbert for language arts, too. He summoned his willpower, suppressed the urge to ball up the schedule and throw it across the room, and tried his absolute hardest not to cry on the first day of sixth grade.

His whole life he'd been different. He was a boy who hated sports, the only one of his kind, it had seemed, in his entire elementary school. Textbook nerd material, and with an IEP and a speech therapist and subpar social skills to boot. They'd forced him to be in a friendship group! After school! On the Upper West Side! He was sick of his parents and teachers worrying about him.

On top of all that, he hated how he looked. Wolf was cute, which was the last thing he wanted to be. He had a halo of brown curly hair and a dimple on each cheek when he smiled. When he was younger, his mother would take him to the Met and point out his uncanny resemblance to the Cupids in the European Painting section.

The worst part was that up until that summer he hadn't been allowed to play video games. Not even *Minecraft*, which was practically educational. Not *Fortnite*, which every other kid played. That changed when his parents announced the move. They were so freaked out about how he'd react that they offered him a Nintendo Switch, a (promised but as-of-yet unplanned) trip to Disney World, and first pick of his own room. (Hazel would be leaving for college soon, anyway.) In Maine, they said, they could afford singing lessons and vacations. They would have two televisions, one upstairs and one downstairs. They'd have an upstairs and a downstairs! And—breaking news alert—his parents agreed to buy him a phone.

The move also coincided with his parents taking him to see a psychiatrist. His newly prescribed ADHD medicine had him feeling like a sharper version of himself. He was slamming fewer doors. He'd also been exercising in the morning with his dad—ten minutes of calisthenics and weights. If he wanted to get a lead in the school play, or make friends, he needed to look the part. No more indulging his mom with his *I am a feminist too* T-shirt.

That summer, he became obsessed with self-administering online Myers-Briggs personality tests, and realized he was an extrovert, not an introvert like the rest of his family. (An introverted extrovert, tbh, but an extrovert nonetheless.) He would no longer be the boy who sat alone at lunch, reading. Wolf wanted—needed—to be with other kids, kids who cared about TV and movies and YouTube videos and video games and virtual reality and Reddit.

In Riverburg, Wolf was determined to fit in. His mom's friend Ramona had sent him *How to Win Friends & Influence People* to read over the summer, swearing the book contained the secret to sixth-grade success. The gift felt a little passive-aggressive, but whatever. His parents warned him to check his privilege at the door. Some of his classmates, they said, lived in apartments, not entire houses. Which seemed to mean something different here than it did in New York, where almost everyone he knew lived in apartments.

Since his forced relocation, Wolf had identified another

problem. Being a Jew, while perfectly normal in New York, was weird in Maine. (Duh.) And Wolf was *Jewish* Jewish. Seth Rogen, Adam Sandler, Mel Brooks–level Jewish. As far as he could make out, he was the only Jewish kid in the entire junior high. (In his Brooklyn elementary school, at least a quarter of the class was at least a quarter Jewish.) *Maybe* a couple kids in his grade celebrated Hannukah along with Christmas, but Wolf was the one about to be forced to go to stupid Hebrew School in the synagogue basement.

His parents swore that couldn't be the case—they couldn't begin to grasp or imagine the foreign world they'd forced him into. There were plenty of Jewish people at the College, so they seemed to assume that extended down to the middle school. His father went so far as to say Maine would be a learning experience for him. Like Wolf's *life* was a cultural exchange program. But Wolf hated nature. He hated forests. He missed the subway. His parents had gotten to grow up in New York and California, not in the middle of the wilderness with moose and bears.

Since the move, his mother had gone out of her way to introduce him to a group of nauseatingly wholesome, string-instrument-playing, track-team-joining neighborhood boys, whom he wanted nothing to do with. Wolf wanted good grades, and he planned to get them, but he wasn't going to hang out with nerds, or participate in boring after-school clubs like Student Council or Odyssey of the Mind, no matter how cool his parents tried to make him believe those were. Wolf wanted people to NOTICE him. To see him.

Wolf was meant for the stage.

The bell rang.

During first period art class with Miss Polly (the only teacher who went by her first name, unlike at his elementary school), someone said *this is gay* about the self-portrait assignment, making Wolf reconsider the remedial nature of the poster in Mrs. Gilbert's room. On the other hand, a few minutes later, Wolf overheard a girl with blue hair at his table talking about her girlfriend.

She shot Wolf a look, like she had to worry about what'd he think. Which *of course*, she didn't.

So, yeah, Riverburg was weird.

So. Many. White people. His teachers, so far, were all white. The students themselves varied more than the teachers, but not by much. There were the outliers, but the vast majority of sixth grade boys were wearing polyester sports shorts.

Riverburg, though, was diverse in its own way. Take the pool. For every family affiliated with the College, there were families who seemed, for a lack of a better word, country. Some richer Riverburg families, his mom reported, didn't go to the pool. They were the ones with "camps" (not actual sleepaway or day camps, Wolf learned, but lake houses) or backyard swimming pools. In New York, his world included everyone from homeless guys on the subway to Park Avenue ladies who dressed their dogs in puffer coats and snow booties. But somehow, here in Riverburg, the class lines were drawn more plainly, more in your face.

Who cared. Wolf had bigger problems than the demographics of his new hometown. After chorus, he had to ask a teacher to help him work the combination on his locker. Up next: further and assured humiliation, and what he'd been dreading all summer. Lunch.

And so, Wolf stood frozen in the center of the lunchroom with his brownie bar and water bottle, trying to figure out where to sit in this land of strangers and exile. This was the official worst moment of his life, more painful and terrifying than when he tripped on blocks and bit through his lip in first grade and had to get stitches.

Again, tears clogged his eyeballs, threatening to make the journey down his cheeks. God, why did he have to be such a baby. Sometimes he really hated himself.

Then, like a miracle, a girl called "Wolf!" and waved him

over, saving him from utter social destruction. She wore a red bandana tied jauntily around her neck and her hair in a long braid down her back. Gracie. At least he thought that was her name. He was 90 percent sure. (He was bad with names.) They'd crossed paths that summer at theater camp and played together at the pool when he was brave enough to approach her.

Flush with relief, he joined the girl-possibly-named-Gracie and her group of friends, which included the blue-haired girl from art. Gracie seemed to be in charge. She was loud and bossy, in a good way. Gracie pretty much always sounded like she knew what she was doing, whether she was shouting *Marco Polo* at the pool or discussing best versus worst homeroom teachers over first day lunch. Gracie talked so much that Wolf could simply relax and bask in her glow. He couldn't believe it: The girl-possibly-named-Gracie had summoned him, Wolf Blum, to her table. If he played his cards right, if he didn't say or do the wrong thing and ruin everything, if he could manage not to mess this up, he'd be able to sit at the best table in school for the next three years of junior high.

Lunch lasted eighteen minutes. Then came a series of boring classes. His social studies teacher refused to learn how to pronounce Wolf's last name properly. She insisted on saying it phonetically, rhyming it with *plum*, rather than the correct and simpler pronunciation, BLOOM. On the positive side, the principal announced over the loudspeaker (between sports tryout info) that there would be three plays that school year. Auditions for the winter drama were happening on Thursday. So, there was that.

For end-of-the-day homeroom, the entire sixth grade assembled in the mini auditorium to get a lecture from the principal on how to STOP. 1. Say no. 2. Tell why. 3. Offer an alternative. 4. Promptly leave. The strategy, meant to fend off preteen dangers, could later be useful when refusing to help around the house, or ski, come winter, which was the only reason Wolf allowed himself to bother with the rather pathetic stretch of an acronym. That, and his annoying brain couldn't help but remember—and synthesize!—random pieces of probably useless information.

Once that was rammed down their young throats, the rising sixth graders were forced to watch a seriously depressing video about an anonymous reporting app called Say Something. Everyone was supposed to put the app on their phones in case they saw a classmate showing signs of cutting, hunger, child abuse, suicidal thoughts, or plans to shoot up the school. Nice.

Then it was time for the bus. He sat by himself, took out his phone, popped on his headphones, pressed Play on the *Hamilton* soundtrack, and stared out the window as the bus driver wound through the streets. Why anybody in their right mind would leave New York for this dumpy town in the middle of nowhere was beyond his comprehension.

3

claire moves to maine

Claire had the house to herself. It was the Tuesday after Labor Day, and Hazel and Wolf were back in school. She'd been dealing with the move all summer long—unpacking, setting up house, organizing the children, finding her bearings. Now she sat on the side porch and tilted her wicker chair toward the morning sun. Birdsong punctuated her thoughts as she took sips of her latte and considered the unexpected turn her family's life had taken.

She couldn't believe she was here. The previous spring, her husband Gus had thrown his name in for consideration, on a whim, to a small preppy liberal arts school they had somehow never heard of, despite its ranking and reputation. Within weeks, the College had made Gus an outsized offer their (pathetic) checking account, (nearly nonexistent) savings, and (clinical levels of anxiety producing) credit card bills couldn't refuse.

Claire and Gus remained unconvinced. They didn't want to leave the city. What Claire wanted, for herself and her family, was completely reasonable sounding (to her) yet utterly unattainable (for them)—a skinny brownstone in Brooklyn, a modest country house, a well-edited closet of garments. An annual February vacation somewhere warm. Two weeks in Italy every other summer. Teenagers who didn't share a bedroom.

That was the dream, anyway. A dream that had long since died. She'd have settled for a rent-stabilized apartment with a washer/dryer, a second bathroom, and a living room that didn't face her building's garbage cans.

She'd worked for BuiltGood as a clothing designer; Gus was an American Studies professor at SUNY Rocky Creek. They no longer had the money to live in the city. Gus said their spending, not their salaries, was the problem. But Claire said it was New York, where it felt impossible to leave the house for a dog walk without buying something. Maybe they'd lacked self-control. Or an entrepreneurial spirit? And in a year, there would be college tuition for Hazel. Which they hadn't saved for. Where had the time gone? Claire couldn't believe that her daughter was a senior and almost grown. That Wolf, her baby, was eleven and starting junior high. That, on top of one day losing them, Claire and Gus needed to come up with hundreds of thousands of dollars to send them to college. The College's educational benefit for faculty children—75 percent of their preposterously high tuition, applied to any accredited college or university—had alighted on the Blums like a winning lottery ticket.

Claire would miss New York. Missing New York was unavoidable. But she also harbored a latent fantasy about moving upstate, making a saner life in a cheap, artistic hamlet. She craved nature and affordable housing. And wasn't Maine like upstate, only more so?

They'd make it work. They had to. And why not? Claire's Maine could be a montage of summer weeks spent barefoot and winter weekends snowed in. She'd dress in nautical stripes and white overalls and fisherman sweaters and clogs. In the garden, they'd grow lettuce and peas and tomatoes. Perhaps they would take on a goat from whom, somehow, she'd procure cheese. She'd have an artist's studio. Gus, the quiet he needed to write his book. Their old dog Pickle would have a backyard. Wolf could arrange spur-of-the-moment playdates by ringing neighbors' doorbells and spend evenings catching fireflies and putting together talent shows with quirky, nature-loving friends. Claire and Gus and Wolf would have this one last year together with Hazel.

They had visited Maine the first weekend of May, without the kids. The flight was a reassuring forty-five minutes; Claire hadn't finished her magazine by the time they landed. For dinner they ate surprisingly excellent shrimp dumplings and house-made noodles at a Portland restaurant that claimed, via understated plaque, to be the partial inspiration for Edward Hopper's *Chop Suey* painting. The next morning, they breakfasted on chocolate croissants and coffee from a bakery on a cobblestone street before driving the one hour and twenty minutes to Riverburg. The highway was absurdly mellow, two lanes on each tree-lined side offering postcard coastal views, before they turned inland.

But while Brooklyn bloomed in midspring, and Portland charmed, the rest of a still gray Maine waited out mud season. Claire shivered in her inadequate cotton sweater as they drove north.

"Can you see us living there?" she had asked Gus, meaning Riverburg. He'd been up in April for his interview.

"Not in a million years."

Nevertheless, Gus refused to consider the obvious compromise of living in Portland and driving back and forth. Not through hardcore Maine winters, not after his two-hour commute from Brooklyn to Rocky Creek. He was firm on that. What was the point of taking a job in a college town if you lived seventy-five miles away? They'd either decamp to Riverburg or stay in Brooklyn for the duration.

To their surprise, Claire agreed once she saw what would become their house. It was a white colonial with green shutters and attached red barn on half an acre of land sitting on a prime corner lot down the block from a stream. An 1873 farmhouse in a historic neighborhood, a short drive or doable walk from campus, priced for less than a studio apartment in New York. The house had just gone on the market.

And so, on that fateful, chilly spring visit, after one afternoon of house hunting, Claire and Gus offered the asking price, awed by their ability to afford it. This would be the first time they'd owned a piece of real estate. It was unclear, however, if they'd found a bargain or overpaid. (As city people tended to do.) The town was economically depressed. Housing prices were far below the national average. Their monthly mortgage would amount to a fraction of what they'd been paying in rent. Seduced by wide hallways, multiple fireplaces, and the warrens of rooms upon rooms, they hadn't thought to factor in heating oil and property taxes and snow removal and deck repair and plumbing disasters and the new boiler the house desperately needed. Instead, they marveled at the sunny double-sized living room, complete with a massive library wall and a window seat nook. At the den for watching television, or, Claire mused, listening to old records? At the separate dining room. The square eat-in kitchen with the farmhouse sink, butcher-block countertops, and an enormous window looking out over the ample backyard. An actual white picket fence and a wooden rope swing hanging from a towering pine tree.

She could still get the *New York Times* at the gas station.

They comforted and consoled Hazel and Wolf, packed up, leased a small Volkswagen SUV, and took possession of the Pine Street house keys on July 1. A handyman who'd worked for the previous owners painted the walls Swedish country white. Claire helped. She bought a farmhouse table and Eames-style yellow plastic molded chairs. In the living room, flanking the fireplace, she positioned a high-end, dog-friendly brown leather couch, sourced for $250 at a Fort Greene stoop sale. Across from it, a rose-colored Ikea sofa. She put a sectional in the den for Friday movie nights. Claire wanted to make for her children—at last—the comfortable house, the sort of loving, bookish, musical, alive—and yes!—beautiful family home she wished she'd grown up in.

Riverburg itself was hardscrabble, a former mill town. An old T-shirt factory sat on the river's edge, its broken windows boarded up. Toward the highway was the stretch of strip malls with supermarkets and fast-food places and the Surplus & Salvage store, with discount emporiums and motels and the always packed pizza place with the strange aftertaste. The Pine Street neighborhood, upon closer inspection, was a mélange of single-family homes and landlord-owned ones carved into multifamily apartment rentals. Some were lovely. Others, with run-down porches, had seen better days. The church around the corner ran a food pantry and lunchtime sandwich program like the one in their Brooklyn neighborhood.

In other ways, Riverburg was almost idyllic. The house was an easy walk downtown. Main Street had a library and the Opera House where Wolf had done theater camp, the new hotel with a fireplace lounge in the lobby, a footbridge across the river, and The Riverburg General, a natural food store and café. On Thursday afternoons, a bustling farmers market came to life with an ice cream truck selling chocolate salted caramel better than any Brooklyn cone, a Mennonite baker with the best German pretzel Claire had ever tasted, and an extravagant display of locally grown and delicious produce, from cantaloupe to beets. The town rabbi (there was a town rabbi?) and her wife (they were gay!) invited Claire to a fermentation workshop. In the evenings, Claire sat on the porch and got high on some quality marijuana before tucking herself into bed under the wool comforter and watching *The Real Housewives of New York City* with Gus.

Things could be worse. A lot worse.

* * *

If only Claire knew what to do with her life. She wanted to be happy. And she should have been. She was?

Today was the day she was supposed to stop procrastinating and start working on her clothing line. But Gus and the kids had been gone all morning and Claire hadn't accomplished a thing. She'd invested in a Pfaff sewing machine, bought a secondhand serger, and picked up a dress form, ironing board and steamer. She found a satisfyingly oversized table that once lived in the town library at the Riverburg Swap Meet. Natural fiber fabrics, deadstock and remnants, a collection of antique-shop quilts, and scraps of ideas were stacked on the worktable. An empty corkboard hung at the ready on the wall, waiting for inspiration to strike.

And so far? Nothing.

Claire had gone to RISD and studied textiles. At BuiltGood she was known for identifying emerging trends early on—jumpsuits and then coveralls, wide-legged denim, the return of acid wash, pink—and bringing them to the design team. She studied the outfits of her fellow Brooklyn moms at drop-off outside Wolf's elementary school, or eyed the latest thrift of their NYU or Pratt student nannies on the occasional days she made it to pickup. It wasn't brain surgery, nor was it cheating per se. This was how the fashion world found inspiration—on the street. She could feel herself becoming obsolete, though. Partly it was her age (forty-seven), partly that social media made trends so immediate as to render her eye and taste unnecessary. More and more, she found herself assigned to the team making loungewear.

BuiltGood was a modest step above fast fashion. Occasionally, Claire was allowed to facilitate a partnership or collaboration with a favorite small-batch producer, but she could only do so much within the company's prescribed budget lines. Generally, they ripped off their favorite indie designers. It was legal, if unethical. Or democratic, depending on one's point of view. You couldn't copyright a look.

When her mentor and boss exited the company and moved to a horse farm in Connecticut, Claire realized she could be asked to leave anytime. And then what? When Gus was handed a tenured position—in a cheap town, with the college tuition benefit, in a state with better than average air quality and good produce, a day's drive from New York—Claire knew they couldn't say no.

By going out on her own, Claire hoped to produce thoughtful garments that would last a lifetime. The business details (pattern maker, manufacturer) remained murky. Her initial idea was to base the debut line on *Fiddler on the Roof.* (Wolf had played the original Broadway soundtrack on repeat the previous winter.) A peasant blouse called the shtetl shirt, a milkman vest, Cossack coveralls, and a matchmaker smock. She had a sample shtetl shirt in her studio she was working on perfecting but couldn't get right. Once she'd removed herself from the bubble of New York, she realized it would never translate.

Rooting around for a fresh idea, she was thinking of basing the line on her new (if aspirational, not actual) Maine lifestyle. Utility work jeans. Organic plant-dyed painter's pants. Cotton waffle long-john sets. A special gray sweatshirt. A pointelle sleep set. The perfect simple striped shirt. A quilted vest. The ideal wool cardigan if she could figure out how to produce a knit. But it seemed rather pointless, all that pointelle. The production of more to *wear,* more waste to fill dressers and closets and landfills.

What Claire really wanted to be was an artist. A real artist, one who mattered. Like her college roommate Ramona, a celebrated ceramicist with a following. But starting her own line seemed ridiculous. Impractical. Unaffordable. Narcissistic. And decades too late. Who would care? She wasn't some young cool thing in Bushwick or Ridgewood. She was staring down fifty. Age and finances aside, Claire wasn't even sure if making things made a difference. Was it enough to (try to) create something beautiful, she asked herself every morning when she sat down to work. Was it anything at all?

★ ★ ★

Claire did the breakfast dishes, prepared a second cup of coffee, and carried the steaming mug up to her studio. She stuck her graying hair in a topknot, picked up a pencil, pulled out her sketch pad, put them down, and started searching the local job listings on her phone instead. The College needed administrative help in the foreign language department. And a gallery guard for their museum. The independent movie house was hiring a projectionist, the elementary school around the corner a permanent substitute teacher.

But Claire wanted to make things. She returned to her pencil and sketch pad and started to work. Somehow, the kids were due home soon. Maybe it wouldn't *matter* in the larger artistic sense, but at least Claire could offer something satisfying. Something that someone somewhere would like—love?—to wear. The thing you'd reach for day after day. The opposite of what she'd done at BuiltGood. She remembered a long-ago professor at RISD who'd spoken at length about beauty and utility, form and function. The desire to make and wear something aesthetically pleasing was ancient and biological. People did need clothes. Especially in Maine.

Claire was about to enter the desired state of Csikszentmihalyi flow when she heard Pickle barking and then a pounding, followed by a positively alarming number of texts. She propped open the window next to her worktable, put her head out into the early September air, and saw a figure—a child, a girl, *her* girl—furiously banging on the porch door.

Claire dropped her sketch pad and rushed downstairs. Hazel's wavy brown hair was an uncharacteristically frizzy mess, as if she'd stuck her finger in an electrical socket.

"Hazel? Shit. What happened? What's wrong?"

"What's wrong is I hate you. And I hate it here."

4

hazel says no

What. The. Actual. Fuck.

The principal didn't just *proposition* her, did he? How could this possibly be her actual life?

She figured he must be attempting a sick ironic joke. Or there were hidden cameras. Or was this some sort of a test?

Because how could this be the same harmless dad in baggy swim shorts from the pool? Had she made it up in her head? Was she experiencing some sort of a psychotic break?

He was looking straight at her, waiting for a response. Like he was serious. How could he touch her like that? And how could he say such a batshit thing? The scenario seemed ridiculous. Inconceivable.

Hazel couldn't possibly have heard right. Only she had.

Fuck, Hazel realized. Nobody would believe her. Not ever.

Time stopped. The sound of her heart pounding through her chest an explosion of homemade bombs.

She said nothing.

He said nothing.

Still nothing. Only this horrible man staring at her. Willing her—expecting her!—to say yes. Hazel might be having a heart attack.

Her entire life her mother had warned her about men, and Hazel wouldn't listen. She was from Brooklyn. She'd taken the G train to the L train to high school since the ninth grade. She could take care of herself. When sketchy guys on the subway looked at her for longer than necessary, when they occasionally brushed up against her in a crowded car, Hazel dismissed the brief encounters as minor annoyances. She should have believed her mother; men could be dangerous. But in Hazel's experience, up until that day, adult men had been a nonissue. They were fine, irrelevant. Their younger versions were the ones to worry about. The soccer boys who rated Hazel and her girlfriends from one to ten on face/body/personality at lunch, who had whole group chats dissecting and demeaning them.

Only now, for the first time around a grown man, Hazel felt straight-up fear. She became aware of the red cotton bralette visible beside the thin straps of her dress. Of her exposed shoulders and bare chest and legs and the chipped black polish on her toenails. She felt herself sweating.

For the longest minute (minutes?) of Hazel's life, they both sat there in silence. A staring contest. A game of chicken.

She weighed her options. They each sucked.

"I like you. A lot," he said.

Like her? He was her dad's age.

"You can't pretend we haven't been dancing around each other this summer. Around this—" He motioned to the air between them.

Dancing? God.

"I know you know exactly what you're doing. What you've done."

What she was *doing*? What she'd done? She'd been minding her own business at a public pool. Taking care of her brother.

Reading books. When approached—when interrupted, when asked what she was *reading*—she'd been polite. To her principal! She'd agreed to start an after-school club, not become his Lolita.

"You know we have a connection. You know how much I like you. How much I get you."

She stared down at the floor.

Hazel felt feverish and lightheaded and dizzy. She was about to pass out.

She dug her short, sharp nails into her palms, and ordered herself to feel her feet on the floor, her body in space.

"And what if I don't want to. What if I say no?" She heard herself ask the questions but had no awareness of having formed the words in her brain or giving them permission to leave her mouth.

The principal seemed genuinely hurt. And surprised. Very surprised.

"I don't think that's going to happen, do you?"

"Oh," Hazel said, clutching the bottom of her chair. She took in the biggest breath of her eighteen years. "But what if I do?"

He stood up. He was tall to begin with. Standing, he towered over her. "Well, things could become more difficult for you when it comes time to graduate. Transferring your credits, making sure you get out of here on time. And, like I said, I have that friend in admissions at Vassar—"

He must be having the psychotic break. How was he the principal of a high school? How could he say these things and expect to have a job the next day?

But what if he was dead serious? What if her chances of graduating—of getting into college, of getting a job one day—were dependent on her agreeing to have sex with him? Or touching him. Or letting him touch her. Hazel considered. If you could consider anything this life-changing while trying not to black out.

Maybe the best thing to do was placate him. Give in a little and let him down easy. Flirt. (She knew how to do that.) Assuage. Appease. Bargain? Duck and weave. Make an excuse. (Her period? Her parents? Her virginity?)

To somehow make this go away. Without him feeling rejected. That was key.

Maybe she should be nice? Maybe she should—

Then Hazel came to.

No. This, Hazel decided, would not be the end of her story. She would not be nice.

The principal could go fuck himself.

With that, Hazel released a guttural noise from deep inside of her. An astonishing roar.

No. NOOOOOOOOO.

No!

"No," she said. *No fucking way.*

And with that Hazel got up and ran like hell.

Hazel ran down the hallway, but it felt like she was moving through quicksand. Finding the girls' bathroom, she locked herself in a stall. Saying no was one thing. Saying no was (relatively) easy. What came next?

Hazel knew that whatever she did, she was screwed.

She was also in shock, her mind trying to process the impossible. She had to talk herself down. She *had* to, otherwise she felt like she was going to die.

And so, Hazel told herself that she was okay. That much worse happened every single day around the globe. She had food to eat. A home. A family. A future. Hazel was FINE.

Think about it. Nothing that serious had happened. Had it? She was asked a question, presented with a proposition, and she'd turned it down. On the one hand, what she'd just experienced felt cataclysmic and earth-shattering. On the other hand, maybe it wasn't that big a deal. It's not like he'd forced her to do something. It's not like he'd raped her or anything.

The bell rang, followed by the stampede of feet and the sound of laughter and hallway greetings. She'd missed statistics and was about to miss environmental studies if she didn't get it together. But she wanted to throw up. Or scoop her insides out. She could feel angry rashes forming on her neck and belly. She was possibly breaking out in hives.

This Was Not OK.

His threat about her not graduating: What if he'd really go through with it and fuck with her future? With college? Because if he could put a good word in for her with colleges, couldn't he put a bad one in, too? At Vassar? Where he *knew* someone in *admissions*? And if that's what he said he'd do if she said no—which she already had, she reminded herself—how would he retaliate when she *told*?

If she told. She didn't have to say anything. She probably shouldn't. She didn't want to think about how stressed out this would make her parents. Or how she would show her face at this school for the rest of the year.

What if she waited? Kept this a weird little anecdote she'd pull out in a decade? What if she let herself stay an ordinary girl finishing out high school, keeping her head down, and heading to college next year? That was her right, after all. To not make a mess of her life.

The bell rang a second time. Locker doors clanged shut. Flip-flops shuffled into classrooms. A decision needed to be made. Maybe, despite the arguments in her head and the rational reasons to keep her mouth shut, she couldn't live with herself unless she reported the principal.

Hazel splashed her face with sink water and marched to the guidance office. The main office lady was on the phone. Hazel screamed. But only in her brain. In real life, she waited and started to rethink. Again. It was one thing to say no. And another thing entirely to tell. How could she let this be her first impression with the guidance counselors if she was to survive the year, much less have them help her get into college?

She couldn't. He was their boss. Why would they believe her? She'd already heard how "great" the principal was. How devoted. Her parents had said he'd started the LGBTQ+ club and the wilderness club. Hazel had clocked how people in town treated him at the pool. Like he was some hometown hero. She was the weirdo New Yorker girl.

Why would they take her word against his? They wouldn't.

Hazel dug out her rotating block schedule. Making her retreat, fueled with adrenaline and renewed purpose, she climbed the stairs and headed to environmental studies. Be normal, she told herself, like a mantra. Be. Normal. *Nothing happened.* Finding a seat in the back of the room, apologizing for her lateness, she proceeded to go numb. And with that accomplished, Hazel bare-knuckled her way through the motions of the rest of the school day until 2:45 dismissal, when she could finally do the one thing she'd desperately wanted to do for that entire day.

She ran out of the school and rode her bike straight home.

5

hazel tells (her mom)

"Hazel? Can I come in?" said her mother, with a crisp double knock on the door.

"No."

After losing her shit on the porch, Hazel disappeared to the third floor, where she'd secured the attic bedroom with the one private bathroom in the house, which consisted of an old toilet and stained sink, and a preposterous square metal stall called The Shower King. Thanking the universe that she was on a separate floor from the rest of her family, she peeled off her dress and bra, turning the shower on as hot as it would go. She stayed until the water made her skin pink and then red. She stayed until the hot water ran out and turned cold. In her bedroom she put on a holey T-shirt and boxer briefs and climbed into bed. She then did the only thing that could possibly soothe her anxiety: she clicked on the Vassar website.

"I want to talk to you," said her mother from the other side of the door. "Please?"

"Go away. I'm begging you."

"Tell me what's going on?"

"This has nothing to do with you."

Hazel genuinely felt sick. Her stomach was in knots with what had become the worst period cramps of her life. She needed the heating pad, but it was in the second-floor bathroom, and she had no plans to leave her room for the foreseeable future.

"Hazel. I'm coming in." Her family wasn't the lock-on-your-door type. And her mother could be relentless.

"So much for having my own room."

"What the hell, Hazel. How bad could it have been? You're scaring me."

"You don't want to know," said Hazel, staring at her phone. "Horrible. Terrible. The worst. Imagine the worst thing, the worst day, and it was a million times worse than that."

"What didn't you like? The kids? The classes? The teachers? Is the curriculum pathetic?" Claire closed the door behind her and sat on the foot of Hazel's bed.

"*Look* at me, Hazel."

Hazel slid her phone under the covers. "I *am* looking at you."

"Don't worry, it's one year. You're smart enough already."

"I don't care what I learn."

"We both know that's not true— Wait. Were there guns?"

"What? Guns? Mom. No. Nothing like that. And that's totally classist of you to say against, like, rural white people. Whatever you call the people here."

"Okay, so what's the problem?"

"I can't explain it and if I did you wouldn't understand."

Her mother clicked on the AC. It was the loud, standalone kind with a hose that her dad had jerry-rigged to work with the old-fashioned window. She inspected Hazel for signs of distress and bodily harm, checking her arms and legs. (For what? Hazel thought. For ticks? For bruises?) Claire could be self-involved, but she was a good mother. Or a good enough one. She cared. Too much if anything. And she was sort of, for lack of a better word, cool? More than Hazel would ever be. Hazel vacillated between loving her unconditionally and resenting and admiring her and being intimidated by her. And hating her. Today she hated her.

"Your skin is red," declared Claire.

"Excuse me for taking a shower. Excuse me for being clean."

"Give me your phone."

Hazel handed it over. Whatever. Did her mother think the answers were in there? Or was this an attempt to punish her for wanting her privacy? Absurd. She was eighteen.

"Did something happen to you? Did someone *do* something to you?"

Ha.

Hahahahahahahahahaha.

"Hazel. I'm your mother. I need to know." Claire was starting to freak. "No matter what it is. Talk to me. I promise not to be mad."

Looking back, maybe Hazel wanted to tell. Some subconscious part of her. Maybe she was brave. Or maybe everything that would end up happening that year was because her mother pried the words out of her.

She could have made a different choice, Hazel realized later. Kept that morning to herself. Safeguarded her life. How could she have foreseen that telling would trigger endless reverberations and consequences, like a small rock tossed out into a still lake casting ripples as far as the eye could see? Farther.

Her mother sat at the foot of Hazel's bed and listened without interrupting. Which was unusual in the Blum house. It took time to get her story out. That's what she knew it was already becoming. A story. Though it was the truth.

"He *said* that? He said the word *sex*?"

"How many times can I tell you the same thing?"

"Tell me again," her mother said. She was trying to massage Hazel's foot, but Hazel shook her off. She had that "concerned mother" look on her face that made Hazel want to low-key murder her.

"Do you want me to do an interpretive dance?" Hazel sat up straighter. This was the last time she'd talk about this. Ever. "Okay. The principal called me into his office and asked me to have sex with him. Or be his girlfriend or something. He said he picks one girl a year. He offered to write me a letter for Vassar." She'd forgotten that very last part.

Claire was speechless.

How could this be? Now—after everything? After all the shitty men canceled in front-page headlines and arrested? After all the prison sentences and million-dollar lawsuits? Had the news not gotten to Maine? In what possible world did the principal think he could get away with something so ridiculously wrong? But come to think of it.

"That's horrible!" yelled her brother, who was eavesdropping from his sentinel post in the lower part of the attic stairwell. He climbed the narrow stairs, opened the door, and crawled into bed with Hazel.

"Wolf!" said Claire. She could hardly handle parenting one child right now, much less two. "When did you get home? This is a private conversation."

"She's my sister," said Wolf. "It's my right to know."

At least they had one another, Claire told herself. When the shit hit the fan in Claire's childhood home, after her father's anger subsided, she'd been left all alone—her mother nowhere to be found.

Pickle nosed the door and heaved her old bones onto the foot of the bed.

"You could quit and get a GED?" offered Wolf.

"I'm screwed," said Hazel.

"What are we going to do?" said Claire, to the children, to the ether, to the universe. "Oh God, Hazel. I'm so sorry."

"I told you we shouldn't have moved," said Wolf, who was waiting for someone to ask how *his* day was.

Fuck. Fuck. Fuck. Wolf was right. What had Claire been thinking uprooting her family? When they were perfectly okay in Brooklyn? So that Gus could be *department chair*? So Hazel could go to a *liberal arts* college? So that Wolf could have a *yard?* And Claire could be some sort of *artist*? This was the price Claire would pay for her greed. For her selfishness.

"It doesn't matter where you live," said Hazel, as Wolf cuddled her. "This could have happened anywhere. It happens everywhere. Today it happened to happen to me."

"I'm calling Daddy. I'm. Calling. Daddy!" Wolf saw that Claire had two phones in her hand—hers and Hazel's—and got up to grab one.

"No!" said Hazel, snatching her phone back and securing it under her pillow, which she then sat on. "I don't want to make a bigger deal of this than it is."

"Hazel," said Claire, walking the narrow stretch of floorboard in front of Hazel's bed. "There could not be a bigger deal."

"Well, okay. Yeah. Something happened. Something creepy. But I'm exhausted, and I don't want to deal with it. Can we talk about this later? Can you *please* both go away?"

"I'm calling him," said Claire. "End of discussion. This sociopath is going to rot in jail."

"Do NOT CALL HIM," said Hazel. "I'm done talking about this. Dad can't do anything, anyway. Like, we need to get serious and call a man? Are you living in the 1950s?"

Wolf pried the second phone from Claire's palm. Voice mail. "Daddy! Something bad happened. Call us back right now. It's an emergency."

6

gus is trying to work

Gus ignored his phone. He was trying to work. He was forever trying to work.

Over the summer he'd taken the reins of the American Studies department, where he was the newly appointed chair. The department now consisted of Gus and another, almost retired, seventy-one-year-old professor who split her time between American Studies and anthropology, with the president's pledge of one or two additional hiring lines to come.

Back in Brooklyn, Claire had been pressuring him to ask for a raise from SUNY Rocky Creek, something that was never going to happen, not at a state school running on fumes in an overlooked department with hardly enough money to operate the copy machines. Late last winter, a job description, seemingly tailor-made for Gus, had appeared in *The Chronicle of Higher Education*. On his visit to the campus, the president of the College, Nicole Hill, made time in her schedule to have breakfast with him. Flowers were sent to his hotel room. Two days later: the official offer. A sizeable salary bump from Rocky Creek, a housing bonus for a down payment (if they bought in town), an upgrade from associate to full professor, the promise of a plentiful research account for travel to conferences and archives, and the guarantee of a 2-2 (two classes per semester) course load, so long as he was chair of the department. *We need you*, Nicole Hill had said.

Gus should have been elated about the job offer. But he dreamed of teaching at a top university with brilliant graduate students and world-class thinkers doing cutting-edge work that would shape the culture for generations to come. A University of Chicago. Northwestern. UC Berkeley, where he'd grown up in the shadow of the university. An Ivy? The real goal, of course, the holy grail—and the only acceptable end to their story as far as Claire was concerned—was a tenured position, complete with subsidized faculty housing, at New York University or Columbia.

To outsiders, he was already a success. A professor with a chic and knowing and lovely wife, and two precocious, talented children. But Gus had been holding on by a thread. Finances aside, it was impossible to work in New York. To think. Certainly not in their overcrowded 925 square foot two-bedroom garden apartment (one bathroom, no laundry machines) where Wolf was jumping off the walls and Hazel was slamming doors and Claire was exercising on her trampoline in the living room. The writing that got done happened on the margins. At 5:00 a.m. or after the kids went to sleep. On a (rare) open weekday, between semesters or on his non-teaching Tuesdays and Thursdays, he worked out of the Rose Reading Room at the New York Public Library. Those were his best hours, when he had time to stretch out and become immersed in his work—the days that made everything else worth it. More often, he crammed his writing between lecture and committee prep while stuffing himself onto the Long

Island Railroad, drowning out commuters with drugstore rubber earplugs, his low-rent version of noise-canceling headphones.

Once upon a time he was a good Marxist. But it was difficult to reconcile his leftist politics with his desire for nine-dollar nut butter smoothies. The College was a respectable (in fact, quite good—and hard to get into) liberal arts school where a bright kid would be introduced to Michel Foucault and Judith Butler, and get in some skiing, before being thrust into the capitalist machine four years later. And so, he traded in his toehold in the firmament of New York for a big raise and a big house.

To a non-academic, the status distinction between a research university and an elite college was, of course, meaningless. The College was a fine place to land, wilds of Maine or not. So what if he'd have to do his own grading? Gus was not only department chair, he'd become an endowed professor: The Leon Leonwood Bean Professor of American Studies. Not that he had an actual chair. Gus was sitting on a cardboard moving box, a laptop perched on his knees because his office furniture had yet to arrive, a named professor who was paid well but saw himself as a sad sack with a stalled career.

The phone again. Claire.

He turned the phone facedown and continued pounding out his syllabi. That semester he was teaching two classes—a seminar called Representing the American Family, and an intro course, Deconstructing America. Once the syllabi were done, he'd be up half the night prepping his first day lectures.

Gus specialized in representations of gender and sex on television with a focus on "the family." He'd done his undergrad at UC Santa Cruz, and graduate work at Brown, where he'd written a series of journal articles published during his final year of grad school, most notably, "Praxis of Fatherhood in *thirtysomething*." His theories were well cited, if dimly understood, landing him the Rocky Creek assistant professorship. He'd followed up the Praxis pieces with *Family Man*, a slim monograph—no more than a pamphlet, really—on Herbert Marcuse, the radical social theorist, and how his ideas could be used to deconstruct the gendered consumerist messages in reality television.

At the College, Gus would have a chance to write his big book. His much ballyhooed, long promised, longer overdue, once highly anticipated and since forgotten tome in the making, *Family Matters: The American Marriage on Television*.

In truth, he'd only written ten pages. Settled in Vacationland, as Maine touted itself, Gus hoped to find the elusive peace and quiet he craved, a suitable working environment that would engender the sort of consequential, significant thinking his graduate cohort and professors had once believed him capable of doing. Research for the book entailed watching thousands of hours of television and taking exceedingly detailed notes. Gus expected that with fewer distractions, and a dedicated work-from-home space, he could get the thing written.

The damn phone. Again! Probably Wolf wanting him to cook him an early dinner. He felt guilty for not answering, but Gus needed to get his class prep done. Wolfie would have to make do with Claire's pasta.

He and Claire had met at a coffee shop in Providence on a Sunday morning around the time of her graduation. She smelled of juniper. And she was smart, not necessarily *intellectual* like his grad school friends—but sharper and quicker than the lot of them. Claire was well-read and funny. He was into it. Into her. Seven years, and several breakups and reunions later, when Claire threw up at a New Year's Eve party in Red Hook despite only being on her second glass of wine, they realized something was amiss. A 2:00 a.m. drugstore test confirmed their suspicions. At twenty-nine, she still felt too young to have a child. But Claire hated her parents and longed for a family of her own. Gus's parents, who were older, had died—his mom when he was in college and his father while he was in graduate school. Gus wanted a family, too.

While neither cared about a ring or piece of paper certifying their relationship, Claire liked the idea of being a pregnant bride, and the idea of getting on Gus's better university health insurance plan. On the last weekend of May they were married at City Hall, followed by dinner and dancing at Sammy's Roumanian, the Jewish steak house on the Lower East Side. Gus wore a seersucker suit, Claire, an empire waist lace vintage nightgown, her belly pressing against the material. They honeymooned at Mohonk Mountain House in upstate New York. Hazel was born later that summer. (An emergency C-section at NYU. The most terrifying and exhilarating thirty-six hours of his life.)

For years, the city worked for them. More or less. Gus's modest inheritance—the sale of his childhood house, minus his parents' financial obligations and medical bills—helped pay for after-school programs and babysitters and summer day camps. They hustled their kids all over the city on the subway, and in strollers and then scooters and then short and then longer legs. Prospect Park, Natural History, Russ & Daughters, The Strand, all of it. Claire juggled kids and work (assisting the creative director at BuiltGood, then moving over to the design team). Gus did the same, as his reverse commute to Long Island allowed. They had a decent social life in the neighborhood and ate out and ordered in and told themselves they hadn't given up their inner worlds because they had kids. They used the fumes of his parents' money to afford what his salary couldn't until that money was gone. And then the jig was up.

Their marriage was basically a happy one. They held hands while watching good and bad TV. They made each other laugh. They had sex once a week or so, when Claire remembered, and when they managed to get both kids out of the apartment at the same time—a tactical feat. Gus kept his hair short and his beard long. He had a messy closet stocked with button-down shirts he wore rolled up at the sleeves, jeans in various states of earned distress, and sweaters that lived in a jumbled pile on the floor. He was naturally thin, an early riser with a dependable metabolism, skinny legs, solidly competent arms, and a weakness for crackers. He had gold John Lennon eyeglass frames and a discreet tattoo of an electric typewriter under his right wrist. And one of an old-fashioned television with rabbit ears under his left.

The silenced phone wouldn't stop vibrating. Gus flipped it over again to survey the damage: a squall of Claire texts, and another three calls, plus two from Wolf. This was precisely why he couldn't write his book. Why wouldn't they let him work? Giving up and calling home, Gus remembered that it was the first day of school for the kids and felt like a jerk.

"Hey. Sorry, I wasn't looking at my phone. How'd it go for Wolf? How's Hazel?"

"Gus, where have you been? You need to come home. We have an emergency situation."

"Oh shit. Is Wolf having a nosebleed? Does he need the ER? Stick the clip on his nose and tell him not to move."

"No, not like that. And not Wolf. I think I could handle a nosebleed on my own."

"Then what? Hazel drama? I'm at the office and everyone can hear me."

"Well, they can't hear *me*," said Claire.

"Claire. Is this a real emergency or a the-toilet-won't-flush emergency? Because I'm trying to work here. I teach tomorrow. Just because my office is five minutes away doesn't mean I can come home every five minutes. We talked about that."

"God, Gus. Really?" Claire said. "When are you going to learn that work isn't everything?"

Gus was silent. Work *was* everything. Work, and the children.

"I wouldn't call you twenty-five times if it wasn't important. Something insane has happened, and it's unimaginably horrible and it happened to Hazel."

"What? Now you're scaring me. Tell me what's going on."

"I'd rather not get into it on the phone—the kids are here with me. We need you, okay? Come home."

"I'm leaving right now," said Gus, grabbing his laptop and pulling some dog-eared books out of a moving box labeled TEACHING.

"Hold on."

7

gus comes home

Not knowing what else to do, Claire cleaned the kitchen. Tidying usually calmed her, but Claire's hands were shaking as she worked a sponge over the counter. She could feel her psoriasis flaring up and counted in her head how many more nights of pot she had left before she needed to run to the weed store. She considered texting Ramona in Brooklyn but felt too panicked by the idea of her phone and what she should probably be doing with it. Call Hazel's homeroom teacher? The superintendent? The mayor?

She heard Gus pull his newly acquired, decades-old Volvo station wagon into the driveway, and met him on the porch, a white dishrag with its red stripe hanging over her shoulder, like an epaulet.

"Where's Hazel?" Gus demanded, rushing into the kitchen.

"I told you already. It's not *medical*. She's in her room," Claire said, following him inside. They took their places in the kitchen. Claire at the square pine table, Gus leaning on the baking counter. "Can you sit down so I can talk to you?"

"I don't feel like sitting." Gus began to pace. He was a worrier. The overprotective parent. He had a hard time letting Pickle run off leash.

Claire somehow couldn't get the words out. She redid her messy bun.

"What happened?"

"Okay," she exhaled. "Hazel was propositioned by her principal this morning."

"Propositioned? What does that mean?"

"The principal. You're not going to believe this. He called Hazel into his office, closed the door and told her that every year he picks one girl to have sex with—"

"Richard White said that?"

"That's what Hazel told me."

"Have *sex* with?" said Gus.

"Have sex with," continued Claire. "He told her that every year he picks one girl and this year he chose Hazel."

"What the fuck? Why didn't you tell me?"

"I tried to tell you. I've been *trying* to tell you for hours. You're the one who wanted to move here."

"I'm calling the police."

"Slow down. We don't really know what this is," said Claire. "For one thing, it didn't happen. I mean the conversation happened, but that's it. He didn't touch her. Hardly touched her—I think she said he put his hand on her knee. Or on her thigh? Hazel handled it."

"Handled it? She's a *child*. This is a crime. Statutory rape."

"Hazel is eighteen. It's not statutory anything."

Gus pushed a loose floor plank nail back into place with his heel.

"Maybe it's best defined as hardcore sexual harassment. Or sexual assault?" continued Claire.

"Hi, Daddy," Wolf said, poking his head into the kitchen.

"How long have you been standing there?" asked Gus. "How was your first day?"

"Pretty good. I'm exhausted, though. And starving. Did Mommy tell you what happened to Hazel?"

"Go upstairs. I'm talking to him about it now," said Claire. She tried to close the door between the kitchen and dining room, but their shoe rack got in the way.

"He knows?" asked Gus, starting a stopgap quesadilla for Wolf on the stove.

"He overheard. You try being the stay-at-home parent," Claire said, returning the mozzarella and tortillas to the refrigerator. Gus did the cooking, but she was the one who put things away.

"I'm calling Nicole Hill."

"Really? You're calling Nicole? Are you fucking kidding me? She's not the town sheriff. Why is this your decision, anyway? I'm Hazel's mother."

"You're right. Rephrasing. Let's call Nicole," said Gus. "And can we please not fight? This is stressful enough without you yelling at me."

"We should ask Hazel before we do anything," said Claire. "We *have* to ask her. And I'm not yelling. I said *fuck*. I'm from Long Island, I curse when I'm stressed. Have you not known me for twenty-five years?"

"I'll get her," said Wolf from the dining room table, one room over.

"Wolf!" yelled Claire and Gus, neither of whom had realized he was still listening.

"What? I'm just sitting here. You two are loud, you know."

"This conversation is inappropriate," said Gus. "You shouldn't be downstairs."

"But you're making my food! I was just trying to help," said Wolf. "I looked it up and the age of consent in Maine is sixteen."

"Fuck," said Claire. "Sorry," she added to Wolf.

"Here's your quesadilla. Can you take it to your room and send Hazel downstairs?" said Gus. "And, Claire, can you please stop saying *fuck*?"

"Can I bring my Switch?" Wolf wasn't allowed to bring screens into his bedroom.

"Yes!" said Claire and Gus.

A summoned Hazel appeared, drained of color. She let her father hug her. "Tell me what happened," said Gus, releasing her to the table.

"Didn't Mommy?"

"I want to hear it from you." He propped himself up against the baking counter again and crossed his arms.

"This is the last time," said Hazel, sitting down at the table. "I am so done with repeating this."

Claire and Gus exchanged a look. Reporting this meant she'd be telling her story over and over.

"You're very brave," said Claire, putting her hand on Hazel's arm.

"No, I'm not." Hazel shook her off. "It's not a big deal. Nothing happened. I keep trying to tell you that."

"Your principal propositioned and blackmailed you," Claire said. "This couldn't be a bigger deal."

"Sexually harassed you," added Gus.

"Basically attempted to rape you," amended Claire.

"Whatever," said Hazel.

"Hazel, honey, Daddy wants to call President Hill at the College."

"Confidentially," said Gus, grating cheese for a second quesadilla, this time for Hazel. "For advice."

A former Women's Studies professor, President Hill was a mover and shaker in feminist circles.

"On second thought, let's email," said Gus. "We need this in writing."

They sat down with his laptop at the kitchen table, the three of them, with Pickle at their feet. Gus typed.

Dear Nicole,

We're writing with difficult news, and with a request for help.

Today, as you know, was the first day of school at Riverburg High. Our daughter Hazel, a senior, was called to the principal's office. Richard White proceeded to proposition Hazel, telling her that "every year I pick one girl to have sex with and this year I pick you." He threatened that if she refused, he'd make things difficult for her at school, and that her graduation would be in jeopardy.

Before calling the police, we thought we'd turn to you for guidance.

With thanks, and apologies for adding to what must already be a hectic start to the semester for you.

Sincerely,
Gus Blum (and Claire Greenberg Blum)

"No way," said Hazel, snapping the laptop shut. "The police? Dad! You are not sending that email. No."

"I can take out the part about the police," said Gus, opening his computer back up. "This is just a draft."

"It's not the email. It's that I don't know if I want to make such a big deal out of this. I don't know if I want to tell anyone. Ever."

"Oh my God. Please stop saying that. You can't *make* it a big deal. It *is* a big deal," said Claire. "There's no getting around that no matter what we do."

"Why do we have to say anything? I'm already the new girl. I don't want to be THAT girl, too. It's not fair."

"You're right." Claire pulled Hazel toward her lap, which was unwieldy as Hazel was two inches taller. "It's incredibly unfair. What are you thinking you want to do?"

"I'm going back to school tomorrow."

"What?" said Gus. "No, you're not. You can't."

"If I don't go back to school, then I really won't graduate," said Hazel. Which was reasonable.

"You can homeschool!" Wolf shouted his suggestion from two rooms away. He'd made it back downstairs to the living room and was inching toward the kitchen.

Hazel withdrew from her mother. Wolf came in and sat in his regular chair at the kitchen table.

"You're supposed to be playing video games," said Claire.

"I'm part of this family, too."

"I know you are," said Claire. "But you're not part of this discussion. Or this decision."

"I don't care. Let him stay," said Hazel.

"I guess maybe you *could* homeschool. Until we figure this out. Or switch to another school district?" said Gus. "I think you can do that here."

"There's a solid boarding school an hour away. You don't have to sleep over," said Claire. "They take day students, and the College has a tuition break, and they have a bus pickup right in town—"

"He didn't hurt you," said Wolf, looking up from his phone, a flash of worry furrowing his little brow. "Did he?"

"I'm not sitting in this house by myself homeschooling for my senior year. I'm not going to be a shut-in. And I'm not switching schools. The same thing could happen all over again," said Hazel. "That boarding school is like 30K a year for day students—"

"Twenty thousand for faculty kids," said Gus.

"—and we can't afford that," said Hazel. "I need that money for college. For Vassar. Not that I can even get *in* with a principal who hates me."

"You can get in—" said Gus.

"Besides, it won't help. I read a memoir about a girl who was raped in boarding school. And why should I be the one to have to leave? Shouldn't he get fired or something?"

"Yes, of course," said Claire. "Absolutely."

"Clearly," said Gus.

"Did you know that the age of consent is thirteen in Japan?" said Wolf. "In France, there's no age of consent. It's basically normal for a teenager to date her principal."

"That's disgusting," said Claire.

"Send the email! Send the email!" said Wolf.

"Stop," said Hazel, kicking Wolf under the table.

"Did it ever occur to any of you that without rules and repercussions, society would fall into mass chaos? Have any of you ever heard of *anarchy*?" said Wolf.

"Seriously. Go back to your room," said Gus.

"What about school tomorrow?" said Claire.

"She can't go," said Gus.

"Neither can I," said Wolf.

"I have to go," said Hazel, leaving the table, like she was done talking, like it was decided. "I'm going. My first quarter grades are the last ones Vassar will see for my early decision application. I can't get behind. I'm taking four APs."

"No, this is crazy. I'm sorry," said Claire. "Maybe we really should call the police."

"Let's send the email first," said Gus.

"We're calling the police."

"Something's burning," Wolf pointed out.

"*Mom.* Can you just give me a chance to figure out what I want to do?" said Hazel. She stood in the doorway between the kitchen and dining room. "With my own life. Please?"

"What *we* want to do," said Claire. "This is a family decision."

"No, it's not. I'm eighteen years old. It's my body. My choice."

"That's true," Wolf said. "It *is* Hazel's body."

With that, the smoke alarm went off.

"Shit. Hazel's quesadilla," said Gus, so neurotic about burning the house down that he'd made Claire swear not to use any of the fireplaces.

Wolf, who was sensitive to most mildly unpleasant noises, started screaming. Pickle barked. Gus doused the charred tortilla in the sink. Claire opened the window.

"Wolf! Go upstairs right now. Hazel—" Claire turned, and found her on the back deck, calming the dog. "I love you. I know you're eighteen. That doesn't mean you can or should figure this out by yourself."

A part of Claire didn't want Hazel to say anything, didn't want her daughter's life to veer off course. Her job was to protect her daughter, not to fix an unfixable world. Claire knew how these cases worked. Every day men did much worse and got away with it.

Gus was quiet. This was out of his purview. This one should be Claire's call. And Hazel's.

Claire returned to the kitchen. "Let's give Hazel the night to think. We'll wake up with clearer heads," she said, deciding on a nondecision.

"Okay," said Gus. "Should I make pizza?"

8

say something

Wolf did what he was told. Sort of. While his dad made dinner, Wolf went to his room. He took his phone, since screens in his room were suddenly NBD, got under the covers and downloaded the Say Something anonymous reporting app mentioned during assembly. He created a password, entered Riverburg High School, and went down the list of options: Anger issues, Animal Cruelty, Bullying/Cyber-Bullying, Concern about an adult, Cutting/Self-Harm, Depression/Anxiety, Domestic Violence/Child abuse, Drug Use/Distribution, Eating Disorder, Gang Violence—

Wait. He'd skipped it. *Concern about an adult.* Got it. The screen changed.

Call 911 if this is an emergency. Noted.

What's going on? The more info, the better.

Who are you concerned about? This person is…

There was a drop-down tab, and a choice between two options: The victim. The offender.

Easy. The offender. The principal. No need to give Hazel's name.

Next. *Attachments are super helpful. Upload one here.*

Hmm. No, not happening.

Then came a green Submit prompt, and a warning.

Note: If you provide your name and/or contact information, you acknowledge that it will be provided to assist in resolving the concern or threat you are reporting. If you deliberately provide false information or use this system to threaten or harass someone, you may be subject to criminal prosecution.

That made this sound serious, like Wolf could be the one to go to jail. He wasn't exactly known for his impulse control. Given that he was still down on calories *and* his meds had probably long worn off *and* he could feel his anxiety cresting to a new high, it wasn't necessarily the ideal point in the day to take a potentially life-altering course of action. But Wolf knew wrong from right, he told himself, and he loved his sister, and the principal was a rapist, or at least a jerk, and his parents were being stupid.

Rules were rules. A principal should *not* be allowed to get away with this. What were his parents and Hazel thinking? They *had* to report this. And if they wouldn't? Well, then Wolf had no choice but to take matters into his own hands.

He went back up to the *tell us about what happened* portion. How to put this? *The high school principal asked a student to have sex with him today.* That seemed about right. And it didn't mean that anybody would ever find out the student was Hazel. He hadn't stipulated a gender or a grade. It could be anyone in the entire high school. This way Hazel remained anonymous and protected, and the principal would get what was coming to him.

Satisfied, Wolf clicked out of the app and went downstairs looking for dinner.

Later that night, Gus sat in front of his laptop at the dining room table, waiting for Wolf's water to boil for chamomile tea, trying to come up with a lecture for Deconstructing America. He hadn't taught it for years. No matter what the family emergency, unless he was dead, he had to teach tomorrow. It was the first day of classes. He was department chair. Yet it felt preposterous to pretend this was a normal Tuesday night when Hazel had been violated that morning. He couldn't concentrate. Hazel's well-being was at stake. Her safety! Her future. The email was sitting there, ready to go, in his drafts folder. Fuck it. He wasn't going to be talked out of protecting his daughter. He typed in Nicole Hill's address, taking Claire's off the cc. His finger lingered on the Send button. He tapped it, like he was tapping out a nuclear code.

9

claire can't sleep

Back when they lived in Brooklyn, Claire had a hard time with sleep. Either she couldn't fall asleep for hours, or she would right away, only to wake up in the middle of the night, filled with anxiety, preoccupied by to-do lists and the mental gymnastics of managing the family's schedule and finances. Some nights her meditation app worked, and her mind quieted. Other nights not. She was an anxious person, Gus said. Claire blamed New York. The nightly sirens from the old age home across the street when a resident died. The pair of mice scurrying across her kitchen. The energy of the city seeping under the windows, promising something outside their apartment, something better, that Claire could or should be doing. That first summer in Riverburg, safe with the knowledge that there was nothing out there for her in the dark, Claire had slept.

Until that night. After seeing to Hazel's delayed dinner, Claire snuck onto the porch and belatedly smoked her semi-regular three hits and one extra, as recompense for the horrible day. She watched some TV with Gus and read herself to sleep. She woke up an hour and a half later, her tank top twisted around her neck, her chest steaming like a stovetop grill, her pajamas soaked through, as if she had the flu. The heat a new, hellish twist to her insomnia. So, this was perimenopause?

Claire grabbed for dry pajamas and padded down the stairs to the kitchen, where she proceeded to guzzle grapefruit juice and spoon gobs of peanut butter into her mouth. Back in bed she resorted to her version of counting sheep. She planned her outfits. She planned their weekend excursions. She planned the outfits she'd wear on their weekend excursions. But it didn't work, because who cared what she wore, or where they went, when her daughter's life was crashing.

She gave up on sleep and moved through the darkness to her studio to find her phone. Gus had unplugged hers from the charger and plugged his in its place. His was at 100 percent, hers at 67 percent. It was one of those things that didn't matter but annoyed her to no end.

"Asshole," Claire said under her breath.

That was unfair. Gus was no asshole. As a professor, he tended to profess, but he was a good person—a good husband. She couldn't help it that the little things got to her. Using up the last of the toilet paper in the bathroom and not replacing it, muddy sneakers left in the middle of the kitchen, jeans on the bedroom floor, beard hairs in the sink, not dumping the espresso capsules. She unplugged his phone and plugged hers in, checking the time—4:57 a.m.

Lately, Gus had become part of the scenery, like the kitchen table. Sturdy and hardworking and taken for granted. But Gus was indefatigable. He could stay up when Wolf's insomnia struck, walk the dog at daybreak, and then teach a packed lecture hall. He had the immune system of an ox. He would get sick for an afternoon, take a nap, and be himself again. More than that, there was an ideological purity to how he saw the world. Gus was a thinker.

Ramona said he was a "prince among men." *That* was pushing it.

Claire considered his phone in her hand. Her general policy was not to snoop on her husband. If he wanted to cheat on her he could go ahead. She wanted someone who wanted her. Not that she was worried—Gus wasn't the dick pic type; he wasn't on social media. He had a thing about the surveillance state. There wasn't much danger of finding anything compromising. Sometimes, though, it was instructional to glance through his emails, as he didn't always remember to tell her about out-of-state conferences he'd penciled in, or the next day's early-morning faculty meeting or work dinner. And because you never knew what else you'd find. Knowledge was power.

She pressed Gus's code, Wolf's birthday digits, into the phone.

There it was. An email in Gus's sent mailbox, timed 9:29 p.m. Subject: family emergency. What the fuck? Gus had sent the email to Nicole Hill behind Claire's back. Behind Hazel's back. He hadn't so much as bothered to hide his phone or delete the email. He'd watched *television* with her! Rage coursed through Claire's veins. Alongside, she had to admit to herself, some relief. Part of her had wanted him to do something. Part of her knew he would, no matter what she'd told him the night before. This was a very Gus move. She clicked back to his inbox. In real time, she saw President Hill's response come in. She thumbed the message open.

Come see me in my office this morning first thing. Can you do 8? Bring your wife and daughter. We have resources for emotional and staff support. We can connect you with the appropriate authorities. I am so very sorry this is the way you are starting out at the College. My heart goes out to Hazel.

Claire was wrong. Gus *was* an asshole. He'd lied to Claire and betrayed Hazel. But maybe he'd done the right thing? They were out of their depths. Maybe Nicole Hill could help.

10

hazel wakes up

Hazel slept fitfully. It was as though she hadn't slept at all, really, but she must have, because when her dad barged in and opened her blinds, the attic filled with sunlight.

"Hazel, time to wake up."

"Coming," she said. For thirty seconds she was regular Hazel, and then she remembered the day before, and became screwed Hazel. She pulled the thin summer blanket over her head and let herself descend back into sleep to the time before this was real.

"Hazel?" It was her mother. "Come down to the kitchen for breakfast, okay?"

Hazel grunted into her pillow. If only she could stay in bed forever.

"You said you wanted to go to school today. And we need to talk."

Fine. She threw on a short-sleeved sweatshirt and followed her mother down the stairs. Wolf was eating an English muffin and watching a video on his phone. Her father had his laptop open on the kitchen table.

"What can I make you?" her mother asked.

Hazel didn't normally eat breakfast. And if she did, she could get her own. Her mother rarely asked what she wanted. Her parents were too busy catering to Wolf. This morning was different. Claire handed Hazel a bowl of warm oatmeal with banana slices and honey on top.

"Pancakes?" asked her dad, holding a spatula in the air like a conductor's baton. He seemed awfully cheerful given the circumstances.

"How much do you think I can eat?" said Hazel. "And I know exactly what you're doing."

"What are we doing?" asked her mom.

"There's no point in trying to talk me out of it," said Hazel, between bites. It was helpful to get out in front of things when maneuvering around her parents. "I'm going to school," said Hazel. "If you didn't want me to go, you should have let me sleep in."

"Hazel, listen," her dad said, turning his back to the pancakes. "I did something and you're not going to like it. But I hope one day when you're a parent, you'll understand that I didn't have a choice."

"You had a choice," said her mother, grinding a citrus. "Maybe you felt you had no choice."

"Claire—"

"We said last night—we decided, *as a family*—that we would wait for Hazel. It's not like you did it without asking us. We'd already said no."

"What do you mean? Said no about what? What are you talking about?" said Hazel.

"The email?" guessed Wolf. His favorite board game was Clue. *The professor, with a phone, in the den.*

"God," said Hazel, refusing the orange juice her mother was trying to hand her. "You did *not*."

"She's a big deal in town," said her father. "Like the de facto czar. And she'll help us navigate this."

Hazel wasn't the kind of girl to break down and cry at the kitchen table. She prided herself on a certain toughness, a certain stoicism. Her father's email, though, his betrayal of her *very* clear wishes, was more than she could handle. Also, the idea that now there were sides to take. Which meant some people would be taking his side, the principal's side.

"I can't believe you did this to me." She pushed the rest of the oatmeal away.

"Not *to* you, sweetie. *For* you. To protect you. You shouldn't have to feel scared to go to school," said Gus.

"I never said I was scared."

"There's something else," said her mother.

Hazel felt herself turn numb again. Her feet were cold as icicles. She couldn't feel her fingertips. This was a new thing, this ability to go blank, to feel nothing, to make her insides disappear. Whatever this new version of her reality was, she couldn't do anything to stop it.

"We're meeting with the president. On campus. Her office. At eight," explained her dad.

"At eight? This morning? How many times do I have to say *I have school.*"

"I'm coming, too," said Wolf. "Hazel's my sister."

"Wolf," said their mother, "you're leaving for the bus in ten minutes and going to the junior high where you belong. Go brush your teeth. Or no screens for the rest of the school year."

"What?!" said Wolf.

"Can you stop?" asked Hazel. "Like, all of you?"

"Go get my toothbrush."

"Wolfie, you can get your own toothbrush," said her mom.

"You guys, can everyone calm down?" asked her dad.

Somehow, by 7:15, Wolf was at the bus stop, teeth brushed, school supplies in his backpack. By 7:40, Hazel and her mother were dressed and the three of them in the car on the way to campus.

"She runs early," her dad said.

Unlike scruffy Riverburg, the College's campus was manicured and pristine, fastidiously kept up by a grounds and custodial staff. Georgian-style brick buildings positioned on the greenest of lawns, nestled between rolling hills. The library bell tower—once the tallest building in the state—pointing up toward the September sky.

"Hazel, welcome," said the president with an outstretched hand. Unlike most people in town, Nicole Hill was Black. And unlike anyone else in town, she looked like she'd stepped out of a glossy magazine's Women in Power issue. (According to Hazel's dad, she worked out six days a week with a trainer and made five times as much money as any professor did.) The president was dressed in a perfectly fitted pantsuit with a silk top underneath and heels on her feet, like she worked in Midtown Manhattan. Hazel's parents said on the ride over that, one day, Nicole would run for Senate.

"Gus, thank you for coming in. Claire, so nice to meet you. Hazel, I'm Nicole Hill. Before we begin, do you have any questions or concerns for me?"

The president's office was supersized and more corporate feeling than Hazel would have imagined. Lots of wood. A long conference table. A large desk. Framed photos faced out with politicians and, Hazel was surprised to see, a notable actor slash activist. This was the second time in twenty-four hours, Hazel realized, that she'd been called into a head person's office. Why was she being treated like the one in trouble when she'd done nothing wrong?

"President Hill, I haven't decided if I want to report this," said Hazel. Her ears were ringing and muffled-feeling, like she was on a plane. "I don't think I want to."

"Call me Nicole. To be totally transparent with you, we do need to communicate with the authorities, Hazel. Legally. The College does. I'm sorry to have to tell you that."

"Wait," said Hazel. "Are saying it's not up to me?"

"I'm a mandatory reporter, Hazel. So is your father."

"What does that mean exactly?" asked Claire.

"It means that faculty and staff at the College, and at the high school for that matter, are legally obligated to report this…" she hesitated "…this type of abuse—to the police."

"If I may chime in. That's when it comes to campus incidents. Sexual assault and the like," said an older man coming in from the hall. The College's in-house attorney, he said, introducing himself. "This situation is murkier."

"It's complicated," continued Hill. "This is new terrain for us. You're not a student, but you are a member of our college community."

"What if that's not what I want? I mean, I'm still trying to figure this out. It happened yesterday. I don't *know* what I want."

The president paused. Her eyes welled. This made it a lot harder for Hazel to hate her.

"Hazel, I feel for you. I can't tell you how much. You shouldn't have to go through this. No young woman should. No student should. That said, I can't unknow what I know. I don't think you can, either. Your parents were right to come to me. In any case, from a legal standpoint, and not to mention an ethical one, given the other young people in school with you, we do need to talk to the police—I do."

President Hill was laser focused on her. "Hazel? Are you still with me?"

Hazel nodded but really, she wasn't.

"I have something else to tell you that's going to be difficult and painful to hear." President Hill exchanged looks with the lawyer guy. "We made some calls first thing this morning.

Richard White is saying that you were the one to propose a sexual relationship."

"What?" said Hazel.

"He's denying it."

"What are you talking about?" said her mother. "How is that possible?"

"Where are you getting this from?" asked her father. "If I may ask."

"The superintendent already knows what happened yesterday—or knows, at least, that something out of the ordinary happened. White told his assistant principal, Hazel, that you put your hand on his thigh. That you—this is his phrase, not mine—'came on' to him." She added air quotes and a sympathetic eye roll.

"That is ridiculous," said her father, standing up and pacing the length of Nicole's office.

"He's lying," Hazel said.

"This is textbook rape culture," said her mother.

"Your mom's right," explained Hill. "A predator will often turn the accusation around on his victim as a preventative strategy, an anticipatory self-defense."

Hazel hated that word. *Victim*. She wasn't a victim. Nothing had happened. She was *fine*.

"I'm sorry, Hazel. Truly." President Hill came around from the desk and kneeled beside her.

"I've been there. Not exactly there. Something like there. We'll take every step we can to protect you."

Oh God. What if people believed him?

"I don't want anyone to know it was me. Do they have to know? Can you not use my name? Can the whole thing be sealed or something?"

"We'll try our best," said President Hill. "Legally, your anonymity is supposed to be protected. But the story may get out. Unfortunately—"

"It will?" asked Claire.

"Not necessarily your name, but—eventually, probably sooner rather than later, people in Riverburg could start hearing something about this."

Perfect, thought Hazel.

"What can we do?" her father asked.

"Gus, take the family time you need. Let's inform the dean of faculty, so you can have some leeway. Hazel, here's a phone number for a therapist in our counseling office. She's wonderful. Why don't you call and book some appointments—you'll need a space that's confidential to talk things through." The president gave Hazel's hand a sympathetic squeeze, ending the meeting. "Here's my card. I'm putting my cell phone on the back. Don't hesitate to reach out, and I mean that."

Claire and Gus and Hazel walked down the stairs and gathered themselves in the carpeted lobby. It was 8:20.

"I hate to say this," said Gus, "but I have to go prep my class and teach." He ushered them out to the lawn in front of the administration building, steering them toward the faculty parking lot.

"But Nicole said—"

"She didn't mean I shouldn't *teach*."

"What about Hazel?"

"What about me?" said Hazel.

"I mean, it would be certifiably insane for you to go back to that high school today," her mother said. "Wouldn't it? Gus?"

"Can you *please* listen to me? You can't stop me from getting an education. That would literally be illegal. It's not like I'm going there to hang out with him. We're not spending the day together. He's not my new boyfriend. Also, don't say *insane*. That's really disrespectful to people with mental health problems. Like our entire family."

"Hazel," said Gus. "Can you do me a favor and lower your voice? At least until we make it to the car? I work here."

"I don't know. Maybe you're right. Maybe it's okay," said Claire. "For today. After that, we'll see. Don't talk to him."

"Keep your phone on you," said her father. "If he approaches you, make a video."

"We have to keep our phones in our lockers," said Hazel, buckling up in the front passenger seat.

"Yeah, well I'm pretty sure school principals are not allowed to have sex with their students, so if anyone gives you a problem about your phone, have them call me. Okay?" He closed her door.

"Are you okay?" asked her mother as they reversed out of the lot and headed past the campus gates. "Are you sure you want to go back there?"

She fiddled with the window lever. As her mother ferried her to some unknown but likely cataclysmic fate at school, Hazel wanted nothing more than to go home and crawl back into bed. She wasn't going to let herself. If she stayed home one day, she'd stay home a week and then before she knew it a month, and then a semester. She'd miss her entire senior year. She'd miss her life.

"Can we stop talking about it?"

When Hazel said no to the principal, she'd thought that was the end of the humiliation. Only now did she realize this was, maybe, only the beginning.

PART TWO

official oppression

11

gus gets canceled

Gus was running on empty. The terrible, enraging business with the principal had consumed him with worry about Hazel and left him completely spent; he'd hardly slept that night. Now he had to put all of that aside.

The time had come to "Deconstruct America." In half an hour, he'd be standing in front of a classroom packed with students. Claire could criticize him as much as she liked for going back to work that morning. She'd quit her job. Someone needed to make money.

Teaching his first class of his first semester would take everything he could muster. Lectures were a performance. Day one, like opening night. He'd be panned or praised. His reputation on campus formed or spoiled. Gus needed to sparkle.

After grabbing a cup of lukewarm black coffee at the snack bar in the student center, Gus crossed the quad, walked into the classroom, met the AV person who showed him how to work the projector and mic, and assumed his position behind the podium.

The classroom had tiered rows and three huge green chalkboards. At the appointed hour, Gus's charges filed in and took their seats, and opened their sticker-laden laptops ready for a lecture that would be worth their parents' ungodly tuition dollars.

"Welcome to American Studies: Deconstructing America. I'm Professor Gus Blum. This semester we'll be looking at American culture through the lens of the TV sitcom."

Gus hadn't taught this introductory course for many years. At Rocky Creek, he and his colleagues in American Studies typically hired adjuncts or visiting professors or corralled one of their almost graduated and on the job market PhD students for the task. The real professors preferred upper-level, discussion-focused courses, or better yet, graduate seminars, both for the intellectual rigor and because they could shepherd a class discussion instead of having to write lectures and prepare PowerPoints.

The first day of an introductory lecture class, as Gus taught it, came down to a scholarly seduction. An invitation for his students to stop being mere consumers of culture and to refashion themselves as cultural critics. There were problematics to be unknotted, theoretical vistas to be opened. There was so much for his students to question. The intransigent family paradigm. The glorification of suburban conformity. The multicamera setup.

Popular culture—television, in particular—was a reflection of society. A narrator, if an unreliable one. A funhouse mirror. The themes that appeared and reappeared on millions of television screens across America refracted the nation's anxieties, its problems, its collective unconscious. Its *gestalt*. The job of the critic was to interpret plotlines and characters, settings and worlds and dialogue for the broader societal messages and meanings they encoded, in the same way a psychoanalyst might interpret a dream. His students would learn how to connect those dots, joining the ranks of the chosen few who could watch and understand and see television, and therefore the world they lived in—and therefore "American" culture—for what it really was.

To get his students started on their intellectual rite of passage, Gus would show how sitcom depictions of the American family across the decades linked up with big cultural changes, social movements—and fears—of the period. He had a decade-old lecture on this from when he last taught the class at Rocky Creek, complete with clips from various shows. In an ideal world he would have prepared a new lecture. But this was *not* an ideal world. It had been a mad scramble that morning, between breakfast and walking Pickle and the meeting at the president's office. Miraculously, he'd found a crumpled printout of his ancient class notes and a memory stick abandoned in the inside pocket of a (rather smelly, rather ridiculous, and therefore rarely worn) Claire-thrifted barn jacket buried in a forgotten laundry bag with some of his to-be-dry-cleaned shirts. He'd had just enough time after the meeting at Hill's office to switch out the Rocky Creek logo for the logo of the College.

He clicked on his first slide.

"*Leave it to Beaver* aired from 1957 to 1963. Your classic depiction of the stereotypical 'American' family. The white, comfortably middle-class, breadwinner husband with the suit and briefcase off to the office, mom in her apron happily managing the two children and the household. We refer to this show, for some with nostalgia, for others with disdain, as representing and meaning something beyond what it was. What did it symbolize? And, perhaps more importantly, what did the show try and *do*?"

Gus walked to the right side of the classroom where a chalkboard wall stood unobstructed by the screen.

"Anyone?" he asked. An expected silence followed. Par for the course on the first day of class. It was Gus's job to warm the crowd.

"Let's free associate," he suggested. "There are no wrong answers."

"Tradition?" a kid in the front eventually volunteered. "Like, family values or something?"

"Yes," said Gus. "Someone else?"

"Housewives?" said another.

"Absolutely—and not the kind we're used to seeing on TV these days."

"Patriarchy!"

"Good!" said Gus, writing.

"Heteronormative family."

"You got it."

"Capitalism?"

"Indeed," affirmed Gus, adding to the list on the board. He was pleasantly surprised. These were great first day answers. The students seemed sharp.

He ran the *Leave it to Beaver* clip, then offered a long aside about how images of the idealized family soothed people's anxieties in the aftermath of World War II and during the Cold War, speaking indirectly to the growth of the suburbs and white flight from urban centers.

Things were going well. He was back in the saddle. He felt his sea legs beneath him. Next up, the 1970s.

"Flash forward to Archie Bunker. *All in the Family* debuts in 1971. We're in a living room in Queens, New York. Right? A white guy with a cigar sits in a recliner spewing racism. Yeah?"

A couple of the savvier kids nodded. Most young people, he knew, wouldn't have encountered Archie Bunker before.

After showing a clip and explaining the show's premise, Gus said it was common knowledge that the show was about generational change and the tensions surrounding it. But it was also innovative, Gus said, because it tackled racism from a white perspective, telling the story of all the Archie Bunkers out there who felt left behind. Later in the semester, Gus said, they'd look at how the white backlash to the civil rights movement of the 1960s foreshadowed the rise of contemporary right-wing extremism.

Making his way toward the home stretch of the late twentieth century, Gus took a sip from the dregs of his coffee and glanced at his frayed notes. His job now was to usher his students into the era of his youth, the '80s.

Cliff and Clair Huxtable flashed on the screen.

Jesus. Cosby was in his lecture? He'd almost forgotten. If he'd had more time to properly review his notes the night before, as was his habit, he'd probably have cut Cosby. He hesitated and considered advancing through the Cosby section—before deciding to press on. If he stopped teaching about every bad man there'd be nothing left to teach, and no one left to teach about.

"*The Cosby Show*," Gus explained, trying to play it cool, "ran from 1984 to 1992 and shaped American views of the city, reenvisioning Brooklyn, New York, and therefore cities around the country, as family friendly. And, more importantly, American audiences were introduced to their first ever, and long-ignored, Black professional-class family. And to a post Mary Tyler Moore *marriage* of equals. Clair, a lawyer, and Cosby's Cliff, the more home-based parent, an ob-gyn with his office in the family basement."

Although most of the students seemed to not care—or be oblivious to Gus's wrong turn—an undeniable undercurrent of dissent rippled through the classroom.

"Now, I know what you're thinking," he said, improvising, suppressing his growing thrum of panic. "Cosby as we know him today is a villain, not a family man, much less a hero. And it's complicated, right, because Cosby was playing a version of himself."

The fact was, Cosby became a cultural icon of the twentieth century, the first Black actor to have a male lead in an American television series (*I Spy*). *The Cosby Show* was groundbreaking, seminal television. But none of that mattered. Cross chatter was catching like kindling in the room. Gus heard a groan. He was losing them.

Shit. Shit, shit, shit. The last time Gus had taught Cosby he was one of a large fraternity of perhaps bad men who made good art. While long-standing allegations and rumors had circulated in whisper networks for decades, in the years since Gus had last lectured on him, there were Cosby's rape trials and eventual conviction; a *New York* magazine cover story of his many accusers; a thoughtful documentary grappling with his tainted legacy and crimes; and of course, the MeToo movement writ large. Bill Cosby had become a complete pariah. Gus may as well have played the opening sequence to Woody Allen's *Manhattan*.

A girl raised her hand, though Gus hadn't asked a question. Woman, Gus corrected himself. Person, he readjusted. Should he have begun class by going around the room and inquiring about pronouns? Even in a lecture format? Stupid Gus. He was a relic. He was supposed to be a scholar. Why did he have to be such an idiot? In any case, his student was ponytailed and heavily banged, not just raising their hand, but vigorously waving their arm like it was an enemy flag.

"Professor Blum?"

Gus steadied himself, gripping the lectern. "Hi there. Your name?"

"Sam, but this isn't about me. Cosby is a serial rapist. He's raped like *hundreds* of women. I don't get it. How can you give him a platform?"

Gus knew that the College's students were different than those at Rocky Creek—more self-aware and self-conscious, and more privileged. And, he'd heard, as far as the humanities students went, more politically attuned and progressive—which he was jazzed about. Like it or not, the luxuriously sweatered Cosby, en famille, took up the whole of the projector screen and stared down at his class with heightened proportions.

As a feminist scholar and as a *father*, Gus would be first in line to condemn Cosby's actions. Obviously! But how can you deconstruct culture if you can't bring yourself to see it? Perhaps he should pivot and center the rest of the lecture on that age-old if thoroughly clichéd debate.

Disgruntled mumbles rose in the room.

This could have been so easily avoided. If he'd had time to properly prepare the night before, he might have switched out *The Cosby Show* for the more anodyne *Family Ties*, looking at the Reagan-loving Alex P. Keaton in conflict with his hippie liberal parents. But, that said, there *was* a valid academic and intellectual argument for showing Cosby to the class.

So Gus stumbled into an impromptu, deeply awkward dive into the essentialness of *The Cosby Show* to his generation. What it meant for Black bourgeois and Black cool. What it meant for conceptions of the city life. How his own wife, his own *Claire*, had become an artist slash designer because of Denise Huxtable's outfits.

"Who cares!" Someone—not Sam, someone else, a guy?—yelled out from the back of the room.

Gus Blum, defender of evil men? This was not who he was. This was the *opposite* of who he was.

"Are you for real?" said Sam, evidently not one to back down. (He hadn't said that last part aloud, had he?) "It's a stupid TV show. It doesn't matter if nobody ever watches it again. Talk about capitalism."

"Yes!" said Gus, brightening at the term. One last attempt to regain his theoretical footing. "Let's *talk* about capitalism! Please! Anyone else?"

"Professor Blum, don't you get it? There are *survivors* in this room. Statistically speaking, there must be. There are predators here on campus. In Riverburg." Sam gestured to the world beyond the campus gates. "Have you thought about that? Don't you care?"

Several students in Gus's sight line began recording the exchange on their phone.

Gus found himself for the first time ever in front of a classroom, speechless. Did he *care*? About *predators*? About the problem of evil? If only Sam knew.

Defeated, Gus ended class early. This was his demise? A *Cosby Show* clip? He was like a gymnast who fell off the balance beam while executing a minor requirement, like a figure skater who fell not on a quad axel but on a toe loop.

12

wolf tries out

Wolf walked into the school's mini auditorium to audition for the winter drama, knowing that what transpired over the next hour and ten minutes would determine the course of the rest of his life. Or, at least, the next three years of middle school. He needed to be cast—students were only guaranteed a part in the spring musical, he'd learned—and he wanted as big a role as he could get.

A motley group of drama kids with a variety of hair colors, skin tones, personalities and sneakers were assembling in the first few rows. While Wolf's stomach churned with nerves, he nevertheless had the rare feeling that he was in the right place. Because here were the kids who—maybe?—didn't play sports. At least not obsessively. Maybe here, in this unlikely, backwoods town, he'd find his people? Something he never could in his old school, where they had called him, good-naturedly or not, The Professor.

He was trying as hard as he possibly could to BE IN THE MOMENT. To not let his mind rest on the disastrous events of the day before yesterday and the stupidest decision he'd ever made. (After agreeing to move to Riverburg.) But he couldn't shake thinking—obsessing—about the Say Something report. It *would* be traced back to him, it was just a matter of time. His parents and Hazel would find out sooner or later. Probably sooner, with his luck. And when they did, they would—well, he didn't know what. He'd never been in really big trouble before.

Which meant that Wolf, while into and (admittedly) more than somewhat intimidated by the drama kids, not to mention *completely* preoccupied by his about-to-be-in-big-troubleness, was inwardly FREAKING OUT when Gracie walked in, with her overall shorts and pigtail braids and confidence. To his great surprise, she casually claimed the seat two down from his, with only his orange backpack between them. Wolf's stomach stopped churning and started flipping, his belly becoming a butterfly house. For three lunches in a row, he'd sat with Gracie and her friends. The girls didn't seem to mind his presence, but he was petrified of screwing things up and being banished to the Dungeons & Dragons table, or worse, having to eat alone. Being around Gracie, with a seat at her table, was enough. And now, this.

Wolf told his ever-ticking stopwatch of anxiety to shut up. For the sake of the audition, for the sake of his future social standing and emotional well-being, he had to stop thinking about it. To not stress. He inhaled and he exhaled, like he'd been taught in theater camp. (And in therapy.) He'd use it—the anxiety, the fear, he had no other choice. The stakes couldn't be higher. He'd funnel his nerves out of his body and INTO the audition. He'd go Method.

Mr. Woods stepped onto the stage. "Welcome to drama club, and auditions for the winter production of *Charlotte's Web*. Later this afternoon we'll be taking turns reading from a couple of scenes. First, let's get to know each other. Please join me onstage."

Omg. Wolf rolled his eyes. E.B. White. Could they get any

more Maine than this? Talk about country. True, *Charlotte's Web*, which according to his mom, was inspired by E.B. White's seaside farm in Brooklin, Maine, was one of his favorite classic books. He was a fan of the original animated film, and the live action version starring Dakota Fanning wasn't bad, either.

Mr. Woods had them sit in a circle and play theater games where they paired off and acted like mirrors. Then they moved around like farm animals before the actual "acting" part of the audition started. Mr. Woods had Wolf read *three* separate scenes. More than anyone else. He was possibly slaying the audition? No. Scratch that. He probably sucked. It was more that, for a few minutes, he forgot to care, forgot to be self-conscious, forgot to worry if everyone thought he was a loser. He forgot *himself*. It seemed like practically no time had passed when the late-late bus driver honked, announcing his imminent departure.

Life was weird. Wolf had been a 1000 percent certain he'd hate his new school. So far, tbh, it was almost fun? Classes were easy and occasionally a teacher said something interesting. The first week, anyway. Contrary to his mother's worries, bullies did not roam the halls. Nobody had sexted or catfished him. Who cares that his science teacher gave an entire lesson on microwave safety? If he wanted to learn something, he'd look it up on his phone.

Mr. Woods said the cast list would be posted the next morning. Wolf had no idea how he'd manage to sleep until then. Maybe he wouldn't try.

That night, Wolf did sleep. Probably because his new psychiatrist had recently prescribed him a nighttime ADHD medicine for his chronic insomnia. Still, he was up by five, before the sun and his dad (whom he promptly woke, asking for breakfast). Wolf prepared for bad news, readying himself to face the humiliation and ensuing depression that would come with not getting a role.

The cast list was posted before Wolf made it to homeroom. He saw a throng of drama kids clumped together by the bulletin board next to the mini auditorium, eyes scanning the page for their name, and ran to join them, pushing through the crowd so that he could see.

What the—?! There it was. His name was first on the list. WILBUR... Wolf Blum. He got the part. HE GOT THE PART. This was the best thing that had happened to him since moving. Scratch that. This was the best day of his life.

Who cared if his first starring role would be in a pig costume?

"Hey, Wolf, congratulations," said a girl a half a foot taller than him. "You were amazing at auditions."

Wolf ignored her and stared up at the cast list, needing to check again that he wasn't making this up. That's when he noticed that right below his name was Gracie's. She was to play Charlotte. Opposite him. Was he dreaming? He felt a hand graze his shoulder.

"Wolf!" said Gracie. "You're Wilbur!"

"And you're Charlotte," said Wolf.

Wolf's shock turned to a speedy euphoria. Was it his morning meds kicking in, or the feeling of Gracie's touch?

"We should run lines," Gracie said. "Give me your phone and I'll put in my number."

He hadn't been hallucinating. Wolf's life truly had changed. Kids were pointing at him. In a good way! Like the scene in a dumb sports movie where a football player is hoisted on the shoulders of his teammates.

Wolf glided through the school day. When it was over, he ignored the directive to wait for his bus to be called and walked himself straight over to the drama club board to quadruple-check the cast list.

The paper was still pinned to the board, flapping from one corner. Wolf stood on his tiptoes and touched it for good luck. He felt the primal urge to kiss his finger, like he'd seen the Riverburg rabbi do with the Torah and her tallit. His name was there at the top, clear as a newspaper headline. He really was Wilbur. Wolf was Wilbur. Unbelievable. He couldn't wait to get home and tell his parents. And Hazel, too. (If she still cared what happened to him?)

"Hey, buddy! Bus line!" A teacher type was yelling at him for being in the wrong part of the lobby.

"Coming!" He took an extra second and ran his finger down the cast list.

There she was. Right below him. Charlotte... Grace White. Wow.

Wait.

Gracie White?!

WHITE? Hazel's principal—wasn't he *Richard White*? No, Wolf must have that wrong. But he swore he remembered the name. Because it was so patently ridiculous—the principal of a mostly white school in a mostly white state—the whitest state! In the entire country!—being named White. His old principal back in New York, Principal Goodman, had one of those last names, too. The kind that describes a person. There was a word for it—

An aptronym, Wolf remembered.

Could there maybe be multiple White families in town? Or could Gracie be, say, the principal's distant relative? Wolf had no idea what Gracie's father did for a job. Kids didn't talk about that stuff. It probably wasn't the same person. White had to be an incredibly common name. E.B. White was named White!

Wolf wasn't good with names. Or faces. There was no way he could have put together that the old guy he saw with Grace at the pool, and occasionally talking to his sister, was the high school principal.

What he didn't know wouldn't hurt him, right? Wolf wouldn't inquire or say a word. He'd play innocent. He was already preposterously lucky. The most he, like Wilbur, could hope for was a true friend. He wasn't going to press his luck with a bunch of nosy questions.

★ ★ ★

On the bus ride home, Wolf convinced himself he was wrong about Gracie. She couldn't be related to the principal. What were the odds? Riverburg was small but it wasn't *that* small. Researching the question during the meandering ride, Wolf was relieved to discover that White was one of the most common last names in the state of Maine.

Wolf rounded the corner to Pine Street and was starting up the path to his house when he saw something strange on the ground. A bag filled with pebbles and a ragged scrap of paper. Like a message in a bottle? Only this bottle was a plastic baggie, the kind he carried his nose clip and tissues in. Maybe it could be something cool. Some sort of a riddle? Part of a scavenger hunt or alternate reality game? Or maybe something bad, like drugs? Was this how dealers got kids addicted? By sending a first batch free? Wolf opened the dirty bag and pulled out the note.

SHUT YOUR BITCH DAUGHTER UP

He searched the street for a wrongdoer, some sort of bad man, but only saw their old lady neighbor across the road, reading on her screened-in porch.

OHMYGODOHMYGODOHMYGODOHMYGOD.

His mother was going to kill him.

Wolf might be an idiot, but he wasn't stupid. It didn't take a brain surgeon to put two and two together. He "said something" and with a few swipes of his phone had ruined his family's life. Well, he'd learned his lesson—he was SO done with reporting. Because telling made things worse. The smartest thing to do was nothing. To not ask questions. To not know more than you needed to know—about whatever this rock bag note thing was, about Gracie's last name. About any of it. This was Wolf's fault. And it would stay Wolf's secret.

Wolf stuffed the hate note in his backpack, rocks included, and vowed not to tell his parents. He'd hold on to the evidence, hide it deep in the basement or the attic or his closet maybe, deep in his subconscious, too, and keep his big mouth shut.

13

riverburg high hates hazel

As her mother drove from the College down the hill to the high school, Hazel didn't say a word. She existed in the numb emotional space located somewhere between shock and disbelief. Was it textbook denial? Or disassociation? Hazel preferred to think of it as a "no feelings allowed" shield—a way to protect herself. She wasn't going to let him mess her up. She was going to ignore these nightmare events and move on.

She wasn't about to let her future be derailed because some guy asked her to have sex. That kind of thing happened to girls every day. This time he was middle-aged and her principal. So what? She didn't need to process or analyze the "trauma" of her half hour in some perverted man's office. Because the next best thing to this having never happened in the first place was never having to think or talk about it again. She didn't need a therapist. Or a new school. Hazel was FINE. She'd get her head straight, get to class, and go about the business of getting a semester's worth of straight A's.

Her plan: white-knuckle it through the school year and get

the hell out of Maine. She'd keep her head down and concentrate on her classes and grades. She'd try not to attract any more attention to herself. Maintain a cordial relationship with her teachers. Get over it, move on with her life, and maybe find a friend. She'd recalibrate, tune out the outside world. Work on her college applications. She just had to make it through this rough patch. By this time next year, she wouldn't remember Riverburg. Or him.

Considering it was the second day of school after being propositioned by the principal, that Wednesday went by uneventfully enough. To explain her lateness, she gave the attendance lady a note from her parents. Nobody in the building seemed to know what happened, or care one way or another about Hazel as she went from class to class and crowded hall to toilet-paper-deficient school bathroom. Hazel planned to live in that suspended bubble for the remaining 179 days of the school year.

Step one to her disappearing act, abstaining from a social life, would be simple. Hazel had a grand total of zero friends in town so far and no idea how to go about making any, given that these kids had probably known one another since birth. Theoretically she *wanted* Riverburg friends, but now she couldn't imagine opening her mouth. Luna was waiting for her in Brooklyn (Hazel's very own friend since birth, thank you very much) and that was never going to change. But finding new friends—real ones—her senior year in this completely alien environment? That seemed about as likely as Hazel becoming a famous writer.

It wouldn't help that she'd basically quit her phone that summer, or at least deleted her social media. Not because she was above technology or anything, but because her phone had come to control her every waking moment and became a source of endless unhappiness. What was the point of stalking her former social life in the city, or thirstily trying to start a new, temporary one here? Living with her phone loaded up with those apps was like someone with an eating disorder spending her entire day standing on a scale. Or an addict walking around with drugs in her pocket.

If Hazel wasn't (yet!) a full-out "Luddite teen" with a flip phone and a reading group in the woods, she did, as a new-ish rule, avoid certain trapdoors and corners of the interwebs like the plague. Instagram was a shopping magazine, Twitter a madman's newsfeed. TikTok an attention span killer. Snapchat a photo bomb surveillance mechanism where girls created fake accounts and harassed one another about their respective lack or overabundance of sexual activity. The social media of Hazel's former classmates from the School of the Future ranged in degrees of cringe from vaguely embarrassing to deeply humiliating. And now that she'd become an off-the-grid outsider to her previous social life, she was lonely AF.

Take this one friend of hers. Or "friend." (They hadn't been in touch since Hazel moved to Maine.) Anyway, Maya was, in real life, a legit supercool person. Smart, socially conscious, ran track. Charismatic, funny. And, yes, she was pretty, too. But her looks were like several rungs down on the list of top ten things that were great about Maya. Anybody who knew her would agree. Then why was Maya's Instagram account a photo dump of Maya in crop tops, Maya taking mirror selfies, Maya basically half-naked, with the lighting on point and filters cranked? And then the comments, which made Hazel want to become Amish. Because like 100 percent of them were concerned with letting Maya know how freaking desirable she was. *Babe, smoking, fire, beauty, could you be hotter no you could not be.* Barf. Hazel decided she was not here on this planet to produce daily unpaid hot-girl photo spreads.

Hazel made a deal with her parents at the start of the summer: if she continued to stay off social media and helped out with Wolfcare they'd buy her whatever books she wanted from an independent bookstore, anytime she asked. That plus a modest monthly thrifting budget. She didn't abuse this deal. She wasn't a *monster.* She still used the library. But if there was something she really wanted, she'd ask, and her parents would provide.

Ever since she taught herself to read, she devoured books. She was the weirdo second grader who was sent to the fifth grade to find "just right" books. It wasn't only that reading was an escape. (Although it was never *not* a relief to take a break from the particularities and anxieties of being Hazel Greenberg Blum.) Eventually, the other kids caught up to her reading level and she caught up to their social mores. Yet even with friends and afternoon clubs and late nights of problem sets and essays and papers, Hazel made time to read. Not because she was some old-fashioned saint or genius. She was neither. Because the world of a good book felt more real than Hazel's "real" life. Complicated and attuned and like it somehow made sense. Like it mattered and meant something. Which was more than Hazel could say for 95 percent of her actual existence.

Thursday, the third day of school.

Riverburg High sat on Brooklyn Avenue, an irony that Hazel was sure only she, out of the five hundred some-odd student body, appreciated. Like one of those kids named Brooklyn who had never been to New York. The squat school building was stationed less than a mile from their house, a fifteen-minute walk or three-minute car ride away from Pine Street, or in Hazel's case, a quick bike ride. The route was flat most of the way before a steep incline at the end. Hazel was sweaty by the time she reached the top.

Once she entered the double doors and walked into the building, the paranoia kicked in. She couldn't shake the feeling that kids were not-so-subtly checking her out. Did this have to do with her dad's seriously ill-considered Cosby lecture, which he'd confessed to the family about over dinner? Somehow Hazel doubted Riverburg High kids followed the goings-on at the College, or cared about her dad, or possibly even Bill Cosby. Was it because she was the new kid? The mysterious transfer student was, after all, your basic TV trope. Or was it because she was from New York? But no, she was only one day less new than the day before. Could it be anything other than the obvious?

Chill, she told herself.

Between classes, Hazel checked her schedule. The building was much bigger physically than her old school, though there were fewer students. She was minorly lost, heading down an empty hallway, finding her way toward the science wing, running late, doing her best to navigate the unfamiliar halls when she saw him.

White. Making his way down the hallway like he was the mayor, favorite teacher, and #1 dad all in one. It happened in slow motion, like skidding on a highway in an ice storm, careening toward the median strip.

He saw her. She saw him see her. Without meaning to, she stopped in her tracks. She couldn't walk. She couldn't speak. She couldn't think. Hazel wanted to scream or call for help or run out of the building, but any of those options seemed impossible given her state of psychic-turned-physical paralysis.

"Hazel," the principal said, nodding in her direction, while continuing to walk. Like nothing had happened between them. As though what he'd said and done to her in his office was no big deal, like *she* was no big deal, like there'd been nothing out of the ordinary to acknowledge or atone for. Like he was some regular principal, and she was the new kid, and Hazel should feel flattered he knew her name.

To White she was nothing. He probably had another girl lined up in her place.

Hazel stared down the tunnel of the hallway ahead of her. Like the worthless coward she now felt herself to be, she continued on to class.

Hazel wasn't one to skip school, barring a fever. On Friday morning, the fourth day of school, Hazel rode her bicycle, a thermos of ice coffee stashed in her bike's water bottle holder and half a bar of dark chocolate in her pocket. She'd gotten herself together that morning. Or tried to. She picked out combat boots and cutoff denim shorts and a plain white T-shirt and tied a flannel around her waist, seventy-seven degrees out or not. She had one more day until the weekend.

She took it minute by minute, period by period. (And, to make matters worse, period cramp by period cramp.) Nobody really talked to her. And she didn't really talk to anyone. This was one way of breaking Hazel's questionable habit of over-participating in class. In environmental studies, her teacher announced that the first meeting of the wilderness club was canceled because White, the faculty advisor, was out "sick." Was that a good thing? A bad thing? Hazel tried to parse the possibilities. Clearly, it meant something. He was the principal, and this was the fourth day of the year.

After sitting through a lecture about how global warming was about to decimate the planet and how Maine was the state where you wanted to spend end times (and where she seemed to be spending hers), she left the classroom for her free block.

She couldn't get through the rest of the day. But she couldn't skip her last class, either. It was raining—a full-on out of nowhere shower. She considered going home to her mom or going to the nurse's office for headache medicine and a nap or texting her dad and asking him to call that boarding school. Instead, she spent the next forty-plus minutes holed up in a dark corner of the air-conditioned media room, reading and silent crying, while forcing bites of chocolate down her throat.

Right before the bell a girl approached her, crossing the clear do-not-get-in-my-force-field vibe.

"You're in my English class. And we have stats together, too. I'm April. Are—are you okay?" She was shorter than Hazel, and had on a pair of cool black eyeglasses, and carried a backpack with a bunch of iron-on patches and buttons and pins.

"Why? I mean, yeah, of course. Totally," said Hazel, wiping her face.

"Are you sure? Not to invade your space or anything but—I saw you the other day. In the bathroom? After you were sent to White's office."

"Okay?" said Hazel, packing her things and checking the time. She was being stalked in the bathroom now. Perfect. Could this be a smaller town?

"Hazel," April said. "If you ever want to talk about it—it's not just you. He's gross."

"We should get to class," Hazel said. She wasn't sure how she was supposed to react to April's offer. Yeah, obviously White was gross. And April seemed nice—she had a sort of energetic ball of light around her. And yeah, Hazel could have used a friend in Riverburg. But signing up for a Dick White victim after-school club wasn't her idea of a good time.

The class chatter in AP Lit stopped cold when they walked through the doorway, and a legitimate dramatic hush fell over the room. The local newspaper, the *Riverburg Record*, a regional daily paper based in town, covering mid Maine and its environs, was sprawled open on the debate team kid Alex Andrews's desk, surrounded by a half-dozen students and Mr. Miller.

Once Hazel saw the paper, she realized what was up. The story must have broken.

"Hazel—hey," said Alex. Why was he even aware of her name? (Hazel knew his because she'd researched the high honor roll list before school started.)

It had to be because Alex knew that White had picked her. And that she'd told. She'd half expected and had mentally prepared herself for stares and behind-her-back conjecture, given that an entire class had seen her go to his office. But a newspaper article was a hundred times worse. President Hill had said they'd protect her anonymity, at least sort of. Hadn't she? Hazel never thought it would last forever—but more than seventy-two hours would have been nice. Or was she being paranoid? Miller went back behind his desk at the front of the room, cleared his throat, ready to start. For the second time in two days, Hazel froze.

A gentle hand pulled on her flannel. April, who was standing next to her. As much as Hazel wanted to collapse into this stranger girl's arms or take her hand and flee the premises together, she brushed April off.

What was she supposed to *do*?

One thing was certain. Hazel wasn't going to pull up a chair and listen while they analyzed the article, like it was the subject of their next literature unit. No way would she wait for the rest of the AP kids to ID her. Or like, stone her to death in the center of town.

She'd taken ninth-grade English. She'd read *The Lottery.* She was Nathaniel Hawthorne's Hester Prynne wearing the red *A* on her chest. She wasn't sticking around for any of that. She *dared* Mr. Miller to call her out for ditching class. Despite begging herself not to look, Hazel read the headline on her way out the classroom door: *Police, School Board Investigating Riverburg Principal.*

Outside, the rain had stopped and the sun had reappeared. She was *not* going to let herself read the article. No way. She needed to get out of there. Out of the classroom, out of the school, out of town. Hazel grabbed her bike off the rack and started to ride. She rode past the stream with the ducks, past the College, out to the country road where neighborhoods became far-apart houses.

She stopped for water, but her bottle was empty. She came close to checking her phone for the article, but instead she kept riding. Her brain was a mess, but her calves and thighs could pedal. She got muddy. She passed a farm, then another. When she got to farm three and saw a hand-painted barn sign with a delusional political message, Hazel realized the obvious: There was nowhere to go. Nowhere! She was marooned. A city girl with no driver's license (much less a car).

That's when she got angry. That's when she wanted to murder him. Okay, maybe not murder him. Hazel wanted to do something—anything. To act. To bring White down. But she felt too afraid of the consequences. If she proceeded with the case, the specter of whatever would come next—the police station? A pair of gruff Maine detectives? A prosecutor driving up from Portland? A trial her senior year? White in handcuffs? Hazel on the witness stand? The inevitable backlash? Snarky Reddit boys like Alex Andrews times a gazillion?—seemed much more awful than the alternative: Saying nothing. Doing nothing.

At the far edge of town she braked, hung a U-turn, and let her bike fall on the dirt.

It was hopeless. *She* was hopeless. There was no way out. She could bike for a year, and it wouldn't change a thing.

Covered in mud and dying of thirst, she was about to break down and call her parents for a ride. She would have if she didn't hate them so much. For letting them convince her that moving her senior year was anything but the worst idea she'd ever heard in her life.

Hazel regretted absolutely everything that had happened to her—every decision she'd made, every dumb word out of her mouth since the day they'd entered this dumb state. She blamed herself, too, but mostly, she blamed her parents. This was their fault.

If only Hazel could do that stupid first day over. A sliver of her wished she'd gotten over herself and just said yes and given him, like, a blow job or something, and saved herself from the rest of this bullshit. Maybe a yes would have been easier? But that was ridiculous. And the second she thought of it, she felt like vomiting. She wasn't going to lose her virginity, oral or otherwise, to her high school principal. What she *should* have done? Say no but keep this a secret. She would give anything to take that part back. To have people not know. Because Hazel could feel it in AP Lit; they knew she was the girl in the newspaper story. Thinking back to the relatively high-functioning, ambitious girl she'd been a few weeks ago at the pool, talking about *books* with White, believing he cared what she *thought*, making a big deal of how she was going to be a writer one day, Hazel felt like a part of her had died.

When Hazel finally made it back to her house, her annoying family was waiting on the porch, each glued to their devices. Proving maybe they did care, because for once in their lives, they were reading the same article at the same time.

"Have you seen it?" asked Wolf.

"What do you think?" said Hazel.

"Where have you been?" asked her mother, inspecting her dirty limbs. "What happened to you? Are you okay? Where did you go? Why didn't you answer my texts?"

"They didn't put your name in," Wolf said. "Or anything about you."

"It doesn't matter," said Hazel. "They might as well have. People are going to figure it out."

"How do you know that?" asked her dad.

"I can just tell."

"You should read it," said Wolf.

"You don't have to read it," said her mom.

"Read it," said Wolf. "Of course you have to read it."

"Give me that," said Hazel, grabbing her brother's phone from him.

"Don't click out of it, though. I only get two more free articles this month. There's one about Daddy in there, too."

"Are you serious?" said Hazel, scrolling down. "Because of Cosby?"

"He's getting fired," said Wolf.

"Daddy is *not* getting fired," said Claire.

"By the way," said Wolf, as he read over his sister's shoulder and played with her sweaty hair, "I got the lead in the school play."

Police, School Board Investigating Riverburg Principal
By Camille Sullivan, Riverburg Record
September 9

RIVERBURG, MAINE—The Riverburg Police Department is investigating Richard White, Principal of Riverburg Senior High School, following reports of misconduct, according to Chief Lawrence Chase. Charges of sexual impropriety involving a student may be at play, say sources familiar with the matter. "All are innocent until proven guilty, and I prefer not to make the specific allegations public out of respect for both Principal White and the alleged victim," said Chase.

The Riverburg school board, led by Superintendent Nick Pelletier, is also investigating the charges surrounding events that are alleged to have transpired earlier this week, on the first day of school. White has been placed on a temporary paid administrative leave.

Richard White came to Riverburg in 2007, after teaching English and then serving as assistant principal at Lincoln High School in Vermont. A native of Long Island, New York, White spent summers in Maine as a boy and has become a beloved fixture in town, according to residents.

White arrived at Riverburg High School at a time of declining enrollment and budget cuts, in the wake of the closing of the Lodge shirt factory. He implemented a free school breakfast program and several new after-school activities including a video gaming club, a wilderness club, and a queer student affinity group. Under White's administration, test scores have improved at a time when they are trending downward statewide.

"I have a lot of respect and admiration for Principal White," said Beth Haskin, whose children graduated from the high school during White's time as principal. "He has gone above and beyond for this community and for our kids. He's one of us. He would never do anything like this. I know that for a fact."

Principal White lives in town with his wife, a child development specialist, and their daughter. By law, he will continue to be paid while the investigation continues. It's unclear what additional steps or disciplinary actions Superintendent Pelletier or the school board have taken beyond a preliminary investigation.

At the time of this reporting, Mr. White and his attorney had not returned emails or phone calls. Chief Chase said that the police department and school district will protect the anonymity of the alleged victim.

Riverburg High School and all planned sports and after-school clubs remain in session during the investigation.

New College Professor In Hot Water
By Camille Sullivan, Riverburg Record
September 9

Gus Blum, a recently hired professor and chair of the American Studies department at the College, has provoked controversy on campus. Blum, who teaches about television and the family, presented a clip from The Cosby Show on the first day of class. Several students walked out in protest over the convicted rapist and once popular comedian and actor. A petition calling for Blum's firing has been circulating online since the incident and has garnered over four hundred signatures of students, alumnae, and some faculty and staff.

"He gave a platform to a known serial rapist," said Samantha Moore, the author of the petition and a student in Blum's class.

A student group led by Moore, calling themselves Fire Gus Blum!, has requested office space in the student center. A smaller group of faculty members have circulated a counterpetition calling for free speech and academic freedom.

President Nicole Hill, when reached for comment, defended both the student group and Blum. "While I wholeheartedly support Professor Blum's choice to discuss a relevant piece of American culture with his class, at the same time, I understand, affirm, and applaud the student group for flexing their activist muscles, and for speaking their minds and their truths. There's room for all of us at the College, and we welcome dissent in scholarship, in the classroom and on campus."

14

hurt people hurt people

It was Saturday morning and Claire missed New York. Gus was off somewhere in the cavernous house, working. The kids were asleep. She should be doing something productive, like deep cleaning the upstairs bathroom or starting one of ten million loads of laundry or organizing the kitchen or planting fall greens in the garden or, at the very least, working out. Or finding a real job. Pretty much anything other than shopping for vintage on her phone. But her desire to search out inspiration, to hunt and gather, to conceive and make garments, to clothe people, felt as natural and necessary and instinctual and compulsive as Pickle's desire to dig a hole in the backyard and burrow her snout down. Particularly when she was stressed. Shopping, Claire rationalized, doubled as research and development and was the first step to building her line. Although, granted, given Hazel's situation, brainstorming the design, manufacture and marketing of, say, bespoke thermal separates or utility jeans was objectively frivolous no matter how you looked at it. She worried that whatever she made wouldn't be good enough, anyway. That she wasn't good enough. She should probably be researching lawyers.

After Hazel, and Gus's disastrous first week of school, Claire's anxiety was cresting. She should never have quit therapy, but Miranda Silverman wasn't licensed in Maine and Claire couldn't imagine telling her complicated dysfunctional family history to someone new. She'd grown up with a sometimes terrifying father, and a mother who hadn't protected her. Around the time she met Gus, she'd broken free of them. But she was old enough to get over her childhood, wasn't she?

What choice did she have? She'd be dead soon! If she needed to obsess over anyone's childhood, it should be Hazel's. But Hazel seemed to have it under control. It was Claire who needed to get a grip.

She would, she promised herself. Claire closed her eyes, settled into her breathing, made a mental health morning gratitude list (her limbs, her children, Gus and Pickle), and told herself that her family was safe. Hazel was resilient. Gus would manage. Wolf had the lead in the school play! There was that. Claire needed to stop obsessing and start appreciating the smaller pleasures of life. She was in Maine, drinking coffee from her favorite mug, potted by Ramona. Seated at the kitchen table, Claire concentrated on sensations: the floorboards beneath her feet, the pleasurable scratch of the Spanish wool cardigan she wore, and how her favorite cotton granny panties and bra top set, responsibly sewn in Oregon, held her underneath her sweatpants. Coffee outside, she remembered, while the weather was still warm.

With that, Claire stepped onto the side porch in her bare feet, Ramona mug in hand, and was surprised to discover a blonde woman in a T-shirt dress and leggings approaching the house, breaking Claire's impromptu meditation with a wave of greeting as she made her way up the drive.

"I hope you don't mind my stopping by. I've wanted to come say hello since you moved in. I don't know where the summer went," the woman said. "I'm Polly. Wolf's art teacher. My husband, Luke, teaches Econ at the College. He knows Gus."

Claire had noticed Polly around town that summer, at The General and the fabric store and once at the library with Wolf. Gus had mentioned the Econ husband.

"I live down the block. Well, around the corner."

"Oh, hi. How nice of you. Come inside," Claire said, beckoning her toward the kitchen. Claire had been thinking about hosting a dinner or housewarming party, perhaps a potluck in the backyard. "Do you want a coffee?" She wished she'd bothered to wear real pants that morning. Or a wrap skirt or something.

"Next time, I'd love to. We need to talk, though. Maybe we should stay here on the porch. This is more for adult ears."

"Did Wolf do something weird in class?"

"Nothing like that. Wolf's an incredible kid. So *smart* that one. I couldn't believe that this little sixth grader knew that Roy Lichtenstein had an abstract expressionist period. I mean, come on."

"He's a bit of a polymath," said Claire. "But he can't tie his shoelaces."

"I really should have come before this. I was going to bring flowers from my garden and invite you to my book club. But okay. Something's been done to your sidewalk, by the front door. I hate to say this, but it's pretty awful. I was walking by with my boys to soccer for an early practice and noticed it. I dropped them and came right back. Here, you should come see."

Claire slipped on her porch sandals and followed Polly down the driveway, cutting a path across the lawn to their official front door facing Pine Street.

The word was waiting, scrawled in red spray paint on the sidewalk in front of the path that led to their door.

SLUT.

Claire froze and dropped her mug, which shattered into a half-dozen pieces of marigold clay.

★★★

Gus was in the kitchen, starting breakfast. Wolf was awake and gaming at the table in his underwear.

"Did you know that Jerry Seinfeld calls YouTube 'The garbage can of content'?" Wolf informed Claire by way of morning salutation, without looking up from his device.

"Gus, I need you to come with me." She motioned to the side yard.

"Can it wait? I'm in the middle of an egg for Wolf."

"It definitely can't wait."

"Okay, give me one minute. There," he said, flipping the pancake omelet and presenting it to Wolf, who started eating it with his hands.

She led him onto the porch and closed the door behind them.

"Please, don't freak out," Claire said.

"Why are you being so dramatic?" Gus asked.

"And don't say a word to the kids."

"About what? What's going on?"

"What's going on is a hate crime. On the sidewalk in front of our house."

A skeptical Gus followed Claire across the lawn.

"Look," she said.

"Jesus." The worry lines in Gus's forehead came out when he was stressed or thinking hard. "Okay. Okay—we need to call someone. We need to text Nicole."

"Enough with Nicole. I need you to get me some cleaning supplies. And can you hurry please? Before either one of the kids come out here?" said Claire.

"We probably shouldn't touch it," said Gus.

"Why not?"

"We'd be tampering with evidence."

"Evidence! What about Hazel? What about Wolf? We can't let them know about this, can we?"

Gus sat down on the front stoop, took his glasses off and

rubbed at his eyes. "I haven't slept since Monday night. I can't stop thinking about White. Or about getting fired."

"Can we focus here? Someone just wrote *slut* all over our front walk."

"I'll be having nightmares about this week for the rest of my life," Gus said.

Claire put saliva on her fingers and started scratching at the *SLUT*.

"It's going to take a lot more than spit," Gus said. "We should call the police."

"It's spray paint," said Claire. "It's not a *bomb*. We are not calling the police."

"How can we not? You called this a hate crime."

"It *is* a hate crime. I'm not saying it's not. I'm saying I don't want either of the kids to know about it."

"They're smart kids," said Gus. "They'll find out eventually."

"I blame myself," said Claire. "We never should have come here. We never should have left Brooklyn. I can't believe you let me buy a house. I can't believe I let you give up a tenured job in New York."

"Not New York," said Gus. "Long Island."

"We should have moved there if we wanted a house so badly." She couldn't believe Maine had her pining for Long Island.

"It's too late. There's no point in going backward."

"It is *not* too late. Don't say that. We should be fleeing the state," said Claire, spinning out. "The country! Driving to Canada. I want to move to Montreal. Can you try and get a job at McGill? I'm serious."

Gus was ignoring her, staring into the abyss of his phone. The petition, probably. He'd been researching the signees, neurotically, ever since a couple of faculty members had joined the bandwagon. "You don't speak French. Neither do the kids."

"We can learn."

"We're not moving to Montreal," said Gus. Complaining

about Riverburg and the College was one thing, abandoning tenure and trying to sell a house they had just signed the papers on was another. "We're not moving anywhere. We just got here. And you're right, the petition is probably going to blow over."

"Forget Cosby," said Claire. "I'm not talking about the petition. I'm talking about Hazel and White. I'm talking about this." She motioned to the sidewalk. "How can we stay here?"

"Being a professor isn't something you can quit. I'd never get an academic job again. And no, I can't just get a nonexistent job at McGill. It doesn't work that way. We can't let some deranged asshole dictate our life choices. What lesson does that teach our kids?"

"Are you serious?"

"This is terrible, but it's graffiti. Probably the work of some drunk teenagers defending their principal's honor or something. It's not like Richard White came and spray-painted our sidewalk himself. Let's try and keep it in perspective? Vandalism is a low-level crime. Nobody was murdered. We weren't even robbed. We can talk to the school and make sure Hazel never has to see him again. We're okay." A bluebird flew down and lingered on the step next to them.

"Hazel is okay," said Gus, as if repeating that made it true. "And you love this house. We had such a good summer. Didn't we?"

They had. They swam off the College's dock. They ate corn and peaches and tomatoes.

"Hazel is *not* okay. She goes to school with those teenagers. That man is her principal. Can we please deal with the sidewalk? Before Hazel and Wolf see?"

"We really should report it," said Gus.

"I don't get you. You want to stay *and* you want to report it?"

"Yes! I want to fix this!"

"Reporting is only going to make things worse. What happened when you told Nicole Hill? A couple days later and Hazel's story is in the newspaper. No way. Don't give whoever did this the satisfaction of making it into some bigger deal. I want Hazel to have a normal weekend. I want her to have a normal life."

"It's not like people know for a fact that Hazel's the girl in the story," said Gus.

"Have you seen our sidewalk?" said Claire. "People know."

"Fine," said Gus, too tired to keep arguing. "If that's what you think."

"The only way I'll consider staying is if you let me clean this up," said Claire. She meant it.

"Okay."

"Promise me you won't call the police?"

"I won't call the police."

"Thank you." Claire exhaled. Paint was in her wheelhouse. "Okay. I need you to go to the hardware store. I need paint thinner and sandpaper, a bristle brush maybe, some mineral spirits. We probably need a pressure washer, too. Before you leave can you bring the rags and cleaning stuff at the top of the basement stairs—and the mop. Check the bathroom, I think I have some nail polish remover. The longer this is on here the harder it will be to cover up. And fill the bucket with hot, soapy water. Let me see if I can deal with this myself."

15

the record

A Town Divided as Riverburg High School Principal Suspended
By Camille Sullivan, Riverburg Record
September 17

Following an accusation of sexual misconduct on the first day of the school year, Richard White, principal of Riverburg Senior High, has been suspended, according to Riverburg superintendent of schools, Nick Pelletier. "We thought it best to act with utmost caution and prudence in this matter while we wait for more information," said Pelletier. As local authorities investigate the case, Riverburg is left divided over a trusted administrator's denial and a high school student's accusation.

White appeared at a public hearing held Monday evening in the high school gymnasium. Reading from a prepared statement with his wife, Agatha White, and his attorney Michael Taylor by his side, White once again repudiated the accusations.

"I absolutely deny these charges," said White. "I have done nothing wrong. I have always put the welfare of my students first. The truth is this student, a senior and legal adult, was inappropriate with me. My mistake was not talking about what really happened publicly sooner. I was trying to protect this troubled student."

A vocal group of students, teachers, and parents came out to support White. After making his statement, White was given a standing ovation by some members of the audience.

"I have three kids who've been through this school system. None of them have ever talked about a teacher or administrator like they do about Principal White," one high school parent, Melissa Schraeder, told this reporter.

"He's there for us 24/7," said Evan Dorchester, a tenth grader active in the outdoor club founded by White. "There's no way this is true. He took us rafting."

Others attended in a show of solidarity with the anonymous alleged victim. April Hunt, a senior at Riverburg High, asked, "Why would she lie? What would be in it for her? I don't get why people think that."

Lauren Levin, an assistant professor in the art department at the College, says that while her daughter currently attends the Community Montessori School, she came to the hearing to register her concern. "As a town, we can't allow the old boys' network to make decisions affecting the safety of our children."

It will be up to the district attorney's office to determine what charges White may face.

Chief Lawrence Chase confirmed that the student in question is 18 years old, a legal adult, and has made a brief statement to the authorities. Chase would not comment on whether gross sexual assault, a charge often used in cases involving educators, would be applicable. One difficulty, Chase noted, is the "he said she said" nature of these allegations. "We're working hard to conduct a complete and thorough investigation. After that, the district attorney takes over."

Profile of a Fallen Educator
By Douglas Martin, Riverburg Record
September 22

A charismatic and once-beloved high school principal in Riverburg has become embroiled in a controversy splitting the foundations of this central Maine town. Richard White, 41, has been suspended without pay by the Riverburg Schools superintendent's office and remains under criminal investigation for an alleged incident on the first day of school.

White grew up in Long Island, New York, during the school year, and spent his summers in northern Maine at his extended family's camp on Moosehead Lake, near the Canadian border.

"Those cousins ran free. Like boys do," said a former neighbor, Paul Gardener. "Later on, he met his wife up here when they were teenagers. They were summer camp counselors."

White played varsity baseball in high school, where he was student body president and editor of the yearbook. He attended Brown University, studying education and English, and was the first person in his family to earn a bachelor's degree.

White became something of a rarity in central Maine: an educator with an Ivy League pedigree and local roots. Before coming to Riverburg High, he was an English teacher and then assisstant principal at Lincoln High School in Vermont.

The position at Riverburg High allowed White to fulfill

his longtime dream of living in Maine year-round. During his years at Riverburg High, he was promoted from eleventh- and twelfth-grade English teacher and department chair to assistant principal before becoming principal. He and his wife, Agatha White, who studied child development at Middlebury College, are parents to a school-age child and live in town.

By most accounts, White took to the community, and the community to him. He was known to love the outdoors, and to be active in community skiing and sporting events. "We all know each other here. You'd always see Dick around town. He came to all the games. He's a good man," said Ray Brady, a former Riverburg High student and current parent.

Some Riverburgians expressed shock at the idea that White could have done this. "Dick has been nothing but wonderful with my girls and has fixed a broken school," said Bree Murray, a mother of a tenth and twelfth grader at Riverburg High, interviewed during a high school soccer game yesterday.

"Why was the office door closed? I don't see why a girl would agree to that," said another parent, Jen Stone, a former math teacher at Riverburg Junior High. "You can't have it both ways."

Nadine Krause, a professor of women's studies at the College, disagreed. "Teenage girls do not make this type of thing up. A history of sexual misconduct in this country teaches us that perpetrators deny far more often than victims make false accusations."

16

wolf quits

Unlike the rest of his family, Wolf was going to forge ahead and live his life. He had a semi-secure place at the popular-adjacent lunch table and a lead in the school play. He had possession of a phone and was angling for a gaming laptop for his birthday. His math teacher gave out extra credit points for handing in assignments early, which he took full advantage of. It's not like he was happy, exactly. Being a normal kid took hard work. And being thrust into the spotlight and starring in the school play was a ton of pressure. Middle school—especially as the new kid—was *a lot.*

Still, come Mondays, Wolf was almost relieved to be back in school. He wanted to worry about himself for once. Because he was sick of thinking about his sister and Principal White. He was sick of pretending not to know about the spray paint. (As if he hadn't heard his mother yelling that morning and watched through the den window as his parents scrubbed the sidewalk.) He was sick of keeping track of all THE THINGS WOLF WASN'T ALLOWED TO KNOW.

As if he didn't read the *Record*, too.

As if *he* wasn't the one who'd found the hate note!

As if this wasn't Wolf's fault. Because of his stupid Say Something report, the principal was now suspended without pay and possibly going to jail. Which were both good things? But nothing that Wolf wanted to be responsible for.

Most of all, despite worrying about his sister, Wolf was sick of his parents treating Hazel like she was the most important person in the world because she'd had a sucky first day of school.

The first Monday in October, a few weeks later, some of the kids were already onstage when Wolf arrived at the mini auditorium a couple of minutes late for *Charlotte's Web* rehearsal, after frantically stuffing textbooks and assorted newly fraying folders into his locker. Mr. Woods, the drama coach, was leading them in warm-ups. Yoga, it looked like. At the start of every practice, Woods taught them a new, generally kooky, way to stretch themselves—theater games, improvs, karaoke-offs, relaxation exercises. Today they'd literally be stretching.

"Wolf, come join us," he said when he spotted his swine star. "We're saluting the sun." Wolf put yoga squarely in the category of annoying stuff his mother liked.

"Wolf, hold on," said Gracie, stopping herself midsalute. "I need to talk to you." She jumped off the stage. Gracie seemed mad at him. Great. Wolf mentally rewound through his day, searching for social skill blunders. He couldn't think of any.

"Is that okay?" she asked Mr. Woods.

"Can it wait? You know that warm-ups set the tone for the rehearsal." She shook her head no. Mr. Woods was skeptical about the urgency of this discussion, but let them go, pointing to the seats. "Don't leave the room, guys."

Gracie was in her signature denim short overalls, worn over black leggings since the weather had changed, purposefully mismatched high-tops (one color per foot), and red bandana tied around her neck. She was so perfect. So intimidating. She was also much taller than Wolf, forcing him to crane his neck, posing a practical impediment to their friendship. Gracie led him to the back row.

"The thing is my mother has decided I can't be in the play with you, and I need to be in the play, and that means you need to quit." She said the words fast and bunched up in a row, like she'd memorized them.

"Wait, what?" Wolf needed Gracie to slow down. "But I have to be in the play. I'm Wilbur."

"Wolf, I *know.*"

"Know what?"

"Wolf. Stop it."

"What?"

"You knew already. Didn't you?" said Gracie.

"Know what?"

She was either going to cry or curse at him. Or both.

"About my father. About my family. I bet you knew this whole time."

Wolf picked at his chapped lips and tried to figure out whether or not to lie.

"Do you think I'm dumb?" demanded Gracie.

"Of course not."

"Do you know who my father is?"

"No, not really." He wasn't positive. He didn't have proof. Only a last name.

Well, maybe he subconsciously knew. He'd suspected. Gracie had left the room crying during rehearsal that one time, and once in chorus. There were whispers at school. But he'd chosen to not investigate. He wasn't Sherlock Holmes. He didn't want to lose his friend.

"Don't lie to me."

"I'm *new.* Remember?"

"He's the principal. Of the high school. Your sister is trying to get my father fired."

That wasn't technically true. Hazel had no power over Gracie's dad's firing. The school board would decide what to do with White.

"My mom has made my dad sleep at our camp for the past two weeks." Gracie was glaring at him, her arms crossed, waiting. Onstage the kids were done with yoga and making their bodies into a machine, each one adding a part. The machine was getting louder by the person. Gracie and Wolf slipped out the back door of the mini auditorium and stood in the main lobby.

"Okay. You're right," he said, "I do know something." He was a terrible secret keeper. The absolute worst. "You can't tell anyone. You can't tell your parents. You have to swear you won't."

Gracie nodded.

"My sister is the girl from your dad's office."

"Yeah. That's the *whole point*. Haven't you been paying attention? That's why I'm not allowed to do the play with you."

"There's something else." Wolf felt helpless in the face of Gracie's anger and hurt. He couldn't hide anything from her. His earnestness, his penchant for the truth was inborn. Ingrown? Like a toenail.

"What? I'm listening." She was so angry. Wolf hated this.

"I'm the one who told on your father. It wasn't Hazel. Okay!?" Wolf was about to lose it.

"What?"

"Do you remember the thing about the Say Something app? On the first day of school, we had that assembly about it?"

"No way. You didn't." Now Gracie was the one who was about to start crying. "How could you do that to me? How could you *ruin my life*?"

"I didn't know I was doing anything to you! I didn't know he was your father. I swear." Wolf couldn't look at her. He crumpled and recrumpled a deflated potato chip bag he'd grabbed off the floor. "It was stupid of me," he added. It really was. "If I could take it back, believe me, I would."

"Do you have any idea how serious this is? My dad could lose his job. I might have to move. My mother is talking about getting a *divorce*. My father could go to jail, Wolf. Do you understand that? My life is RUINED. And you're telling me this is because of you? Because of your big stupid mouth?"

Wolf wanted to remind Gracie this was not because of him. The entire sequence of events was set in motion by her father, not Hazel, and—guilty as he felt—not Wolf, either. If you see a murder and call the police, are you the criminal? In the subway, the announcement said if you see something, say something. He was doing what any concerned citizen would. Or should.

But he wasn't going to convince Gracie to hate her father. It would be like Wolf signing the student petition to fire *his* dad. Sometimes, it wasn't about right or wrong. You just had to be on the side of the person you love. No matter what. Gracie could blame Wolf and Hazel. She *should* blame them. Because the alternative, believing Hazel, meant believing and accepting that her father was a terrible human being.

"Gracie, I'm really sorry." He wanted to rewind time. Or better yet, to be in the parallel universe where she was Charlotte, and he was Wilbur, and they were best friends for life. "I'm *so* sorry."

"You're sorry?" Somehow the words made Gracie angrier. "You're *sorry*?"

"I am! I'm sorry for what I did. I'm sorry this is happening. To you and my sister, too." Issuing a heartfelt apology worked with his family 99 percent of the time.

"I don't care about how you *feel*, Wolf. I don't care about *you*, okay! And I'm *sorry* but I don't care about your sister. *Sorry* to be selfish."

Wolf hadn't seen this side of Gracie.

"My father says your sister is a liar. And I believe him. If your stupid family had never moved, *my* family would be fine."

"If I could take it back, I would," said Wolf.

"You can't be in drama anymore. You can't be Wilbur."

"No, please don't say that."

"I can't play Charlotte if you're Wilbur—I'm not allowed. My parents said so. And if you won't quit, then I'll have to quit." Gracie wrapped a braid around her hand, tight. "The other kids in drama won't like that. They're my best friends."

Wolf wanted to do whatever would make Gracie feel better. Whatever would make her stop hating him. She was being *so* mean. But Wilbur was a lead. His big break.

"One more thing," Gracie said. "I never want to talk to you again."

Wolf might die of shame and hurt. Right there.

Mr. Woods was in the mini doorway, pointing to his imaginary watch, beckoning them back in. "Wolf!" he said, with an unexpected sharpness to his voice.

Forget it. He couldn't pull off being scene partners with someone who hated him, who was going to ignore him for months on end. This was Gracie's turf. Her school. Her town. He knew when he wasn't wanted.

"Okay," Wolf said. Now he was mad, too. "Forget your stupid play. You win. I quit." The drama kids were annoying. Playing a pig was degrading. Besides, there was no such thing as a kosher pig.

Mr. Woods was disappointed but didn't want a lead who didn't want the part. He gave the role to the kid previously slated to play Goose, a dependable if uninspired actor, and the reigning eighth-grade student of the month. Wolf's parents went from worried to "very concerned" about him but couldn't physically force him to be in the show. They had no idea that Charlotte was being played by the principal's daughter. Hazel knew Gracie from the pool, but Wolf hadn't told her they'd been cast as costars. (What was one more secret, he'd figured.) Hazel thought Wolf had stage fright or panic attacks or something.

In chorus, Gracie wouldn't look at him. Sparing himself the public humiliation of being ignored at her lunch table, he opted for another, sliding into a spot at the end of the junior high principal's nobody-else-wants-to-sit-with-these-kids-so-they-sit-here-with-me table. Wolf was officially friendless. In language arts, he had to partner with the teacher during a peer review breakout. On the bus home, the string-playing neighborhood boys didn't acknowledge his existence.

Soon his mom started picking him up from school—he'd convinced her that the twisty bus ride home made him seasick. They drove straight home. There was nowhere else to go—which was fine by Wolf. The quicker to melt onto the couch in the living room, fingers on his phone, the better.

He started reading *Atlas Shrugged* sometime around then, because you could only game so many hours of the day before your eyes bled, and it was the only book in the entire Riverburg bookstore that his mother didn't want to buy for him. Never mind that it was a million pages long. Or that the plot sounded highly convoluted. As soon as he held up that gigantic doorstopper for his mother's inspection and saw her reaction, there was no other book that would satisfy him.

Wolf couldn't stop reading it. He loved (and was borderline obsessed with) not the writing or the characters, but the ideas. The author, Ayn Rand, tackled topics ranging from the downfalls of religion and collectivism to the upsides of looking out for number one. His related descent into rabbit holes and nether regions of the internet began with an innocent dip into *Atlas Shrugged* discussion forums. From there, it was a hop, skip and jump to find them: the Libertarians and anarcho-capitalists.

He was sick of everyone treading on him, telling him what to do. His parents. His sister. His school. Gracie. The government. He wanted to control his own life for once. He didn't want to have to worry about anyone other than himself. And if that meant he was selfish? Maybe he was.

His parents accused him of isolating, of escaping the "real" world and hiding out inside his phone, but that's because they didn't get it. Online, Wolf was witty. He was respected. His posts got likes and upvotes. There, within days, he was part of a community. He could say snarky things, or sentimental things, and nobody would know he was the mean one, or the corny one. Online, it didn't make a difference that Wolf was eleven. Online, Wolf mattered. And Wolf was Very Online.

Which was driving his parents crazy.

Despite having way too much time on his hands—without drama club he was home by 2:15 on weekdays and wouldn't leave the house on weekends—he wasn't about to bike ride or play in the backyard, much less help around the house. But there was one chore he couldn't get out of—the afternoon Pickle walk. She'd nap next to him on the couch, and when she stirred, his mother would make him take her around the block, confiscating his phone and sticking it on top of the fridge until he complied. His only exercise, his mom insisted. As if going to school wasn't tiring enough.

Wolf agreed to the dog walks because he had no choice, and, also, so that he could be the one to find and hide the notes. They weren't always there. Each time a few days went by without discovering anything, he'd think it was over. His parents were oblivious—they drove in and out of the driveway or walked Pickle in the early morning or late-night hours or let her do her business in the backyard. Wolf, closer to the ground, was perpetually looking down.

The latest plastic baggie was especially dirty, wedged between the toppled-over recycling bins where the gravel met the sidewalk. The hate note delivery boy must have been feeling lazy that day. While Pickle sniffed, Wolf opened it, pulling a paper from the pebbles. The letter, if you could call it that, was, as usual, handwritten in all caps and black marker. But this time the message was way, way worse:

TAKE YOUR LYING SLUT AND GO BACK TO JEW YORK

OHGODOHGODOHOGOD. Wolf's head was about to explode. Were there actual Nazis in Riverburg? Or just run-of-the-mill Jew haters? Calling Hazel a slut was terrible and mean. It didn't even make *sense* given the situation with the principal. And to bring up their being Jewish??? And to call his city a bad name?

Wolf ignored Pickle's poop and stuffed the papers into the pocket of his sweatshirt, praying his mother wouldn't notice the parts that poked out. He would never EVER tell his parents. Not when this WHOLE ENTIRE THING was his fault. Not when his parents would kill him if they knew that he'd reported the principal on Say Something. It's not like his parents could stop white supremacy or the rise of fascism. They couldn't even stop Richard White.

At bedtime, when his parents wouldn't let him have his phone, in the lonely interlude between brushing his teeth and lights-out, when no one could see him, Wolf sadomasochistically read *Charlotte's Web*—sometimes the book, and sometimes the photocopied script Mr. Woods had placed on his homeroom desk that first morning before rehearsal—torturing himself with memories of Gracie.

He went through his days like a sixth-grade robot, occasionally forgetting himself in a small moment of normalness—reading time in language arts, learning basic algebra. He collected his 98s and 96s and 100s and 110s with extra credit points. He let his mother fawn on him; he let his dad wait on him. But he never forgot how lonely he was. Seeing Gracie in chorus was the worst. Even though they were both altos, and sometimes forced to share sheet music, she continued giving him the silent treatment.

It took Wolf another couple of weeks to find the HeyYo app. He hadn't heard of it before—a sort of hyperlocal social media for people living within six miles of one another. HeyYo, whose motto was "small is beautiful," had recently become a thing on college campuses, and, to a lesser extent, in small Podunk towns like Riverburg. He'd overheard some kid at school talking about it. Wolf duly clicked on the site. And yeah. His sister covered the home page like wallpaper. His dad came up, too. His family, no joke, was topic #1.

Wolf scrolled through each entry. HeyYo posts were called logs, as if Riverburgians and the College's students were living on a ship, stranded together in this pathetic excuse for a town. He saw the haters and the attacks first. Also, a surprisingly vocal minority of defenders. It was maybe 70 percent pro principal to 30 percent pro Hazel. But the ranting and meanness of the worst of the posts felt as toxic and lethal to Wolf as the hate missives, because these weren't anonymous evildoers, these were regular kids at Hazel's school putting her on blast. One of the more popular posts was titled "It's Okay to Be White." An offshoot, College-focused section of the HeyYo was about how much his dad sucked for playing that TV show clip.

Wolf wouldn't lie idly by while his sister and father were defamed. This was wrong. Why was Hazel being blamed for what the principal did? What was she supposed to do? Shut up and have sex with him?

It was really messed up. Wolf needed to defend and protect his family now that his sister's identity was out. Because not only did Gracie know Hazel was the girl in the principal's office. According to his HeyYos the whole *town* knew. Wolf had no choice but to tell Hazel.

She wasn't going to like it.

17

hazel is not okay

Hazel was not okay. She should have texted back Luna, who was worried about her, who would have let her check in and complain and cry every single day after school if she would only not ghost her. She should have talked to April in the library during their free period, when April asked about New York and Hazel's old school, instead of acting like she didn't know how to form a sentence. Or make a friend. She should have probably called the therapist at the College. Or tried a meditation app. Or journaled. Or done anything to deal with the inescapable feelings building inside of her. She didn't.

For the first numb days post principal's office, post finding out about the sidewalk spray paint from Detective Wolf, post *everything*, she could get away with telling herself what happened was no big deal. She could trick herself into acting normal. By week three, when she wasn't in school, she was in bed. She'd grown up believing that academic and extracurricular achievement guaranteed a baseline level of personal fulfillment. That her clubs and A's, that her perfectionistic nature, would lead to something essential and real. Something approaching happiness? Something that made this shit worth it. Like Wolf's idea that if he made the high honor roll every single quarter from sixth through twelfth grade, he'd get into film school in Los Angeles, or God, maybe Harvard or something, and the hole inside of him would fill. How childish! How naïve! How privileged! Only Hazel sort of thought that way, too. It's not that she believed accomplishing things would make her happy, but she was convinced that the opposite, *not* accomplishing these things, would make her unhappy. That if she didn't grow up to be someone special, she may as well not exist. The strange thing was Hazel no longer cared, not in her normal (borderline obsessive) way, about long-term plans or her future. Getting through each day outside of her bedroom was like climbing a Himalayan mountaintop without proper gear or supplies. An exhausting exercise that would end in the inevitable: death.

She didn't want to *try* anymore. She wanted to be left alone.

Taking President Hill's advice, Hazel had spoken to the Riverburg police. A female detective had come to her house to take a statement. Hazel recounted what happened in the principal's office. When the detective pressed her for more details, she started shaking, filled with self-doubt and fear. It wasn't anything specific the officer said, so much as the thought of making things even more official. After a few minutes—twenty? Thirty? Ten?—she had to ask to stop. However long, it was a horrible experience she never wanted to think about ever again.

Hazel wasn't going to meet with the DA or otherwise be part of the criminal investigation—much less testify against White in court. Why should she have to? She already felt like she was on trial.

By the end of October, Hazel was full-on depressed. The kind of depressed that made washing her face feel like taking out the grarbage, showering practically impossible. The kind that made her not care about accomplishing anything ever again. The kind that made her resort to stupid teenage girl self-harm bullshit. Not *cutting*, nothing physical. But cutting herself down. Like, verbally. Inside her head.

Shewasstupidshewasuglyshewasfatnobodywouldeverloveher-shewasatotalfailureandloser.

Each weekday morning, her father came upstairs to the third floor, coffee cup in hand, acting fake chipper, opening the curtains, saying good morning. As if her life hadn't ended. When she wouldn't get out of bed, he'd offer an I-love-you-now-get-over-yourself pep talk and try to compare their situations. If he could face the unfriendly fire of campus cancel culture, then she could face the sexism of small-town America. *He* was the one who would have to live in Riverburg for the duration, he'd laugh with gallows humor, taking a sip of his espresso.

Please. There was no comparing his cushy day within the bubble of the College to Hazel's daily grind at the institutional sausage factory that was Riverburg High.

Because school was a shit show: *Riverburg Record* articles covering the case dropped almost daily. Guessing White's accuser was topic #1 on the bathroom walls and she was the top contender. Some kids were passive-aggressive, others were under-their-breath rude. Most steered clear of her, especially the girls, like she was contagious.

Not that everyone in Riverburg was necessarily anti-Hazel. The same small group of kids followed one another from AP class to honors class and had stared at her long enough that the novelty was wearing off. A bunch of them were anti-White and made it known they were, at least ideologically, on her side. A few of the kids were legitimately okay. Alex Andrews could be halfway decent when he turned down the dial on his snark—or directed it appropriately. Maybe he wanted to hook up or something? Which was not happening. Hazel wanted no boys near her ever. Mira Sharma, who had a bunch of indie band stickers on her laptop, invited Hazel to their study group. Hazel went, forced by her mother, who was a new patient of Mira's doctor mother and had clearly orchestrated the invitation, but it ended up being the three of them, Hazel and Alex and Mira, spending a supremely awkward school night in the Sharmas' dining room studying their phones instead of their science textbooks.

April was different. They didn't talk much, but they had a free period together and both spent it in the school library sitting at opposite ends of an oval table doing their own thing, sometimes discussing homework or an upcoming test or paper. April was genuinely great, a good egg, as Luna's mom Ramona would say, and April was trying, despite Hazel being weird back to her. But Hazel could tell that what April really wanted to talk about was White, and that was the last subject she was ready to address in the middle of her school day. Or ever. Hazel would rather be friendless and burned at the stake.

The general vibe in the building, though, was pro-White and low-to-medium-key anti-Hazel. How strange to remember that Hazel used to like school. She flashed back to the days in New York when she'd walk the halls, bookstore tote on her shoulder, an innocently ambitious, basically doing okay overachieving wannabe creative class Brooklyn kid.

Teachers were a mixed bag. A couple acted like she was any other student, all business, neither sympathetic nor antagonistic. A few of them—Ms. Harding who taught environmental studies, and Mrs. Marquette, her government teacher—were straight-up nice. Her AP English Lit & Comp teacher Mr. Miller, however, did for real, no exaggeration, hate her and hated her writing more. She used fragments; she started sentences with "and." She broke the rules before she had earned the right to. In their short creative writing unit, he'd had them work on flash fiction, and he'd given her a B minus. She'd never gotten a B minus in English in her entire life. The way he made her feel in class, so dumb and untalented and pathetic, so worthless, was somehow nearly as bad as how White had made her feel. Almost as terrible as she was making herself feel.

Weed seemed a viable alternative to feeling. Stealing her mother's marijuana was simple. Her stash lived in a glass jar in a storage container in the cobwebby basement laundry room. When supplies got precariously low, a refill magically appeared. As if pot were toilet paper or milk or one of her mother's ten thousand moisturizers. Hazel bought rolling paper on Main Street and watched some tutorials on how to roll a joint. Her parents made her take Pickle for an evening walk, and she started smoking them while the dog sniffed her way around the neighborhood. (Behind trees at first, and then out in the open; Pine Street wasn't well lit.) After a couple weeks, the effects of the first few puffs leveled off and she dared to smoke inside her room with the window cracked once more before bed. The pot really helped. More than talking would. And it wasn't like it was addictive or anything. It was a *plant*.

Okay—there were two or three (or four) mornings (a week) when Hazel took the leftover end of a joint and smoked it on her way to school. Not enough to be sleepy or totally out of it or red-eyed, but enough to take the edge off another day of being stared at and hated. It was no different, she told herself, than the coffee she drank in front of her parents. One made her wake up, the other helped her mellow out. She wasn't out drinking and getting wasted and giving blow jobs. She was hardly getting high. Plus, Wolf was on pharmaceuticals. As was her father. She was merely borrowing her mother's pot. She wasn't exactly a coke smuggler.

Her mother seemed to prefer the Indica strains, which Hazel soon learned were the mellowing-out kind. The pot produced a sense of calm and slightly lowered stakes which came as a relief but made it easier for Hazel to put off dealing with her college essays. Hazel hadn't meant to procrastinate on her application. She wasn't ignoring November 1. She hadn't somehow simply *forgotten* about Vassar's early decision deadline. She was lying when she told herself she didn't care. She did care. She thought about it every waking second of the day. Procrastination happened because she cared too much, not too little. She'd worn in the digital grooves on the Vassar website. She'd held a personal screening of movies and TV shows filmed there (*The Muppets Take Manhattan, Frances Ha, The Sex Lives of College Girls*). She'd read Mary McCarthy's 1963 novel about eight Vassar grads, *The Group.*

Hazel visited the campus twice the previous year. Once, with her family at the peak of fall foliage. They left Wolf in the city with Ramona and stayed at the Alumnae House for an informational interview and the college tour and the other official parent-sanctioned things. Later that spring, Hazel was allowed to return on her own, taking the train and sleeping on a friend of a friend's dorm room floor. Vassar was turrets and towers and gates and a pond and a Shakespeare garden, with tendrils of actual ivy climbing up the old buildings. The library was an enchanted castle of stacks and reading rooms, complete with vast rectangular tables where hushed students worked with their books laid out and laptops open and clicking. In the student center there were signs about protests and marches and boycotts and mutual aid funds. The world was on fire and here's where you could learn what to do about it. That's what Hazel should be worrying about: books and changing the world and falling in love. Not some disgusting Principal White.

She remembered walking around campus that Sunday morning, sleep-deprived and hungover, in a post-bagel haze, believing she could be enough for the admissions counselors. And then she'd gotten freaked out about tuition and her imperfect grades. She would never get in. If she somehow did manage an acceptance, her parents wouldn't be able to pay for it. She'd have to take out a predatory student loan and end up living with roommates until she was ninety-two.

In a cryptic parental power play, they'd taken Hazel at face value when she begged them to stop harassing her about her college essay. She persuaded them that if she was going to one day make it as a writer, she needed to do this on her own and be responsible for meeting her deadlines.

But now? Now that it was go time? Hazel was clutching. How to explain herself in few hundred words? Given that Hazel was applying as a prospective English major, the essays had to be perfect. And she didn't have a word.

She'd never had writer's block before. Her fingers reliably worked whenever she sat down at her laptop. But now—nothing. She couldn't *read* much less write. It's like the principal had picked her up that day and dumped all the magic liquids from inside her brain before righting her again. She was there, she was in one piece, but she was empty.

Mr. Miller, the AP English ogre, was right. She was a hack, a teenage dilettante who had nothing to contribute to the literary world and would be lucky to land an online marketing pyramid scheme job after college. Hazel was sure she'd lost any inkling of talent she'd ever possessed. She couldn't possibly handle plumbing her psychic and imaginative depths to transform her real-life experiences and thoughts and feelings into some perfect little admissions office consumable essay.

Fuck it, she'd say each evening between dinner and homework and sleep, giving up. She'd take Pickle and a newly rolled joint around the block. What had once seemed so urgent—her future?—felt pointless. Each morning she told herself she'd work on her essays after school, and each night she put the writing off one more day. Time had run out. It was Thursday night, and the application was due the following Friday. She had one last weekend.

Meanwhile, her brother had turned the living room couch into his personal mission control, from which he monitored the rise in global authoritarianism and the White/Hazel news stories. He sent Hazel links to the *Record*, as if she didn't already check the site like her horoscope. Which was why she didn't think twice when Wolf texted her a link, asking *have u seen?* Maybe it was something about their dad? Hazel could care less if a student website gave her father a chili pepper for his hotness or whatever and didn't bother clicking.

The alarm set in when Wolf made the journey from the living room to the attic. He wasn't one to climb stairs unnecessarily. He took her phone, went to the app store, punched in the family ID code, and handed Hazel her phone back. *Look*, he said, and showed her the HeyYos. The Richard White controversy completely dominated the "fire" page of most popular logs in their radius. Hazel was very much named. Seeing herself in post after post, she gave up.

I am so fucked, she said to herself over and over, scrolling through.

So no, Hazel wasn't okay.

"I thought you should know. Since everyone else does. Are you mad?"

"Thanks, Wolfie. Not at you. But get out of my room, okay?"

After diligently abstaining from social media reactions to her for weeks, Hazel was going to read every dirty disgusting piece of shit comment about her. She didn't want to be smart or good or disciplined anymore. She wanted to breathe in the most poisonous comments, as if overdosing on them could somehow build up her immunity. She stayed up late binge reading, and when her dad came to wake her and turn the lights on the next morning, she categorically refused to go to school.

18

schooled

Countless times that fall Gus had felt like giving up. On what, he couldn't say precisely. On his family? Of course not. On Maine, then? Sure. On being a professor? God, yes. He had half a mind to quit. (And do what exactly? Law school at fifty?) But Gus didn't have the luxury. He had a family to feed, two kids to put through college, a daughter recovering from her brush with a nefarious principal, a son who'd become permanently affixed to the sofa, and a wife in the middle of a midlife crisis. On top of that, he had a cancelation to overcome.

And so, on a Sunday night when Gus would have much preferred an evening at home enjoying and analyzing prestige television, he found himself at the College's library in a parlor set up with cookies and herbal tea for his weekly reading group.

President Hill might have his back, but that didn't mean she wasn't pressuring him to make things right on campus. Founding a campus reading group had been the only thing he could think to do. He'd screwed up his teaching with the stupid Cosby reference, and now he'd have to teach his way out of it. The reading group would provide more opportunity for him to convince his students that he was a good professor who had simply made a mistake.

Sam and Noah, his Deconstructing America students, and several others, settled into their seats. One or two College kids he didn't recognize—they may or may not have been his students—straggled in at seven on the nose. If only they knew what a fraud he felt like half the time. To them, Gus was some sort of totem: the liberal arts professor. A tenured one, and chair, at that. These kids had worked their asses off since kindergarten to get into this room with him. And look at them, here they were, a few practically salivating, waiting for him to lead them through the brambles and thickets of what had become, in recent years on campus, the almost impossible thorniness of a free exchange of ideas.

The fact of the matter was, Gus was no genius. He was smart, sure. Workably so. He could write a paper; and his hermeneutics were spot-on. But he lacked the clarity, speed, productivity, and big thinker brainpower of a true academic powerhouse.

Early on he'd had one good idea and had managed to turn that into *Family Man*. But that was it. Now he was finished, before he'd really got going. He was a one-hit academic wonder, a serviceable lieutenant of the academy, but no five-star general. He hated to have his dissertation advisor, a God of American Studies, see him like this, unfooted and flailing.

Gus poured a chamomile tea and tried to pull himself together. This was the third session of their small group and this week they were reading *Monsters: A Fan's Dilemma* by Claire Dederer, an exhilarating roller-coaster ride of astute criticism about how to handle the work of men like Cosby. There was no way out but through, a truism his wife told the kids when they were having a bad day.

What surprised Gus—once the Sunday night conversations began, and in truth, in his classes too, on a good day—was how much he *liked* teaching. The smaller classes at the College, in contrast to the larger anonymous lectures at Rocky Creek, allowed for a Socratic back-and-forth with students, a real and meaningful dialogue. There was something pure about the intellectual innocence of these fresh-faced undergrads as compared to the older, more demanding, and typically more neurotic, grad students Gus had worked with before.

The setting didn't suck, either, with its stately brick buildings and comfortable lounges and eating halls, its freshly refurbished athletic center and newly built theater and performance hall.

While the commotion around his cancelation had begun to die down—the Fire Gus Blum! petition remained posted but had stopped attracting new signees—Gus needed to be vigilant. As a father, as a husband, as a citizen standing up against predation and exploitation. And as a teacher.

Gus held his copy of *Monsters* high, like an auction paddle. Or an errant Frisbee.

"And now," he said, settling into a leather armchair in the corner, "let's begin."

Monday morning, Hazel was sitting in her usual seat by the door of Mr. Miller's AP Literature class. Having her favorite subject ruined by a terrible teacher was the icing on the cake of her annus horribilis. But today the class was bringing their poetry unit to a close by sharing their original compositions. As a wannabe writer, Hazel felt like she was expected to write something incredible, but the truth was she wasn't much of a poet. Maybe she was dead inside. Or maybe it was because she'd never fallen in love? That's what poetry seemed to be mostly about.

Miller shushed the class and said Mira was up first. Of course, as with all Mira did, her poem was sort of amazing. Funny and self-deprecating and smart and touching. Did this girl ever sleep? Not wanting to be outdone, Alex went second. His poem was dumb. It was silly and rhymed, which Miller seemed unduly impressed by, but felt like a cop-out to Hazel.

April gave Hazel a look. They had a weird sort of agreement between them. Like Hazel, April struggled in stats and preferred English as a subject. Both girls blamed Miller for ruining what should have been their best class of the year.

One by one the rest of the students read their poems. The minutes on the clock above the doorway ticked by slow and loud. In quality, nobody's poem approached Mira's. Most were tepid and dull. No one was really trying.

"April? Hazel?" said Miller, checking his grade book. "You two are the last up. Read your poems so we can get out of here and call it a day."

What was Hazel going to do, freestyle? Or pull out her truly embarrassing draft of a sucky poem? She was ignoring Miller while inwardly freaking out when April spoke up.

"I don't think it's fair that we should have to read these to the class," declared April, tugging at the strings of her hoodie.

"Fair?" said Miller, from behind his desk. "It's your homework. If you don't want to do your assigned work, you shouldn't be taking an AP class."

"Poetry is different," said April. "Poetry isn't something you can be forced to perform on demand. It's something you feel. You're trying to put a number grade on our creativity."

"Yeah, and the number I'm currently thinking of for you is zero," said Miller.

April strapped on her backpack. "Mr. Miller, I'm very sorry but I just got my period. May I go to the nurse's office?"

Miller shook his head just as the bell rang. "That, folks, is our poetry unit," he said. "For next time, please read the first two chapters of *The Red Badge of Courage*."

Hazel caught up to April in the hallway. "Hey," she said. "Thanks for saving me in there."

"I was saving myself," said April. "No way in hell was I going to read my innermost thoughts to a jerk like Miller."

"Way to think fast. The word *period* really shut him down," said Hazel. "What was he going to do, make you prove it?"

"The funny thing is?" said April. "I think I did just get mine. That guy stresses me out."

Hazel suddenly remembered how she'd had her period on the first day of school. The tampon in her tote bag, how White had made her cramps exponentially worse. She was about to say something, to confide in April about the last couple of months—or at least to ask for her phone number so they could text about homework and school stuff—when the bell rang again and April ran off to her next class.

Her mother was in the kitchen folding laundry when she got home later that afternoon. Hazel was sick of being lonely and lost and she was pretty sure her mother was, also. But neither of them seemed to know what to do about it.

"Why aren't you in your studio?" she asked her mom.

"Uh. Thanks a lot. It's nice to see you, too. And how was *your* day?"

"I didn't mean it like that," said Hazel.

"You sure?" Claire put some dish towels and napkins in a drawer and began unloading the dishwasher.

"It's just that you used to love your job," said Hazel, trying again. "And now you seem—I don't know, kind of sad? Maybe it would help if you worked more."

"I'm not exactly sad. I'm incubating. I'm waiting."

"Waiting for what?" asked Hazel.

"For inspiration, I guess. Being creative takes time."

"How long exactly?" asked Hazel.

Claire shrugged. "Good question."

"Honestly, you seem like you're depressed," said Hazel. "You should take one of those online diagnostic tests."

"What if I am?" asked Claire. "Isn't that okay? For me to have feelings, I mean. For me to go through something. Everything isn't always about you."

"Wow, sick burn. Seriously?" Hazel said. "That's really mean."

"Sorry," said Claire. "That came out wrong. Like something my mother would have said."

"Do you ever miss your parents?" Hazel asked. This was a dangerous question. Her mother would talk about almost anything, but only rarely about her childhood family. Hazel used to resent her mother for not letting her know her grandparents, but now that she was older, it was more like a peculiar feature of her life, a family idiosyncrasy that she'd come to accept.

"No, not really," said Claire. "Sometimes, sort of. Like around Thanksgiving or the Jewish holidays."

"Why? Was it better during the holidays?"

"No, babe. It wasn't better… It's really hard to explain."

Claire and Hazel studied the silence for a minute.

Claire, like Gus, had grown up an only child. Her parents, both teachers in Claire's suburban town, seemed normal enough on the outside. Inside the house, her father drank and raged and called Claire names and threw things. He hit her. Her mother, cold, made excuse after excuse for him. Claire focused on school and on her friends, and basically lived in the art teacher's room during open studio hours on evenings and weekends. After meeting Gus, she simply stopped talking to her parents. Slowly, painfully—and then completely.

"It could have been a lot worse, though," Claire finally continued. "And now I have you. And Wolf and Daddy."

"Then why are you depressed?" asked Hazel.

"I don't know. Honestly? I guess I'm worried about you. And maybe I'm figuring some stuff out for myself here, too."

"You don't have to worry about me," said Hazel. She didn't sound very convincing.

19

the other mother

Fall came fast and hard to Maine. Claire was already turning up the heat, enveloping herself in layers of cardigan, her holey cashmere scarf wrapped around her neck. Without a place to be in the morning, she'd taken to wearing monochrome with thick wool socks and Danish house shoes. Her feet remained cold. It was only the end of October. How was she going to make it until spring?

Mornings were still special, despite everything. The light had a clarity to it. While the luxury of a quiet weekday morning at home was not wasted on Claire, whenever she brought her coffee to her studio table and tried to work, her mind scattered or went blank or returned to obsessing over Hazel or worrying about Gus.

Concerned that their daughter had been permanently damaged by her encounter with the principal, Claire and Gus had started seeing a cognitive behavioral therapist who was covered by their health insurance and had the mien of someone recently returned from a silent retreat. He was nonreactive to a fault, acting like what happened to Hazel was an everyday parenting challenge. So far it wasn't helping.

On a Wednesday morning, Claire should have been sketching and researching and sourcing fabrics but was lingering over an episode of *Fresh Air* and almost relieved to hear a knock on the kitchen door. Polly? Claire wondered with a flicker of hope. They'd hiked the nature reserve two Friday afternoons in a row, the sun setting behind them.

Another knock. A package perhaps. Claire went to check. It was a woman around Claire's age. She looked athletic, like she'd played field hockey and tennis as a girl.

"Are you Claire? I thought about calling, but I couldn't find your number."

Claire felt herself brace.

"I was hoping we could talk—" She seemed to be summoning her courage. "I'm Agatha. White. Can I come in for a minute?"

Claire considered the alternatives to inviting her in. She could slam the door in her face. Sic Pickle on her. Tell her to get the hell off their property. Or call the police? But Claire had worked hard to tame her Long Island instincts. Instead, she opened the door, held it ajar with her hip, and gestured to the shoe cubby.

They sat down at the kitchen table, assessing one another.

"Did you make your necklace?" Claire heard herself ask. She couldn't help but notice satisfying things. The twists of pink-and-cream yarn like something either a child would make, or that might be carried by a shop on a cobblestoned street in Norway.

"This?" Agatha touched it. "Oh. I forgot to take it off. Finger knitting. On rainy days I craft with my daughter."

Other than the necklace, Agatha was no-nonsense, her hair pulled back in a tight low ponytail, black yoga leggings and a plain crewneck sweater.

It was strange to meet someone whom you'd stalked online.

Someone who you didn't know but had decided you hated. Claire had heard that Agatha worked as a school counselor before becoming a stay-at-home-mom. She pictured a girl of four or five, sitting at one of those low children's play tables stocked with yarn and glue and crayons and colored pencils and paper and sundry supplies, Agatha seated beside her, squeezing her legs underneath.

"I like it," said Claire. The moment the words left her mouth she regretted the compliment.

Claire watched Agatha study the kitchen. The *New York Times* sections left over from Sunday. Wolf's drawing pads and pens on the windowsill. A trio of small potted succulents that needed watering. Bills. A dish towel crumpled next to the stovetop.

"I was hoping to talk to you about my husband," said Agatha.

"There's nothing to say."

The two women sat there for another long minute.

"I want to be practical about this," Agatha began again. "I want us both to be practical. For the sake of our daughters."

"Practical," said Claire, crossing her arms and legs.

"Nobody will ever really know what went on in that office. Other than Richard and Hazel."

"Please. We know exactly what happened," said Claire.

"I think—I *know*—there's been a misunderstanding," said Agatha.

"Seriously? What has he told you?"

"We haven't talked about it," said Agatha.

"You haven't *talked* about it?" Claire repeated, her voice rising to borderline inhospitable. "How is that even possible?"

"I get why you're angry. I'm sorry for what Hazel thinks or believes or feels she experienced."

"What she *feels* she experienced?"

"I'm sorry for whatever was said, by either of them, to get us here. But your family is fine," said Agatha. "Your daughter is fine. Nothing happened to her, right? I wish I could say the same for mine."

Through her hatred, Claire noticed how drained Agatha looked. How worn and worried and sad. How tired. She was younger than Claire, by a good five or ten years, but her skin was starting to line.

"Why are you here?" asked Claire.

"I thought maybe you could talk to Hazel. Whatever miscommunication they might have had, Richard is an excellent principal. I want you to know that."

Claire couldn't believe this gaslighting was happening in her kitchen. "Excellent principals do not proposition their students."

"Have you heard anything about what Richard did for that high school? It was a mess before he got there. Being the principal in Riverburg, it's like running a social services agency and a school at the same time. These kids are dealing with so many challenges before they've walked into the building."

"That has nothing to do with what he did to my daughter—or any other girls."

Agatha stood. "There are no other girls."

"Why the hell are you here?" asked Claire.

"Because I want to know if Hazel is telling the truth."

"Are you for real? *Of course* she is. Why would anyone make something like this up?"

"I didn't say she's making it up. I feel like there's a real chance that this is some sort of a miscommunication. That Hazel read the situation the wrong way. Richard tends to be close with his students. And maybe for her, as a kid from New York, that somehow crossed an emotional line. But being friendly and being sexually inappropriate are two very different things. There are two sides to every story. We know that. There is no objective thing that happened that day. It's all about interpretation. Projection, even. Do you know what I'm saying?"

"No," said Claire. Unbelievable. "I really don't. You should go."

"Has Hazel ever lied about anything else? Or shoplifted? Or cheated on a test? Because teenage girls can be quite—expansive—with the truth. It's a normal part of their development. This stuff can happen. It's a confusing time, being a teenager. Especially with social media. Kids make things up sometimes. Exaggerate, or somehow confuse reality with fiction. It doesn't mean they're bad people. I'm not trying to blame Hazel."

"Hazel is *fine*. Hazel is not the problem."

"Well, either way, hasn't Richard been punished enough?"

"What are you talking about?" said Claire. "He hasn't been punished at all." He was on leave, that was it.

"Do *you* believe Hazel?" asked Agatha. "Are you one million percent sure she's not embellishing or exaggerating any of this?"

"I have not the tiniest shred of doubt in my mind," said Claire.

"Because we're talking about twenty minutes versus the rest of Richard's life."

"I mean you could say the same thing about murder, right? Bad things can happen in a short amount of time."

"Richard hardly murdered Hazel."

"You admit then, something happened."

"Look, Richard claims your daughter was inappropriate with him. She came on to him. She told him she'd do anything to get into college."

"That is nothing like what Hazel told me."

"Exactly! That's my point. Like I said, there are two sides to every story. Why do we automatically believe hers?"

"Number one, Hazel is not a liar," Claire said. "Hazel is a supremely trustworthy kid. Number two, she doesn't need help getting into college. Whereas your husband—"

"What about *your* husband?"

"*My* husband? What about him." Speaking of murder, speaking of husbands, Gus was going to kill her for talking to Agatha.

"I read the newspaper, too." Agatha walked to the shoe cubby and slid her feet into her boots. "All I ask is you consider that this may not be what you think. My family matters as much as yours."

"Are you seriously comparing Gus's Cosby thing to what your husband did to Hazel?"

Agatha didn't answer.

"Get out," Claire said, opening the yellow door and pulling her cardigan tighter around her.

20

be very afraid

Wolf woke up on Halloween morning feeling like a kid on Christmas. Because he had no Christmas. This was it. His favorite holiday of the entire year. In New York, Halloween meant a Saturday school fair where overly zealous TV and film industry parents turned the auditorium into a Haunted House, a seriously cute dog costume parade in the East Village, a free oversized grandma sprinkle cookie at the Italian bakery, a paperback at the library for trick or treat, dressed-up drunk people on the subway (lots of boobs), the occasional stretch of stoops handing out candy. Which was all well and good, but Wolf wanted a classic Halloween. A Charlie Brown spooky neighborhood, honest-to-goodness real Halloween. A Halloween in Riverburg might do—so far, the town definitely seemed creepy and fraught with danger. Supposedly their new neighborhood was the place to be, if only for this one night. People at the College warned his parents to prepare for a deluge of trick-or-treaters. Kids from surrounding, more rural towns where houses were too far apart came to Riverburg for candy. And not just Riverburg, his neighborhood specifically. Well, the block around the corner, River Street. His dad had gone to the supermarket and bought a thousand mini candy bars. A thousand!

Wolf needed this. Suffering through junior high with no friends while intercepting the hate notes was wearing him down. Was it supposed to help things that the chorus teacher had added an embarrassingly Jewish medley of "Hanukkah O Hanukkah," "Oseh Shalom" and "Hava Nagila" to the list of Christmas songs and old-fashioned winter ones about sledding? Wolf was a fluorescent Jewish highlighter in a box of gentile pencils. (And by the way, it's not like his family was even religious!)

The junior high kids were allowed to wear costumes to school. (No masks, though. Too scary.) He'd do one costume for day and another for trick-or-treating. Last year in fifth grade, he'd gone as Zeus with a sheet draped around him and hand-me-down sheepskin boots. He used to be into Greek mythology, back in the days when he was a dork. This year for trick-or-treating he wanted to be something macabre and bloody like a zombie or the grim reaper. In the Halloween aisle, he saw a headless horseman costume and settled on that. For the school day, *maybe* Spiderman? The nerd to superhero character thing felt borderline played out. Maybe something simpler like a vampire—he could throw on a cape over black sweats.

The larger issue was who to trick-or-treat with. His mom kept bugging him to "find a friend" and go with them. AS IF. The chances he'd be asked to go trick-or-treating by anyone in stupid Riverburg were about the same as being struck by lightning while taking his evening bath. Less. How he wished he was still friends with Gracie. If only he could go back in time—or cross the metaverse—and undo the colossal mess he'd made. But since he had not ONE friend in the state, the best he could do, the least mortifying prospect available to him, was convince his sister to take him.

Wolf knocked on Hazel's door Halloween morning.

"Go away," she said.

"It's me," said Wolf.

"What do you want?"

"To talk to you? Which is why I'm doing this thing called knocking."

"Come in, I guess. Close the door behind you," Hazel said. She was supposed to be getting ready, but was wrapped in a blanket, wearing pajamas, her laptop open.

"Aren't you going to school? Are you going to pretend to be sick again?"

"I'm running late. Working on something. What do you need?"

"It's Halloween."

"Yes, I'm aware it's October 31st. Exceedingly aware."

"Can you take me trick-or-treating tonight? Please?"

"You know I would but my ED deadline for Vassar is November 1. Otherwise known as tomorrow."

"How can you not be done yet? You've been working on that for months," said Wolf. "You told Mom and Dad you were done."

"I have some last-minute edits. Don't say anything, okay?"

"Can't you finish it in school or something?"

"Are you kidding? Why don't you ask a friend? You made a friend, didn't you? That girl Charlotte?"

"NO." God. She played Charlotte. Her *name* wasn't Charlotte!

"Go with Mom. She's only like a couple of inches taller than you. Maybe people will think you're with some cool eighth grader."

"Yeah right."

Hazel returned to her laptop. "This is my life here. My entire future rests on this application."

"Hazel?" said Wolf, from the doorway.

"What?"

"Can I ask you something else?"

"If you must."

"You know how the principal says you put your hand on his leg?"

Hazel closed her laptop.

"Yeah?"

"Did you?"

"Ew! Wolf, shut up."

"I'm your brother. It's my right to know. Did you put your hand there or what?"

"Wolf. Use your ninety-ninth percentile brain. What do you think?"

"No?"

"Why would I touch him?"

"They're saying you came on to him." Wolf half mumbled his accusation and couldn't look at Hazel. He was uncomfortable talking about s-e-x with his family members.

"In what universe would I be interested in having sex with my high school principal?" She looked pissed.

"That's what I figured," said Wolf. He'd been worried, though.

"Why did you wait like two whole months to ask me that?"

Wolf didn't answer.

"Did you think I was lying this whole time? Whose side are you on?"

"I was making a hundred percent sure. Due diligence, you know? Don't be mad."

Claire insisted they go ahead with Halloween. Otherwise, Wolf would never forgive her. Gus wanted to leave the house dark and turn away trick-or-treaters but had followed her instructions and wasted far too much money on decorations. She had to hand it to him: The house looked incredible. Strobe lighting, Styrofoam cemetery headstones, a skeleton hanging ominously from a hook on the front door, cobweb goo. Claire added a homemade sign of black and orange block lettering strung on a black ribbon spelling out: BE VERY AFRAID.

Claire *was* afraid. She'd managed to remove the awful word from their sidewalk, but the memory of the graffiti haunted her. Opening the door voluntarily to all the denizens of Riverburg and beyond didn't sound like the smartest idea in the world. But she was trying to be festive for Wolf's sake. She was setting up a speaker to play new wave quasi-Halloween music when Gus appeared in the foyer.

"You're not dressing up?" she asked him.

When the kids were younger, Claire had made them wear family costumes. One year, Gus had gone as a ketchup bottle, Wolf as a veggie burger, Hazel a French fry and Claire a chef. She missed those days. Hazel a curious and magical child; Wolf a preschooler who always wanted her. She was trying to cling to the orange buoy of their childhood for dear life.

"I'm a professor. See?" Gus was wearing his usual jeans but had put on a brown corduroy. The one with the suede patches he'd complained about when Claire bought it for him on final sale. He usually got annoyed when she styled him like a cinematic version of a college professor.

Claire itched to criticize Gus for his lack of costume effort but managed to stop herself. Not that Claire should talk. She was "dressed" as Rocky Balboa in the gray sweatsuit that had become her second skin, with the added flourish of a red terrycloth sweatband.

"I'm worried about tonight," said Gus.

"Please don't tell me you bought more candy."

"About what could happen. Do you really think it makes sense for us to be answering the door for trick-or-treaters? The entire town will know where we live."

Claire wasn't going to admit that she was worried, too. Wolf needed Halloween and Claire was going to provide it for him. "We've been over this. They already know. We're not canceling

Halloween. The kids have lost enough already. Besides, Halloween is happening—whether we like it or not."

Hazel came down the stairs wearing an oversized Vassar hooded sweatshirt and bike shorts. "What are you talking about? Why would we cancel Halloween? Because of me?"

"Because of the situation. To be safe," said Gus.

"We're not canceling anything," said Claire. "Do you want to destroy Wolf?"

"Seriously," said Hazel. "This is Wolf's first Halloween outside of the city. He lives for this shit. And you decorated the house, which is basically an engraved invitation to trick-or-treaters."

"Hazel, honey. Don't you need pants?" asked Claire. "It's freezing out. And I'm sure Wolf would rather you wear a costume."

"Oh, I'm not personally planning on leaving the house."

"You're not going with Wolf?"

"I can't. Homework."

"On Halloween?" said Claire.

The sky went from blue to pink to gray before becoming one of those luminous fall evenings in Maine where the darkness is a deep indigo and then black, the stars twinkling, the moon a storybook crescent. The little kids came first, a Noah's Ark of animals with chubby legs. Then preschoolers gave way to elementary schoolkids in plastic superhero and princess costumes with parents hanging back by the sidewalk.

Claire's work at the door was interrupted by Wolf yelling his fake bloody headless horseman head off trying to figure out how to retain consciousness with his face encased in industrial grade rubber. Once he stopped freaking out long enough for Claire to poke some air holes, he ate three candy bars, stuck his head back on, and pronounced himself ready to go.

"Just watch the door for a second," said Claire. "I need something from upstairs."

Claire ran up to the playroom and grabbed an oddly lifelike wolf head purchased years ago at a costume shop in the city, adding it to her lackluster Rocky Balboa, turning from underdog to predator.

"Gus! Door!" Claire yelled. Gus had disappeared again, presumably hiding in his small home office behind Wolf's bedroom to get some work done. Gus said holidays were a construct.

"We're leaving!"

The constant doorbell ringing made the dog crazy. Wolf was about to implode from overexcitement, candy, and social pressure, too.

"You're in charge of candy. And Pickle."

"No problem."

"And, Gus? It's Halloween. Can you not be on your phone the whole time?" said Claire. "It's really cute out there."

"In here, too. You both look great. Wolf, you're terrifying."

"Well, we're off," said Claire. Vibes 4 your homework, she texted Hazel.

Claire and Wolf entered the crowded darkness. She was trying with him. She really was. Wolf used to resent her for working too much. Once, during a bath when he was little, he'd begged her to quit BuiltGood. *Mommy, be a full-time mommy*, he'd said. She explained, of course, that she was always his mommy, whether she was at work or at home. But she knew what Wolf meant. He didn't want a babysitter in the afternoons. He wanted Claire.

These days he resented her for being around *too* much. When she walked into the kitchen, he grabbed his phone or video game thing and walked out. She'd been warned of the terrible tween boy years, but somehow, she'd believed, Wolf would be different. That a perimenopausal mother should have a preteen entering puberty was a terrible stroke of hormonal timing.

"Feel free to pretend you don't know me," offered Claire.

"Deal," said Wolf.

River Street, the once handsome avenue around the corner from them, still boasted large houses owned by professors and longstanding Riverburg families. The western side of the street's houses backed up onto a stream. Russet leaves carpeted the sidewalks. Traffic was stopped for the evening in either direction. Volunteers gave away glow stick bracelets. A haunted alley came complete with sound effects. Themed houses were the thing. One was a pirate ship, another had severed heads growing from trees. Some families had constructed whole live action mise-en-scènes in their front yards, casting themselves as ghouls and ghosts. At a house on the corner of Pine and River, classic horror films were projected onto a sheeted garage door. Claire spotted a séance. The block was transformed; Wolf was spellbound. One offshoot cul-de-sac had orchestrated a performance art–like Wizard of Oz tableau, making a yellow brick road out of a circular driveway. Was that Polly as Dorothy?

Midway down River Street, Wolf stopped cold in the middle of the crowd.

"Is that you?" he asked.

He was talking to a girl. She was unusually edgy-looking by Riverburg standards, dressed in a homemade Wonder Woman costume, complete with fishnets and long-sleeve leotard and pleather zip-up boots and a felt eye mask. Claire had trained her eye to notice the cool, the sparkly girls, the ones with *it*, and to note their clothing choices. She'd made a career out of it.

"It's me," said Wolf, from inside his headless horseman head. The excitement and strangeness of Halloween must have made him forget himself.

"Who are you?" Wonder Woman asked the horseman.

I'm nobody! Who are you? thought Claire. Hazel had given her an Emily Dickinson collection for her last birthday.

"Is this a friend of yours?" Claire asked Wolf.

"I'm Gracie," the girl volunteered.

"Gracie? Gracie, as in *Charlotte's Web*?" Claire still didn't understand why he'd quit the school play.

"Who's the headless kid?" asked Gracie.

"It's Wolf," said Claire. "Wolf Blum." With that, Claire pulled the top of his costume off. Maybe this chance encounter could turn into Wolf's first playdate since the move?

"Mom!" said Wolf.

Claire's eye wandered over to look at the girl's parental companion. She felt a weird energy, a rush of cold, biting wind, a blast of the winter to come, followed by the fury of recognition.

"Agatha?" said Claire. She wasn't certain. The night had been full of apparitions.

Met with silence, Claire realized that she'd been rendered anonymous by her rubbery head. She took the thing off.

"Claire, I thought that was you," said Agatha, eerily calm. "Hello."

Unbelievable. This woman had sat at her kitchen table and somehow hadn't thought to mention that her daughter went to school with Wolf. That their children were friends?

That's when Claire noticed him, lurking a few steps behind.

It was *him*. The principal. She'd memorized White's face from the newspaper photos. This was the face of her nightmares. Agatha and Richard White, trick-or-treating like they were Mr. and Mrs. America. Or, at least, Mr. and Mrs. Riverburg. How dare they have the nerve to come to her side of town? Not that she had any idea where they lived, come to think of it. Maybe this was their side of town, too.

Claire wanted to take her house key and poke his eyes out so that he could never so much as look at her daughter, or anyone else's daughter, again.

★★★

Wolf looked back and forth from his mother to Gracie to Principal White.

GAME OVER.

"NO!!!" Wolf screamed, a bloodcurdling scream into the Halloween night.

His mother grabbed his arm and pulled him across the street to the corner of River and Pine.

"Ow," said Wolf. "Let go of me!" There were hundreds of trick-or-treaters on the blocked-off road. Older kids, now that darkness had fallen. Wolf's howls were absorbed by the night. By the moon.

"Wolf. Jesus! Do you know who that is? Do you know who her father is? *Do you?*"

"She's not my friend anymore. She won't even talk to me, okay? I didn't do anything wrong. Let go. You're *hurting* me."

She let him go. "Sorry. I didn't mean to hurt you. But this is serious. We need to go home. Right now."

Hazel felt like a dick for disappointing Wolf, but she had bigger things to worry about than Halloween. She was already exhausted, having been up since six for school, and nowhere near done with her application essay.

She picked at a PMS pimple. She needed coffee. Lots of coffee. And Halloween candy. Hazel went down to the kitchen for supplies, made an iced latte and grabbed a handful of peanut butter cups. Back upstairs she sat on her bed, propped her laptop on a pillow, crossed her legs, pulled her hair into a bun, and attempted to psyche herself up. She felt her fingers take their place hovering over her laptop keyboard like a pianist in the moment before beginning a concerto. She was ready to be transported, to transport her reader, to tell a story that, while resonating personally with the admissions counselors, would simultaneously speak to larger, broader generational—maybe even timeless!—themes, thereby securing her place in the college essay pantheon. While waiting for the caffeine to kick in, she reviewed the already filled-in application basics. Her New York extracurricular activities painted the picture of a creative, intellectually engaged and pleasingly overextended student. Her Maine fall semester, on the other hand, made her look like a loser who'd never make it out of her parents' basement. Or attic, in her case. If only she'd volunteered to work on the school newspaper, her original plan. If only the principal *had* really called her into his office to start a literary magazine.

Well, too late. She couldn't change any of that. The one element of her application—of her life—she could control was this one page of writing.

She read the questions for the thousandth time.

The common application, used by Vassar and a host of other schools, gave prompts that could encompass pretty much any topic on the planet, 101 variations on: *Recount a time when you faced a challenge, setback, or failure. How did it affect you, and what did you learn from the experience?* (Lol.) If that didn't work, there was a completely amorphous choose-your own-adventure style topic, too. *Share an essay on any topic of your choice.* (Write about WHATEVER in 250–650 words? Thanks for narrowing it down!) Vassar requested an additional short essay asking prospective students what they might contribute to the campus environment, aka the "Why Vassar" question. There was also a Your Space page that you could do absolutely anything—or nothing—with. A short film? A short story? Photography? Poetry? A digital link to a dance you'd choreographed. Anything!

She'd considered submitting her best old short story. A sex-positive, self-deprecatingly comic, self-consciously Jewish, autofictional send-up about her first (kind of major, no sex) hookup, a supremely awkward pas de deux performed in a canoe during her July program month at Bennington. The piece had opened the school literary journal in the fall issue of her junior year.

But ever since her sexist jerk of an English teacher Miller had torn apart her creative writing assignments that fall, she'd gotten down on herself and come to the conclusion that her writing was kind of stupid.

She'd tried for months to write a personal statement worthy of Vassar. Her laptop's desktop was strewn with the go-nowhere attempts. Any rhetorical path she started down felt either intellectually fraudulent and trying too hard, or facile and simplistic. The word limits were killer. As if each of the words needed to be a smooth shell plucked from the beach of her mind. A few paragraphs, however taut, could never sum up who she was. Or the years she'd spent (wasted?) studying and stressing and raising her hand until her arm cramped and losing hundreds of hours of sleep on homework and generally trying to be perfect.

Had she considered writing about the principal? She had, of course she had, but she couldn't make herself go through with it. Whenever she tried, she felt completely blocked. Writing about him felt too risky, too scary, too real. Too personal. Too vulnerable. She didn't want to feel any of those things. She *couldn't* feel those things. If she did, she'd wind up a *Girl, Interrupted* in a psychiatric hospital, not Vassar. Also, it felt cheap, like cheating. She didn't want that one morning in his office to define her.

The usually sleepy neighborhood outside her attic window wouldn't shut up. In a few hours it would be November 1. Despite the iced coffee, she didn't feel alert or focused, she hadn't had one jolt of creative inspiration. All she felt was burned-out and sleepy. Like she didn't even care whether she got into Vassar anymore. But applying early decision would save her a lot of work later on.

And so it was time to put words on the page, to produce *something* no matter how half-assed. Since she'd proven she could NOT write a decent personal statement to save her life, Hazel calculated she could either write something new and last-minute that would inevitably suck or go the safer route and repurpose an old class assignment. She found her earbuds and blasted music, willing herself to stay awake while clicking through her documents folder.

There it was. Her eleventh-grade social studies essay, "On Reckoning with (my) White Privilege: Defining, Understanding and Interrogating Whiteness." Hazel knew the essay was a pedestrian attempt at understanding the subject matter—a self-congratulatory performative project. Virtue Signaling 101. But adults seemed to love it. She'd gotten an A plus.

The term paper was too long, massively so, but she could fish out the better bits and string them together. Add an introductory sentence or two about moving to Maine, and a concluding paragraph about wanting to become a writer (or journalist?) so she could help end oppression. Stick a quote from *Between the World and Me* or possibly Toni Morrison up top. The essay would be #basic. Not exactly the work of a literary genius. But it was doable, and when she finished her cutting and pasting and word collaging her pastiche, she could allow herself some sleep.

Because Hazel was tired. SO tired.

Or. New idea. She could go to sleep now, get some rest, set her alarm for 4:00 a.m. and wake up fresh to do the editing then, along with the Why Vassar part. Because while she needed to take courses like "The Art of Reading and Writing" and "Thinking Short: The Story" and "Making Waves: Topics in Feminist Activism," she was too groggy to remember why.

It sounded like a decent plan, so instead of writing anything, Hazel scrolled through selfies to pick a profile photo. She settled on an image of herself in a purple-and-white Indian block print dress standing in front of a community mural by a bookstore in coastal Maine. She was looking at something out beyond the camera, and laughing at Wolf, who'd taken the photo. He'd captured her with his first and last shot of the day. She'd miss that kid next year. *If* she somehow managed to finish this application and get into college. She couldn't keep her eyes open one more minute. She closed her laptop, pulled the comforter over her, and let go. Hazel slept deep and hard.

Gus was sitting on the stoop with Pickle on a leash secured by his boot, manically grading midterms by flashlight while eating a mini chocolate bar. Claire was right. He'd bought three times the candy they'd needed, maybe four times.

"I need to talk to you," said Claire, approaching the house with Wolf lagging behind her.

"I'm manning the door," said Gus. He needed to finish his grading. "Can this wait?"

"Wolf, time for your bath," said Claire. (He still took baths.)

"Bath?! But I haven't had my dinner yet—"

"Wolf. Go to your room," Claire said, pointing up. She could hardly keep her shit together.

"You want me to eat in the tub?" asked Wolf, who started crying.

"Not in the tub, in your room," said Claire. "Gus, can you come see me in the kitchen?"

"What about the doorbell?"

"Ignore it."

Wolf traipsed upstairs as he was told. Gus followed Claire into the kitchen.

"Remember how Wolf made that friend at school?" Claire said. "The one who plays Charlotte?"

Gus remembered, of course. Not her name, but the fact of her existence.

"Gracie?" reminded Claire.

Names weren't his forte. He cooked dinner. Claire kept track of the children's social lives.

"You're not going to believe this. Gracie is Richard White's daughter."

"What?"

"We ran into them. He and his wife are out there trick-or-treating together. They're a block away."

"Jesus," said Gus.

"That's what I said."

"Wait. You talked to them?"

"We didn't exactly have a conversation with them. But that's not the point. That girl is Wolf's best friend here. His only friend. This must be why Wolf quit the play. Why he won't get off the couch." She hadn't been able to figure it out before then, his turn against the drama club.

"I'm going out there," said Gus, reaching for his boots. "That pervert should be in prison."

"Calm down. This isn't a TV show. You can't go after him. Do *you* want to get arrested?"

"Why tell me this if you don't want me to do anything about it?"

"There's nothing to *do* about it. It just is. And it's not Wolf's fault. It's not the daughter's fault, either. Gracie. I feel bad for her. She's—adorable, honestly. I mean, can you imagine? Having that man as your father?" Claire knew something about bad fathers.

"How did you not figure this out before?" said Gus.

"How did *I* not figure this out?"

"You're the one who talks to Wolf about his friends."

"Oh my God. This is *my* fault?"

"I don't care how adorable she is. Wolf is never seeing that girl again," said Gus.

"Her name is Gracie," said Wolf, reappearing in the kitchen, having shed his costume.

"I asked you to go upstairs," said Claire.

"I'm *hungry*. You promised to bring me food. And you can't CANCEL AN INNOCENT PERSON."

"You really need to stop eavesdropping," said Claire. "We're not canceling Gracie. We're trying to look out for you and Hazel—"

"Can you two stop fighting? You're about to give me a nosebleed."

"Wolfie, I really don't think it's a good idea for you to spend time with Gracie," said Gus.

"We can't forbid them from seeing one another," said Claire. "She's his best friend here. For all we know he *likes* her. This isn't Shakespeare."

"I DO NOT LIKE GRACIE! I'M NOT FRIENDS WITH HER ANYMORE!" shouted Wolf. "She won't *speak* to me!"

"Wolfie, why did you quit the play?" asked Claire.

"Gracie is NOT MY FRIEND."

Wolf ran to his room and slammed his door. Hard. The house shook. The dumb old paint peeled an inch more. He didn't care if the whole house burned down. His parents were terrible people. Total hypocrites. Not that he could have a minute's peace to feel sorry for himself. His mother was knocking.

"Sweetie? I want to talk to you," she said through the bedroom door.

"Don't come in."

"Please?"

Wolf didn't answer. She came in and sat on the end of his narrow twin bed.

"This is all your fault," said Wolf.

"I'm so sorry." Deep down, Claire thought he was right.

"You made us move here. Don't you get it! None of us belong here! I don't belong here. Isn't that obvious? And now I'm trapped for eternity in this frostbitten hellhole."

"It's forty-five degrees out, Wolf. It's not even winter yet."

"Exactly!! Why do we live in this barn?"

"I was trying to do the right thing. For Daddy, so he could stop commuting four hours back and forth a day to work. For you and Hazel. I wanted to give you a house, and a college fund."

Wolf grabbed his phone off the bookcase by his bed and stared into the Reddit abyss. "Liar. You did this for *yourself.* So you could quit your job and buy more stupid clothes."

"That's not true." Or maybe it was.

"Why should I have to suffer because you like big houses and fresh air?" Sometimes Wolf wished he'd never been born.

"It's going to be okay. It's going to get better. Just give it time. You do belong here. We all—"

"Get out! You don't care about me. Maine is a terrible place!"

Downstairs, Gus was writing out a note that said TAKE THREE and dumping candy bars into an oversized aluminum bowl. He killed the porch lights, left the bowl on the stoop, locked the front door and headed to the kitchen to make Wolf some dinner.

"How did you know it was them?" asked Gus.

"What do you mean?" said Claire. She retrieved the broom from the kitchen pantry and started sweeping.

"The Whites," said Gus.

Claire hadn't planned on saying anything. But not telling him suddenly felt impossible. "Agatha came to see me the other day. She wanted to talk to me, mother to mother or something like that—"

Gus turned off the water he was boiling for pasta and looked at her like she was crazy. "Richard White's wife came to our house. And you didn't tell me this because why?" How the hell had he not been *fired* yet?

"Because I knew you'd get like this," said Claire.

"I hate this town," said Gus.

"That's what Wolf said," said Claire.

"We should have never left New York."

"You didn't have a job in New York."

"I had a job in New York."

"Sort of."

"Rocky Creek is in New York."

"Long Island is not New York," said Claire. She should know.

"Moving here was your idea," said Gus, "Don't put this on me."

Neither of them said anything. Every couple had a knotty, mostly unspoken issue between them. Privileged and petty as it was, Gus's lack of a New York City professorship was theirs.

Claire hated when they fought. She moved into the living room, took a blanket off the couch, and wrapped herself in it. Gus followed, sitting down next to her and putting his wrinkled brow in his hands. "Why wouldn't you move to Minneapolis when we had the chance?"

There had been a job offer from the University of Minnesota when they were pregnant with Wolf. It was a reputable department in a real city. Claire had flatly rejected the idea.

"We could have been happy there," said Gus. "We could have afforded a life."

"Gus, I'm in fashion," said Claire. "I can't live in *Minnesota*."

"So Minneapolis isn't cool enough for you, but somehow you're fine with moving to the fashion hub of Riverburg, Maine?"

"Let's move back, then. I'll beg BuiltGood to give me whatever they have. Let's move to Queens like we should have done years ago. Let's move to New Jersey. Let's move to Staten Island for all I care! Let's put the house on the market and move back to New York right now."

"That's impossible," said Gus, checking his phone. For what? Claire thought. A job offer?

"Because you refuse to do it. You know everyone! Can't you pick up a visiting professor gig for next semester? A class or two? Call in a favor."

"As an adjunct? Making $4500 a semester? Do you like having health insurance? And housing? And food?"

"Ask for your Rocky Creek job back," said Claire.

"There's no way in hell they'll rehire me. That ship has sailed. To say nothing of the fact that a vocal portion of the College's student body is trying to get me fired."

"Cosby? That's mostly blown over. Hasn't it?"

"Not entirely, no," said Gus. "You'd know that if you bothered to ask."

If so much hadn't been happening, she *would* have. But when it came down to it, she was more worried about Hazel than Gus. She supposed that made her a bad wife. "Can we at least move to Portland?" she asked. "I mean, doesn't that make sense?"

"We bought a house here. A few months ago! And Portland is expensive."

"We'll rent out the house," said Claire.

"I'm hanging on by a thread at work," said Gus. "I need to show my face on campus four or five days a week. That's why they hired me. I'm the chair. We moved here partly so that I wouldn't have to commute, right? I want to be here for the kids. For you."

"Hazel won't even be here next year." The thought terrified Claire.

"That's the other thing. Hazel's tuition. Do you want to be the one to tell her we can't afford to send her to college next year?"

So they were stuck. Claire gave up. She really did.

While Gus retreated to the kitchen, Claire unwrapped a bar of chocolate from her personal stash—the extra dark kind with almonds and sea salt—and sank deeper into the pink couch with the throw on her lap. She opened her phone, hoping to anesthetize herself with the annual Halloween envy scroll. She thumbed through costumed babies and toddlers set atop white Carrara marble kitchen countertops, grade school siblings close enough in age to gamely trick-or-treat together (why had she let Gus talk them into waiting so long before trying for their second?), clever homemade costumes conceived and executed by her RISD and BuiltGood friends (why hadn't she sewn costumes this year?). All these happy families in Brownstone Brooklyn, living the very lives Claire and Gus had been unable to provide their progeny.

Upstairs, Gus was tucking Wolf into bed. He'd be okay. Kids were resilient, weren't they? Or maybe that was a lie parents told to make themselves feel less guilty and terrified. Maybe Wolf and Hazel would be scarred for life.

When she'd scrolled until there was nothing left to scroll, long after Wolf's light was off and she'd waited an extra half hour to make sure he (and hopefully Gus) had entered an unawakenable dream state, Claire was ready for sleep, too.

The exact moment she started up the stairs she heard an enormous crash.

She ran to the den and found shards of broken glass strewn everywhere. Claire could hardly believe it. A rock had been hurled, destroying the bay window. Some of the window's glass remained, but most of it was shattered.

In a sort of trance, Claire unlocked the porch door, hit the lights, and went out to investigate the damage from the other side. On the front stoop, the stupid dollar-store ghost was still on, moaning and glowing. Styrofoam headstones knocked in the wind. When she turned around, what she found waiting for her on their door was the most terrifying, hateful, shocking thing that had ever been directed at her family.

21

jews in maine

Claire and Gus had been awake since Halloween morning, some twenty-six hellish hours ago, and were running on anxiety and adrenaline. The house was now filled with strangers. At dawn, several hours after the rock had been thrown and Claire discovered the swastika, Gus had called the police. Chief Larry Chase showed up with a pair of detectives as the school busses made their lurching routes past River and Pine Streets and toward the elementary school. Hate crimes, unlike predator principals, were taken seriously in Riverburg.

They decided to let the kids sleep in and skip school. The longer they slept, the longer they wouldn't have to know. Gus had texted Nicole Hill, who wanted to come by. Someone must have alerted Sarah Abraham, the local rabbi, who emailed Claire that she was on her way, too.

By 8:00 a.m., people were everywhere. Chase and his cops out front by the door, snapping photographs and dusting for fingerprints. Nicole Hill and Gus conferring on the sidewalk. Their older neighbor from across the street had dropped off a bouquet of yellow flowers. Claire was with Rabbi Abraham in the kitchen. A pair of untouched salt bagels, baked by Sarah's wife, sat on a plate before them. Was it normal for rabbis to make house calls? Claire had no idea.

Awakened by the commotion, or perhaps, by his conscience, Wolf soon appeared in the kitchen, bleary-eyed, Halloween candy hungover in his striped pajama set.

"What's going on?" he asked. "Who are you? Why didn't anyone wake me up for school?" Wolf didn't handle change well; he liked his routines. He needed them.

"This is Rabbi Abraham."

"Oh, right. Your wife is my Hebrew School teacher. And you came to my language arts class," said Wolf.

"I talk to the sixth graders every fall around the high holidays. I like the children to know about being a Jew. What it means."

"It was embarrassing."

"So, Wolf. Something's happened. Something shameful. Baruch Hashem, you're okay and your family's okay, and our town is a mostly nice place filled with mostly nice people. But there are a few—" she shrugged and lifted her hands "—not so nice people who sometimes do bad things." Rabbi Abraham was a good ten years younger than Claire but gave off a wise-beyond-her-years vibe.

"I already know about my sister."

"This is something new," said Claire.

"Something new bad?" clarified Wolf, who seemed to have lost his advanced vocabulary in the face of this strange morning. He began alternately picking at the wool on Claire's sweater and drawing a picture of some sort of serial killer on the yellow legal pad she'd set in front of him to doodle on.

Claire didn't trust herself to break the news about the swastika. She let the rabbi talk while she made Wolf fried eggs and toast. (Oddly, he did not like bagels.)

"Something new bad," said Rabbi Abraham. "Listen, the

truth of the matter is once every year or two we have an incident of AS." She refastened her kippah to the back of her head and adjusted her low ponytail.

"AS?" asked Wolf. He looked worried. Stressed. He had every right to be, thought Claire.

"Antisemitism. Sometimes at the College. Once someone painted a swastika on a big rock in the park across from the library."

"God," said Claire.

Wolf became quiet. It had to be *really* bad for the rabbi to come.

"Are you hanging in there, Wolf?" asked the rabbi.

He didn't answer. Instead, he began pulsing his right leg under the table. Then he started systematically shredding his drawing, letting bits and pieces of it fall to the floor.

"I know. It's terrible. I'm not saying it's *not* terrible. But this can happen anywhere," continued Rabbi Abraham. That was true, Claire considered, even in Brooklyn. There'd been a swastika the year before, at Luna's German school, which was housed in a former synagogue.

"Antisemitism is, believe it or not, much less of a problem here than in other places."

"Really?" asked Claire. That didn't sound right.

"Why can't anyone tell me what happened?" Wolf asked.

"This is hard to talk about," began Claire, wishing the rabbi would jump in and rescue her, but Sarah only nodded seriously. Claire exhaled. There was no way to make this anything other than awful. "Someone put a swastika on our door last night. Halloween vandalism, we're thinking."

"Because of Hazel?"

Wolf looked like he was about to cry. Or scream.

"Well, yeah. That's what we think."

"And because we're Jewish." Scream, Claire was guessing.

"Our being Jewish is just—I don't know how to explain it.

It's an excuse. A way to be hateful and blame Hazel for what the principal did. That's not the real reason."

"I hate it here," said Wolf, finally. "I refuse to live here one more day."

Claire read Wolf's face. Maybe he simply couldn't handle another horrible thing. Once he got like this, there was no turning back. But it didn't stop her from trying. "You heard what Rabbi Abraham said, this could happen anywhere."

"That's a LIE. You are a LIAR. And I HATE YOU!" With that he stormed upstairs, slamming doors and stomping his bare feet along the way, passing the College president and police chief in his wake.

"Sweetie!" Claire called after him, too late. "I'm so sorry about Wolf," she said to the rabbi.

"It's okay. It's perfectly reasonable for him to feel this way," said Sarah, checking her phone to afford Claire a moment of privacy. She'd probably seen worse. Claire hoped she had.

There was a knock on the kitchen door. It was Polly, holding a tray of coffees.

"I was teaching when I saw your text," Polly said, putting the flowers and coffee on the counter and giving Claire a hug. "I have a couple of free periods now. What do you need? What can I do?"

Neither Sarah Abraham nor Polly could *do* much of anything. But they could talk. Claire could cry. It was a comfort to be in the warm kitchen with them. Claire wished she could do the same for Wolf. Dealing with the fallout from his sister was one thing. The swastika was a whole other level. What if this was the childhood trauma he'd never get over? That he'd be discussing with his therapist in ten years? In twenty?

The police had dispersed. President Hill must have gone back to campus. Gus, who was deep in the throes of denial, as far as Claire was concerned, and still saying he wasn't going to let white supremacists drive him out of town, was nowhere to be found. Today of all days, Claire wasn't going to pretend to work. She went to the basement and collected Wolf's clothes from the dryer, brought them up in a hamper to his room, slid in after an efficient knock and started folding.

Wolf was hiding under the covers.

"Mommy?" he asked, from underneath.

"Yes?" Claire's heart pinged when Wolf reverted to his younger self and called her that.

"I did something bad. Something really, really bad. You're going to be so mad at me."

Claire wondered what else could possibly go wrong as she flicked through her mental Rolodex of Really Bad Things. Vaping? Drugs? Cutting? Bullying? Sexting? That all paled next to what had already gone down.

"Whatever it is," said Claire. "It's okay. It doesn't matter."

"No, you're wrong," said Wolf. "This matters. A LOT."

"You won't be in trouble. I promise."

She tried her best to channel the Zen of their therapist. But it took every single ounce of self-control she had to not completely lose her mind while Wolf confessed what he'd been hiding. Because Claire's list of tween misadventures hadn't included an entry for *a secret series of hate notes filled with rocks hand delivered to the driveway which Wolf hadn't bothered to tell his parents about.*

For the rest of the morning—for the foreseeable future—Wolf was allowed unlimited screens. YouTube, video games, TV. Whatever he wanted. Claire made another coffee and sat at the kitchen table and texted Ramona. A long series of messages about Gracie and Wolf and Gus and Agatha White. And about the swastika and the hate notes, which, the police and the rabbi and Nicole Hill said, were not necessarily evidence of an actual hate group in town, but more likely the work of some deranged Richard White supporters. Either way, writing it out she saw how serious it all was.

Ramona wrote right back, unusual for one of her studio days. Two words:

Come home

I wish

Come

Gus doesn't want to

Come without him. With Hazel and Wolf. The three of you. You can stay in the garden apartment until you figure something better out. We're between renters.

We can't afford rent + mortgage

I'm not going to charge you!

For real?

Of course. This shit is toxic. We need to get you out of there.

Gus wouldn't go for it, Claire knew. The garden apartment was a tiny, light-challenged one-bedroom. Haters or no haters, Gus still had his job and wouldn't be separated from his children. Besides, Wolf had school. Hazel had school. Transferring back midyear would mean more chaos for them.

But maybe Ramona was right? She usually was.

The morning after Halloween, the day her Very Important Vassar application was due, Hazel did *not* wake up when her alarm went off at 4:00 a.m.

Because nobody had bothered to wake her, she slept past the start of school, too.

When she eventually came to, the school day was practically over, she was freaking out about oversleeping, and wandered downstairs expecting an empty house, but instead saw a police car parked in their driveway and was gingerly informed by her mother about the rock through the window and everything else. She proceeded to vomit in the downstairs bathroom and then pass out into a weird sort of dissociative nap before waking up again two hours later, eating a sliced banana and getting herself together enough to deal with her essay and send in the application. She had a piercing migraine and was shrouded in brain fog. For five minutes she considered writing about the swastika. The application wasn't due until midnight, so technically she had time. But Hazel couldn't think straight much less write. There was simply no way she was going to write a personal essay from scratch now.

She'd have to go with her plan to throw something together, something half-assed. Against her better judgment, Hazel copied and pasted a truncated "best lines of" her old eleventh-grade paper about white privilege.

And then Hazel went back to bed.

She may as well have slept for the next six weeks. As the November mornings turned grayer and colder and drearier, she biked to school, somehow making it through the day before riding home and climbing back into bed. Sunset came at 5:00 and then 4:30 and then 4:00. There was nothing left to do but attend her classes, keep up her sagging grades, and wait fatalistically for Vassar's decision. Some afternoons, she fell asleep rereading novels—which was a consolation and reprieve since she hadn't been able to read a book (that wasn't assigned) since the first day of school. Most afternoons she pawed through paparazzi photos or binged shows and numbed out. Then she got really sick, which bought her a week off from school. To save her life, Hazel couldn't remember how she had ever mustered the energy to be her old, overly involved, New York City self.

At least the hate had taken a break. No more notes appeared in their driveway or on their sidewalk or on their front door. A gang of neighbors and College students had banded together to keep an eye on Pine Street. Armed with family dogs, the ragtag group seemed to be an effective deterrent, for now. Or maybe the bad men, as her brother called them, couldn't survive the November frost.

Thanksgiving in Riverburg was bleak. Neither of Hazel's parents had families. The lack of an extended family used to be sort of okay, because they had each other, blah blah blah, but they also had New York, which was like an extended family, not just the people they knew there, but the city itself. The fact of it. The schlepping, the people watching, the eavesdropping, the subway and sidewalks.

In Maine they were alone. Stranded. And her parents were acting a little weird with one another. It was like they were co-parents, coworkers, but they didn't seem to be married-married anymore. No more catching them kiss in the kitchen. And while it was too cliché for Hazel to believe their problems were her fault, she felt or knew or worried, depending on the day, that they were.

Then the news dropped.

New Allegations Emerge for Riverburg High School Principal; White Wife Files for Divorce
By Camille Sullivan, Riverburg Record
November 30

Further allegations of sexual misconduct have emerged in the case against Richard White, the embattled Riverburg High School principal currently suspended without pay. According to Vermont law enforcement, two former students from White's years as an English teacher in Vermont have come forward.

Richard White taught at Lincoln High School in the Green Mountains of Vermont. One alleged victim says that she and White had sex around the time of her graduation. A second former student handed over to police a trove of hundreds of pages of letters she says were written by White while she was at the school. In the letters, according to the police report, White "declared his love for her" and references their "taboo" relationship. She was 16 when the letters began, and 17 when their alleged sexual relationship took place, according to officials.

The age of consent in Vermont is 16.

While sexual intercourse between a teacher and current student is legally prohibited, said Roy Gagnon of the Addison County Vermont sheriff's office, this is a complex set of cases, and the elapsed time remains a significant roadblock to the investigation and possible criminal charges.

In a separate development, Agatha White, Richard White's wife, filed for divorce Friday morning at the county clerk's office. Michael Taylor, White's attorney, told the Record, "There is no connection between the filing and the allegations. This matter was in the works for some time. My client and his wife remain dear friends and loving co-parents to their daughter and ask for privacy during this difficult time." Mrs. White has declined to comment.

While Richard White continues to deny all allegations, the Record's investigation finds that his defense in the Riverburg case has shifted. Initially, White denied asking for sex, and claimed that the Riverburg High student in question propositioned him. In recent days, White and attorney Taylor have begun stressing that White never engaged in non-consensual sex with a student, and that he's never had sexual intercourse with a minor, offenses that carry more serious sentences than having a sexual relationship with a student who is over the age of legal consent.

Taylor has repeatedly emphasized the alleged victim's age in the more recent Riverburg case, as well as underscoring the point that no sexual contact took place between his client and the Riverburg High School student.

"Any out-of-state accusations or claims should have no bearing on the allegation in Maine," Taylor told the Record.

Hazel had known, intellectually, that she wasn't alone. She knew there must have been other Riverburg High girls before her, students who presumably hadn't felt like they could say no. White had said so himself, had bragged that he did this every year! He'd *told* Hazel that. (And April had called White gross, which had to mean something.) But nobody in town seemed to be thinking about those girls. Hazel had to admit that she hadn't thought much about them, either.

The Vermont allegations changed all that. The idea of those sick AF letters, "declaring his love," made her skin crawl, of course it did. Here was proof, before her eyes and on her phone, that she was one of many.

Nobody could say that she was a liar anymore. People in Riverburg would have to believe her. Which was something of a relief. A relief that turned itself inside out into shame. Hazel felt guilty for feeling like it was a good thing, a positive development that there were other girls. Girls, who were now full-fledged adults.

When Wolf sent the link to the latest White article in the *Record* a couple of days later, she almost ignored it. If nobody else cared, Hazel wouldn't care, either. Besides that, she was stoned.

FIRED texted her dad.

For a split second Hazel thought her dad meant *he* was fired? Because, Cosby? Then her mother responded to the family group text with a bunch of congratulatory cake and party blower emojis that made Hazel's screen burst with confetti.

White was fired, Hazel realized. She clicked and read. The school board had voted to dismiss him, six to one.

White's firing was something, Hazel told herself. Although that might be it. Criminal charges-wise, the best-case scenario was called Official Oppression: *Maine Title 17-A. A person is guilty of official oppression if, being a public servant and acting with the intention to benefit himself or to harm another, he knowingly commits an unauthorized act which purports to be an act of his office. Class E Crimes are punishable by up to six months in county jail and a fine of up to $1000. A misdemeanor.*

A misdemeanor. What bullshit.

This was exactly why Hazel had refused to go to the police and file a victim's report. Even if there was a trial it would come down to a he-said, she-said standoff. Her family could pursue a civil suit—sue White directly for damages—but by then the principal would no longer be collecting a salary, and presumably would be in debt with mounting legal fees, and there was probably nothing to get out of him. They could sue the school system, but collecting money from a poorly funded, low-income school district sounded too messed up, her parents agreed, talking it over with Hazel.

The next day, there was more breaking news: White was surrendering his Maine teaching credentials. In exchange, charges would be dropped.

It was over. But to Hazel it felt nothing like justice.

On the appointed December early decision day for Vassar, Hazel scrounged some more of her mother's pot, rolled a joint and smoked half. At the specified hour, Hazel checked the Vassar portal link nine zillion times.

Deferred.

PART THREE

main character energy

22

hazel needs to get her shit together

Hazel wasn't angry. Not exactly. It was more that she kind of hated herself. What she felt was shame and the weight of her inadequacies—not so much the deferral, which was standard-issue teenage disappointment, but how she'd handled the entire principal situation from the moment she walked into his office. How she'd basically ruined her family's life. How she let one pathetic man asking one pathetic question derail her. She didn't blame Vassar. She'd been the one to drop the ball. The girl she had been from the start of kindergarten through the end of eleventh grade would never have handed in that personal statement.

Not that getting deferred didn't suck. It did. A deferral was, possibly, more of a mindfuck than a rejection because it meant the anxiety of waiting would continue for months. She'd have to apply to a full slate of other schools to make sure she didn't have to live in her parents' attic for the remainder of her sad life. She would end up somewhere, though. She didn't really know why this was hitting her so hard. Hazel had known that an ED admission from Vassar was a reach. But would it have been so terrible to have a dream that came true?

The worst part of the deferral was having the universe, or at least the Vassar admissions committee, prove that Hazel had been right all along. She wasn't special. And now her parents would know it, too. Hazel dreaded the look of pity on her mother's face, and the disappointment on her father's, when she told them she was a loser at the college admissions game. So, she didn't tell them. Not in person. She texted them. (One word: *Deferred*.) Then she tucked her phone in her underwear drawer and went to sleep.

Overnight her parents had sent her a series of flowery, supportive, emoji-laden texts. They didn't seem to care that she was a failure. If anything, they seemed relieved, once she came downstairs and confessed, over a big breakfast, about her writer's block and the half-assed essays. There was a *reason* for the rejection, one that could be addressed and overcome for the larger January application round. Annoyingly true to form, her parents blamed themselves. Her dad felt guilty for having suggested she use the term paper. Her mom, for not "overseeing" (meaning, micromanaging) the application timeline. Don't take it personally, they agreed, these schools were crazily competitive. To stand out you needed either wealth and connections, or a one-in-a-million story.

"Their loss," her dad said, pressing a long shot on the espresso machine.

"You're not mad?" Hazel asked.

"It doesn't really matter where you go to college," said her mom.

"Choosing a college is like buying an SUV," said her dad. "These liberal arts schools look a little different on the outside but they're basically all the same."

Her mom nodded and gave Hazel a hug. "It's more about

what you make of it, you know? Lots of schools can be great. There's no one perfect place."

Hazel suspected their nonchalance was an act informed by a *New York Times* parenting article. Nevertheless, their seeming lack of concern was comforting. At least they hadn't, like, cried or something.

She'd already texted Luna who, while sympathetic, didn't totally get it. She was applying to The New School and NYU's Gallatin School and FIT and Brooklyn College and Hunter's Honor College and Fordham because she didn't want to leave New York and would be fine with wherever took her.

All told, nobody other than Hazel cared that she'd gotten deferred. Except of course for her pain in the ass brother.

"Guess you did all that studying and homework for nothing," Wolf said when he wandered into the kitchen and heard the news.

"You'll get into a fantastic school that's perfect for you," said her mom. "Lots of them, I'm sure."

"What if you don't get in anywhere?" said Wolf. "What happens then?"

"Shut up," said Hazel, and neither of her parents told her not to talk to her brother like that.

Hazel returned to her room, made her bed, and took out her laptop. Clearly, there was no longer a point in visiting the Vassar website. Nor did she feel like compulsively researching her second and third choices. But if she wanted to get into college—period—her grades, unfortunately, still mattered, so she pulled up the homework she'd been procrastinating on. For government, she was supposed to study and write about an historical event from two perspectives. One of the options was the Anita Hill trial. Hazel knew Clarence Thomas was a nightmare Supreme Court justice, but she didn't know his history and what Hill had done to stand up to him. So she read. Then, because she had nothing better to do, she researched Christine Blasey

Ford and Brett Kavanaugh, which she vaguely remembered hearing about when she was younger.

Nothing even remotely in that universe of bad had happened to her, but finding out about the two women shifted something inside of her.

That Sunday Hazel woke up sick of being depressed. She was determined. She was going to get over herself. The sun was shining. Fuck it, she thought. Hazel put on her warmest leggings and went for a run. Even though it was freezing out. She jogged up the hill to the College and back down. Just a couple of miles. It felt amazing. On Monday she went out after school, which felt good, but not quite as exhilarating and mind clearing as a morning run, and so on Tuesday she set her alarm for 5:30 and ran through the predawn dark. Running made her mind feel free for the first time in months. The next day, she ran again. Each day she grew stronger, tracing her route once and then twice over by the end of the week. Faster, too. That Thursday, she took the right down the country road by campus and ended up running past farms and cows and horses as the sun rose over Riverburg.

Over the next two weeks, when she wasn't running, or sitting through school, or plowing through homework, she broke her reading slump.

Hazel ordered books from the College library off her dad's account, remembering how good reading made her feel—grounded and alive. She'd read as much as she could before college. Virginia Woolf and bell hooks. Jhumpa Lahiri and Lauren Groff. Celeste Ng and Lorrie Moore, Curtis Sittenfeld and Chimamanda Ngozi Adichie and Elena Ferrante and Sheila Heti and Min Jin Lee and Jennifer Egan and more Zadie Smith.

She read in the afternoons before homework, and at night afterward. In the early mornings she ran.

On a Friday in the middle of December when her shins ached,

she took the morning to sleep in before school. (If you could consider 6:45 sleeping in.) When she came down for her oatmeal and coffee, she found her father in the kitchen. Until she'd gone all Olympic marathoner-in-training, he'd been the early bird of the family.

"You didn't run today?"

"My legs are sore."

Her dad had a weird expression on his face.

"Okay. So, listen. The College is hosting a big talk. It was scheduled before I was hired, and I've been reluctant to mention it with everything else going on. I'm not sure if you'll want to go. But I've noticed the books you've been taking out and—"

"Who's coming? Is it going to be boring?"

"Quite the opposite. This is huge for the College. Maxine Joy."

"*Maxine Joy* is coming to Riverburg? Why?"

Hazel was impressed. Maxine Joy was *the* feminist author (slash personality) of the moment. Gus got out his phone and showed Hazel the invite.

"She's speaking about her next book. The talk is called 'Making the World Less Terrible: Can Things Possibly Ever Get Even a Little Better?'"

"Bleak," said Hazel. "I appreciate that."

"It's the annual Jane Fonda endowed lecture, the last big event of the semester before finals. Most of the College will be there, everyone they can pack in the chapel. There's the talk, and, afterward, a cocktail party for faculty at Nicole Hill's house. I have two tickets for the talk, and I RSVP'd yes for the reception. I was planning to go with Mom, but you're welcome to come instead. You don't have to, though. You could always just read Joy's books."

Her dad's new thing was being "present" on campus. Post Cosby debacle, he'd invited Sam Moore and the rest of the Fire Gus Blum! student group to a series of "listening coffees," and then taken part in a couple of larger campus-wide "difficult discussions." The Sunday night reading group he'd organized at Hazel's suggestion was maybe working? At least he was complaining less about the Cosby thing and seemed a little less freaked out about his perceived cancelation.

"I've *read* Maxine Joy. I've been telling you to read her for like a year, remember?"

"Well, now I have. Or I will have, by the end of the day." He pointed to her latest, sticking out of his backpack.

Why hadn't her father mentioned this before today? Though, truth: if he'd asked a week ago, she would have refused. As she'd passed on every other outing or activity meant to cheer her up that fall. But if she was going to stay up late rereading *Thirsty Feminist* or go on YouTube and watch Maxine Joy speak at other college campuses, she might as well see her in person. Running had given her energy. And maybe a touch of courage.

"I assume the answer will be no. No pressure," said Gus.

"*Obviously* I want to come. To the lecture. Probably to the party? I'm not sure."

"Really? That's terrific, Hazel. Be ready at six. I should have asked you about this earlier. Maybe I could have arranged a private meeting for you two."

"Dad. Stop," said Hazel.

23

main character energy

The drive to campus took five minutes; finding a parking spot near the packed chapel took longer. On their way into the building, Gus flashed his faculty tickets like they were VIP passes to a Taylor Swift concert and Hazel was twelve. Hazel's throat hurt and it was eighteen degrees outside and pitch-black and it would be weird to be the only high school student at the talk, but she didn't want to *not* go, either. She'd worn a flannel shirtdress and her mom's huge wool cardigan with bone buttons. It was the Friday before finals week and the whole campus had taken a study break to come out for the lecture of the year. Students, faculty, and staff filled the chapel floor and the side and upper galleries. Her dad had texted his older colleague from American Studies who'd arrived an hour early with papers to grade, saving them two seats right up front.

On the stage sat an armchair and a love seat complete with mic stands and a small round table with water bottles and a flower arrangement—a cross between a living room and a talk show set. At seven o'clock sharp, a thirtysomething poetry professor, her wrist stacked with gold bangles, gave the introduction.

"Thank you for joining us at the Jane Fonda lecture. Tonight, we gather for a powerful conversation with a groundbreaking leader of our time. The acclaimed writer, activist, artist and professor, Maxine Joy. Joy is a thinker and advocate who has inspired a generation—and a movement. You've read her books, you probably follow her on social media, and now here she is in Riverburg, Maine. The Gender Studies, American Studies, African American Studies and Creative Writing departments are proud to be your sponsors for a talk about what I believe to be the most pressing question, not just for your generation, but for all of us. How do we make the world less terrible? Professor Joy, welcome to the College."

Maxine Joy took the stage to a thunder of applause.

"Well, hello, Maine." More applause. "The original title of my talk was How Do We Unfuck a Fucked-Up World. But that didn't quite make it past the host committee." Joy winked. She knew how to work a crowd.

"Now, I don't have children myself," Joy began. "But I do have students, and I have nieces and nephews and mentees, and I've been bottling up some unsolicited advice I'd like to drop on you this evening. How does that sound?"

Appreciative claps.

"What I want to say to you? Don't be an NPC."

A slow building, uncomfortable wave of laughter washed over the students; the tenured faculty looked confused and turned to their younger colleagues for translation. Hazel took pity on her dad and whispered in his ear.

"Non-player character," she said, but Gus remained confused. "Like in a video game."

"Ah," he mouthed, and nodded.

Professor Joy dove in and talked about activism and how grassroots organizing can be promoted and supported by people with privilege and platforms. Then she talked about her work as a writer and cultural producer, and about the importance of speaking out against injustice. How it was basically your duty as a human, if you had the chance.

"I repeat! Don't be an NPC. We can't sit by and eat our gummies and stream reality show content and watch the world get worse and do nothing. Here's what I implore you to ask yourself. How can you be a main character? How can you maybe even be a hero? And yes, I mean you—and you and you and you.

"Here's what it comes down to. Stop being a passive observer in your own life. Save the world! At least your corner of it! Can you do that for me? Can you at least try?"

It felt like Maxine Joy was looking right at Hazel.

"Now, I need to tell you about something," Joy said, as if the crowd were a singular being she was speaking to. "Something I'm finally writing about." If she was going to take her own advice, she said, she needed to confront a piece of personal history. To deal with the trauma of having been groomed and preyed on by a teacher at the elite prep school she had attended. And what happened when she spoke up and the school tried to silence her. Joy needed to come to terms with being a survivor.

Hazel was getting sweaty with self-awareness. She'd felt a drumbeat, a pounding in her chest that was getting louder and louder by the day. That maybe she couldn't keep being quiet. That maybe she couldn't live with herself if she didn't do something more than simply mentioning the principal's advances to her mother and answer a few questions from the police. What if Hazel could somehow change things? What if Hazel could make a difference?

"Okay," Joy concluded, with a lively clap. "Who has a question for me?"

Before her brain could register what she was doing, Hazel stood and accepted a microphone from one of the AV techs wandering the chapel. She was shaking. She was full-on out of body. In her periphery, she saw her dad tense up, but she ignored him.

"I'm not a student here," she said tentatively as she heard her voice boom over the speaker.

"Okay," said Professor Joy.

"I don't know if it's wrong for me to be taking up a question."

"Appreciated. What brings you to the mic?"

"My name is Hazel. My pronouns are she/her. I'm a senior at Riverburg High School. Oh, and I loved your last two books."

"Just the last two?" Maxine laughed.

"I'm from Brooklyn. We moved this summer because my dad works here."

Hazel glanced over at her father. Gus had his legs crossed and his chin resting on his cupped hand with his professorial listening-and-learning face on. She wondered if he'd be mad at her for drawing (more) attention to their family. Given the Cosby situation. Hazel couldn't tell whether she was in big trouble or making him proud.

"I see you."

"This year something messed up happened at my new school between me and the principal. He—he sort of came on to me. But I guess he sort of respected my boundaries? I mean he let me physically leave his office."

"Wow. I'm sorry to hear that. Do you feel comfortable saying more?"

Not really, thought Hazel. But she could try. "He asked me to have sex with him. He said he picked someone every year. I told him no and then I said something, and part of me wishes I hadn't. Not hadn't said no, I mean, I know that was what I needed to do, but wishes I hadn't turned him in."

"The principal?" Joy asked. "Are you the girl who told the high school principal to go you-know-what himself?"

Hazel flushed. "Yeah."

"I read about that business in the paper on my way up here.

I wouldn't call what he did respecting your boundaries. I'd call it sexual harassment and attempted assault."

"That's not how people here see it. Half the town hates me. More than half. Somebody spray-painted the word *slut* on the sidewalk in front of my house.

"And then something worse happened," Hazel continued. "Something scarier. I don't know if I'm allowed to talk about it." She shot her dad a worried look. "My younger brother started finding hate notes in our driveway. The notes were pretty awful, super sexist and antisemitic. We don't know who's responsible."

"So the principal says this horrible thing to you, and then your family starts getting harassed."

"And then, like almost two months later, on Halloween night? Someone threw a rock at my house. A big one. Through our window. And spray-painted a swastika on our front door."

The room fell hush. Someone let out a groan of lamentation; someone else a *damn*. College students didn't read the local paper. Most of them hadn't heard about White. And for those who had, it was different to witness this shit play out.

"And there were all these other girls before me. Women. He's been doing this for a long time. I guess what I'm trying to say is that I'm so incredibly sick of hearing about stuff like this in the news for basically my entire life, and since I started reading more and learning about how this is practically *normal*, how it's like an everyday thing. And when I think about this happening to other girls in other schools and—you know, everywhere—to other women, other people, to kids, and how instead of getting angry and doing something about it, I end up being more and more depressed about how much the world sucks and how these men get away with their bad behavior and here I am just kind of watching it get worse and sitting in my room and staring at my phone. Because when you said the thing about not being an NPC? That's exactly what I've been doing. Like, with the case here? The criminal charges against the principal were dropped, so yeah, he was fired but otherwise he just sort of got away with it."

"Come on up here," Joy said.

Everyone was looking at Hazel. She felt a hand on her back encouraging her toward the stage.

"It's okay," said Professor Joy. "If you want to come up, you can come up. Or you can stay right where you are."

Hazel hesitated, took a deep breath—and decided to go for it.

As she stood on the stage, to her deep embarrassment, she began to cry. She pulled her dress down and her tights up.

"You said your name is Hazel? You've been through it, haven't you, Hazel."

Hazel nodded. Tears were now falling down her face. She'd blown her last crumbs of anonymity. Her parents were going to kill her.

"The worst part is he said *I* came on to *him*."

"I bet he did," said Maxine Joy. "They usually do."

Hazel nodded and wiped her tears with the sleeve of her sweater.

"You might not feel like you have lots of support in town. But guess what? These people right here live in Riverburg, too."

Joy turned to the audience. "Make some noise if you believe Hazel. Make some noise if you think Hazel is a badass for saying no to that disgrace of a high school principal."

The chapel exploded in cheers. Students were stomping feet and letting out encouraging yells and whistles and exclamations of solidarity. The room was wild and electric.

"Hazel," said Professor Joy. "You're resilient. You are more than what happened to you, and you are so much more than what this man said to you or tried to do to you. Now sit yourself down and let some others come up here."

The line to speak wound from the chapel's center aisle and wrapped around the room. Joy could have stayed at the Q&A all night. Turns out, Hazel wasn't the only one with a story.

"Hazel. My God," said her dad, who took her hand when she returned to her seat. He had maybe been tearing up a little, too. "You were incredible up there. What do you think? Should we go to the reception?"

"I feel like I might pass out."

The president's house, where the cocktail party was held, sat on a hill a short walk from the epicenter of campus. A team of caterers in black polyester pants and white button-down shirts passed pigs in blankets and mini tarts and bite-sized quiches and butter cookies and offered white wine and sparkling water.

Maxine Joy broke away from her group when she saw Hazel.

"That was brave," said Professor Joy. "Really brave. How are you feeling?"

"I'm not sure."

"It's hard to be a public person."

"I'm not," said Hazel. "Not at all."

"You are now," said Maxine. "Here, at least. What do you want to do with it? What are your plans?"

"College? And I maybe sort of want to be a writer when I grow up."

"Okay, then!"

"I mean, I'm not very good. I doubt it will happen."

Joy stopped her before she could neg on herself more. "You want to be a writer? Then, you need to write the hell out of this. This is your story, right? Write it. And send it to me."

"Wait, really?"

"Give me your phone." She took it and put in her contact info under JOY and then handed it back.

And that's how Hazel's life changed for the second time.

24

noah

"Hazel? HAZEL!" The next morning, Wolf was screaming from the bottom of the attic stairs like the house was on fire. He flew up the stairs and burst into her room.

"HAZEL!!!"

"What? I'm sleeping."

"Someone's here to see you. Get up! It's almost eleven! He's waiting for you."

"What are you talking about? Who?"

"Daddy says it's one of his students and you need to come downstairs."

That was strange, but Hazel threw a sweatshirt on over her pajamas and followed her brother.

A guy in a beat-up parka and jeans that came low over narrow hips was leaning against their porch. He was her size. Maybe a couple of inches taller.

"Hey. I'm Noah. Can we talk?" He introduced himself as a student reporter from the *College Caller*, a first year. He'd been at the chapel hanging out with his editor, who was covering the event. But, after seeing Hazel speak, Noah wanted to do an article on *her.* He was taking Deconstructing America with her dad, he said, and had been following her case in the *Record.*

"It's not my case," said Hazel. "It's the state's case."

"Can I quote you on that?"

"Why would you want to?"

"I'd like to interview you and ask you a few questions if you have time."

"Now?" asked Hazel. "I woke up like three minutes ago."

"We could go for coffee?"

He was in college, and she was in high school, but since she'd started kindergarten late, they were probably around the same age. It *was* a Saturday. She'd grown overly accustomed to staying in on the weekends. To having no IRL friends. To not speaking outside of class or her house. Unless you counted April, who Hazel didn't count, because they only spoke in the library during their mutual free period and hadn't exchanged numbers to text or anything. Maybe having a Riverburg social life—or at least, a coffee with some College kid—could be part of her new and improved Hazel thing?

"Where?" she asked. Did he want to lure her back to his dorm room to show off his pour over and vinyl collection?

"How about The General?" suggested Noah.

She thought for a moment. He was a reporter. So, no. On the other hand, she'd been feeling supremely lonely.

"Um. I guess so. But I need to get dressed, okay?"

It had started to snow by the time she'd picked an outfit and put on her coat and boots.

Noah had parked in the driveway. Many of the student cars Hazel noticed on campus and around town were Subaru SUVs or BMWs or Range Rovers with out-of-town license plates. Noah drove an old, beat-up Ford Ranger pickup. Contrary to her previous idea of a kid from the College, he wasn't rich or preppy or a mediocre jock. He wore canvas skateboard sneakers in the snow and majored in art history, possibly the least practical major at the College, next to her father's department. Which, as a prospective English major, Hazel respected.

"Should we walk downtown?" Hazel suggested. "We'll get warm that way."

"Excellent," said Noah. He was cute, she realized. Very. Kind of perfect looking, in fact. And Hazel could be tricky when it came to that sort of thing. She'd only kissed three people; and one of those was during a drinking game at a party in Cobble Hill the previous spring.

"It's not far," said Hazel, trying to keep it cool. But she was probably already embarrassing herself.

Hazel remained quiet as they made their way down Pine Street, but Noah was chatty. He was interested in ancestry, Noah said, offering that he was part Quebecois on one side, part Mayflower Pilgrim and Native on the other. He was from Downeast Maine and grew up in Jonesport. His grandfather and father were, for many years, lobstermen with a once sturdy if exhausting family business. But these days his grandfather was retired. Noah's father had died when he was in eleventh grade. (No, Noah didn't want to talk about it.) Noah said he wanted something different for himself. He wasn't quite sure what. His mother wanted him to get a real job, a real major. Anything but art history. He was on a full scholarship—a free ride—at the College. He volunteered at the Teen Center downtown. His interest in journalism was relatively new; his high school had been too tiny for a newspaper.

Hazel listened intently, taking mental notes. Things were starting to feel weird between them, she noticed—charged.

At The General, they took a table by the window and nursed cups of coffee before ordering tuna melts and fries. When they were long done eating, after another round of coffee, The General began closing for the afternoon break. They decided to walk down by the river.

"I thought it was dope that you could get up there in front of everyone," Noah said, at the start of the penny bridge.

"I was dying," said Hazel. "I totally idolize Maxine Joy."

"Can I ask you something? About what happened at your school, I mean."

"I guess so," said Hazel, though she was sick of talking about it.

"How did you feel when he asked you?"

"Is this for your newspaper story?"

"No," said Noah. "For me."

Because it seemed like he actually, possibly cared, she told her story again. This time, Hazel felt like Noah was the first person to listen—truly listen—to her. To hear how the whole situation made her feel, rather than immediately jump to horror at what he did. He could make a good reporter one day, Hazel thought. Or a therapist.

Noah wasn't trying to fix the situation or Hazel when they talked about what had gone down and he wasn't drooling over her, either. He probably wasn't into her or anything. Hazel didn't know for a fact if she was completely straight. Or if he was into girls, for that matter. But she knew that when Noah stood six inches away, she could feel the heat between them, and she wanted to pull in closer. She wanted *him*. Which was a new thing for her. They kept talking, leaving the topic of the principal on the penny bridge and moving on to books and movies and TV shows and music and a little bit of politics so Hazel could make sure he wasn't a bro in disguise.

Hazel was experienced, like as a subway rider and a reader, but she wasn't "experienced." For the record, Hazel was still a virgin. Like half her city friends, some of whom had never even kissed anyone. Hazel knew her worth and wasn't about to squander her first time on some high school kid just so she could feel grown up, like the Molly Ringwald character in one of her mom's John Hughes movies.

As Hazel and Noah talked, they walked, through the falling snow from downtown back to her house. Noah admitted his feet were wet and cold, and the sun was already setting which meant it was almost four and that somehow they'd spent the entire day together. (Her mother had texted her approximately a million times until Hazel texted back that she was *fine*.) So *this* was what it meant to like someone—the heat rushing up her veins and skin bursting like radiator pipes emitting steam.

When she said goodbye on the sidewalk and was about to pivot and walk down her driveway, Hazel remembered what Joy had said and called back to Noah.

"What about your story for the newspaper?" Hazel asked.

"Forget the story. It might not be the best idea."

"No?" asked Hazel.

"Yeah, I've been thinking about it. I'm in your dad's reading group and his class, so— It could be awkward. He still has to give me a final grade for the semester."

"Oh," said Hazel. He could have thought of that before showing up on her porch.

"Yeah. It's finals week. Then I'm driving home for Christmas. Maybe I'll see you next semester? Classes start back up again in early February."

February? Really? That seemed like an eternity since it was December and he said he was from Maine. But, okay.

"I'm going to India for Jan Plan."

Hazel was jealous and impressed. And let down. And frozen. She readjusted her hat and scarf, along with her expectations.

"I should probably get back to the library," said Noah.

"Okay."

Was that it? It was like that Ethan Hawke movie on the train her mother made her watch. A low-key magical day together and then nothing. He could ask for her number. People did *text* in India. Then again, she could ask for his.

"See you around?" she said, for lack of something better.

"For sure," said Noah. "Merry Christmas, Hazel."

25

rough draft

The morning after Hazel's walk with Noah, two mornings after meeting Maxine Joy, Hazel decided to write something. Nobody might ever see it, nobody might ever care, but at least she was going to try.

She wanted a dedicated writing space. A desk of her own. So she walked downtown, sidestepping patches of sidewalk ice, to the Habitat for Humanity store, thrifted a wood desk for $22 and a farmhouse-y chair for $9, and called home for a ride. A clerk helped Hazel and her dad lug the mismatched set to their station wagon, and her mother helped haul them up the stairs where they fit right under her window. On the wall beside her workspace, she tacked a Polaroid of her and Luna on the subway. She deposited her old school Oxford dictionary and thesaurus on the right-hand corner of the desk.

Over Christmas break, free from the tyranny of AP assignments, a routine formed. She ran, she read, and she wrote. In the mornings she piled on layers and ran outside until she was sweaty enough to wrap her fleece around her hips. When the weather turned the streets into icy death traps, she went to the

College's indoor track. Upon her return, after devouring thick slices of toast with peanut butter, she observed Sunday shopkeeper hours, writing diligently from eleven to five. After an early dinner, she streamed something with her parents and Wolf. She went to bed by ten. Come morning she was back at it. In the hush of new winter, high on caffeine and endorphins, Hazel meant business. While it might be too late to make a difference with Vassar, Hazel set out to write the essay she should have written in the first place. Why not? She had a virtual stack of applications due on January 1 requiring a personal statement, and a story that *Maxine Joy* (?!) said she wanted to read.

She started with a shitty first draft. Afterward, Hazel turned to work on each sentence and paragraph, deliberating over structure and word choices. She printed her pages and edited them with a pen, then made serious cuts and rewrote and began the process again. She let the words rest in her brain and set on the page, like Ramona did when putting a newly formed bowl in the kiln and then on the shelf to cool. Then she broke it and started over.

By the end of December, when she ran her eyes through the essay, she found fewer passages to streamline, fewer things to fix, fewer somethings to tinker with. She worked through it with her eyes and fingertips once more. She read the draft aloud to Pickle. She realized that if she kept on changing it, she'd make it worse, not better. It was done. Hazel knew she wasn't the best writer, neither flowery and lyric, nor spare and gritty, nor caustic and cool. But maybe Maxine Joy was right, maybe she had something important to say.

On New Year's Eve Day, Hazel exhaled and hit submit on her common app, sending her new personal statement to a slate of schools from Columbia University (ha ha ha) to the University of Maine. She didn't want to bug, bother, or harass the Vassar admissions committee—but she figured she might as well send them the new essay also. Which she did, along with an apologetic email asking them to please consider reading it.

Even though Hazel wrote the essay partly to get into college, she liked to think she would have written it, anyway. It was the one thing in her life to date that she'd *needed* to write. The completed version now burned like a white-hot coal in her documents folder. She wanted someone beyond an admissions committee member to read it. To have someone see her. And so, she composed one more email.

Dear Professor Joy,

You probably don't remember me. I asked you a (sort of) question when you came to the College in Riverburg, Maine. I'm the high school girl who said no to her principal. You gave me your email? I know you must be terribly busy and have so much going on, and I don't expect you to read this or respond but I'm sending in this attached essay with my college applications, and I wanted you to see it, too. If you feel like it. You inspired me to speak up. Or, if not to speak up, to write it down. Feel free to ignore!!

Yours, and thank you,
Hazel Greenberg Blum

After that, Hazel took a shower and washed her hair. She put on a sample clarifying mask she'd stolen from her mother's bathroom cubby (better than stealing her weed, right?) while playing Sufjan Stevens off her phone. It was time for a nap. Or a pathetically early bedtime. She climbed into bed with her phone to text Luna and find out what she would have been doing come midnight if she weren't living in exile. And there it was. An email from Maxine Joy.

Hazel,

Of course I remember you. This is good. Really good. Admission committees will eat it up. Beyond that, I'd like to forward the essay to my editor at The Clip. No promises. She might want this, she might not. But I have a feeling. You game?

HNY.—MJ

Holy. Fucking. Shit.

The Clip was the *New York Spectator*'s feminist take on a fashion magazine. Their stable of journalists wrote about politics and style, beauty and career advice, celebrity and media gossip, and power, broadly defined. The *New York Spectator* itself was a storied bimonthly reporting on arts and culture and food, with longform pieces on politics. Its illustrated covers were recognizable not only across a subway platform, but across Midwestern boardrooms and Silicon Valley open plan offices and in fancier doctor's waiting rooms. *The Clip* was published mostly online, but every few months there was a print issue tucked inside the regular *New York Spectator.*

Dear Professor Joy,

Yes, please!!!!!!

Thank you forever,
Hazel

Thirty-two minutes later she received an email introduction to Emma Park, an editor at *The Clip*, with her essay attached.

Subject: Hazel Greenberg Blum < > Emma Park

Emma—I met Hazel while on a campus speaking gig in Riverburg, Maine. She's a high school senior (a precocious one) with a story to tell. This is her college app essay. Maybe you can do something with it. Hazel—meet Emma Park.

Happy New Year,
Max

Hazel paced around her room and reread the email until she had it memorized. After that, she didn't know what to do with herself. This was the best thing that had ever happened to her. By far! She was feeling a touch manic. Or was this what happiness felt like? She wasn't sure.

Not that anything had happened. Or would. This was just an email into the ether. Maxine Joy being nice to a kid. No way would Emma Park read anything Hazel wrote. The idea was laughable. But the slim possibility of having her writing considered for *The Clip* was a lottery ticket beyond anything Hazel had imagined for herself.

She should maybe tell Luna, but it was a lot. High school kids did not have their writing in *The Clip*. And Luna might not even know who Maxine Joy was. She didn't want to say anything to her parents, especially not her father, who would make way too much of what would probably amount to nothing. She thought about getting in touch with Noah, since he was a student journalist and at the chapel that night, but that would come off like she was bragging, and she didn't have his number and would have to resort to his college email address which would make her seem like a stalker. Not having anyone else to tell made her feel semi-pathetic. Maybe making a friend should be her New Year's resolution. She found her mother in the den, knitting in front of a Diane Keaton rom-com, and watched the last half with her. Which was sort of like taking a sedative.

26

hazel gets clipped

Hazel was in school on a random Tuesday morning in late January, surreptitiously checking her phone between classes, when the email appeared.

Subject: Hazel Greenberg Blum < > Emma Park

Max, Thank you SO much for thinking of us. You're the best. Emailing you separately about an interview we'd like to assign you if you're up for it.

Hazel! Sincere apologies that it's taken me this long to get back to you. Typically, I respond right away if I'm interested. My inbox has been bananas as of late. (We went to press before Christmas with our seasonal print issue and then we closed for the holiday, and I was in Tulum for a short vacation and then the flu.) All to say, sorry for the delay. I love your piece. I want to run it. Our usual procedure is a back-and-forth editorial process, but your voice is wonderfully fresh and young, and the piece is so short that my instinct says let's go with it as is. Pretty much. I'm doing a light edit and polish. PS We pay $500. Sending contract.

Best,
Emma

Hazel's mind was officially blown. Maxine Joy had sent her essay to Emma Park nearly a month ago. Each day that had passed since then made the likelihood of hearing back seem exponentially smaller. Hazel figured Joy had been humoring her, making her feel good because she was a kid who'd had something shitty happen to her. But this email? It was like she'd time traveled past college and a decade of paying her dues and bringing her boss coffee, struggling to make rent and publishing in obscure literary journals, and had somehow telekinetically propelled herself into exactly the situation she'd dreamed of. The point was that she, Hazel, a high school student (!!!) was about to become a published writer.

Sure enough, after a few more emails with Emma Park, and after compulsively checking her phone a gazillion times, that Friday morning, Hazel fucking Greenberg fucking Blum's byline was there on *The Clip*'s home page. They'd used a stock photo of a girl with long brown hair and a forlorn expression breaking her pencil in two, and another of a man who eerily resembled Richard White (crossed with Jason Bateman), sitting at a desk, with a red bank stamp–style NO across his forehead.

My High School Principal Tried to Have Sex with Me And (Basically) Got Away with It
by Hazel Greenberg Blum
"Every year I choose one student to have sex with, and this year I pick you."

Hazel's words read differently in *The Clip*'s distinctive font—more real. Overnight, she'd gone from a twelfth grader with no friends in a hundred-mile radius to precociously published. Not that anybody she knew would necessarily end up seeing this. There were, truth be told, quite a few articles on *The Clip* Hazel never bothered to click on. Maybe she didn't need to tell her parents? A lie by omission was no harm, no foul. It's not like her essay was going to be in the print issue. Her mother would probably miss it. Her father didn't read very much online, besides the news, preferring his cultural studies journals. He definitely didn't read *The Clip*. Realistically, someone, some friend of her mother's or colleague of her father's, would eventually notice. Hazel wondered how long she had before her parents found out. Days? Weeks? Months?

Make that minutes. An incoming text flashed from her mom.

Do you know you're in The Clip?!?!?!

She started texting back Obviously, but before she could finish, her mother was calling.

"Mom," Hazel whispered, closing her locker. "I'm at school. I'm not supposed to be talking on the phone. Do you want me to get detention?"

"We have bigger things to worry about than detention."

"So you're mad? I was hoping, I don't know, that maybe you'd be excited for me?"

"I'm not mad. I'm concerned. There's a difference. Daddy, though, is going to freak out. Why didn't you say anything?"

"Dad was the one who took me to see Maxine Joy. This was her idea." Hazel looked around to make sure there wasn't a teacher who would confiscate her phone.

"It was? When did you write this?"

"It's my common application essay," said Hazel.

"You used this for your applications? Are you serious?"

"So? So what? What happened to trusting me?"

"I do trust you, but people your age can't necessarily make the best long-term decisions. And you've made a big one."

"I've made it into *The Clip*. I'm more than okay with that. In fact, it would be nice if you would be proud of me."

"I'm *always* proud of you. You have no idea how much. Also—"

"What?"

"Your piece. It's unbelievably powerful. And beautiful. You're an amazing writer. You're so talented."

The bell rang. Hazel hung up on her mother and gave herself three more glorious minutes staring at her essay before running to her fourth-period class and grabbing the last desk within the two-minute grace period her stats teacher gave them to settle down. For the rest of the day, she went through the motions, keeping her profile low. Hazel told herself that having the most personal of personal essays up on *The Clip* was no big deal. (Sort of like, okay—exactly like, what she'd told herself on the first day of school, after the principal had done what he'd done.) She was in shock, she supposed. A good kind of shock, the best kind of shock. The delirious with excitement kind of shock. Not many people were published for the first time, at age eighteen, in the *New York Spectator.*

School ended, and Hazel's piece was still on the home page of *The Clip.* She checked her rarely used lurker Pinkhorizon account. She had literally zero followers and had never posted a word, but followed a bunch of writers. It was bonkers. Her essay was everywhere. A link had been "pushed out" three times by *The Clip*, gathering a multitude of likes and views and posted—with comments!—by Emma Park, a bunch of cool publishing people Hazel idolized including the book world icon Lisa Lucas, the *New York Times* writer turned TV showrunner Taffy Brodesser-Akner, the *New Yorker* writer Naomi Fry, and, by the time she biked home, none other than Maxine Joy herself. Hazel clicked over to Instagram. Without an account it was harder to figure out, but she started searching around and saw that a bunch of big deal writers on there, including *New York Magazine*'s Emily Gould, had posted about her essay in their Stories.

She had seventeen new texts, including several successively more excitable and aggressive ones from Luna:

Um the clip??

lol yeah

HOLY SHIT?!!!!!!

it weird, but nbd

U R famous now

Uh, NO

Do you still know me?

Ha but is it okay by the way? Kinda embarrassing to have it out there

RU 4real? It's fire!!!!

You sure?

Fax, babe, FAX

As Luna hyped and reassured her, Hazel ignored the avalanche of messages from her father, and clicked over to her email, where her inbox was overflowing, including two heartfelt letters from other teenage girls who'd correctly guessed her email address and who had similar stories of their own. One email was from Emma.

Hazel!!
Your piece is blowing up. Passed your email to a publishing world friend. She's the best. Here if you need me.—Em

Another was from someone named Sadie Lansky.

Dear Hazel,

Emma Park shared your email with me. I'm Sadie Lansky, and I have a small—but mighty!—boutique agency called Lansky Literary. Your inbox must be inundated with admiring notes. Deservedly so. I missed my subway stop while reading you in The Clip this morning. Your piece, and your story—you!—are inspiring and necessary. You can speak for so many young people who've been forced to deal with this sort of violation at school. That you're 18 and a current high school senior makes this feel special and fresh. Like lightning in a bottle. All of that, and I like the way you write. A lot. I'm wondering if there's a larger, longer story here? I'd love to take you to lunch to discuss. If that's a conversation you're interested in having? Let me know the next time you make it down to the city. My list includes everything from journalistic nonfiction to essay collections and memoir to fiction that bridges the literary commercial divide. What I care most about are stories. Send me your address and I'll have my assistant send you some of my books.

Yours truly,
Sadie

Was this real life? People were *reading* her. On the subway! People she didn't know. Not just people. A *literary agent.* Not just an agent—*Sadie Lansky.* Hazel, of course, had never heard of Sadie Lansky, but her name smacked of bookstore readings and book parties. A quick look at her authors, listed on the agency website, left Hazel breathless.

Gliding home on foot over the snow and ice, she deposited her things on top of the dining room shoe cubby and prepared to deal with her mother, who was in the kitchen with Wolf. Hazel couldn't believe she was published. She'd felt so alone in her attic room these last months. Suddenly, Hazel felt seen.

"Who wants a milkshake?" Her mom was in the kitchen with Wolf, filling the blender with chocolate milk and ice cream before noisily running it and handing a mug to Wolf, who took his after-school snack into the den. She gave a second mug to Hazel, who drank hers in two big gulps.

"Mom, I need to go to New York."

"I mean, same. We said we'd go in April over your spring break. Remember?"

"No, I need to go immediately. Today."

"What are you talking about? You have school."

"I need to go there for a lunch."

"A *lunch?*"

"You said we'd go back all the time. April isn't all the time. We haven't been back *once* since we moved. We could leave now and be in Brooklyn by bedtime."

"It's five degrees out. And six hours away."

"I *know* that."

"Hazel. We're not driving to New York today. What's your rush? Is this about your article?"

"There's someone I need to see."

Hazel pulled up Sadie Lansky's email and placed the phone in her mother's palm.

"Is this real?" asked Claire, reading it for a second and then a third time.

"No, I faked it," said Hazel.

"A longer story? What does she mean by that?"

"I don't know," said Hazel. She wasn't 100 percent sure. "A book?"

"How can you write a book? You're eighteen."

"It's not like drinking. There's no age requirement. Sadie Lansky seems to think I can. She wants to be my literary agent."

Claire couldn't quite imagine why Sadie Lansky would want her twelfth-grade daughter to write a book. Hazel *was* a good writer. For a teenager. But still.

"I don't get what the book would be about," said Claire, before realizing how unsupportive she sounded. But she really didn't.

"What happened with the principal," said Hazel. "Duh."

"How can that take up a whole book?"

"I don't know, but I want to meet Sadie and hear what she has to say. If nothing else, maybe she can write me an extra last-minute letter of recommendation or something. Or give me an internship one day. She's a good connection for later. Mom, please."

"Let me think. You have your February break coming up and Daddy has to teach that week. What if I take you and Wolf and we go to the city then? I'll have to check hotel prices. Or ask Ramona if she has room for the three of us. I miss New York, too. Weather in the forties will feel like a tropical vacation after this polar vortex."

"We can't wait until February. I need to go to New York now."

"February break is in three weeks, Haze. You can't wait three weeks?"

"Okay, fine. But no Wolf? Please? He's a nightmare on trips."

Wolf wasn't a *nightmare*, but, Claire conceded, his ADHD flared when traveling.

"I'll have to talk to Daddy."

They both knew Gus wouldn't go for the idea of Hazel meeting Sadie, not at first. He'd been trying to get literary agents interested in his writing for years and had eventually given up. Writing about television for academia turned out to be different than writing about it for the *New York Times* or the *New Yorker*. Or the *New York Spectator*. The rejections had made him turn against mainstream publications. Also, Gus was old-fashioned. He didn't believe that children should have social media accounts, or screens in their bedrooms, much less viral essays in *The Clip* or literary agents.

"Fine, talk to Dad," said Hazel. "But honestly? I'm going with or without you. So, let me know, okay?" She could borrow the bus money from Wolf, who hoarded his birthday cash.

Hazel left her mother in the kitchen and went up to the attic, sat at her desk, opened her laptop and wrote:

Dear Sadie,

Thank you so much. I would love to have lunch with you. I'll be in the city for my February break.

Yours truly,
Hazel

The reply came within minutes.

Terrific! Thrilled to meet you in person.

How would you feel about a late lunch at Schvitzhaus? I'm a member, and they have these ridiculous sandwich melts in their Café Nosh I can't seem to stop eating. Send me your dates, and I'll get us a reservation.

Hugs,
Sadie

Hazel had wanted to go to Schvitzhaus, the women and femme and nonbinary identified members-only bathhouse and coworking club with a ten-thousand-person-long waiting list, since it opened. Last winter, Ramona had treated Hazel and Luna to the sidewalk to-go window's famous $18 cup of turmeric matzah ball soup.

There were more emails piling up in Hazel's inbox. Texts accumulating on her phone from School of the Future kids and Brooklyn neighborhood friends wanting to know if she was okay. Rabbi Abraham wondering if she'd like to meet up for a walk or a coffee. A note of concern and congratulations from the social studies teacher at her old high school. Her former lit magazine advisor asking if she needed to talk—and if she could maybe do a Q&A with the club about how to get published? A dozen or more emails from girls across the country with stories like hers, but worse. Much worse. Back on Pinkhorizon, STEPHEN KING had shared her essay. What was happening?! She checked *The Clip* one more time. *My Principal Tried to Have Sex with Me* was the lead story and the #1 most popular article on the site. Hazel dropped her phone like it could give her a third-degree burn.

27

skinny brownstone

A "luxury" bus shuttled twice a day between Portland and New York City, offering complimentary water, snacks, and Wi-Fi. The first Saturday of February break was sunny and bright, a bracing eleven degrees at noon. The bus ride took forever but Claire didn't mind. It was a physical relief to leave Maine. In the seat next to her, Hazel, content with earbuds on and laptop open, returned to her longtime status as the easy child. Claire caught up on podcasts and Howard Stern interviews, pretended to read a novel while pre-shopping online, and made restaurant reservations.

By the time they drove through Harlem and then down the east side of Manhattan, Claire felt something like the anticipation and exhilaration and freedom she'd experienced as a teenager on special Saturdays, taking the Long Island Railroad to Penn Station. The city! While Maine hibernated through winter, comforting itself with pajama and ski days, battling colds and flus and Seasonal Affective Disorder and blizzards, Manhattan was alive. No matter where Claire went, the city was still here. She could move to Maine or Alaska or Mars. She could die. New York would exist with or without her. Who *hadn't* felt this way upon returning to the city, whether from a week or a decade away? In any case, this trip wasn't about her, Claire reminded herself as the bus arrived at Forty-Second Street and First Avenue. This was her daughter's adventure.

Claire spotted Ramona—who'd insisted on picking them up in her husband Christian's van—and felt another wave of love and recognition. Ramona put her hazards on, popped open the back, and came around to help with their bags.

"We'll do a proper hello in the car. This isn't a real spot."

"Where's Luna?" asked Hazel.

"Oh, she's finishing something for school."

"During February break?" asked Hazel.

"German school," said Ramona. "Germans don't do President's week."

Claire's suitcase was the XL oversized kind on rollers meant for a Real Housewife traveling with her glam squad.

"Damn," laughed Ramona.

"Sorry," said Claire. The night before, instead of spending quality time with Wolf, she'd frittered away the evening gathering her toiletries and strategizing her wardrobe for the trip. In the end she threw a bunch of options into her largest suitcase.

From the driver's seat Ramona offered both cheeks to Claire and reached her hand in the back to squeeze Hazel's.

As per usual, Ramona was wearing something incredible. A gardenia-colored silk blouse with precariously high-waisted and wide-legged denim that buttoned up the sides. A faux fur winter coat slung over her shoulders, halfway between a blanket and a superhero cape. She should have been the designer, thought Claire.

"Who made that top? Ulla Johnson?" asked Claire. "You look gorgeous."

"Dôen."

"How much?"

"$79. Originally $298. I waited in line for hours at their last sample sale. I was so hyped the night before I had to take an Ativan to fall asleep."

Ramona pulled onto the FDR Drive. "Thank goodness you're here," she continued, checking to see that Hazel's pods were back in her ears. "How is she?"

They texted, of course. But it wasn't the same as being in each other's presence.

Out of necessity—Claire's—Ramona had become a better correspondent since Halloween. She sent a steady stream of missives about cheap vacation spots and expensive facials. She texted about DC rallies and New York City protests. She texted about the hypocrisy and allure of fillers, tips on surviving perimenopause (progesterone, patch and vaginal estrogen, herbal supplements), about acupuncture mats, ketamine therapy, must-read novels, and the unheralded benefits of fiber cookies. On occasion, they texted about their husbands, though Ramona loved Gus and tended to take his side and Claire wasn't a huge fan of Christian, which made those exchanges less satisfying. Mostly, Ramona sent reassurances. *You've told me about at least three people you envied who then turned out to be having a very hard time; Of all the marriages I know, yours is the one where emotional labor is treated as equal to wage labor; Fanny packs are infinitely expanding. Buy one.*

Since the first day of school, they'd maintained a continuous text conversation about Hazel's situation. Ramona was ready to strangle Dick White. But they hadn't communicated much about Claire, her creative block, her fears that Maine was a mistake. How Claire was ashamed of herself for making her family move.

"Hazel seems like she's doing okay, actually," Claire said. "Given the circumstances? But I'm not sure it's working out for the rest of us."

"Which part?"

"Maine."

"Dickwad White? The Nazis?"

"That. And Gus. And, when I'm not terrified about Hazel, I'm bored."

"It's boring here, too. In an exhausting way. *Life* can be boring. Being a parent can be boring."

"Even in New York? Remind me."

"Even in New York." Ramona pulled off the FDR and onto the Brooklyn Bridge. "How's your line coming along?" she asked.

"What line?"

"That bad?"

Ramona knew how to make a dizzying array of things. When she saw a prohibitively priced sweater, she knit a version for herself. When she wanted a sauna in her backyard, she built one from scrap materials. She was a creature of the city, born and bred, who decompressed in the country—at her cabin in upstate New York's Western Catskills. She dared to light the candles on her personally-chopped-down Christmas tree. Her tiny one-woman pottery studio had a cult following, and her ceramics sold out within minutes of dropping online. She refused to scale, and limited stock made her pieces more longed for and desired. Ramona had a keen sense of personal style, a way with the conversational arts, and a head for real estate. Through a series of shrewd moves (and a down payment from her father), Ramona and Christian, a German-born painter turned high-end-contractor and occasional late-in-life model, had gone from renters in '90s Williamsburg to residents of a skinny Brooklyn brownstone.

They got to Ramona's block and double-parked.

"I'd kill for this brownstone," said Claire. Ramona laughed.

A typically sullen Christian came out and gave Claire a polite kiss on the cheek, lugged her suitcase up the stairs—grunting his displeasure—and then fled for the rest of the night. They'd picked up pizza on the way home and Hazel took one of the two pies to Luna on the top floor so they could eat and do whatever teenagers did the weekend before one of them was about to meet with a literary agent. In the living room, Claire and Ramona made plans to see an exhibit at the Guggenheim and started in on the other pie—mushroom. Claire took a bite and tried to swallow her envy.

"Great piece," said Ramona, nodding to what Claire had on. "So cute."

Claire was wearing a lavender boilersuit with white buttons up the front over her fleece tights. A collab she'd worked on for BuiltGood.

"Gus says I look like a cheesemaker in this."

"What's wrong with being a cheesemaker? Isn't that the dream?"

Claire strained to remember her original fantasy of life in Maine. It *would* be something to make your own goat cheese. Or, perhaps, an artisanal cottage cheese.

"Really, though. How's Maine? Besides boring? And aside from child predators?"

Claire hesitated. The previous spring, Ramona had warned her not to move there. "Maine can be beautiful," she'd said. "But the ocean's too cold for swimming. Even in August." As a girl Ramona had summered at her stepfather's vacation home in Deer Isle. Claire didn't learn until college that summer could be a verb. She was lucky to get two weeks at 4-H camp.

"Portland, Maine, is the new Portland, Oregon," said Claire.

"Is it?" Ramona asked.

"Truth? I hardly go to Portland. I rarely leave the house or see anyone," Claire said, sinking deeper into Ramona's love seat. "Wolf refuses to take the school bus, but I stay in the car at pickup."

"How's Wolfie doing?" Ramona asked.

"Not great. C plus? The meds help his ADHD. He's on the

high honor roll but he's not making any friends. Neither of them is, really."

Ramona went to the kitchen and returned with a bottle of red wine and a corkscrew.

"I pick him up at two and then he sits on the couch until bedtime doing who knows what on his phone."

"At least he's downstairs on the couch," said Ramona. "He could be hiding out in his bedroom, like Luna."

"I guess so."

"What's the latest with that piece of human trash?" asked Ramona, meaning White. "Is he going to jail or what?" She poured them each a glass.

"Ha. Or what. God, I hate him. Can we please talk about something else? I'm sick of thinking about him."

"Of course. Tell me anything. How's the house?"

"We bought a Japanese infrared space heater for the kitchen. Gus won't spend the money to fix the fireplaces. He says they cause cancer. I guess I got what I wanted but I want more?"

"'Aspiration is suffering.' I think I'm quoting a Gwyneth profile. Or the Dalai Lama."

"What's the matter with me?" said Claire. "I should be happy. Or happy enough."

"You've been through a trauma."

"I guess so. Can you believe Hazel made it into *The Clip*?"

"It's wild."

"She's meeting with an agent the day after tomorrow. I mean?"

"Our children are cooler than we are." Luna was a drummer in a neighborhood garage band. "That's for sure."

"We're old," declared Claire. Ramona raised her wineglass, and they drank to that.

"How are things between you and Gus?"

"Decent? Sometimes he gets fed up with me moping around the house. He's on this Riverburg kick. Like he thinks he can single-handedly defeat white supremacy and fascism by being a good teacher."

"That's admirable," said Ramona.

"I guess so," said Claire.

"What about the petition? I can't believe those spoiled brats are tormenting him. That college is so lucky to have him. He wrote *Family Man*, for fuck's sake."

"Gus is fine. Gus has tenure." Claire shrugged. "Aside from worrying about Hazel, I mean. And swastikas. And being 'canceled.'" She air quoted the canceling with her fingers. "His main complaint is that he never has time to write."

"Why not? I thought that was the whole point of moving to Maine."

"He preps his classes like he's teaching on Broadway. Or at the Sorbonne or something. He's had to start some Sunday night reading group, so they don't run him off campus." She undid her coveralls and started trying on a pile of clothes Ramona had left for her on the coffee table. "Ooh," she said, holding up a pair of cotton canvas sailor pants. "Are you really giving these to me?"

"They look amazing on you," said Ramona, handing her a thin floral print top to try next. "Do you know how the rest of my friends feel about their husbands? They hate them. They're waiting for their kids to go to college and just praying they can afford a divorce one day. My studio assistant hasn't slept with her husband in three years."

"How does that even work?"

"You know what I think of Gus," said Ramona. "He's a prince among men."

Claire laughed. She'd heard that line before.

"I mean it. He's an intellectual who gets up with the kids every morning and cooks dinner seven nights a week. It's like you have a personal chef. And you like the way he smells."

"True," Claire admitted.

"Maybe it's not Gus," suggested Ramona. "Maybe it's Maine.

Or maybe it's Riverburg? Oh, I keep forgetting—I was talking about you during my shift at the food co-op the other day. Supposedly there's a good Riverburg vintage place?"

"Please. There's nothing in Riverburg."

"The woman who told me about it is a stylist with a Substack and a summer house in Maine. Says the owner finds these little old Waspy ladies and goes through their closets with them. You should check it out."

"I get depressed whenever I walk downtown. We never should have left Brooklyn. What was I thinking?"

Ramona looked like she felt sorry for Claire. Which was even worse than trying to help.

"You can say I told you so, you know," said Claire. "That's allowed."

"Never," answered Ramona.

Ramona could say the thing that hit Claire's funny bone squarely, making her laugh and feel understood. Ramona *got* Claire. And being gotten was the rarest and best feeling in the world, which helped make it okay that Ramona had what Claire wanted. This home and life in New York City.

On that February night, Claire's covetousness was temporarily resolved. With Hazel and Luna out of sight upstairs, the ladies bundled up and smoked pot on the steps that led to the garden, and then back in the living room drank wine while listening to Stevie Wonder and Fleetwood Mac, trading complaints and compliments. They talked clog boots and gray hair and skin regimens. Claire tried to convince Ramona to order a gallon of jojoba oil and moisturize with it from head to toe, Ramona said that sounded messy and she was not as into hydration.

"Who needs more clothes, anyway," said Claire, circling back to her stalled line. To her stalled life. "I mean, look at you. Giving me all this good stuff so you can simplify. While I'm talking about making *more*. It's so dumb and pointless."

"Well, I wouldn't say that. Being naked is nice, for sleeping.

Plus, less laundry. But during the daytime, I do appreciate having something other than my peach fuzz. Those pants don't fit me anymore, by the way. I'm not becoming a monk. Can I ask you something?"

"Of course. Anything."

"What do you *want* to make?" asked Ramona. "Meditate on it. What if you made something you loved? Maybe you should close your eyes and visualize that for a minute. Should I pull your animal cards?" Animal cards were like a cuter tarot. Ramona had a way with them. She could make you see your life differently.

Claire twisted her anchor necklace. "Will you come visit this summer?"

"Promise."

28

schvitzhaus

Hazel walked up the stairs of Schvitzhaus wishing she'd had a lighter touch with Ramona's perfume, which had left her smelling like a firepit. An oversized, faux-distressed mirror on top of the welcome desk confronted her with the words *imagine future pleasures.*

"My name's Hazel Greenberg Blum and I'm here to see Sadie Lansky, but not for an hour," Hazel said to a staffer wearing a puffed-sleeve lilac sweater with matching beanie.

Light streamed in. Vases with wildflowers and cacti adorned the marble check-in counter. The staffer, hardly a couple years older than Hazel, said "ooh" and that since Hazel was meeting Sadie—a very special member—she was welcome to *literally* come right in.

"Would you like to try a water circuit or a schvitz or even a hammam scrub on the house?" she asked, offering Hazel a thick striped terry-cloth robe, and pointing out the baths on the lower level. "Did you bring your bathing suit?" A cleansing ritual, she added, was about to begin in the sauna.

Hazel, who was not planning on getting undressed, politely declined.

The staffer shrugged her shoulders and grinned, as if Hazel had given the correct answer. "Okay. Why don't you go have a seat and make yourself at home while you wait for Sadie."

In the lounge, two leather sofas with cream- and coral-colored tasseled pillows surrounded a fireplace. Hazel took in the scene, glad she'd done her research. A coworking space filled with long library desks took up one wall. At a round kiosk an aproned person was selling Jerusalem sesame bagel toasts, and at the back of the lobby, a broth and juice bar served their signature overpriced sip drinks. Café Nosh was on the upper floor; the baths and saunas and cold plunge and hot tubs at ground level.

Seated in a bouclé swivel chair, Hazel noticed an unusual number of brunette bangs and clear pink oversized eyeglasses and yellow popcorn sweaters. Like all the trust-fund Veronicas in New York City had gathered in one place. An uncanny number of women carried bookstore totes. She spied an actress she liked typing away on her laptop in aviator frames and noise-canceling headphones, and a model turned writer, wearing a navy newsboy cap, taking a virtual meeting.

Two nights before, Hazel and Luna had not gotten high. As their mothers did whatever mothers do downstairs, they'd searched the center drawer of Christian's desk looking for pot and found his contraband American Spirits, attempting smoke rings—before deciding that cigarettes were, in fact, disgusting. Instead, they streamed the horror film *Carrie*. Which seemed fitting given Hazel's high school hellscape in Maine.

"Are you really going to write a book?" Luna had asked, biting off a nail and then picking at her guitar. Hazel was so jealous of Luna's chill. She took things in stride, including Hazel's drama.

"I don't know," said Hazel. "Maybe?"

"I think that would be so cool."

It didn't seem real, though. Not like Luna's band, which had actual gigs. Hazel felt like she was making the whole thing up. She changed the subject and showed Luna her text chain with Noah. He was back from India and starting a new semester and had gotten her number off her dad. They hadn't seen one another, though he'd been on campus for two weeks and lived ten minutes away. Luna said that didn't mean anything. Hazel knew better. She and Hazel traded massages and fell asleep a third of the way into the movie.

The next morning was Sunday and the day before Hazel's big meeting. Her body was missing her morning run and she was contemplating heading to Prospect Park. But when the girls wandered down to the kitchen, they found that their mothers had planned the entire day. Surprising exactly no one, Claire and Ramona insisted they spend Sunday shopping for a "meet your literary agent look."

"Sadie Lansky doesn't care how I look," Hazel said, and immediately realized she was probably wrong. There was a reason why the teenagers who "made it," whether as actors or influencers or YouTubers or even activists, were always camera ready.

"I find that when I feel happy with what I'm wearing I say smarter things," volunteered Ramona.

Hazel liked clothes, too. She wasn't *dead*.

Beacon's Closet was an enormous consignment store in Greenpoint, Brooklyn, filled with cast-off treasures. A mother ship of thrift and vintage, beloved by a certain type of chic-and-dollar-conscious New Yorker. Claire and Hazel and Ramona and Luna worked through the dozens of circular clothing racks organized by color. They lifted items for one another's inspection. They were diligent; they were adept. Eventually, her mom plucked Hazel a dress. *The* dress. Trying it on, Hazel had to admit it was perfect. An above-the-knee rainbow-striped silk number—vintage Diane von Furstenberg—with an ironic pussy bow at the neck. A little much maybe? She could dress it down with tights and her Docs.

When she came out to show her mom and Ramona and Luna they oohed and aahed.

"You're so beautiful," said her mother. The longer layers of Hazel's hair grazed the top of her shoulders.

"Mom. Can we not?"

By Sunday evening, Sadie had written to confirm that their lunch the next day was on.

Five minutes after 2:00 p.m., a woman in a belted black jumpsuit with an artfully managed mess of dark curly hair approached.

"You must be Hazel," she said, offering a firm handshake. "I'm Sadie."

Whereas the celebrities Hazel had been trying hard not to stare at appeared dewy yet somehow more humanlike in person, Sadie Lansky breezed into Café Nosh looking approximately five billion times more glamorous and intimidating than the bookish soul Hazel had imagined while studying her Lansky Literary profile photo and the brainy list of authors she worked with. Hazel probably should have let her mom come to the meeting.

"We're in luck," said Sadie, sitting down and placing her bag on a hook under the table. "They gave us my favorite spot by the window. So, what do you think?" asked Sadie.

Of what? Hazel wondered. Of Sadie?

"Of Schvitzhaus, I mean," clarified Sadie.

"It's amazing," said Hazel.

"You're not in Maine anymore, Hazel."

"I mean, I'm from New York. I hardly know Maine."

"Oh right! Projecting! In my alternate life I live on a farm in Maine by the ocean. No bath can compare to the sea, right? I'll have to come visit you one day."

Hazel smiled.

"Let's order. Are you hungry? I have a big buzzy debut novel coming out this summer and we had a media breakfast for it this morning, but I didn't have time to eat a bite."

"Wow. You wrote a novel? On top of being an agent?"

"Oh! No. Not me," said Sadie. "I could never have the patience to write a book. A client of mine. I'll send you an advanced copy."

Hazel would have felt dumber than she did if she hadn't read that Sadie, on top of a law degree, had an MFA in fiction. Who knew what Sadie could or couldn't do?

"You need to try one of their open-faced sandwiches with cheese and lox. And, also, you *must* order a German pretzel. They get their breads from a new bakery down the block that is bonkers delicious."

Sadie waved over a server and ordered. After the coffees arrived, she began quizzing Hazel on the day at the principal's office, her life in Brooklyn, why her family had moved to Maine, her favorite writers and literary influences, her college reaches and safeties and what she might study, and whether she thought she could write a book in the next year.

"A memoir?" asked Hazel.

"A memoir, yes."

"I've always wanted to write a novel," confessed Hazel.

"You will. One day. For now? Having something salable to pin a memoir on, that's a once-in-a-lifetime opportunity," said Sadie.

"Aren't I too young for a memoir? It seems presumptuous, don't you think? Like, who cares what I have to say. I'm only eighteen."

Sadie took a swig of her coffee. "You'd be surprised. Youth sells. Especially right now. Believe me, you're more than old enough. And I can help you. Once we sell it, your editor will help, too. If you feel uncomfortable writing on your own, we could pair you with a collaborator."

Hazel must have looked confused.

"A ghostwriter. That's super common. You'd have to share your advance but that would take some of the pressure off you."

"No," said Hazel, with unexpected force. "I don't want anyone else to write my book for me. I want to be a writer one day," said Hazel. "It's not about the money for me."

"Hazel," Sadie said. "Your piece is all over the internet. You're already a writer."

The server came with their food. Hazel tried her sandwich. It was the most delicious thing she'd eaten in months. Years. Ever?

Sadie groaned after her first bite. "Ancient grains are really having a moment, aren't they?"

"But what would the book be *about*?" Hazel asked. "A whole book? I mean, I met White over the summer at the pool, but we only talked about what I was reading. That first day of school I was in his office for less than half a class period. And then I saw him once in the hallway, and then I never saw him again."

"Think about it this way," said Sadie. "Each line in your *Clip* essay could be a chapter. Or maybe each paragraph. We'll have to brainstorm. You'd start with what happened and make your way back. Write about growing up in Brooklyn. Readers can't get enough of a New York City childhood. Then the move to Maine. City girl in the country. Fish out of water."

Hazel nodded.

"Have you seen *Northern Exposure*?"

Hazel shook her head no, trying to keep up. Should she be taking notes?

"Stream it. And *Gilmore Girls* should be a touchstone. For the hints of small-town whimsy."

"*Gilmore Girls* is my favorite show."

"I bet. You're such a Rory. Do you watch *Schitt's Creek*?"

Regrettably, Hazel didn't.

"It's the best. Canadian! You must watch *Sex Education*, too. For a more modern take on the small-town drama thing. Anyway!

Once you're in Riverburg, slo-mo back to the day in the principal's office. Take us there. What did it smell like, feel like, sound like, taste like? Well, not taste like! What am I saying? But the point is: Show don't tell, etc. You know the drill. You're a reader.

"Then, you get into what happened in your town. Riverburg, right? From there, MeToo from a teenage girl's perspective. And the backlash, that's really important. What made you speak out and then write the essay. Set us up for why this was your breaking point, your last straw.

"As I said, I love Maine. New Yorkers in general, we're obsessed. But we don't know the *real* Maine. We know lobster shacks and lighthouses and chilly summer nights, you know? We don't know winter in Maine. We don't know the red part of purple state Maine. That's what makes this interesting. All the meaty issues you touch on in your piece. Town versus gown. Working class versus middle class. Left versus right. Racism, antisemitism, sexism. If I can let us dream big? I'm picturing you in *Teen Vogue*. Hell, I'm picturing you on the cover of the *New York Times Magazine*."

"I don't know if I can do it," said Hazel half to herself.

"Well, don't worry. *I* know you can do it," Sadie said. "But," she continued, finishing her coffee, "I'm not here to push you. Don't do it if you're not ready. Writing a book isn't for everyone. It's hard. So is having your name out there."

"I should probably talk to my parents," said Hazel.

"One hundred percent. I thought about asking your mother to come today. Then I said to myself, this young woman takes down sexual predators. She stands up to white supremacists. She speaks at college campuses. She goes viral. She can handle Sadie Lansky."

Maybe she could, thought Hazel. Though *viral*, Hazel knew, was Sadie being generous. Wolf had said it was more like her essay had a bad cold. (Though weren't colds viral? Hazel couldn't remember.)

"Listen," said Sadie, pulling out her phone and checking emails and texts and the time and weather like she was done with the conversation. "If your mom wants to meet, let's do that while you're in the city. Or if you want time to think. Take it. Now. Before we write a proposal and sell this. I want you to feel comfortable."

Hazel had a last bite of pretzel.

"Before I head back to the office—if you don't mind my asking, has anyone else approached you about representation?"

"I've gotten a couple of emails," said Hazel. One agent had written her twice, which felt a bit aggressive. "Don't worry, I didn't write them back."

"You should, if you like. You need to find the perfect fit. You should meet with them."

Hazel knew she wouldn't. She didn't want to wait, or meet other people, or think or hesitate or leave things unresolved. She needed Sadie. She needed to *be* more like Sadie, too. Confident. Self-assured. Badass. Because as stressful as all of this was, as much as she craved what she now realized was the safety and serenity of her attic bedroom, Hazel didn't want any of it to stop.

Goodbyes were said and hugs exchanged. Despite not having used the baths, Hazel floated out of Schvitzhaus feeling cleansed and buffed and fortified and like she was living her best life. Was Sadie her agent? Was Hazel for real writing a book?

Filled with adrenaline, Hazel decided to walk the Williamsburg Bridge back to Luna's house, and was two-thirds across, when an email showed up in her inbox.

Dear Hazel,

It was SO lovely to spend the afternoon with you. I believe in you as a writer and important young feminist voice. I would love to represent you. While we haven't officially teamed up—and I fully respect your process and timetable—on my way out of Schvitzhaus I happened to run into Evie Vogel, the Making the Rounds with The Clip podcast host and we started chatting about you. Exciting news! She wants you to do their show. You'd tape in studio tomorrow morning. What do you think? I'd love to have that in hand for the proposal. It'll be nice for prospective editorial teams. Lots of editors, especially the younger ones I'm thinking we should submit to, love Making the Rounds, meaning some of them will have already heard you by the time we're ready for submission.

Xx Sadie

29

the phone call

Meanwhile, back in Maine, Gus was not pleased. He was working his way through a sleeve of saltines while trying to make headway on a long overdue essay for an edited volume, and he still had to prep his class for the next morning. With his book, he'd made no progress whatsoever. When he fell asleep at night, or tossed and turned before dawn, he convinced himself that if he could work for a solid three to four focused, uninterrupted hours a day he could pound out a draft and then spend a year revising and finally—finally!—be done with it. He was a cliché, a failure, a joke, he knew. He was fully aware. His graduate school cohort had run circles around him publication-wise. Nobody cared that he was a good *teacher.* This wasn't high school. This was academia. His best grad school friend Charlie, now tenured at Princeton, had his name consistently splashed all over the newspapers, quoted in trend pieces and features on gender and society. The difference between Charlie and Gus? The reason Charlie was productive and lauded while Gus labored in obscurity? Charlie and his husband Frank had decided not to have children. Instead, they had money to spare and well-groomed beards and good wardrobes and better restaurants and *Europe* and passed their weekend mornings in thick terry-cloth bathrobes *getting their fucking work done.*

Making matters worse, his student nemesis Sam was enrolled in one of his spring seminars. She was a major, and a senior, and the course was required. It wasn't like she wanted to have Gus as her professor again. But they were stuck with one another. Which meant that Gus, rather than drilling down on his writing that winter, was walking on eggshells and pouring himself into pedagogy. When he wasn't at the College, or preparing to be there, Gus spent his every waking moment attending to Wolf, whose cooking skills were limited to toast.

So, no, Gus was not pleased. Claire had been gone for six days and he was sick of doing everything—the shoveling, the laundry, the dog, Wolfcare. Claire could talk all she wanted about the "mental load"—a term he'd taught her!—of family scheduling, and keeping on top of the children's schoolwork, or emotional labor and kin work, but Gus was the one who cooked dinner and got up with the kids every morning since they'd moved to Maine. While Claire slept and exercised and made macramé and waited for inspiration to strike.

But Gus wasn't about to ask for anyone's sympathy. He knew that nobody in the world had a small enough violin for Gus Blum. And now, on top of the humiliation he felt amongst his peers for agreeing to come to the College, for stepping off the academic star track once and for all—to have his daughter, his eighteen-year-old child, go *viral* with 650 words? He was immensely proud of Hazel, but something about the way this whole chain of events was playing out didn't sit right with him.

Despite his misgivings about the job, Gus wanted to stay—at the College, and in Riverburg. For the first time in almost twenty years, since leaving the graduate school nest, he could breathe. It was the trees, sure. The vastness of the Maine sky.

But 90 percent of it was his bank account. (That, and his five-minute commute.) Even with Claire unemployed, they were better off. It was simple math. He was—they were—making more money in a much cheaper place. Besides, if he let the Dick Whites and the misogynistic hate note leavers and the swastika spray-painters of the world dictate his moves, where would that leave him? Where would that leave any of them?

At least Claire and Hazel were coming home today. He had a plan: Gus was going to pick them up from Portland, give Hazel a hug and Claire a kiss, drop them at Pine Street and hightail it back to campus, lock the door, and not come out for a week—or until he'd written three new book chapters, whichever came first. He was grabbing for his coat, heading home to make Wolf a quick dinner before driving down to the bus station in Portland when the phone rang, his office landline.

"Hi. This is Becky Singer. I'm a reporter with the *New York Times*. Is this Professor Gus Blum?"

"Hello. Of course, I'm familiar with your work."

A wave of relief with a foam of rapture washed over him. Huzzah! This was it. It had taken them long enough. Singer must have seen his latest journal article or gotten wind of the forthcoming edited volume. At long last, his work, his theories, *he* would be quoted in the newspaper that mattered most to him—the paper of record. Whenever Gus tried to get a word in edgewise at dinner, to share some theoretical point of interest, only Wolf leaned forward, while Hazel's eyes glazed over and Claire accused him of pontificating, saying *professors gotta profess* and pulling out the newspaper. Years of that made Gus feel like the only way to get Claire to take him seriously was to be *in* that paper.

He held the phone aloft and gave himself a millisecond to clear his throat, regain his composure, and speak. This was what he'd been waiting for.

"Gus Blum. At your service," he added with a flourish and a

tip of his figurative cap, hoping to sound simultaneously ironic and helpful. Thank god he'd answered the phone. Academics were notorious for not responding promptly to media calls. Gus understood the news cycle and the deadline pressures journalists faced. If he played his cards right, he could become *the* guy, *their* guy, the go-to quotable figure on American culture. To the extent that a straight white man could or should.

"How may I help?" he asked. He grabbed a pen and notepad.

"I'm looking for Hazel Blum—"

"My daughter?"

"—I'm hoping to speak with her about what happened in Riverburg with the former principal, and about her essay, but I couldn't find her number or email. Yours is listed on your website for the College."

Gus dropped his pen and somehow managed to bang his foot on the desk while retrieving it.

"Sorry, why do you want to talk to Hazel? You're not thinking of writing about what happened, are you? This must be pretty small-town news for the *Times*."

"Well, you're right. This isn't a high-profile Hollywood or DC case. Unfortunately, though, what happened to your daughter is not unusual. Nor is the pushback that follows when students have the wherewithal to say no. More and more, schools are becoming battlegrounds over sexual harassment. That's what I'm hearing, and what I'm hoping to learn more about."

"Oh," said Gus. "I see." American Studies professor or not, he hadn't been thinking about what happened to Hazel, or their family, as anything other than a personal catastrophe.

"Your daughter was quite brave to stand up to that principal. And to write about it. When I heard Hazel on *The Clip*'s *Making the Rounds* podcast—"

He was surprised Singer had listened. *The Clip* was a fashion blog, wasn't it?

"Hazel spoke a bit about there being a backlash in town," said

Becky. "I'm so sorry about the swastika. This must be a very difficult time for your family."

Gus heard typing. Was she IN the *Times* building?

"You should probably wait and save your pitch for Hazel, or her mother," Gus said. He didn't mean to be rude, but the indignity of this long-awaited call skipping a generation was too much. "I'd feel more comfortable commenting as an academic, than as a parent," he added, a final last-ditch attempt, which he then regretted and wished he could take back. He'd never answer the phone again. Email was far superior. Speaking extemporaneously was not his thing.

"Well, I'd love the chance to talk to Hazel. And her mother. Claire Greenberg, yes?"

"Greenberg Blum," corrected Gus.

He rolled his chair back from his desk and swiveled to face his bookcase. "You say you found my email on the department website?"

At least she'd seen his areas of expertise, then. And his publications. "Send me your contact information. Hazel can make up her own mind."

Gus hung up with Singer and called Claire, who said they were just passing the Portsmouth bridge, which meant Gus should leave Riverburg soon. She was whispering.

"What's up? I can't really talk. Hazel fell asleep, and I think there's a no talking rule on the bus. It doesn't say that anywhere, but nobody else has been on their phone for the last five hours."

"You're never going to believe this. The *New York Times* wants to do a story on Hazel."

"Really?" said Claire. "That's cool, I guess?"

"Are you serious? Because I think it's a terrible idea."

"But you're obsessed with the *New York Times*."

"That doesn't mean I want my child to be *in* it."

"We can't keep her in Bubble Wrap. She's eighteen. These are her decisions. We talked about this in therapy."

“It doesn’t matter how old she is,” said Gus. “This has been really stressful and it’s going to get worse if the *Times* covers it.”

“Or maybe it’ll get better? Maybe this is Hazel’s chance to make the world a better place. I wish I had that chance. Don’t you?”

Gus sighed. A forty-nine-year-old sigh. Maybe it was time to get over himself. “Can we stop saying ‘she’s eighteen’ like that makes her an adult?”

“Agreed,” said Claire.

“We should stop arguing all the time, too,” said Gus. “It’s not healthy for the kids.”

“It’s not healthy for us,” said Claire. “I missed you, by the way.”

“What do you want for dinner?” asked Gus.

“I’ll take anything, Thank you for cooking for me. I actually got sick of eating out, believe it or not.”

“You’re lying, but that’s sweet.”

“Can I tell Hazel about the *Times* or do you want to do it together?”

“Go for it,” Gus said. “I’ll cheer from the sidelines.”

30

charlotte's web

Wolf hated everything. Especially his family. His mom and sister had ditched him for New York City—his real home—and hadn't thought twice about it. His dad was busy on a mission of atonement, trying to win over students lecture by lecture with his theoretical charisma and encyclopedic knowledge of TV culture, and by his philosophical refusal to hightail it out of town, as Wolf would have preferred.

Some February break.

And no, Wolf did NOT want to learn how to cross-country ski. He could care less if ski club was a good way to make friends. He didn't want to be cold or try something new. Or go outside! He didn't want to face-plant onto the snow and be the laughingstock of Maine.

All Wolf wanted was to sit on the couch, warm and dry, petting Pickle, noise-canceling headphones on, reading the news on his phone. Because what his parents didn't understand was that *he had tried* to make friends and—news alert—nobody in the state of Maine, or at least the town of Riverburg, wanted to be friends with him. Nobody but Gracie. Who hadn't so much as said hi to him since Halloween.

Wolf hated himself for betraying her. *He* was the one who told on Gracie's father. All Hazel did was tell their parents. He told THE WORLD. Wolf had learned his lesson. He would never in a million, trillion years "say something" again.

But at least it was a week off from school. If #couchlife was occasionally boring, and sometimes full-on depressing, at least it wasn't life-threatening. Without Gracie around, junior high was worse by an infinite magnitude. At school it was like he had a kippah on his head. He was Riverburg's resident Albert Einstein, and not in a good way. His parents were completely clueless about the lion's den of working-class resentment they'd thrown him into, so that they could feel moral and upright for sending their kids to public school.

With nobody to hang out with and nothing to do, Wolf nestled under the couch blankets and typed snarky comments into his phone, debating politics and policy ideas with randos on Reddit's urbanism boards, commiserating over their shared hatred of car culture and rural life. Occasionally, he got inadvertently sucked into MRM (men's rights movement) videos. He remained a follower of Ayn Rand, studying *Atlas Shrugged* as his ancestors might have studied the Talmud, though lately the author's theoretical reasoning wasn't making as much sense to him.

That was his February vacation. Phone. Reddit. Couch. TV break. Repeat. The more alone he was, the more alone he felt. And bored. Desperately bored.

So, you know what? Maybe Wolf would try something new. Maybe he'd break some rules. On purpose. He considered his options: Get drunk off the wine in the cabinet above the refrigerator? Somehow get ahold of a vape pen? Or break through the parental controls on the internet and check out You Porn? Or something worse? Not that his family would notice. Or care.

He was *this* close to becoming a juvenile delinquent—but

then! On the Friday afternoon before school started back, while his father was off somewhere (his office? Wolf hadn't been listening when he left and said where he was going), Wolf randomly checked his grades and noticed an incoming item in his school email account. Inbox: An emergency message from Mr. Woods. (Aka the director of *Charlotte's Web.*)

Drama club needs you! read the subject line.

In a different state of mind, perhaps Wolf would have said no to Mr. Woods. If he hadn't been so bored, he might never have seen the email in the first place. Presumably, Mr. Woods would have reached out to his parents by the end of the night. But this way, Wolf got to be the one to make the call—and the decision.

After months of rehearsal, the new kid playing Wilbur, Wolf's replacement, had the flu, a fever of 104, and was developing bronchitis. Maybe pneumonia! The show was two days away—that Tuesday. The drama teacher said the show must go on and that *the only way* was for Wolf to play the part. *Did he remember the lines? If not, they could put some script sides up in the barn.*

Did he? Did he ever! He basically had a photographic memory. A useless party trick 99.9 percent of the time, nothing compared to soccer field or basketball court prowess, but handy in this case.

Wolf wrote back and said he'd do it, he'd take on Wilbur, but only if Gracie said it was okay.

This was Gracie's suggestion, replied Mr. Woods. She says you should text her.

Wolf was shocked when he texted Gracie and seconds later, she wrote back. A TON. It was the longest text exchange (outside of his family group text) of his life.

Do you care if I do the play?

Heyy. You have to bc nobody else knows the lines!!

But you're not allowed to talk to me

My mom said it's ok

Acting involves talking?

I know that. But we need you for the show to go on

hmmm

I don't know how much longer I'm going to be at RJH anyway

What???? They're making you QUIT SCHOOL?!?

Not quit, move

Oh

Yeah

Why???

The divorce and stuff. Me and my mom are moving in with my grandma

I'm really sorry

Me too

Wolf didn't have ANY grandparents, which sucked. But probably not as much as having your parents get divorced because your father tried to sleep with your friend's older sister?

My mom says the schools are better in southern Maine

I heard that

Closer to Portland

Yeah

My grandmother lives in Cape Elizabeth

Cool

There are beaches and lighthouses

You're lucky

Not really

I know, sorry

I'm the one who = sorry

You didn't do anything wrong, it's not your fault

I'm sorry about my dad I mean

I'm sorry about my sister

No that's dumb

I'm sorry she made this into a big deal

She definitely didn't do anything wrong!!

I know but I'm sorry I couldn't keep my big mouth shut

I know

I'm sorry we moved here

I'm not. So, will you do the play?

Yeah

TX Wolf

I guess I'll see you at drama?

And lunch

That's okay. I like sitting at the loser table HAHAHAHHAAHHA

You can SIT with me Wolf

Really?

Tbh we're moving right after the play is over. Friday is my last day.

Oh. Bye Gracie

Byye

"DAAAAAAAADDDDDDDDDYYYYYYYYYYY!!!!!! I NEED MOMMY!!!!!!! She's not answering her phone IT'S AN EMERGENCY!"

"What's wrong? I'm driving to Portland, remember? I'm picking up Hazel and Mommy at the bus station."

"I'm Wilbur! Again!!!!! CALLLLLLL MOMMMYYYYYY!!!! SHE NEEDS TO COME HOME!!!!! We need to RUN LINES. RIGHT. NOW."

Wolf was NOT going to miss the biggest moment of his entire life. And this time, he wasn't going to let either of his parents stop him. When his mom came home, he pled his case and they relented. She and Wolf ran lines past his bedtime and again early the next morning. That weekend, Wolf attended a two-day marathon dress rehearsal.

A sold-out performance of *Charlotte's Web* followed. While Wolf trod the boards, his family sat in the second row, his mother holding supermarket flowers. (Embarrassing, yeah, but it had secretly felt good.) It was the first time since Hazel said no that Wolf saw his mother happy. Even his dad kept it together. In an out-of-character show of chill, he accepted the school district's decision that Dick White could attend if he sat in the last row—sex offender or not.

Dick White wasn't the White who mattered that night. Up onstage, Wolf transcended his Wolfness and—somehow—*became* Wilbur. It was like E.B. White and Wilbur were both speaking directly to him, and almost *through* him. Act Two. Templeton, played by a rather intimidatingly large eighth grader named Camden, said Wilbur was probably scared enough to faint. It was Wolf's big monologue and he remembered, he FELT, every word.

"Whatever will happen, will happen. I may not live as long as I'd like, but I've lived very well. A good life is much more important than just having a long life. So starting now, I'm going to stop worrying about myself. There are more important things than just thinking about yourself all the time."

Wolf had never felt as alive as he did that night onstage. So at home in his skin. He'd never felt more himself. And from pretending to be a pig! All that energy and attention, laser-focused on him. E.B. White, author extraordinaire, telling him exactly what to say and how to act, Cyrano de Bergerac style. The standing ovation wasn't too shabby, either.

Hazel said Wolf should be a theater major in college. (Yeah right.)

The one thing about the show that sucked was that at the end of it, there'd be no more Gracie. Her house was packed in moving boxes, she said, at the after-show backstage juice and chips party. She and her mom were moving that weekend.

31

the general

Hazel very much *did* want to talk to Becky Singer. Singer, along with her fellow reporter Erin Flattery, had taken down a hugely powerful Hollywood mogul—and told the truth about a Supreme Court justice. They'd won the Pulitzer Prize! Their #MeToo reporting had been made into a *movie.* The idea that she was interested in Hazel was nuts. Sadie said the story, if it turned out the right way, could make the sale of her book (?!) inevitable, as close to a sure thing as they came.

Becky and Hazel spent a solid hour on the phone the next afternoon, Hazel sitting at her desk with a blanket wrapped around her, snow falling peacefully. She'd had to pee for the last half hour of the call but felt awkward about asking for a break, so she went with the mute button on her phone, praying it would work. Becky was kind and warm, supportive yes, but also businesslike, asking Hazel to tell her story from the pool to the first day of school and on, step by step. Unlike her parents, but sort of like Sadie, Becky made her feel like she could handle hearing whatever Hazel had to say. Hazel figured that as an investigative reporter, she must have been through this with dozens—hundreds? thousands?—of other women. Toward the end of the conversation, she said she'd like to come to Maine on a reporting trip and how did Hazel feel about that?

The plan was to meet Tuesday after school at The General. Hazel half figured the incoming snow would stop or possibly postpone Becky's arrival, as seven to ten inches were expected sometime early in the week, and that was on top of Sunday's snow dump. Yet Becky materialized as promised two days later. She could have been a Mainer, a transplanted one at least, in her regulation shearling-lined L.L. Bean duck boots and puffy parka and her no-nonsense wavy hair styled only by her plain wool beanie. Hazel realized the half hour she'd spent debating her look for the meeting had been unnecessary and, in retrospect, completely embarrassing; something her mother might have done. She and Becky were here to change the world, or at least repair a tiny corner of it, not put on a fashion show.

They found a booth.

Talking to Becky was a lot easier than dealing with an unsympathetic judge and jury or mounting a protest. Hazel didn't have the constitution of an activist. She was an introvert, more comfortable in her third-floor attic bedroom with a book than in a town square with a bullhorn. She could, however, sit at The General and tell Becky what had happened, slowly and precisely and quietly and accurately, over tea and chocolate chip cookies. That much she could do. Besides, this would probably work better.

"In your essay, and on the podcast, and again now, you said Richard White told you he did this every year."

"Yes," said Hazel.

"That's part of what I'm here to find out more about. The pattern of students before you. Who else, if anyone, he propositioned and blackmailed. Whether they said yes or no or were forced into a sex act through coercion or physical force. What other inappropriate behavior, if any, took place."

"Okay," said Hazel.

"We've learned that a couple of earlier attempts at uncovering White were squashed by the local school board and superintendent. Small town or not, that's a very real system of complicity and entitlement. An old boy's network. Which means things could get harder here for you when our piece comes out."

Hazel gulped her tea. *Harder?*

"I know *The Clip* essay was a lot. Are you prepared to have more attention directed at you? Do you think you're ready for it? Because there's #MeToo, right? And then there's the backlash. What you faced here. Do you have the support you need?" asked Becky. "Those are the questions to think about."

"I have enough, I guess," said Hazel. There were her parents. Luna. There was Ramona, in a pinch. Wolf, if she was desperate. Noah, sort of. Did Pickle count?

"Because there may be more to this story," said Becky. "Other students with something to say."

"Here?"

"We'll have to see. That's what I'm doing this week. Reporting this out. My colleague Erin is working on the story with me. We're looking into this not because it's unusual, but because it happens every day. We've been talking to students in similar situations across the country."

"You are?" She hadn't realized.

Hazel went to the counter for a refill of hot water. Maybe this wasn't about her, after all. Maybe it wasn't about fame or a book or press hits. When she came back and slid into the booth, Becky was texting furiously and had her coat and hat back on.

"I'm off," she said, standing up. "I'm going to try and beat the snow."

"Back to New York?" Hazel asked.

"Vermont," said Becky. "To find out exactly what happened

with White and those two students there. That's between us, okay?"

The person behind the counter was cleaning up for the night. After refusing Becky's offer of a ride the few blocks home, Hazel lingered over her second mug of tea. She emailed Sadie, figuring she'd hear back the next morning.

Sadie texted two minutes later. Incredible news. Here for you. This will be a game changer. Call me? Hazel's head was splitting in two. It wasn't just White. It was—life? She needed a dark room and five hours of comfort TV and ten hours of sleep. And possibly, to find where her mother had moved her stash of pot.

Tomorrow? Is that okay? Hazel typed. She put on her winter things and flipped her hood to brave the short walk home through the frigid air across Main Street, past the tattoo parlor and the vintage store and the used record shop and the library and the town park where an old cannon (technically a German Howitzer captured in World War I, according to Wolf) was covered with frost.

Her family was sitting in the kitchen at the remains of dinner as if there were nothing terribly unusual about Hazel meeting with a Pulitzer-Prize-winning journalist.

"How was it?" asked her father.

"What was Becky like?" asked her mother. "What was she wearing? What did she say?"

"Who cares?" said Wolf, who considered print a dead medium. "It's not like you're going to be on TV," said Wolf. "Will you?"

"TV? No," said Hazel. "I don't think so. The article isn't really going to be about me, anyway. It's not really about White, either. Or Riverburg. Becky's talking to a lot of high school kids around the country who've been through something like this. Like I said from the beginning, this happens everywhere, all the time."

32

the snowy day

Hazel woke and dozed and woke again, wondering why her parents hadn't gotten her up for school. Then she remembered the forecast and swiped her bedroom curtain, and there it was. Inches stacked upon inches of fresh Maine snow and a sky filled with fluffy flakes that reminded her of the cutout snowflakes she used to scissor when she was younger. A snow day.

She grabbed her phone, saw the text from Becky Singer flash on her locked screen, and several earlier texts from her parents alerting her to the school closure, didn't click on any of them, and instead pulled on a big sweater she'd stolen from her mother and went down to breakfast, craving coffee and carbs.

If Hazel could never leave the house, if she could stay inside the warm confines of Pine Street and her parents' care, she could pretend for the day that her life was something close to normal. Winter in Maine was like living inside a snow globe. Long johns and wool socks and pointy icicles hanging down their windows and her mother forcing her thick hand creams on them, and weekend upon weekend with nothing to do. Mornings with

Wolf staring out the kitchen window watching the snow fall and cling to the branches of the backyard pines. Pickle snoring by the stove. Her mother weaving an actual RUG for Hazel's dorm room. The reality of what she'd set in motion so far away. During the long winter it felt like everything came to a stop.

Hazel had known that the story was coming. She'd met with Becky weeks ago and had spoken on the phone with her and Erin a bunch of times since. They'd let her know when the piece would run and made sure she was okay with what it laid out. But it was one thing to understand in the abstract that you were about to appear in a *New York Times* story and another thing entirely to see your name on their home page. At least she wouldn't have to show her face at school for another twenty-two hours. Hazel doubted that many kids at Riverburg High read the *Times*, but they'd see this.

She wasn't ready to read the article, at least not before breakfast. As Hazel put up her toast and made coffee, her phone buzzed on the counter. An incoming call followed by a voice mail followed by a text. Sadie. She turned the phone facedown.

"You're in the *New York Times*," Wolf said, without looking up from the video game he'd been playing.

"It's out?" said her mother. "Let me see that. When did this happen?"

"Do I look like a clock?" said Wolf.

"Why you didn't tell me?" continued their mom. "While I've been sitting here the whole time?"

"Your phone," said Wolf. "Someone's calling you."

"I *know*," said Hazel. "I have *ears*."

"Who is it?" asked her mother. "Is it press? You don't have to answer."

"Must be someone old," Wolf guessed. "If they're calling instead of texting."

"I guess so," said Hazel, checking. "It's Sadie."

"Oooh. Your 'agent' is on the phone," said Wolf, pausing his game to deploy air quotes.

Hazel gave him the finger while her mom wasn't looking.

"Are you avoiding her?" asked her mother.

"I'm not *avoiding* her. I just woke up."

"You don't have to do anything you don't want to do," said her mother, while anxiously reading her phone and making weird noises at different points in the article.

"Yes, you do," said Wolf. "We want your money."

"What do you care? This has nothing to do with you."

"The more you get for the book, the less Mom and Dad need to spend for your college, the more they can spend on me."

"It's touching how much you care about me."

"Ha ha. But seriously, you should know that child stars rarely make the transition to adult fame."

"I'm not trying to be *famous*, Wolf."

"I don't get why this is even a story. Isn't #MeToo over?"

"Don't be naïve. That shit's never going to be over."

"Shh," said her mom. "I'm trying to concentrate."

"What do you mean you don't want to be famous? You want to be a writer, don't you?"

"They're not the same thing. I'm into books, okay? I happen to like *to read*. So yeah, maybe I want to be a writer. I'm not out to be some influencer."

"You can't make a living as a writer," said Wolf.

"I haven't even gone to college yet. Why don't you quit sixth grade and go to business school if you're so worried about money?" said Hazel.

"Who cares about some principal in Riverburg? I don't see how you can write a book about something that didn't happen."

"Well Sadie Lansky disagrees with you," said their mother. "She thinks Hazel has a book in her. Hazel. My god. This is incredible. You killed it. You're a rock star. Take that, Dick White! I just hope this snow isn't getting in the way of the newspaper deliveries to the supermarket. I have to tell Daddy to get every copy of the paper he can find on his way home."

"Why do we need print copies? For kindling?" said Wolf. "Are we literally living in the nineteenth century?"

"Wolf, go put away your laundry."

"In a minute."

"That's what you said yesterday. And the day before."

"My clothes are fine in the hamper."

"Dad says putting things away in drawers is a social convention," Hazel said, taking a bite of toast. She'd lived this battle.

"I'm glad to hear you two agree on something. Can you both please enjoy your snow day? And, Wolf, congratulate your sister? This is a big deal. It's not every day you're in the newspaper. Hazel, sweetie, how do you feel about the story?"

"I haven't read it yet."

"'Cause you're so into *reading*," said Wolf.

"Wolf, be nice or no screens."

"Okay, okay. Sorry," said Wolf. "Hazel, seriously. Congratulations. It's cool."

"Um. You two are making me truly uncomfortable. I'm going back upstairs. I have a paper due Friday. Can you please be normal?"

"Will you call Sadie back? And Daddy is desperate to talk to you, too."

"Mom. Please. Calm down."

She wasn't so much avoiding Sadie as avoiding the article. Still, in what universe was she not taking her literary agent's calls? She brought her coffee up the two flights of stairs and was debating whether to read or not when her phone rang again.

"Sorry to stalk you. It's Sadie."

Hazel hadn't been to Sadie's office yet. She imagined walls lined with bookshelves, everyone in black-framed glasses and blazers with strong shoulders. "Did I get you in trouble by calling during school?"

"No, it's okay. We have a snow day. There's supposed to be two feet."

"Oh! How Ezra Jack Keats. Here we're having flurries but nothing's sticking. It'll be sludge on my boots by lunchtime," said Sadie. "So! Let's talk. What do you think of Becky and Erin's story? Are you happy with how it turned out?"

"I haven't read it yet," said Hazel. "I woke up a few minutes ago."

"You haven't? Well, it's good, Hazel. It's really, *really* good."

Hazel's stomach turned.

"—Hazel, this changes things. I want to take you—your book, your proposal—out as soon as humanly possible."

"But I don't have a book. I don't have a proposal. Sadie, I'm so sorry but I haven't really started on the stuff you told me to write—I don't even have one of the sample chapters—"

"Let me stop you right there. I'm rethinking all that. After *The Clip* and how well you did on *Making the Rounds* a few weeks ago and now Becky's story... I'm thinking we don't need an overstuffed seventy-five-page proposal. We have your original essay. We have the *Times* piece and all the coverage that will get. We have *you*. I can see us going to auction and then looking at how much interest we can generate in LA. And I do think this is highly optionable. A limited series with one of the streamers, ideally. We could go straight to the studios. Or we can see if a creator slash producing partner like Piper Clarkson wants to buy it. Which would be amazing for your book, too. Given her book club. Why don't you sit down and pound out some pages? Five pages. Ten pages, whatever you can manage. An About the Book section explaining why it matters. Chapter summaries. Super short. A couple sentences each. I'll help you. We'll write it together. We can do it tag team in a Google Doc. How does that sound?"

"I don't know. I have an AP social studies paper due on Friday and a stats midterm next Monday."

"Hazel," said Sadie, sounding like a cross between her mother when she was annoyed at her for not cleaning her room, and Luna, when Hazel wasn't up for an after-party at some random's apartment. "I don't want to take you out of your day-to-day. I truly don't. But this is a once-in-a-lifetime thing. Could you talk to your teachers? Could I? Could your parents? It's your second semester senior year."

"I don't know if my parents really want me to do this," said Hazel. "My teachers definitely won't understand."

"I could try? With your parents," said Sadie, "but maybe that's too much. I want to work with you, but on your terms. I want to meet you where you are, but you have to want it. Because writing a book is really hard."

Did she have anything more to say? Did she have the energy left to say it? Maybe what she wanted was to go back to being a normal girl. She needed to think for a second.

Maybe she was okay with not being special. Maybe she didn't want to be the brave person everyone thought she was. Maybe she didn't want to be famous. Maybe she didn't even want to be a writer. Maybe she wanted to stay in the Pine Street attic snow globe forever. Or, at least, until college.

But also? What if this was her big shot? A once-in-a-lifetime one, like Sadie had said. Maybe this was her literary destiny.

"I want it," she answered.

The energy on the phone line shifted. She imagined Sadie swiveling her chair.

"Hazel Greenberg Blum, let's get you a book deal."

Hazel got off the phone and into the shower and returned to the bedroom with a towel wrapped around her body and another around her hair and checked her phone for new incoming messages from Sadie. She considered plundering her mother's pot stash—something she hadn't done in a while—but fumbling around in the basement in pursuit of a 10:00 a.m. wake and bake seemed a little too hardcore stoner.

Instead, Hazel got back into bed with her laptop. *Fuck it.* She pulled up the *New York Times* article. She forced herself to read it—a fast scan, bracing for anything truly terrible, and a second time through, digesting the weight of the story. Sadie and her mom were right. It was brilliant. Becky and Erin reported on what happened to Hazel and then went deeper into investigating Richard White's pattern of behavior at Riverburg High, and how White had pulled his pedophiliac teacher act before with the two high school girls in Vermont. They profiled other small town school districts, one in Oregon, and another in Texas, where something similar had happened. She was about to write a thank-you note to the reporters when she received a long-awaited (to the point of almost being obnoxious?) message from Noah (!) wanting to know, of all the things, her shoe size.

7, Hazel texted back.

I'll come to you. Noah wrote. With snowshoes and cross-country skis. You can try both.

You're prepared. Do you run a ski store in your spare time or something?

College has free rentals. I'll throw them in the back of my truck.

Don't you have class?

Only one today and it's canceled. My prof lives in Portland.

She started typing... I have this thing to do for my and then deleted and started over. How many times would someone she'd been thinking about every night before bed for months offer to take her clomping through a full-on winter wonderland?

K, come

On my way

Before she could change her mind or dwell on the fact that she *didn't know how to ski*, or that Noah, a student journalist, had reached out to her the day her *New York Times* story had dropped, Hazel got her mom's permission to wear her recently acquired vintage cherry-red Bogner snowsuit. Hazel was pulling on a base layer when her phone pinged.

Look out the window

Already? Noah was below, holding up a pair of snowshoes. They weren't the old-school wooden ones Hazel imagined; they were plastic and purple. Hazel waved, and then let the curtain drop from her hand and turned to the mirror to give herself a hard look. She brushed her hair and eyebrows with her fingers and smoothed on lip balm and plunked a pink pom hat on her head and that would have to be that. Running down the two flights of stairs, she grabbed gloves out of the warm things bin and took a gulp of orange juice from the fridge on her way out.

"Where are you going?" said Wolf.

"Snowshoeing. Or maybe skiing," said Hazel.

"Cool. With who? Your imaginary friend?"

Hazel didn't exactly keep a full social calendar in Riverburg.

"A kid from the College. You don't know him."

"I think it's great that Hazel made a friend," said her mother, rather patronizingly, Hazel thought, as if she and her brother were condemned to be social pariahs for life.

"You're going *outside* with *a boy*? It's a blizzard," said Wolf. "Are you crazy? You'll die out there."

Hazel laughed. "Live a little, Wolfie."

★ ★ ★

She made her way through the already knee-deep snow to where Noah was waiting, leaning on his truck parked on Pine Street at the tip of the yet-to-be-plowed driveway. He wasn't looking down at his phone, which impressed Hazel. He was studying the tree branches, heavy with white.

"Hey," said Noah.

"Hey," said Hazel.

Noah was wearing jeans.

"My mom says jeans are death cloth in the snow. Aren't you afraid you'll fall?" Hazel asked.

"I won't fall," said Noah. "How are you feeling about this? If you're stressed, let's start with snowshoeing—it's basically walking, but with bigger feet."

"I'm not stressed," said Hazel. But she did feel ridiculous in her one-piece snowsuit, like she was dressed for a day on the Alps. "Where are we going?"

"I thought we could start here. Since they haven't plowed yet."

"Here? Where?"

"In the street. We can ski your neighborhood. You'll see. It'll be fun. Trust me?"

"Why don't you start by showing me how to put the skis on? I've never done this before."

She fell. A lot. The puffy snowsuit came in handy. It said something about Noah, Hazel thought, that he wasn't a dick about teaching her to ski. In fact, he was patient. Sweet. A good teacher. Hazel attempted the mostly flat, empty streets around her house, with Noah behind her making sure she was okay. And she was. With his instruction, after several false starts, she made it through one complete pass around the block without falling, and experienced a minute or two of feeling like she was gliding, like she was one with the snow. An hour or so later, they circled back and sat down on the porch, unclipping their skis, Hazel's cheeks as pink as her pom hat. She unzipped the front of her snowsuit.

"You're a fast learner," said Noah. "Do you want to try the snowshoes? It's much easier. We could snowshoe downtown. See what's open?"

"Maybe?" she said.

"Maybe?" Noah turned to Hazel. He brushed the snow off her hat. She put her hand on the leg of his jeans, near his knee.

"Are you cold?" she asked. He didn't answer. Instead, he placed his hand on the small of Hazel's back, sending wintry fireworks down her spine and goose bumps up her arms. She moved her hand two inches up his thigh. Noah's lips were plump and pillowy. She slipped her hand into his back pocket and pressed herself closer to him. Noah brushed Hazel's hair to the side of her neck and began doing something mysterious and wonderful around her right ear, tracing a path with his nose and tongue and breath down her neck and across her collarbone. Hazel kissed Noah and Noah kissed Hazel and neither could have said who kissed who first. All she knew was that if she didn't kiss him in that snowstorm, Hazel felt like she would have died.

"Do you want to come in?" she asked eventually. "For hot chocolate?"

Noah nodded and kissed her one more time.

They shed their boots on the porch and went into the fortuitously empty kitchen and warmed Wolf's chocolate milk over the stove.

"Why did you come to the College? You seem, I don't know..." Hazel let her voice trail off.

"What? Weirder?"

"Cooler," said Hazel. She blushed and backtracked. "I mean, less standard."

"Well, thanks. Once you know me better, you'll see I'm basically a big dork. Just not in the normal way of people at the College. I do yoga in my dorm room. I came because of the art history department. There were some professors here I wanted to work with. That, and the huge scholarship."

Hazel had forgotten Noah was on that much financial aid. He had his truck, not a late-model luxury SUV, but she figured that was because he wasn't a douche. Nor had Hazel considered coming to college to work with a particular professor. She thought of professors as her father's friends.

"That's cool," said Hazel. Could she even speak? Could she come up with anything other than *cool*?

"By the way, I read your essay. And I heard your podcast, too. They were dope."

"Oh," said Hazel. Her stomach dropped. Was that why Noah called? For her story?

"Did I say something wrong? We don't have to talk about it. I'm just standing here in awe of you and so I wanted to get that out of the way."

"Don't be," said Hazel. "You would have done the same thing. Anyone would have."

"Doubtful. Where's your dad, by the way? Are your parents home? Will they think it's okay that I'm here?"

"I don't know. Maybe? They're around. They're always around."

"I have to say I was really into your father's class. I tried to take him again this semester, but there was a wait list. He's a great teacher. Maybe the best I've had at the College so far."

"For real? He can be kind of annoying at home."

Noah reached toward her and pulled some fuzz off her shirt. Hazel got shy and turned her back to him, pouring the hot chocolate into mugs.

"Sure. Parents can be. You're lucky to have two who love you, though. And who are both, like, alive. And together."

Oh shit. Hazel had somehow temporarily forgotten about Noah's father. She was such an asshole. Hazel had never thought about her parents that way. She supposed she was lucky.

"Hey," he said. "Come here."

Noah was leaning on the kitchen counter and pulled her toward him. She hoped her mother was far away working in her studio or doing laundry in the basement and that Wolf had his headphones on. She hoped her breath was decent. Noah exuded a sort of feral heat that burned her fingertips when she touched his skin. Or even his clothes.

"On second thought," said Hazel. "Let's not do the kitchen." She took his hand and led him toward the barn, where nobody would think to look for them, but they started kissing again and got sidelined by the slightly lower baking counter, which was the exact right height for their work.

He unzipped her snowsuit to her waist. She shrugged off his sweater. They were down to base layers, his hand moving up to her bra, when she flinched. Something felt off. Hazel couldn't put her finger on it, but she couldn't ignore it, either. Maybe it was that the huge window to the backyard and street beyond was right there? Maybe it was the suspect timing. Becky's article publishing and Noah's text on the same morning felt like it couldn't be a coincidence. Or maybe Hazel was paranoid.

"Noah, I can't." She pushed him away an inch or two.

"What's up? Am I doing something wrong?"

Was he doing something wrong? Part of her felt he was perfect. Part of her thought Noah might as well have been wearing a press pass around his neck.

"I'm sorry," she said. She pivoted and got up off the counter, crossing the room to the kitchen door.

"It's okay."

"I'm just tired, I guess. From skiing? I think you should maybe go?" She'd probably hate herself for this the minute he left. What was she going to do instead? Watch more *Gilmore Girls*? But it was true, she didn't want him to be there anymore. She didn't know why.

33

shit keeps happening

From the New York Times. *I'm Michael Barbaro. This is* The Daily. *An hour and twenty minutes north of Portland, in Riverburg, Maine, population 14,700, a town has been rocked by a scandal that started on the first day of school. Today, I spoke with my colleagues,* New York Times *reporters Becky Singer and Erin Flattery, and we'll be hearing some of their conversation with high school student Hazel Greenberg Blum. It's Monday, March 18.*

Hazel turned the car radio off.

"*Mom*. No way. Not with me in the car."

"Sorry."

Since the temperatures had dropped to subfreezing subhuman lows, her mother had been driving her to school. (Hazel really needed to get her license.) Becky had let her know that *The Daily* would be running the episode on their story that Monday morning. But hearing the pod on the way to school was too much. Unsettling, bordering on panic-attack-inducing. By the time Hazel made it to her locker and gave her phone a last check, her email was once again exploding.

President Hill had written a note both congratulating her and checking in. Rabbi Abraham texted (again) wanting to see how she was holding up and asking if she was free for a shabbat walk that Saturday, or a coffee at The General one afternoon earlier in the week. There was a note from Maxine Joy, too. This was the first time Hazel had heard from her since their back-and-forth about *The Clip*.

Dear Hazel,

Well done. So glad that worked out with The Clip, and terrific to see Becky Singer's piece in the NYT. Important work—both of you. The Hazels of the world will save us all. Keep in touch?

Cheers,
Max Joy

Keep in touch?! Hazel hardly had time to process. Emails kept coming in, filling her inbox. Emails that were making Hazel LOSE HER SHIT.

From: Michelle Ruiz
To: hazelgreenbergblum@gmail
Subject: Vogue

Dear Hazel,

I hope you don't mind my reaching out. I was moved by your story in the NYT and inspired by your essay in The Clip. I'm working on a piece for Vogue about young activists making their mark. Do you have time for a phone interview sometime this week? PS How would you feel about being shot by a Portland-based photographer?

All my best,
Michelle

From: Stella Bugbee
To: hazelgreenbergblum@gmail
Subject: NYT Styles

Hi Hazel, I'm the NYT Styles editor. I'd love to have one of my writers profile you for the section. And I'd love to say hello and tell you more. I'm available to chat by phone or Zoom or text or WhatsApp or any other mode of modern communication. Can't wait to talk if that's something you're up for! Stella

Subject: possible Talk of the Town piece for the New Yorker
From: Naomi Fry
To: hazelgreenbergblum@gmail

Hey Hazel. I'm a new fan of yours, and a staff writer at the New Yorker. I write about popular culture and am wondering if we could talk. Are you familiar with the Talk of the Town pieces we run at the front of the print magazine? A reporter spends some time with a subject, usually hanging out in her 'natural habitat' (mine would be my couch with my laptop burning my thighs, for example, ha) and writes a short profile. I want to write about you!! What do you think? Could be in Maine or in Brooklyn, since you're from here. I'm up for a road trip. Are you by any chance into thrifting? N

Fuck YEAH. Hazel kicked her locker triumphantly. Was this real life? To think that in a matter of months she'd gone from random Brooklyn kid to someone the *New York Times* and the *New Yorker* wanted to talk to?? And VOGUE WANTED TO SHOOT? This was next-level, are we living in a simulation bullshit.

By lunch, other requests—forwarded from Sadie—were piling up: The *Portland Press Herald* wanted a comment. Jewish publications like *Lilith* and *The Forward* and *Hey Alma* were working the Jewish girl in small-town "interstitial antisemitism" angle. Cup of Jo wanted to chronicle a week of Hazel's outfits. (That one was just weird. Did their readers really need to see her rotation of leggings and sweatshirts?)

There were also emails from girls and women who wrote thanking her, telling her their stories, about teachers and coaches and *parents* and stepparents who had done to them what Dick White tried to do to her. Some of them had told and most of them hadn't.

Hazel stuffed her phone into the bottom of her tote and made it to class by the bell. Nobody at school said anything about the *Times* article aside from Alex and Mira, who offered their awkward congratulations after AP Gov. But Alex maybe liked her, and Mira had to be nice because her mother was Hazel's mother's doctor. The rest of the student body, and the entire RSH faculty: 1. Didn't care? And 2. Minded their own business. Which was fine with Hazel.

But while the kids at school didn't read the *New York Times*, somehow they'd gleaned that Hazel was now temporarily famous. Pockets of support were emerging for her—among the orchestra and chorus kids, the LGBTQ+ club, drama kids, the speech and debate team, and more. The haters were out there, too, but they were less vocal. Alex Andrews wrote a long, gushy story in the school paper. Mira asked her over for another study group.

She appreciated the change, sure. But it felt cheap and fake. How was she supposed to know whether people were into her or her newfound attention?

Which is why Hazel was surprised when April approached her. April had been low-key nice to Hazel since school started but their conversations had never gotten very deep. Sort of like she had with Noah, Hazel felt guarded and skeptical. (Was this her new thing? To distrust anyone who was nice to her, or showed an interest in her? Thanks for the memories, Dick White.)

"I need to talk to you," said April, putting her backpack on both her shoulders and pointing to a dreary corner of the library, away from the table where they normally sat in companionable silence. "In private."

Hazel had the feeling that she was in trouble. "Okay," she said, following April.

"To be honest, I've been wanting to talk to you for months. Pretty much since the first day of school."

"You have?" said Hazel.

I need to talk to you about my sister, explained April. White had done this to her, too. Three years before, when Dakota was a senior. Had Dakota gone through with it? Was she okay? April didn't elaborate on the details, and Hazel didn't press.

And then April asked Hazel a question. *Would Hazel maybe like to meet her?*

Did she? Possibly. But she wasn't sure.

34

in

Hazel was in.

Hazel. Got. In. To. Vassar. VASSAR!

She didn't get in everywhere. She was rejected from Columbia, which was, whatever. Fine. She was rejected from Brown, too. (Not that she wanted to go to Brown. She'd applied last-minute because her father asked her to a gazillion times.) But she was in at NYU, Oberlin, Wesleyan, Bennington and Iowa. She only cared about Vassar. Which, while arguably not "the best" school on her list, was where she saw herself becoming Hazel. Where readers became writers. Where a twenty-dollar commuter train could take you to the city for the day and back again to your (almost) ivory tower.

A few days later, Bennington sent a certified letter offering her a merit scholarship. In conjunction with the College's tuition help, that would leave Hazel and her family with a zero-dollar tuition bill—a virtual free ride (there was still the not insignificant cost of room and board)—making it cheaper than attending the University of Maine. Hazel started wavering until later that same day when Vassar's dean of admissions called to personally apologize for the early decision deferral: an *oversight, one they felt terrible about.* Oh, and Vassar wanted to know what aid packages she'd received elsewhere, saying they'd *work with her* and that cost *shouldn't be an obstacle.*

It was over. All the stress. The migraines. The itchy skin rashes. All the studying and paper writing and homework doing and late nights and worrying. High school math! Hazel was relieved but also overwhelmed. As the acceptances poured in like hot lava during an eruption, none of it seemed 100 percent real.

Her parents were over the freaking moon. (Particularly her father, who evidently had been lying when he'd said all colleges were the same.) They made her and Wolf drive an hour for Japanese food to the coast to celebrate. Her mother talked about how, when Hazel was a baby, she'd insisted on being read the Robert Louis Stevenson poems in *A Child's Garden of Verses* over and over, and how she was destined for "literary greatness." While Wolf made barf noises, her dad let her have a few sips of sake and toasted her "stunning achievement."

Except it wasn't hers. Not at all. It was his. Dick White's. Because Hazel knew, and her parents had to know unless they were kidding themselves—and the whole world probably knew—that Hazel had taken a few (legitimately screwed-up) terrible minutes of her life and squeezed them dry like her mother squeezed her morning grapefruits. Down to the pulp. She hadn't gotten in to Vassar on her own. She'd needed the principal's help.

The real question was: Who would have wanted her if White hadn't?

35

auction

It's time, Sadie texted Hazel late one school night in early April, like they were about to have a baby, or try Molly or something.

Hazel and Sadie had gone back and forth on a million versions of the book proposal, draft after draft, until Sadie declared they were done. Turned out a tight ten pages took a lot of work. The plan was for Hazel to come down to the city for meetings with interested book editors at their publishing houses. Sadie said she was too mediagenic not to introduce around in person.

Sadie had already explained the submission process to Hazel. Sadie would come up with her list of editors to send the proposal to—and make calls and send out emails to make sure said editors wanted to see it. (And *they will*, reassured Sadie. She'd been hyping Hazel over breakfasts and lunches and drinks, and editors were practically begging to be on Sadie's submission list.) They'd have a few days, or a week or two tops, depending how the timing played out, to read, fall in love with the proposal (and Hazel), and convince their bosses to get behind the idea of making a substantial bid. They might have three interested editors, or five or—who knows?!—eight or ten. There could be an auction for the book. Or there might be a preempt—a take-it-or-leave-it offer put on the table before the auction. Anything could happen, Sadie said. Some editorial teams might be skeptical about Hazel's age, or the thinness of the proposal, or question whether her story was enough to become a book. Some editors would drop out before bidding began, others during. Others would pass altogether.

"All we need is one offer," Sadie had said, when she sent her submission list to Hazel the previous Friday afternoon. Hazel had no idea if she was keeping expectations low or being overly optimistic. The idea that a big deal editor would want to buy her (unwritten) "book" seemed somewhere between doubtful and absurd.

It's happening, Sadie texted that Monday morning. Now.

Hazel wasn't supposed to come to New York for meetings for another week. She was going to ride the bus down herself, and Sadie (via Lansky Literary) was putting her up at a scene-y hotel in Brooklyn. Her first time ever in her own hotel room. Or in a hotel in New York City for that matter. She and Luna were planning the sleepover to end all sleepovers.

Should I buy my bus ticket? Hazel texted.

There's a LOT of interest. I think we should move the auction up. I'd like to skip the meetings and do this first thing tomorrow morning. Are you okay with that?

...

Hazel started writing back, then stopped.

Sadie called. "Hey, HGB? Are you with me? Are you okay?" Sadie was basically the only person Hazel spoke to on the phone, besides her parents calling her down to dinner.

"I'm fine," answered Hazel.

"You sure?" asked Sadie. The nice thing about Sadie was she really cared. Or seemed to.

Hazel performed a quick inventory. Her head hurt, her throat was sore, she was stressing about not hearing back from a text she'd gotten the nerve to send Noah (an emoji of hiking boots and another of a mountain). She was sick of her family and simultaneously scared to death of living on her own next year, much less of having to write a *book*. And she couldn't stop thinking about her conversation with April.

"I'm okay," said Hazel. "Totally okay." The last thing she wanted to do was disappoint Sadie.

"We're good?" said Sadie. "We're on the same page here?"

"We're good," said Hazel. But deep down, she wasn't so sure.

"Okay!" She heard Sadie start typing on her laptop. "Let me go work my magic."

The next morning, six editors, representing their respective publishing houses, entered the auction. Hazel kept up with the action on her phone, hidden inside her textbooks, and during illicit, liberally self-bestowed bathroom breaks and between classes. By environmental studies and the second round, three remained. Don't worry, texted Sadie. By AP Lit and the third round, there were two final offers on the table.

Hazel felt her phone's insistent Sadie buzz in the back pocket of her jeans—her phone was now basically a walkie-talkie with Sadie—and took the call in an empty corner of school hallway, silently daring White's temporary replacement, Mr. Fowler, to walk by and have a problem with it.

Two editors had, with Sadie's guidance, landed on the same number. One was an older man with a long history of nonfiction *New York Times* bestsellers. The second, according to Sadie, was a younger powerhouse executive editor at a covetable and prestigious imprint, Now Books, and exactly where they wanted to be.

Hazel was sort of embarrassed by the offer? She couldn't dare speak the number. It was the kind of money one shouldn't touch at her age. Except for the obvious. College. Whatever the details of the financial aid or scholarship package she wound up with, between the book deal and her dad's tuition benefit? She could pay for Vassar herself. Only now that the book money was on the verge of being hers, she felt frugal and thriftier with it. Like giving it to a private college was throwing it away.

The best thing that had happened to Hazel in her entire life—that might ever happen for the rest of her life!—had just gone down.

So why did she feel like a fraud?

36

hazel takes meetings

She woke to a delicious darkness. She was alone. She had no idea what time it was. It could have been four in the morning, or noon. She knew she had to pee. For a split second, she forgot who she was. Then she remembered and reached for the remote, which opened the scrim-like curtains covering floor-to-ceiling windows to reveal a panorama of the Hollywood Hills complete with palm trees and a clear view of the Hollywood sign. She was met by an unwavering, almost oppressive, California sunshine on the other side of the curtain.

Hazel grabbed her phone and made it to the bathroom. Her parents and Wolf were downstairs getting coffee and hot chocolate.

We didn't want to wake you. Back in room in 5! Want an overpriced juice?

Hazel couldn't believe she was here, at The Edge Hotel in Koreatown, the four Greenberg Blums heading later that morning to meet Sadie Lansky at the Chateau Marmont. Lately things had gotten rather out of control. The *New York Times* article. The Talk of the Town *New Yorker* profile. But *this*? LA was next-level.

Because Hazel had *meetings* to take. Hollywood meetings. She showered and dressed, met her family in the lobby, and the Greenberg Blums got in their rental car and drove.

Hazel didn't need, or necessarily want, her parents to accompany her to the Chateau, much less tag along with her for the entire day. She definitely didn't want Wolf involved. But there they all were, pathetically enough, because her mother and father had insisted, and Wolf had begged and cried and yelled that they were RUINING HIS FUTURE AND HIS ENTIRE LIFE if they didn't let him come, too.

Parking on Sunset was a nightmare, but her dad somehow found a space. Claire was wearing one of her denim jumpsuits, Gus was in jeans and a rolled-up-at-the-sleeves pink button-down, his usual, but with sunglasses and desert boots. Wolf had on sweat shorts and a T-shirt because that's all he'd brought to California.

Hazel was unexpectedly sweaty in her pussy bow dress. Sadie awaited them in the front courtyard—also jumpsuited, hers a lighter, more LA-friendly fabric than her mother's, an oatmeal linen—staring into the abyss of her phone.

"Hey there," she said when she saw them, hugging Hazel and shaking hands with Claire and then Gus, and half-jokingly with Wolf. "Are you folks ready? What a day this is going to be!"

First up was this breakfast with Sadie's go-to film and television agent, Josh Berkowitz. Whose assistant had texted, with apologies, that—traffic—Josh was running ten to twenty behind schedule, giving Hazel a welcome chance to catch her breath and be briefed by Sadie, who reported the latest while they waited.

Sarah Silverman, supposedly, was "obsessed" with attaching herself to the project and had requested a one-on-one with Hazel later that day. Kathryn Hahn had expressed real interest in the role of Claire, too, though she was said to have top secret, non-negotiable scheduling issues. There was talk that Mikey Madison would make a great Hazel. Or perhaps the young star of *Yellowjackets*. Most importantly, Piper, the actress-turned-book-club-maven-turned-producer, as they knew, had *loved* her package (the clips and the book proposal Sadie had put together), and her entire team at Morning Glory was said to be "hungry" to tell Hazel's story. It was Piper's producing partner who had suggested the trip out west.

"Hellllloooooo!" said Josh, entering the garden courtyard, offering cheek kisses to Hazel and Claire and Sadie, and hugs all around to everyone but Wolf, who got a fist bump.

"How *are* you guys? How were your flights? Did you sleep? Hope this is okay?" He gestured around the storied hotel restaurant as if it was his local diner. "Since you're staying on the east side, I figured the Chateau made most sense. We'll make our way to Piper's offices in Santa Monica after the traffic clears up. And then circle back to West Hollywood."

He handed out copies of the day's schedule, one for Hazel and one for each of her parents. They ordered breakfast. Eggs and potatoes and toast for the kids. Huevos rancheros for Gus. Juices and pastry for Claire and Sadie. The smoked salmon plate for Josh, with the inside of his bagel scooped out.

Josh acted like he'd known Hazel forever. He'd read everything. The *Clip* essay, of course. The Talk of the Town. The *NYT*. Even the *Record*. He'd listened to the *Making the Rounds* podcast, or claimed he had. Which was more than she could say for her father.

"Hazel," said Josh, while raising a friendly hand toward the waiter and pointing to his almost empty coffee, "I love you."

"You do?"

"Well, what you've done. How brave you are. Chutzpah, am I right?" He looked to Gus for Jew backup.

"Well, she hasn't written the book yet," said Gus, skeptical. Whether of Hazel or Josh, or Hollywood as a whole, it was unclear.

"Not to worry," said Josh, brushing a swoop of hair off his face. "We have full faith and confidence in Hazel's ability to pull this off. And we'll have people working on the screenplay or breaking scripts in the writers' room, whatever form this ends up taking." He turned back toward Hazel. "Hazel, this is *your* life. *You* should be involved in every decision. At least the big ones. At least initially. Here's the question. What story do you want to tell? And are you open to all platforms? Because it's best to be open."

"Me?" said Hazel.

"Yes YOU. Who else? These producers and development people want to meet YOU. They've read about you. They've been following your story. They see their daughters in you."

If Hazel wasn't the one who would write the TV show, she didn't see why meeting her mattered. Wasn't Hazel, or her character anyway, a sort of stand-in for an everygirl?

"I never want to overpromise. In fact, my *thing* is not overpromising. But I think we have lots of potential for an adaptation. As you know, Piper Clarkson is our first stop this morning. Well, not Piper herself, she's filming today, unfortunately, but her producing partner Prudence Lopez and their development director Cassy Altman are in town. If not for Piper to act in, for her to produce. Piper is literally the best when it comes to adapting books for screen. Have you seen *Mrs. Dalloway*?"

"My mom watches that show."

"Lisa Bonet is the coolest," said Claire. "I inhale it."

"We'll head there in five. Anybody for an iced coffee to go?"

They caravanned to Santa Monica: Sadie's kind of ridiculous, kind of awesome rented convertible, the Greenberg Blums' normal person boring sedan rental, and Josh's BMW SUV. The Morning Glory offices were like a West Coast Schvitzhaus with natural light and potted succulents. On white furniture with pops of empowering color, stressed-out industry twenty- and thirtysomethings typed on laptops while nursing caffeinated drinks in oversized mugs.

The crazy thing about the Morning Glory meeting with Cassy and Prudence was that *they* were trying to sell *her* on working with *them*. They introduced Hazel around the office as if she was a big deal. They embraced Hazel (literally and figuratively) and talked about her as though she'd done something. (There was a lot of discussion of her "story" that day. And about it "mattering.") Which felt sort of amazing? But, also, like she was on a mushroom trip. After she'd met half a dozen staff members and said hi to some assistants, Hazel was seated with Sadie to her right and Josh to her left at the glassed-in conference room's oversized rectangular wooden table ringed by white chairs on rollers. She glanced at the shelves filled with color-coded hardcovers of *Piper Picks*, a designation that pretty much guaranteed a book becoming a bestseller.

"Hazel," began Cassy, stretching out the syllables before clapping her hands once in a combination of yogic prayer and kindergarten teacher enthusiasm. "Just for fun. What are you thinking when it comes to actors for these roles? What's your vision? Who's in your dream cast?"

"I've always felt a certain kinship with Mark Ruffalo," Gus admitted.

"They're both political," explained Wolf, putting political in air quotes.

"We're excited about Sarah Silverman," said Claire. "She's super interested in playing Claire. I mean, me? She sent me the most amazing letter. She says she's been looking for a meaty Jewish role for a really long time."

Josh shot her a look. Hazel glared at her mom. She knew it was a terrible idea to let her parents come.

"Is she?" said Prudence. "Well, that's fantastic. Good for her. Good for you. We love your story. We love you! And we are *in* love with Sarah. Though, we don't necessarily see her for this role. We're thinking bigger. We're thinking—now, don't quote me on this—maybe Piper herself. Or Jen."

"Aniston," clarified Cassy.

"Aniston. She's got the right mix of gumption and vulnerability. Or we could go to Julia."

"And SJP?" added Cassy.

"That's an idea! If Piper and Jen are busy. You see where we're headed? Claire is going to be a coveted role for an A-lister in her forties or fifties. And the ingenue part—you, Hazel—that's perfect for young Hollywood to vie for. We don't want to attach ourselves to the wrong name. Or the right name but the wrong, maybe less than totally ultra-perfect actor for this part, you know? Sarah is amazing but she's a much quieter choice. She's more of an indie pick when it comes to acting. More niche."

"She's still very much associated with the comedy space," explained Cassy.

"I had thought I might be more of a Rachel Weisz type," Claire said, half to herself. In her dreams.

"Mom," shushed Hazel.

When the morning was done, Josh debriefed Sadie and Hazel and Claire and Gus (and fended off a barrage of Hollywood career questions from Wolf) over a late lunch at Canter's Deli on Fairfax. For each of the Greenberg Blums, the day was exhilarating and exhausting, but Claire, for her part, felt they were in capable hands. Sadie had skills, on either coast; by the end of the day Josh proved himself to not only be a Hollywood baller but a surprisingly kind and empathic listener, contrary to Hollywood agent stereotypes. Even Gus had been charmed. Claire managed to keep her anxiety at bay about how she and Hazel would come off on film and she hadn't monopolized the conversation as Hazel worried she might. Wolf exhibited unusual impulse control. Hazel didn't say anything too revealing that she'd beat herself up about later.

For dinner, the Greenberg Blums ordered in three pizzas from a place on Melrose and ate them in bed while watching their preferred shows on separate screens, putting themselves on low-power mode, and recharging their respective, dimmed introverted extrovert (Wolf), extroverted introvert (Hazel and Claire), and introverted introvert (Gus) batteries. Before flying home, they'd give Wolf his promised two days at Disney, and Claire her three days in Palm Springs, at a hotel with a gigantic pool and rooms with patios and firepits. But that night in Koreatown, they slept like the dead.

37

mud season

On the first Sunday in May, Hazel woke to an epic, end times thunderstorm. She went to turn her light on, but the bulb was out. Her desk lamp wouldn't work, either. An electrical outage, she realized. She released the blind. An enormous tree had fallen across Pine Street, taking down part of an electrical pole. Where was her family? She remembered something about a doctor's appointment for Wolf. Therapist, probably. He'd need it—thunderstorms were one of his top five phobias. Before heading downstairs to scrounge for caffeine, she grabbed her phone and scrolled through her new normal cyber touchstones. For some strange psychic reason, she clicked first on the *Riverburg Record*.

FUUUUUUCCCCCKKKKK.

There it was. The thing Hazel hadn't realized she'd been dreading. Richard White had written a "Maine Voices" opinion piece.

An Open Letter to My Community

Dear friends and neighbors,

I have stayed silent for long enough. While a student I had a handful of conversations with has gained fame and fortune, I have lost my livelihood, my marriage, and my home.

The 18-year-old young woman in question here in Riverburg? She did not cry in my office that morning. She did not call for help. She did not argue or otherwise protest. She didn't seem particularly offended by our conversation. On the contrary, she was the aggressor. She put her hand on my knee. She told me I was attractive. If anything, she was the one who came on to me.

The system has declared I have done nothing illegal. All charges have been dropped.

Much has been made about other drummed up, unsubstantiated allegations. To be clear, no criminal charges have been filed against me in Vermont. In my younger teaching days, I admit, I made mistakes. It was certainly inappropriate of me, and a regrettable lapse in judgment, to exchange personal letters with a student. That said, it was a different time, and the correspondence, and our friendship, was innocent and entirely mutual. The Vermont student in question was 17. (I was in my twenties at the time.) She was the one who started the friendship between us. We shared nothing but a kiss before she came of age.

I have never assaulted, much less raped anyone. I have never forced anyone to do anything with me she didn't want to do. I have never had sex with anyone under the age of consent. Ever. Not in Maine, not in Vermont. These were consensual encounters, stupid and wrongheaded as they may have been, between myself and adult women, who had every right to say no.

That said, I take responsibility for my behavior. I pledge to learn from my mistakes. I apologize for any feelings that may have been hurt and for any harm I may have inflicted. I regret my poor judgment and apologize to my school community and the town of Riverburg.

More than anything, I apologize to my beloved daughter and my former wife and will continue to do so every day of my life. This has been a living nightmare that no girl should have to endure. She deserves privacy and respect, despite my having lost those rights myself.

I believe I have more than paid the price for my transgressions. I have been through hell and back.

When you think of me, I hope you'll remember the good along with the bad. I am still the man that was here for you and your sons and daughters, cheering on the games, managing a building renovation, adding AP classes and technical courses to the high school curriculum, organizing Soup Kitchen volunteer days. My heart will always be with the town of Riverburg, and Riverburg Senior High School.

I leave you with one note of warning. Be afraid for your husbands and your brothers and your sons. Because the Hazel Blums of the world are coming for them next.

Richard White
Riverburg, Maine

Hazel couldn't breathe. She couldn't think.

Everyone was going to believe him. At least everyone who wanted to believe him. He sounded reasonable, likable. Contrite.

Never mind that he'd admitted to seducing high school students.

Did White really think he was going to win people over with this letter? She couldn't believe he was defending his sleaziness—and coming after her—after everything he'd done, and after the Vermont women had come forward. And after the *New York Times* story! Once again, Dick White was making her feel like she had to throw up.

Reading this was worse than the day in his office. At least then the door had been shut. And she'd felt more in control of the conversation. She'd said no. Now her name had been smeared in the public record, in the *Record*. How could she show her face in Riverburg? How was she supposed to finish her senior year and graduate high school?

On the other hand, what did she expect? Especially after going public?

This was what abusers do, she reminded herself. They deny, they rage, they counterattack. They lie. They talk about witch hunts.

Hazel was sweating. The thunder and lightning sounded like they were growing closer.

Had she said or done something to make him choose her? Had she subconsciously or unwittingly come on to him? Did she put her hand on his knee without realizing it? Had the strap of her dress fallen off her shoulder, allowing her red bra to peek out? Or maybe her mistake was made earlier, that summer at the pool when they talked about books, when she admitted to maybe wanting to become a writer one day. Maybe her mistake was being friendly.

Then Hazel snapped out of it.

That was precisely his sick game. To make his victims think it was their idea. Their fault. How many times had he done this? With no repercussions? To how many girls?

Women, Hazel corrected herself. Because White had been doing this for years. Hazel was just the latest. She was determined to be the last.

Then Hazel did the worst thing: She clicked on the comments. There were forty-nine so far. (Just about all of them hateful, whether toward her or White.)

She was halfway through reading them, falling deep into a pit of despair and self-loathing, when her phone rang. A 207 Maine number not in her contacts. Without thinking, she answered. It could be nothing. A robocall from school. Or Noah calling from a random landline on campus? More likely, Hazel realized the second she picked up, it was some reporter looking for a comment. She hated herself for answering.

"Hello?" the girl on the other end said, so softly Hazel could barely make the word out. "It's Grace. Gracie White."

Shit. Shit. SHIT. *Gracie.* It sounded like she was crying.

"I hope it's okay to call? Your brother gave me your number."

"Oh, hey. Hi. Gracie, oh my god." WTF. Maybe Wolf could have *warned* her?

"I'm calling," Gracie continued, her voice straining and catching, "to ask you a favor."

"Did your dad ask you to call?"

"What? No."

"Okay. Sorry." She could feel Gracie gathering her courage.

"The stuff with my dad. I just—I don't know. I don't think I can handle it anymore. I'm calling to ask you. Can you please make it stop?"

"What's going on Gracie? Are you okay?"

"No. I'm not okay. And my mom is not okay. That's why I'm calling." Gracie was acting brave, but she was Wolf's age.

"I know you don't owe me anything, and I know what my father did was terrible, like truly terrible, but he's my dad and I'm basically like begging you. Hazel, please. Stop talking to the newspapers. Stop writing about what happened. *Please.* Stop. For me?"

As horrible and guilty as Hazel felt, she wanted to explain that this wasn't *her* fault. It was Gracie's father who was the predator, not Hazel.

"Gracie. I am so so sorry. I don't know if that's possible."

Hazel had a book deal. And everyone already knew about everything. Hazel had the right to write about what had happened between them. Didn't she? White wrote the stupid *Record* letter.

"Please?" asked Gracie.

Fuck, thought Hazel. "Let me think about it," she told Gracie.

Hazel stuck her phone in her underwear drawer and crawled back into bed, and for the first time in what felt like months, she let herself cry. Big, messy, snot-filled sobs.

38

mountain day

It was Mountain Day at Riverburg High, the annual late-spring rite of passage when classes were canceled and seniors were bussed to Camden Hills State Park. Theoretically, this should have been a good day, an improvement on sitting around school doing nothing, as Hazel's teachers had basically stopped teaching after last week's AP exams. Perfect weather, the great outdoors, nature is healing, blah blah blah. In practice, Hazel wished she'd called in sick.

Ever since they'd moved, her mother had been trying to get the family to do the Mount Battie hike, a steep ascent that eventually led to scenic coastal views. Wolf was a hard pass. He didn't like nature. Or being outside. Summer was too hot, fall too windy, winter too snowy, spring too muddy. Maybe he had a point? Hazel hadn't run in weeks and the trail felt surprisingly precarious.

The more Hazel hiked, the more her system went into neurotic overdrive. A couple of days after Gracie had called, yet another *Record* bomb dropped, this one completely enraging and maddening and unthinkable and generally crazy-making, and Hazel couldn't stop thinking about it. The newspaper reported that White had been hired as a "part-time consultant" by the school board. Because she was more than semiconscious, Hazel knew how much fucked-up shit happened in America. And something fucked-up had already happened to her in Riverburg. But the idea of people in town closing ranks to protect White was particularly vomit-inducing.

It had been a backroom deal; there'd been no opportunity for public input or discussion. A supposed "common sense" and "pragmatic" hire, or so said the school board chair when pressed for comment. White was being brought on to advise the interim high school principal on how to address falling standardized test scores and a rash of recent discipline problems. It was insane and absurd and everything that was wrong with the world. Why wasn't Riverburg up in arms about this guy?

Once again, she was wasting her time obsessing over White when she was supposed to be happy. Not just happy—ecstatic. Euphoric. Her wildest dreams had come true. She'd written an essay for *The Clip*. That had gone viral. She had a literary agent. And a Hollywood one. She'd been profiled in the *New Yorker* and had her story reported in the *New York Times*. She'd sold her "book" and at age eighteen, she had enough money from her publishing deal to not go into student loan debt and maybe even make a down payment on a studio apartment in Queens.

But Hazel wasn't happy. To be perfectly honest? With every unbelievably good thing that happened, Hazel felt more worthless.

Which, Hazel understood, made no sense. This was what she'd hoped for. She'd *wanted* to be famous. Like Wolf said. Hadn't she? No, Hazel remembered. She'd wanted to be a *writer*. Were those the same thing? Did a writer have to be famous to write? Look at Emily Dickinson. She'd kept most of her poems unpublished while she was alive. *Publication is the auction of the mind* she wrote in one. Ha. And weren't most writers normal, unfamous people? (Hadn't Kafka been an insurance clerk?) But at least part of her must have craved fame. Otherwise, she wouldn't have written the essay. Right?

Because it was so fucking important to Hazel to feel like she was special. She had to do something incredible. Noteworthy. Fame-worthy. To fulfill her parents' unmet dreams. As if her family and her house and her approaching fancy college education wasn't enough. She needed her fifteen minutes, too. She couldn't just write in her journal.

Now, suddenly, it was all too much. It wasn't only that she didn't want the spotlight; she couldn't take it anymore. Like, if she kept going and feeling this way and letting it get worse and worse by the day and hour and minute, she was going to die.

Maybe she had a hole to fill and for that year the drama around White had filled it. Maybe she didn't want to be a writer if being a writer meant sacrificing Gracie. Or giving away a piece of herself.

Alex and Mira were holding hands walking up the trail, which made Hazel a little jealous. Perhaps Alex hadn't been into Hazel or had simply moved on. Mira was the better pick. Smart and sporty and drama-free.

"Hey," said Mira. She'd cut her hair into a chin-length bob and was heading to Dartmouth and looked intimidatingly chic.

"Hey," answered Hazel, redoing her bun.

"My mom said you're seeing a guy who goes to the College. We should all hang out sometime."

Hazel hadn't heard from Noah in a couple of weeks. They'd gotten together a few times after skiing, and then he had term papers and finals and had probably lost interest. He'd texted something annoying about her "still" being in high school. An autobiographical fact she couldn't change for another month. Though, come to think of it, she was the one who owed him a text. Ever since White's letter to the editor, she hadn't felt up for one of their epic hangouts, anyway.

"Yeah, sure, maybe," Hazel said.

"What's the latest on your media tour?" said Alex, his old soccer sneakers caked in mud. Mira punched him in the stomach.

"Don't be a dick, Alex."

"Sorry."

"You're fine," said Hazel. She would never ever live this down.

No matter what Sadie said to convince or reassure her, Hazel kept feeling, in the pit of her stomach, that she was too young to write a memoir. After the auction, she'd delicately brought up these concerns to Sadie, who'd proceeded to school Hazel on the difference between writing one's *memoirs* (like Michelle Obama or Prince Harry) and writing a *memoir*, a memory, of a moment in time. Sadie pronounced "mémoire" a second time with a French accent, and assured Hazel she could produce a draft the summer between graduation and the start of college. Hazel wasn't so sure. She remembered her literary magazine advisor at School of the Future saying 1. that memoir, by nature, was a borderline self-indulgent genre and 2. that memoirists needed time to have passed between whatever happened and writing about it.

Sadie said she could do it. Sadie said she was a good writer. That she stood for so many other girls. That books—the best of them—could change lives. That Hazel should grab the chance to become an author while she had it. Sadie said she had friends from grad school who were super talented and would give anything for a book deal of their own.

Sadie said she deserved it.

Which was ridiculous? Or? Maybe Sadie was right? Maybe Hazel did deserve it? Nobody helped her write that essay. She'd sat in her attic room over Christmas break and revised the shit out of that thing.

"It's fucked-up about White," said Alex. "The consultant thing is total bullshit."

"Yeah," said Hazel.

"Have you thought about suing or something?" asked Alex.

Hazel was in decent shape from running, but the climb up the rocky trail was a workout. When they reached a mountain brook and some kid said they weren't halfway yet, Hazel had to concentrate. Her thighs burned.

She wondered what Maxine Joy would think. Professor Joy had given Hazel *The Clip* editor's email so she could tell her story, not so she could make money. Or were those two, in the publishing world, one and the same?

What if Hazel didn't deserve the book deal? It dawned on her that she'd met Maxine Joy because her father was a professor at the College. Would she have thought to read Joy's books if she'd had different parents? Certainly, 100 percent, she wouldn't have gotten her hands on a ticket to the College event. Nor would she have had the nerve to stand up and speak. She wasn't intimidated by college and professors the way she might have been, because she'd grown up with her father's friends and colleagues. Like her dad, they were normal people who were (maybe?) 10 percent smarter, had studied longer and harder, and, as her mom liked to point out, called themselves Marxists and revolutionaries while spending Julys in Mallorca and Sicily and Augusts in Fire Island and the Catskills.

It was also her father who'd taught her how to write and edit. And her mother who had read to her constantly when she was little. She wasn't born with a book in her hand. Or a pencil for that matter.

If not for her dad, she for sure wouldn't have been invited to the reception following the chapel event. She might not have known how to craft an adult-enough-sounding email back to Emma,

The Clip editor, or to Sadie. Because of her mother, she knew how to walk into Schvitzhaus and act like she belonged there.

And why were those book editors in New York willing—vying!—to give her so much money? To trust Hazel? To invest in her? Think about it, Hazel commanded herself. Why did her story merit six figures? She knew it was because she was the perfect victim. Because she was young and white and pretty. Because she was considered desirable. Believable.

The same energy that made the principal want her, that made him choose her, made the editors and their bosses, the publishers, want her, too.

They were almost at the top of the mountain when Hazel's foot slipped on a rock. She tripped and had to catch herself from full-on face-planting. A hand reached out for her. April. Hazel had been avoiding her ever since April told her about her sister Dakota.

"You okay?" April asked.

They walked the rest of the way together to the lookout point, where massive slabs made for a gigantic platform. Hazel asked about April's college plans, which was all the AP kids were talking about that spring (other than Hazel and White). April had been offered a full ride to Bowdoin; she said she couldn't really leave Maine or her family yet, for reasons that sounded difficult and complicated and private. Instead, they finally talked about April's sister, and the women her sister had connected with in recent months, thanks to Becky Singer and her reporting.

Panoramic views opened of the picturesque town below and Penobscot Bay—and the ocean, the world—beyond. For the first time that year, Hazel talked, really talked, to a kid from school. And had the urge to *do* something, not for herself or her personal ambitions or ego, but to stand up for what was right.

Together, Hazel and April came up with a plan.

39

school board showdown

The Riverburg High School media center was packed by the time Claire and Gus arrived. Standing room only. Claire motioned Gus to an open space on the carpeted floor.

The weekend before, Hazel and April and her sister Dakota had met with another survivor from Riverburg that Dakota knew, plus a woman named Amanda who'd driven in from Vermont after considerable coaxing. Hazel and Dakota and April had convinced them to get together to share their stories—and figure out if there was something they could do to block Dick White's reappointment by the school board. Gathering awkwardly in the Greenberg Blums' living room, they sipped milky coffee and strategized. Later, Claire passed out pizza and listened during the group's call with Becky Singer, who argued that their experiences mattered, no matter how awful or long ago. Giving voice to those experiences, Becky said, was an important step toward change.

Despite all they'd been through, nothing had prepared the women for the power and strength they felt coming together face-to-face that weekend. Hazel, the youngest of their small group, was the one the least had happened to, and the one the world knew the most about. Claire worried about her. About all of them.

"For a long time," Dakota said, "I thought it was me. Something dumb, like the bathing suit I wore on the rafting trip. I mean, I could have been wearing a wet suit and he probably would have gone there anyway. But, for a long time, that's what I told myself."

April hugged her sister from behind while Amanda listened and played a mellow tug-of-war with a graying Pickle, grabbing a beaten-up rope toy.

"He was my teacher for three years in a row," Amanda said eventually, after ice cream had been served. "It was a really small school and he taught almost all of the honors English classes and a social studies class. When we started getting close, or I don't know what to call it. When we started spending time together after school it wasn't weird at all. He was my brother's age. It wasn't like he was some old man or something making a move on me. Is it gross to say we had stuff in common?"

If things had been different, Claire thought, Hazel could have fallen for him, too. Not for him, but for his bullshit.

School board meetings in Riverburg were a top-down affair where community members had to sit, quietly seething, while a board chair ruled with a heavy gavel. Ostensibly, there would be time for questions and comments at some later point in the meeting agenda, but by then business might already be voted on and done, including the vote to approve Richard White's consulting work. In the days leading up to the school board meeting, Hazel and April had been doing boots-on-the-ground activism. Or, more aptly, fingers-to-the-laptop activism. They'd been building support for their cause and asking everyone they knew to turn out.

Claire surveyed the crowded room and couldn't believe it. Hazel and April's outreach had worked. It felt like everyone in Riverburg had shown up. Parents and students and teachers. President Hill. Rabbi Abraham. Student activists from the College, including, Gus pointed out, members of his Sunday night reading group, Sam among them. The *Record* reporter. Noah. Everyone but Richard White, who was clearly too much of a coward to make an appearance.

Claire had never been to a school board meeting before. Not in New York, and not since moving to Riverburg. Local democracy made her itchy. It was both monotonous and vaguely terrifying. All that power in the hands of whomever decided to donate their weekday evenings to tedium. The meeting disturbed her more, oddly, than having her daughter's story in the *New York Times*. Without the protection of journalism and editors and the emotional boundary separating writing from reality, here the Greenberg Blums were exposed. Shit could go wrong fast. And Hazel was at the very center of the potential shitstorm.

At the front of the room, a horseshoe-shaped table had been set up for the board members. Priscilla Stewart, the chair, opened the meeting by defending her decision to offer the job to White. She noted that he had apologized. She invoked the value of forgiveness and spoke about second chances. She said that the high school needed White. He was data-driven; this wasn't personal. He'd work with administrators and teachers, in *an advisory capacity*. He could stay physically off-site. He wouldn't be alone with the kids ever—certainly, Priscilla clarified, not alone with any female students.

The audience grumbled. Several parents raised their arms forcefully, demanding to be heard. Stewart banged her gavel. "We will get to comments when we get to comments. Please see the meeting agenda for the order of operations."

The women weren't given an official speaking slot. The plan was for the White survivors to use the three-minute increments allowed per community member at the end of the meeting to make their statements. But first came an interminable hour during which administrators and the board went over budgetary line items. Would the board approve five hundred dollars for new shin guards for the girls' soccer team? $6200 for new football jerseys? A new ed tech at the rate of $20.71 per hour?

When the chair at last called for community comments, it wasn't Hazel and her friends but Ed Miller who was first at the speaker's podium. "Most of you know me as Mr. Miller. I've been teaching English at Riverburg High for the past twenty-two years and working alongside Richard White for much of that time. Despite all the noise this year from families with their cushy gigs up at the College, my opinion of Richard hasn't changed. Ladies and gentlemen, Richard White, whatever you've heard, is a good man. A solid educator. He's the reason half of us at the school haven't quit our jobs yet. I'd like to see him rehired as principal, to tell you the truth. But if that's not going to happen, then I think the consultant position makes good sense."

This fucking town, thought Claire. No wonder Miller had been such a dick to Hazel all year. She saw Hazel and April squeezing hands hard, shaking their heads in disbelief.

But then a man in utility jeans—the real kind—called out, "Miller, you're full of shit." Another guy, in mechanic's overalls, who looked like he'd come straight from work, yelled, "Let the girls talk!"

"If you can't be orderly and quiet, you will be asked to leave. If necessary, I'll have you escorted out by Chief Chase and his officers," said Stewart, banging her gavel again.

Chase, chagrined, stood off to the side by the new acquisitions table, like he wasn't exactly thrilled to be the board's lackey. He had a daughter who went to Riverburg High, too.

Wolf did NOT want to stay home. He could handle a school board meeting! And so, against his parents' wishes, he abandoned his Pickle-watching duties and started walking the few blocks to the high school. Did they not realize HE HAD LEGS?! Though, to be fair, his legs had atrophied that year in Maine. Too much time on the couch. Too much time passively reading *Atlas Shrugged.* Which, he was coming to realize, wasn't what it was cracked up to be. Ayn Rand's philosophy could only take you so far. What would Rand say about a Dick White? Anarcho-capitalists didn't support an age of consent. It's not like *Atlas Shrugged* could have helped Hazel. Or these other women. Plus, it was too heavy. His arms hurt from holding it.

Even so, there was one lesson he'd learned from the book: it was his right, his *duty* to stand up to a tyrannical government. Wolf was sweaty and huffing and puffing and thirsty and STARVING by the time he got to the high school fifteen minutes later. On the walk over he'd formulated a plan: he'd charge the podium and lecture the town on the dangers of ignoring pedophiles and extremists. Yes, some part of him knew that it wouldn't necessarily be appropriate, and that his parents and sister might not fully appreciate his rant. But all winter long he'd sat on the couch and held his tongue, and he was sick and tired of it. These redneck hillbilly lobster-catcher bureaucrats were going to get a piece of his mind. Like it or not.

Pushing through a sea of adults, without stopping to see his parents, he hightailed it to the speaker's podium. "Out of my way," he mumbled, but not so loud that anyone could hear. As he went to pull a chair over so that he'd have something to stand on, in order to be visible from behind the lectern, Rabbi Abraham intercepted him.

"Wolf, hey. Can I talk to you in the hallway for a minute?" she said.

As angry and upset as Wolf was, he couldn't very well say no to the rabbi, on the off chance there was a God.

In the hallway, Wolf went off on grown men. The rabbi just listened. Then Wolf digressed into a meandering criticism of

Riverburg's downtown redevelopment plans. It would never work. Who would want to move their business to such a crappy town? "Mmmm," said the rabbi. Then the two of them stood together in silence.

"You done?" the rabbi asked.

Wolf nodded. "You know this meeting isn't your time to speak, right?" said Rabbi Abraham. "It's about the survivors." Wolf studied the Velcro tabs on his sneakers.

"I know," he said.

What Wolf saw when he followed the rabbi back inside surprised him. That entire year, he had felt like there was nobody in Riverburg who cared about him, his sister, his family, justice, or democracy, period. But as he looked around, settled in a beanbag chair, he saw his teacher Miss Polly and his drama coach and his English teacher. There was the College president that his dad was constantly talking about, and his mom's new doctor friend. He saw the guy who lived next door to them and mowed lawns for a living. And his family's across-the-street neighbor, whose brother had once been an actual United States Senator.

When at last the time came, the women, one by one, walked up to the podium and told their stories of being groomed by White. Hazel had decided not to speak; she felt like she'd said enough already. For the others, this was the first they'd talked publicly about what they'd been through.

"What's hard," began Amanda when it was her turn, "is that in a lot of ways, Richard White was really good to me. He cared when nobody else did. I know it's a cliché to say he made me feel special, but he made me feel special. It wasn't until I was older that I realized what he did to me was wrong."

Dakota got up, visibly shaky and trying to hold herself together. She was a part-time nursing student at the University of Maine. April had mentioned, in confidence, that Dakota struggled with depression. She'd been reluctant to speak but at the last minute had decided she would. "He said I wouldn't graduate if I didn't sleep with him. I just sort of shut down. During, and for a long time after, too. Once it happened, he said he'd tell my parents if I said anything.

"I have nightmares," said Dakota. "Most nights."

The room was pin-drop silent. Hazel was reminded of the chapel and Maxine Joy. The stillness that came with a rare collective clarity.

When Hazel's group was done, Priscilla Stewart tried to end the meeting but was thwarted by Riverburgians who approached the podium and formed a line that soon snaked around the media room, with current and former parents and students, and teachers too, demanding to speak in what became a growing chorus of support for the survivors, and against White's reinstatement.

After another forty-five minutes or so, Stewart said, "Enough." The meeting couldn't go on indefinitely.

Miles Franco, a board member who represented the Blums' neighborhood, called for a vote on terminating White's new consultant contract. The call was seconded. And just like that White was out, in a five-two decision, with Stewart abstaining. It should have been unanimous, but sometimes vanquishing the forces of evil, even incompletely, was the best you could do.

PART FOUR

summer in maine

40

a lucky break

Gus was melting in his cap and gown. It was eighty-eight degrees and graduation day at the College. Hotter than the sun, by far, was the email in his phone burning up his pocket. NYU Abu Dhabi, New York University's Middle Eastern outpost, had contacted him the week before—with a recruiting feeler so subtle he couldn't tell if it was one. Ever since, he and the Arts and Humanities dean, Sheila Nadaar, had been doing an ever closer and more forthright correspondence dance.

He was flattered. While sentiment on campus had shifted and his cancellation was, Gus prayed, in the rearview mirror, he couldn't help but be tempted by the idea of a fresh start halfway (or was it more?) across the globe. He'd arrived to robe in the library at nine. The email landed in his phone's inbox minutes later. It was official. Sheila wanted him to come for a job talk—the academic version of a job interview. They'd fly him (business class!) from Boston to Dubai. Once in Abu Dhabi he'd get the lay of the land, meet students and possible future colleagues, and present a lecture on his latest research. Tour the local British private school that NYU paid for faculty kids to attend. Check out the apartment complex where they'd live on campus, rent free.

Professor Nadaar preferred that Gus make the trip in the "coming days" during the brief summer semester that ran for four weeks from late May to late June. After that, she and her colleagues fled the region for cooler environs until classes started up again at the end of August.

The prospect of an NYUAD position was exciting, dazzling even, if seen in the right light. Free housing. Free private school for Wolf. The chance for his family to see the world, while paying off their debt and saving for retirement. Flights back to the States once a year for the family. Wolf could learn Arabic!

To be followed, Gus hoped, by his triumphant return to The Real NYU. That was going to be his bargaining chip once Nadaar came through with her offer. He'd agree to put in five years in the desert in exchange for an eventual transfer back to New York and everything Claire had been nagging him about since she found out she was pregnant with Hazel. NYU housing, NYU benefits. Abu Dhabi might be a circuitous route to Manhattan, but he'd take it if he had to. Which, clearly, he did.

Gus hadn't mentioned the opportunity to Claire. At first, there was nothing to tell. Then he hadn't wanted to pull focus from Hazel's upcoming graduation. As his exchanges with the NYU dean escalated, he'd felt increasingly panicked, like he was cheating on Claire. And cheating on the College.

Claire, he knew, would fixate on the negatives. The hundred-degree heat, the lack of fresh vegetables, her not being allowed to wear shorts. Having to smuggle in their menorah and shabbat candles. Not like they were religious. But they did own such things. He knew, too, that she would state the obvious. What did NYUAD need with an American Studies scholar? And what did an American Studies scholar want with NYUAD?

He was lost in a reverie somewhere between fantasizing about his new life in the Middle East and feeling sorry for himself that his wife probably wouldn't support his desert dreams when he noticed an insistent tap on his arm, accompanied by a voice at his ear. People were looking in his direction. Applauding. Pointing. What had he missed? Gus turned around, and then forced his attention to Nicole Hill on the podium. She was looking straight at him.

"Once more let me invite Professor Blum up here. Please come to the stage, Professor Gus Blum. You've been awarded the Stephen King Teaching Award."

There must be some mistake. A *teaching* award? His *first year*? Gus had never won anything! Teaching was merely something to get through. Writing was the thing he cared about. Until the Cosby fiasco, he'd hardly put any work into his lesson plans. For years, most every lecture he gave was three-quarters extemporaneous, the discussion questions he asked conceived on the fly. But now, since he'd started to make more of an effort—an obsessive one, at that—it seemed the students registered his newfound commitment.

A colleague seated next to him put an encouraging hand on Gus's back, pressing him forward. He made his way to the stage buoyed by goodwill.

Nicole was waiting. The audience, graduating seniors and parents alike, clapped appreciatively. Hill handed Gus a plaque and said something he couldn't quite make out above the noise of the crowd.

Maybe this was it. The mountaintop. Not the Everest he'd been working for and toward all these years; nevertheless, a peak. Being a teacher was a noble profession. How had that escaped him? He had knowledge to pass on, critical lines of inquiry to raise. Young people willing—eager!—to listen and learn. There was value in that, wasn't there? There had to be, even if his grad school friends couldn't see it. As he shook hands with President Hill, a vision formed in his head for what the next few years of his life could be.

Gus would stay. He'd double down on his teaching. If they thought he was a decent teacher this past year, then wait for the next year and the one after that. He'd become the most beloved professor to ever walk the campus. They'd bury him on this hill.

He'd continue to write but take Saturdays off. His legacy would be that his students and, more importantly, his children loved him. That he and his wife managed to stay married, to be happy.

NYU Abu Dhabi would have to find someone else.

At the lobster bake after the ceremony, his plate piled high with crustaceans and potato chips, a student approached, a graduating senior. As they got closer, he realized it was Sam.

"Professor Blum?" she said. "Can I take a photo with you?"

Despite Gus having worked with Sam in the Sunday night reading group, and her taking his class again the spring semester, he remained terrified of her. Of her power. But he respected her, too. She was a strong student. He'd assumed she was a rich kid who'd "prepped" at Andover or Choate or Trinity or Chapin. Turned out, she was on a full scholarship, a public-school kid from Albany, New York. Which reminded Gus of himself.

"Congratulations," said Gus. "How does it feel to be graduating?"

"Good, I guess, thanks. Sort of sad? I just want to say—the Cosby stuff aside, you're an excellent professor. Really good. Like, life-changing."

"Really?" said Gus.

"Yeah. I had no idea what I wanted to do with my life until taking your class. But I'm thinking of applying to graduate school in the fall," she said. "I hadn't realized how much popular culture contributes to hegemony. I'm so grateful you had us read Gramsci."

"He's essential." *Yes*, thought Gus.

See? *See?* The life of the mind mattered. Maybe Sam would

go on to get her PhD, and teach, and be a scholar-activist. And one day, decades from now, another young person would follow in their footsteps. Because of Gus. He'd have academic descendants born long after he was in the grave.

"Let me know what I can do to help along the way. Keep in touch. I mean it. I'm rooting for you."

"A letter of recommendation?" Sam asked. "And maybe, could I possibly run my statement of purpose by you this summer?"

"Absolutely," said Gus. You had to give it to this kid, putting him through the wringer and then asking for a letter. Well, she deserved it. As did he. And with that, he ate up and went back for seconds.

41

kindness creates kindness

It was the last day of school before summer vacation and Wolf's language arts teacher was spending the class period announcing superlatives. While eighth-grade superlatives made it into the yearbook, the sixth-grade ones were just for fun. But they were no less highly anticipated or worried about by Wolf.

Superlatives were voted on by students, and so Wolf braced for humiliation. Democracy would speak. He probably wouldn't get any votes, other than the lone one he allowed himself to cast in the one category he felt was his due. This morning was about to prove once and for all that he was a friendless loser destined to never be loved.

Mrs. Gilbert ticked off the winners. He didn't win for best hair. (Secretly, he'd thought he had a distant shot at that one, given his curls.) He didn't win for most social. Obviously. Or best flirt. No duh. (Only in Riverburg would they still have that one, and after what happened to Hazel.) Not for best dressed or most likely to be president (womp womp). He didn't even win for class clown. He was a nothing, a zero. Invisible. He might as well not even go to this school. By the time Mrs. Gilbert got to the last and best award: *most likely to be famous*, he'd given up.

"Wolf!" she announced. It didn't compute in Wolf's brain. Nobody liked him.

What the?!

More than anything, he felt relieved. He felt recognized. Kids—not adults, who were a thousand times easier to charm, but kids—had voted for him. Maybe he didn't have a bajillion (any?) friends, but his classmates saw something in him. Some sort of shine. They'd known his name enough to write it in.

Wolf couldn't wait to get home and tell his mom and dad, and his sister, too. But the person he most wanted to tell was Gracie. He missed her. She was a true friend. The kind you could text who'd text right back, and if she didn't you knew it was because she wasn't allowed on her phone right then. The kind who saved you a seat at her lunch table on your first day in a new school. Who let you be quiet when you were feeling uncomfortable and didn't judge you for it. She was the kind of friend who didn't blend in, didn't expect you to either and was unapologetic about it. He could cry just thinking about her.

Having Gracie back in Riverburg would be worth all the sixth-grade superlatives on the planet. His mom said you only needed one real friend, and that seemed dumb, like something a person with only one friend might say. But maybe it was true? It was hard to stay friends without seeing one another, though. And Wolf hadn't seen Gracie in months, not since she'd moved.

Riverburg sucked, but his parents didn't seem to be going anywhere. Wolf would bide his time. Six more years. Then he could go off to college—a big school, in a big city. Until then, he'd quit trying to be regular and let himself be Wolf.

Graduation morning and Hazel still hadn't decided about the book. The contract from Now Books remained unsigned. She and Sadie needed to talk. Hazel's rented cap and gown was wrapped in plastic and hanging on her bedroom door. In the attic closet a white eyelet sundress her mother had bought from BuiltGood waited for her. Hazel checked the time. She had an hour before they needed to leave. If she skipped her plan to shower and wash her hair and paint her fingernails gray, she could make it.

Her parents insisted on making a big deal of graduation. They'd ordered a shipment of bagels and lox and sour pickles and rugelach from Russ & Daughters in New York, which made no sense, given the exorbitant shipping costs and that the salmon they got was fished in Maine.

"Hazel!" her mother yelled up the stairs. Had she not heard of *texting*?

"We're leaving in forty minutes."

With a start, Hazel realized that soon there would be no more time reminders, no more homemade dinners during the school year unless she made them herself, no more laundry chutes down which she could throw her dirty clothes, hoping her mother would take pity on her and wash and fold her things. Or hound her until she'd put up a load herself. This was it. The end of her childhood. And time to start taking responsibility for her decisions.

Hazel sat on her bed with her phone in her lap, put her earbuds in, and dialed.

"Sadie, it's Hazel," she said.

"I know!" said Sadie. "Happy graduation day."

"Right. Sorry," said Hazel. "So, I don't know."

"What don't you know?"

Hazel didn't answer.

"You don't know about what, sweetie?"

"About the book deal. I don't know if I can do it. I don't know if this is what I want anymore."

"Those are two different things," said Sadie. "Every writer has days when they don't think they can write their book. Guess what I know? For sure? You *can* do it. The question is do you want to?"

"I don't know if this is the way I want to become a writer," said Hazel. "Writing about him… Actually," she continued, "I do know. It's not."

Sadie was uncharacteristically silent for a scary beat.

"Do you hate me?" Hazel asked quietly. "I mean, you did all this work for nothing. Your fifteen percent? All those emails and phone calls. I wasted your time. I bet you wish we'd never met."

It took Sadie another moment to reply, and when she did, she sounded detectably deflated. Understanding, but deflated.

"Hazel. Please don't say that. I'm not worried about leaving money on the table. There are a lot of books out there. There's only one you."

Hazel hadn't realized how much she'd been trying to please Sadie.

"But this is my big chance. Remember what you said? This is once in a lifetime."

"Did I say that? Shit, I shouldn't have. There's always another chance. Sometimes you just can't see it yet."

Relief flooded Hazel's body.

"If the time isn't right now, so be it. The last thing I want to do is pressure you into something you're not ready for. One day we'll do a book together. You'll see. Doesn't matter when. *If* you want to. Find me when I'm an old lady in a rocking chair and I'll come out of retirement. Have you told your parents?"

"No, you're the first. I don't think they'll care. Except about the money. For my college. So maybe they really will care."

"I can talk to them after you do if you like."

"You would do that?"

"Of course. Now go graduate, tell your parents, and call me when you're done."

The ceremony was being held that morning on the College's baseball field. Hazel's parents and Wolf were in the bleachers. Noah was sitting next to her dad. To Hazel's surprise, President

Hill was there. The new principal, a former chorus teacher, was giving a speech about her attempts that year to foster a culture of empathy at Riverburg High. *Kindness Creates Kindness*, the school's entryway marquee had declared daily since she'd taken over. *Change was hard*, the principal said.

Hazel's fellow graduates were sentimental and sweaty in their metal folding chairs on the turf. The school orchestra played a rather grating version of *Star Wars*' "The Throne Room." Hazel stole a look back at Noah. Things remained vague between them. Some weeks that late spring they'd hang out two or three times. Then they could go a week without exchanging so much as a text. They hadn't talked about it. It wasn't that deep. And that was okay with her. Hazel didn't want to show up to Vassar with a boyfriend. And she supposed Noah wasn't up for anything long-distance. He lit her skin on fire, it was true. But she hoped others would, too.

"I have an announcement to make," Hazel said on the car ride home, pulling off her robe and squishing it into a ball.

"What's that, sweetie?" asked her mom.

"I'm not doing the book."

"What?" asked Claire.

"Didn't you sign a contract?" said Wolf, dropping his sister's hand. "You *have* to write it. Or else you'll be in big trouble. You could go to jail."

"Hazel isn't going to jail," said Gus. "You can't go to jail for reneging on a book deal."

"Obviously," said Claire. "But I don't get it. Why don't you want to write your book anymore?"

"I'm not saying I'll never do it. Maybe one day I'll write a novel. I don't know!" said Hazel. Or maybe she'd go to librarian school. Or become a journalist, like Becky Singer. "I guess I just feel…like I'm too young. It's all still happening, you know? And I don't want to be defined by this. By White. I feel like there's so much more I can say but I don't really know how to say any of it yet."

"But all you wanted was to write that book," said Claire.

"You're going to be in such big trouble," said Wolf.

"It's not like I've cashed a check. They can't make me write a book, can they, Daddy?"

"Of course not," said Gus. "Feel free to tell the bastards no."

"They're not bastards, Daddy," said Wolf. "They're capitalists."

Claire allowed her shoulders to sink two inches down and let her legs melt into the passenger seat. Hazel had been through so much that year. Claire didn't know if this was something Hazel would one day regret. If it were up to Claire, she'd take the money and run. But her daughter was maybe a better person than she was. Smarter, too. Whatever Hazel did, she was going to be okay.

42

cape elizabeth

Hazel was struck by the house's windows. They were everywhere—on gables, peeking behind the wraparound porch—keeping watch over the Gulf of Maine.

Cape Elizabeth was an hour and a half from Riverburg, and as they made their way down Route 100, Wolf and Hazel with her new driver's license, they hadn't been sure what to expect. Not this.

Gracie was rich?

"Wow," said Wolf, who was rarely at a loss for words, not getting out of the car.

"Seriously," said Hazel, turning off the engine. "Did you know?"

"Know what?" said Wolf, getting his bearings. Big deal, so Gracie had an oceanfront estate.

"That Gracie's house was like this."

"I'd rather live behind a dumpster in New York," said Wolf. "Plus, global warming. This house will be underwater in ten years."

"Oh okay, Wolfie," Hazel said.

Gracie emerged from the porch with a shy wave. She was barefoot, in denim shorts and her signature braids. A weather-beaten American flag flapped behind her.

"Hi," said Wolf.

"This is beautiful," said Hazel. "You basically live in the ocean."

"Like a mermaid," said Wolf, only half-sarcastically.

This was not the unhappy ending Hazel was imagining (and feeling guilty about 24/7) for Gracie. It wasn't the house, or the view or the town. Which Hazel had assumed was in the middle of nowhere but turned out to be ten miles from Portland. Or that, according to Wolf's research, Cape Elizabeth had the third best school district in the state. It was Gracie. She seemed maybe okay?

"Hey there," said a woman in a linen tank top and drawstring pants, carrying a tray with three glasses of lemonade and a bowl of potato chips. "Welcome. This is my mom's house, but she's out. I'll put this right here on the porch for you. Come in."

Gracie's mother. Hazel had prepared herself for this. She followed Gracie and Wolf up the porch stairs.

"I'm Agatha," she said, offering Hazel a handshake, like she was suggesting a fresh start. Her hand was dry and cool.

"Hi," said Hazel.

What else was Hazel supposed to say? *Nice to meet you, sorry for ruining your marriage slash life, thanks for the potato chips?*

Wolf and Gracie were settling in on a couch; Gracie had taken out a deck of playing cards. She'd dyed her hair pink. Hazel wondered if it was permanent or the kind that washed out after a few shampoos. Wolf was arguing that they should play chess instead.

"I have some work to do inside," Agatha said. She couldn't quite bring herself to look Hazel in the eye. "Should I give you the Wi-Fi password? Or do you maybe want to swim?"

"That's okay," said Hazel, pointing to her tote bag. "I brought a book with me."

"I just remembered that there's something I want to give you," said Agatha. "For your mom. Hold on—"

She went inside and reemerged with a sealed envelope. "I know I could have emailed this," she said. "But this way seemed more appropriate. I owe your mother an apology. I owe you one, too."

Hazel stared down at her ratty plastic Birkenstocks and realized they were the same sandals she'd worn the first day of school.

"No—" Hazel began. She wanted to say Agatha didn't owe her family a thing. It was the Blums who should be apologizing to Gracie and Agatha. Though that wasn't quite right, either. Maybe none of them had done anything wrong. This was on Richard White.

That evening, as the sun set behind the backyard, Claire read Agatha's letter at the kitchen table. Agatha had written a sort of confession to looking the other way. It's not that Agatha knew. She didn't. Not even when she and White left Vermont for Maine. That was a move they'd talked about making for years. But she saw now how she'd ignored clues, dismissed her instincts. A mistake she vowed never to make again. Agatha wanted Claire to know that she didn't hate or blame her family. She was grateful to be free of White. Grateful that at least he wouldn't work in a school ever again. Grace was doing a little better. She was going to be okay. As for Agatha? She was trying to rebuild her life from scratch. Healing, and helping her daughter to do the same. Enjoying living in her childhood home with three generations of women and no men. She felt lighter.

Claire needed to start over, too. Her sabbatical year was almost done. She was determined to figure out her life. For real this time.

43

ramona comes to maine

"Oh. My. God. Look at this place," yelled Ramona from the car window before she'd even gotten out of Gus's station wagon.

"Welcome to my cheap mansion," said Claire.

"Holy shit. It's enormous."

It was June 21, the summer solstice. School was out. June in Maine was heaven. The hopeful, blue mornings followed by warm afternoons, the quality of the sunlight pouring through Claire's studio windows, the birdsong, Pickle living her best life in the backyard, digging holes and chasing squirrels. Summer was a promise, a recompense for the long slog of winter.

And now, Ramona and Luna were here. Gus, wanting a proper haircut and a decent cup of coffee, had picked them up in Portland. Their presence made Claire practically jubilant. That morning she'd tidied the house, laundering extra towels and sheets, and turning the three-season room (the one that was to have been Wolf's playroom, but hadn't seen much playing) into a makeshift guest room. She'd cut wildflowers from the garden and arranged them beside the pair of canvas camp cots she'd found at the Habitat store, placing next to them a much-loved copy of Laurie Colwin's *Family Happiness* for Ramona.

Claire waved with both arms while calling back to the house for the kids.

Ramona stepped out from the front passenger seat. She had a shoulder-length shag with micro bangs and a red roller suitcase, a matching red lip and cactus-green nails, and was wearing an embroidered Mexican beach dress that she'd give to Claire before the week was up.

"I can't believe you came," said Claire, hugging her.

"Of course I came."

When Luna exited the car half-hidden by her jet-black hair and heavy eyeliner, Claire gave Hazel a gentle shove in her direction. The girls hadn't seen each other since February and Claire sensed things may have gotten a little off between them. Hazel and Luna shyly embraced before heading up to the attic.

Years ago, Claire and Ramona had decided that if either one of them died, and Gus and Christian died too, the other would take care of their children. Godmothers, but with death in mind. *There's a word for what we are in Spanish*, Ramona had said when they'd made their wills. *Compadres. Comadres.* Coparents.

"What's this?" Claire asked, feeling the fabric of Ramona's dress.

"From a little tourist shop by my father's house in San Diego.

"Don't worry," continued Ramona, who had a clear radar line for Claire's envy of her wardrobe. "I brought you goodies. For your birthday. I found these incredible white handyman pants at the hardware store. Twenty bucks. We can dye them if you want. And I finished knitting your hat."

Ramona loved to give gifts; Claire loved receiving them. In this way, they were perfectly matched.

For dinner that night, Gus made tofu with a stir-fry of farmers market vegetables. They ate on the back deck, Claire's table set with a lime-green gingham tablecloth and more garden flowers. After dessert, the kids watched a movie in the den while

Claire and Ramona smoked a joint in the backyard, Claire's first in months, talking and watching the light change from pink to blue to black.

The next morning, they convened around the kitchen table over coffee. While hunting for scissors, Ramona noticed two mezuzahs sitting in a kitchen drawer and volunteered to hang them on the front and side doorposts.

"Do you really think that's a smart idea?"

"Why not?" Ramona said. And Claire realized she was probably right.

"What do you want to do today?" Claire asked. "Drive to the beach? It's an hour and twenty each way to the one in Rockland. Or an hour and a half to East Blue Hill, but it's worth it."

"Let's stay in town. I'm feeling lazy. Besides, it's cute here."

Is it? wondered Claire.

"Okay. The College's museum has this amazing rotating permanent collection."

"Yes, please. And I'm hoping we can shop? I really do hear the Maine vintage is divine."

"Maybe on the coast," said Claire, making a face. "Not in Riverburg."

"I want us to go to that place right in town that I heard about," Ramona said, pulling out her phone. "It's half a mile away and my food co-op shift mate says dealers love it, and I'm going with or without you. They open at eleven."

"Do we have to?"

"Invite your new friend. The art teacher? I want to meet your country gal pal."

Claire did as she was told. Polly, who was chronically busy during the school year, said she'd meet them there.

The vintage store was downtown, a ten-minute walk from the Greenberg Blums' house, across from a Lebanese restaurant and next to a boarded-up bakery. Claire wanted to bring the girls, but Luna preferred the Goodwill, and so they dropped them on the way.

Under the watchful eye of the vintage shop owner, an older woman who gave off a punk rock vibe and was playing '80s new wave, Ramona and Claire worked their way diligently and with mounting excitement through organized stacks of wildly well-priced and smartly curated denim, cotton T-shirts, sweaters and sweatshirts, and racks of skirts and tops, day dresses and gowns. They picked through piles of bags and shoes. They went through the men's section, stocked with wool trousers and waxed canvas work wear. For Ramona, shopping was an art, as basic to her humanity as her pottery. For Claire, too.

"I can't believe I didn't know about this place," said Claire, kicking herself for her lost year of treasure.

They found for Claire: real lace-up-the-back wool Navy sailor pants (complete with the name of her sailor marked in); wide-legged, pleated and high-waisted '80s Calvin Klein jeans that could have easily been confused for the current $400 indie designer versions; a handmade Irish cardigan sweater vest Claire knew she'd wear every day the coming winter; Carhartt jean shorts and brown full-length overalls; a "flowers of Maine" T-shirt with a single seam stitch, and a pair of very vintage L.L. Bean cotton skirts. For Ramona, they found: a broad-shouldered, rhinestone-sequined cropped evening jacket; red cowboy boots; two acid-wash yoke-front, pleated mid-length denim skirts, older cousins of the pricey ones she'd been coveting for months; a bustier corset sort of thing; a big black tuxedo blazer to wear over it; and a men's jean jacket with a moose silkscreened on the back.

As Claire was preparing to pay, and Ramona was in the fitting room for a last sweep of try-ons, the bells above the doorway rang. Polly.

She gave Claire a quick hug and took a spin around the store. After a knowing first pass through the women's section, Polly threw some maybes down on the armchair. Without waiting for the fitting room, she took off her T-shirt dress and started trying on clothes over her leggings and bra top.

Claire and Polly had gone from hiking in fall to snowshoeing and cross-country skiing in winter to spring walks. They talked about their children and their marriages and their artistic dreams and frustrations. They gossiped about Riverburg. They talked about Hazel.

"She's going to love college. Did I ever tell you? I almost didn't apply," Polly had once told her. "But I had good grades and my teachers kept pushing. I mailed my application to the University of New Hampshire the day before it was due."

When Polly was busy with her family and with teaching and they skipped their weekend walk for too many weeks in a row, Claire missed her. A lot. Which was strange. Sometimes, Claire still couldn't believe how much she could relate to a softball player from deeply rural New Hampshire.

Ramona introduced herself while Polly pulled a ball gown over her head. Unlike Claire, Ramona and Polly were tall and willowy with coincidentally matching haircuts.

"The stuff here is bananas," said Claire. "Why didn't you tell me about this place?"

"You think so?" Polly held up a pair of silver clogs. "I wasn't sure how it would compare to vintage in New York."

"Are you kidding?" said Claire. "It's ten million times better."

"And ten million times cheaper," added Ramona, bringing her piles to the counter.

"We're for sale," announced Gloria, the owner, as she started ringing up Ramona.

"Oh no!" said Ramona. "Why?"

"I can't make it work anymore. The profit margins. I need to be on Instagram or God only knows what and sell to a national audience, and I don't have the stomach for it. That, and I'm done with winter. My man and I want to move to Arizona."

"Gloria, I can't imagine your store not being here," said Polly.

"Our timing isn't great. The rabbi's wife is opening a sourdough bagel shop next door. She's at bagel school in New Jersey right now. The College is pumping money into the downtown. There's a new arts center coming. Main Street is going to be something in a few years."

"Riverburg is the new Brooklyn," said Ramona.

"I wouldn't go that far," said Claire. "But bespoke bagels? My husband is going to flip."

"Claire's in fashion," said Ramona. "She designed for Built-Good."

"I know who Claire is," said Gloria, writing up a receipt.

Was it that everybody knew everybody in Riverburg? Or was it because of Hazel?

"You should buy me out," Gloria said to Claire. "I own the building, too. The whole package comes cheap. Just enough for me to buy a two-bedroom bungalow in Tucson with a cactus in the front yard."

"No matter how cheap it is," Claire said. "I don't have it."

"Take out a loan," suggested Ramona. "You could sell to students, to parents. To tourists and summer people on their way through to the beach, even. A mix of vintage and very special new. You could sell your line.

"Look. You could put a rack here," Ramona continued. She pointed to a nook by the oversized window facing Main Street.

Claire made a face. *As if.* But she let herself daydream. She pictured an old wood chair flecked with paint and stacked with fisherman sweaters. The rack of her yet-to-be-designed clothes, handmade in Maine. The store, though, would always have reasonably priced vintage and craveable resale as its backbone. There would be a children's consignment section, with Halloween costumes and striped cotton things. She would have stacks of used denim (with plenty years more service left in them) and rows of vintage party dresses and wicker baskets filled with concert T-shirts. She'd hold sidewalk sales.

"I could stay affordable," said Claire, surprised at herself for saying the words aloud.

"You'd have to," said Gloria. "For Mainers, anyway."

"Not quite as affordable as you, Gloria," added Ramona. (Claire's two pairs of pants cost her $25.)

For shoppers from away, Claire could (finally) put her Instagram habit to good use. Open an Etsy shop.

"You could hire someone locally and produce your clothes in the back," said Ramona. "Who knows, maybe Christian and I could come on board as investors? Imagine the time we'd have going out to pick!"

Right there standing in that store, Claire knew. She'd always loved the hunt, obsessively thrifting since she was a teenager. She was ready to do something with her life, something purposeful and productive. Why not steward a place that people in Riverburg could afford and use, and that offered a moment's beauty and respite? Her shop could be a gathering spot, like The General or the farmers market or the library.

People might think it was a twee store. That she was gentrifying Main Street. But then maybe that same person would need something last-minute—a certain color shirt for spirit day at the high school, a last-minute secondhand tote to fill with Easter candy. Practical things, too. A parka!

Maybe she could enlist Polly as her partner? Polly had math skills and could do the books. Maybe she'd like to sell her handmade slippers? Or her watercolors? Ramona could sell her pottery when she had inventory to spare. Maybe Wolf could work the register for a few bucks an hour on the weekends. They'd call the store Pickle, after Claire's dog.

On their last morning together, Claire and Ramona visited the College museum's prized permanent collection of Alex Katz. A special exhibit was on that summer called, of all things, Maine/New York. Alex Katz was an American painter, a Jewish New Yorker who'd gone to art school in Skowhegan, not far from Riverburg. In the 1950s, drawn to Maine's light, he bought a small summer house on the coast outside of Lincolnville, an hour to the east, for $1200. Claire had loved Katz since art school. His work, and what she'd read about him. Making a painting every day. Swimming when he was done. He was approaching 100 and still at it.

The paintings spanned more than half a century. There were seagulls and late-summer flowers and apple trees and blueberry fields and rafts and tube tops in Maine. Dinner parties and office buildings and apartment window outlooks and black cocktail dresses and sparkly sandals in New York. There were portraits and landscapes and friends and children. There was Katz's wife, Ada. There was twilight and darkness.

Claire and Ramona walked through the exhibit silently once, and then again pointing out this or that to one another.

"Promise to come back soon?" asked Claire, dropping Ramona off at the bus station later that afternoon. "Maine's better with you here."

"Promise," answered Ramona.

44

the pool

The Riverburg Pool was not your average town pool. A couple of years before the Greenberg Blums arrived, it had been put through a multimillion-dollar renovation funded by a local philanthropist. Now there was a kiddie section, a shallow end, a middle deep and a deep, along with two gigantic water slides that shot riders out like a cannonball.

It was opening day. Wolf was hot and wanted to swim.

Hazel grabbed a mismatched bathing suit top and bottom from her closet, layered her comfiest, baggiest T-shirt and shorts over them like soft armor, and told Wolf that once he was changed and had his sunscreen on, she'd bring him. Her parents said Hazel could have regular rights to the station wagon if she took daily charge of making sure Wolf had a "wholesome" summer, which was defined as spending a few hours each day off the couch, and off his phone. On the weeks Wolf wasn't in theater camp, that meant Camp Hazel.

Taking Wolf to the pool was like putting a toddler in the bathtub. It occupied and contained him. She texted Noah, who was sticking around for the summer. If he wanted to come swim, he should. She spread her towel out on the cement and checked to make sure Wolf was set before opening her novel.

Hazel knew she would eventually run into him. According to April and Dakota, White had moved into an apartment in downtown Riverburg and was doing landscaping. Gracie's mom had primary custody, but her father had alternate weekends and some school vacations and part of the summer. When Wolf asked Hazel to bring him to the pool that morning, she almost reflexively said no, worried about a White reprise, but then she reconsidered and realized—maybe it would be fine? Cathartic. It's not like she could avoid the pool for the entire summer.

He arrived after the day campers from the Y were shuffled out and the pool's crowd had thinned. He sat off to the side and away, by the deep end, under the slim shade offered by a storage building. He had lost weight, the way a cancer patient loses weight. He'd grown a patchy beard. Hazel could feel him trying not to look at her.

Part of Hazel thought it was unreal that he'd show his face here. But he was still a father who wanted to take his daughter to the pool. And Gracie deserved to swim as much as the next kid. There were oceans and lakes, but there wasn't another town pool for an hour in any direction. Not with slides like these.

It would be easy enough to ignore him. Dick White didn't matter anymore. Not to Hazel. She checked her phone. Noah had work, he texted back—he had a job at the Teen Center—but suggested they have a picnic dinner at the lake outside of town. He preferred fresh water to chlorinated. He said he'd bring egg salad sandwiches. Or avocado, if Hazel was feeling in a vegan mood.

Noah was acting different since she'd graduated. More available. She hadn't realized he'd been bothered by her being in high school. Or maybe it wasn't that. Maybe he was more carefree and ready to hang out because it was summer? Or because she was no longer obsessed with a book deal?

Either way, the more into *it*—their "relationship" (?)—he was, the more into him she became. To be honest, she was maybe falling in love? Just a little. She was thinking about having sex with him.

Lying in the sun, Hazel tried to concentrate on her book. She was reading *Trust Exercise* by Susan Choi, a twisty post-modern novel about a bunch of theater kids, their sketchy teacher, and consent. It hit close to home but was too engrossing to quit halfway. Hazel was feeling less conflicted about everything, and more settled on going to Vassar and being a normal college student.

Gracie and Wolf had found each other in the middle deep. They were playing Marco Polo. Gracie's hair dye had pooled in the chlorinated water, giving her a pink halo. Hazel watched as Gracie did a back walk over in the water and then emerged triumphant like an Olympic gymnast after a gold-medal floor routine.

Hazel finished the chapter she was reading. The sun was turning the concrete under her into a frying pan. She was boiling. Hazel wanted to dive headfirst into the water, and the only place you could safely do that was the deep end. She wasn't going to let him stop her.

Without thinking, Hazel walked over to the deep and dove in, swimming a solid freestyle from end to end, and her faster, stronger backstroke for a full lap. She emerged from the pool's ladder after dipping her head and slicking back her hair. White was there, ten feet in front of her. Where he was drawn and defeated, Hazel vibrated with life, hyperaware of her health and youth.

She shook the water off her hair. She was done with being afraid.

"Hey," he said.

She didn't answer. The thing her father had taught her, the very best thing of all the things, was to not say everything. To give a conversation room to breathe. To outlast your opponent until the silence broke them.

"Sorry," he said.

She didn't reply. Later, in the months and years that followed, she'd think of dozens of smart, biting, eviscerating things she should have said back to him in that moment. On her worst days, she'd replay them when she couldn't fall asleep. But then she'd tell herself that when it mattered most, that morning in his office on the first day of school, she'd said exactly what she needed to say.

45

the lake

The College owned a piece of land on a lake fifteen minutes outside of town. In the late spring, before graduation, it got crowded with student sunbathers, Noah said. But at the end of June, at dinnertime, they'd have the place to themselves. They walked down the forest staircase, one slat at a time. Noah turned back when they reached the bottom step.

"Are you okay?" asked Noah.

"Of course," said Hazel, picking a pebble out of her sandal.

"Are you sure? You seem like… I don't know, sort of removed or something."

"Yeah, sorry."

"Don't apologize," said Noah. "I'm just noticing. Are you not into this?"

"What? No way. I love it here. It's like a painting."

"What is it then?"

"I saw him today," Hazel said.

"*Him* him?"

She nodded.

"Damn," said Noah.

Hazel didn't want to ruin the lake. She definitely didn't want to talk about White anymore.

"You okay?"

"I think so."

"Do you want to be here? 'Cause we can leave—"

Hazel surveyed the picnic tables, the pine trees, the lake. And Noah. "I totally want to be here. Like one hundred percent," she said.

Noah led Hazel by the hand to a shaded spot where a rocky outpost revealed a tiny half-moon sandy beach. He'd brought Scrabble, a small cooler of drinks, and a brown bag with their sandwiches. She wasn't about to have sex for the first time en plein air. Nope. But, she thought, her fingers intertwined with Noah's, maybe later that summer in her attic bedroom. Yes, she decided. With her parents and Wolf out of the house and the shades drawn and a candle lit, and the playlist Noah made her streaming in the background.

And then it was magic hour, the light shimmering over the lake and through the tree branches, and they were sitting on top of the picnic table with the Scrabble board arranged between them. It was her turn, and she had decent consonants, but no vowels. What else was there to do? Hazel leaned forward and kissed Noah. And he leaned forward and kissed Hazel back.

46

one morning in maine

Some nights, Claire dreamed her house was right on the ocean. That waves crested and swelled at her property line. She'd wake up, her chest sweaty, her tank top drenched by the side of the bed, and remember where she was—that Riverburg was an hour from anywhere and always would be. But that was Riverburg's charm. A place didn't have to be at the center of everything—or particularly beautiful, much less celebrated—to be worthy and loveable and significant.

That morning, though, they were headed to the beach. To a house in Brooksville, between Blue Hill and Deer Isle. Their vacation things packed the car to its gills, with coolers and duffels and beach towels and kitchen supplies and more books than four people could possibly read in a month, much less the ten days Claire had planned for them. Pickle was positioned between Hazel and Wolf, her snout drooping sleepily. In two weeks, Hazel would leave for college. Claire wasn't sure how she or the rest of them would manage missing her.

Gus drove them down Route 1 and Claire admired his forearms. His strongest muscle, aside from his brain. All that typing. She played a game with herself. Would she marry him again? If she were rendered suddenly single at forty-eight, would she want to date him?

In Providence, Claire had been with a series of cool kids before Gus. A boy in an indie band, a sculptor, a guy with a massive inheritance and a matching coke habit. Gus wasn't like that. When they'd first met, Claire didn't know what to make of him. Cool he was not. But he was funny, and seemed fascinated when she talked about art and design. Their first morning together he brought her coffee in bed, a perfect French omelet, and a copy of the *New York Times*. It was Gus who'd lent her the courage to stop talking to her parents. Gus wasn't what Claire had gone looking for, but he was just what she'd needed.

She observed him clinically. His lean frame, the muscular arms, the skinny runner's legs, his small professor belly, his thinning hair, the salt in his beard, his thick glasses over hazel eyes, and the way he rolled up the sleeves and tucked a button-down into his jeans. Since he'd won the teaching award, there was something different about him, too—something extra. A confidence, a casualness. A kindness had emerged. Gus had started to resemble the guy in *The Massage Book*, one of those 1970s hippie guides to living she'd collected back in art school. The truth was, they still wanted one another. Would Claire rather be without Gus in New York? Or with him anywhere else? That was easy. Yes, she would pick him all over again.

Claire was excited for the week of anonymity ahead. In Riverburg, the Greenberg Blums would always be known as the College family whose daughter exposed a corrupt high school principal. It's like Wolf had said, *You can't cancel people in a small town.* There aren't enough people to go around, and soon there'd be nobody left. Instead, you watch them learn from their mistakes and change, or watch them never learn and stay the same.

The Cottage on the Lake by the Sea wasn't listed on rental

sites but kept as a valued secret and passed on in whispers. Strangely affordable, ideally positioned on a small quiet lake a scenic twenty-minute drive to a saltwater swim. Polly had told her about it. A last-minute cancellation and they were booked for early August. Claire literally jumped for joy when they arrived. The house was perfect. Comfortable yet satisfyingly rustic. A dock with a private beach, on the lake. A huge wraparound screened-in porch that made the house feel like a ship. A strong Wi-Fi signal for Wolf and Hazel.

They unpacked and got their bearings and ate pizza in a garden plucked straight from Claire's dreams, filled with ripe peach trees and wildflowers. The next day they drove the Deer Isle bridge beneath a full harvest moon. She caught Wolf marveling out the window.

The following morning, Claire woke to the sound of coffee grinding. She pulled her sweater vest over her pajamas and found Gus on the porch working on his laptop, a stack of index cards beside him.

"Shit. Sorry about the noise," he said.

"What are you working on?" Claire asked. "Your book?"

"My lecture for fall. I have some ideas I don't want to forget."

Gus grinned and lifted his coffee in a l'chaim. Claire smiled back and touched his arm. For Gus, happiness meant a productive morning's work, and it always would. Normally she'd care about her sleep, but not here. She wanted to be awake for as many hours of the day as she could, to soak in the short, precious summer before winter came again.

She drove the winding coastal roads to get the paper. At the Brooksville town church, beside the actual Condon's Garage from the classic children's book *One Morning in Maine*, by Robert McCloskey, she happened upon a rummage sale and cadged a near complete dinner set with a mauve floral motif in exchange for a donation to the church's fresh coat of paint campaign. She'd come back to hunt here, with Ramona, for the store.

The days unspooled. In the mornings, they stayed at the lake. Gus canoed with Wolf. Hazel read on the dock. Claire swam with the loons. In the afternoons, they drove to the ocean. Claire had learned of a secret beach past a one-room library; the cove was magical. Majestic. Eagles soared overhead. Sheep grazed by the scattershot headstones on a nearby hill. The surf made a sandy beach at low tide and rushed in and pooled at high tide. Maine had a wild and scrappy beauty.

Gus portaged Pickle over a ravine she was too old to navigate and walked with Claire toward a constellation of smooth boulders under the tree shade. Wolf, who'd complained bitterly that morning about "having" to go to the beach, was hunting for stones and live crabs by the shore. Summer had made him lighter, more like a little kid again. He wouldn't swim with her, though. Not in the ocean.

"Will you come in with me? Please?"

"No. Too cold. *Not* happening."

"You know. Sometimes I feel like you take me for granted," said Claire.

"It would be a problem if I didn't take you for granted," Wolf said.

"What do you mean?"

"I take you for granted because I know you'll always be there for me. Isn't that a good thing?"

"Oh," answered Claire. "That actually makes a lot of sense."

He let her hug him for a good ten seconds before pulling away. Wolf smelled of early teen body odor and late childhood sweetness and the beach.

She looked over at Gus. His head was in a book.

"Come swim," she said to Gus.

"No thanks."

"Don't you like water?"

"I like water. I just don't want to swim in it. I like sitting with you here, on this rock. I like feeling like we're in the same canoe."

"I like sitting here with you, too."

"I'm happy here," he said. "In Maine, I mean. There's room to think."

Fine, then. Claire would swim by herself. She waded in—it *was* cold—and willed herself to submerge. What Claire loved about swimming was everything. She adored the feeling of the water against her skin. How young she felt, a child really, a girl again at Jones Beach on Long Island, as she let herself be taken by the larger waves, jumping over some and diving into others. The feeling of suspension between land and sea. The pleasurable muffle of the water when she submerged, her arms pushing the ocean back, until she shot up for air.

Hazel earmarked the page of the book she was reading and tucked it in her tote. She climbed over the boulders toward the water where her mother was floating on her back. The water was cryogenic, but she should probably seize the moment. She wouldn't be in Maine much longer.

"Hey," said a girl around her age wearing a bathing suit and an oversized shirt, chilling her ankles. "Are you going all the way in?"

"Maybe," Hazel answered.

For a long minute the two girls, strangers, stood side by side staring into the ocean. They were quiet. The water looked formidable. Who knew what was in the deep, what murky secrets it held?

From somewhere in the water, her mother appeared—like a witchy, middle-aged sea nymph.

"Hazel," she called, waving her arms. "What do you think? Would you like to swim?"

Would she?

Claire reached out her hand.

Hazel said yes.

★ ★ ★ ★ ★

acknowledgments

Henry Dunow, I am forever grateful for your dedication, knowing reads, sage advice, big heart, and for making me laugh. You're the Sadie to my Hazel. Working with you has been a highlight not only of my writing life, but of my life-life.

John Glynn, your magical combination of enthusiasm and confidence, sensitivity and editorial brilliance is one of a kind. Thank you for loving Hazel from the very start.

With so much appreciation for the fantastically supportive and creative team at Hanover Square Press and HarperCollins. Eden Railsback, for your sunny emails and hard work; Peter Joseph, Margaret Marbury, Heather Connor, Randy Chan, Pamela Osti, and Emer Flounders, for everything. Kathleen Carter, thank you!

Danielle Friedman, your generosity is boundless, your instincts indispensable, your friendship a precious gift. Thank you for making me better.

Cassandra Neyenesch, best art friend. Thank you for the sharp-eyed comments; for answering a steady stream of texts about character development, plot points, lines, and jokes; for BuiltGood; and for telling me what you really think.

Mara Altman, your literary taste is perfection. Our texts and calls, and your dropping everything to read, made all the difference.

Karen Levin, for reading again and again with A+ notes; Jen Marshall, who pointed a way out of the woods; Sara Verstynen, who told me not to quit; and Nora Knoepflmacher, for Hazel insights and expert assistance. For reading early drafts in Maine, special thanks to Holly Hubbard, Rabbi Rachel Isaacs, Amy Murphy, Elizabeth Hoffman, and Sarah Braunstein. Katherine Brennan cheered me on, like she has since we were girls.

Thank you Marla Apt and Lucy Sullivan for health and care.

Grazie di cuore to Alice and Giada Cancellario at Heloola and vielen Dank to Bastei Lübbe in Germany.

Orly Greenberg and Jason Richman at UTA—working with you is my dream come true.

Alex Lash, you knew it.

RIP Salem. Frannie forever.

Neil, an endless thank-you for a gazillion edits, book conversations, dinners cooked, bills paid, the countless mornings you woke early with child and dog so that I could sleep and then write, and for thinking my writing was worth it. I love you.

Lucien, for saying I should write a novel, and for conjuring, plotting, chainsaw editing; for reading, watching, exploring, swimming, believing, celebrating, growing, and dreaming with me. You are the sweetest and smartest in the land, and more, you are good and kind, and I am happiest to be your mother. This is for you.

Discussion Guide Questions

1. Hazel says "no" right in the title. How did you feel about the inciting incident coming so fast and dramatically at the end of chapter one? Did that feel different and new?
2. Were you hesitant to pick up and continue reading a book that begins with such an upsetting incident of sexual harassment? If so, explain. What made you want to continue reading?
3. Do you think Claire and Gus have a good marriage? What do you think of their parenting style?
4. Was Wolf wrong to *say something*?
5. Was Gus wrong to teach *The Cosby Show*?
6. Hazel says no multiple times in the novel, before saying yes. Discuss the different ways and times Hazel says no throughout the novel—from the principal's office to the publishing world—and how each shaped her as a character.
7. Have you ever been in a situation where you had to say a big (and scary) no? What consequences did that have?
8. When Hazel is asked to write a book about what happened to her, did you feel excitement or concern? What was your emotional response to Hazel saying no to the book deal?
9. What role does humor play in *Hazel Says No*?
10. Beyond the Greenberg Blum family, *Hazel Says No* has a variety of vivid characters, from Sadie Lansky to the rabbi. Who were your favorites? How did you feel about the contrast between the Mainers and the New Yorkers?
11. Agree or disagree—and discuss! The Greenberg Blums aren't very religious or observant, but they are very Jewish. How so? In what ways do they think of themselves as Jews? And live their Jewish identity? What does it mean to be a secular or cultural Jew?
12. The novel considers the contrast between small-town life, often dreamed of and desired by many, and life in a big city, seen as more stressful and dangerous. Do you think this view reflects reality?
13. What do you think happens to each of the Greenberg Blums after the novel ends? Do you think they will stay in Riverburg? Will Hazel become a writer one day?